RAVELED ENDS
OF SKY

RAVELED ENDS

OF SKY

LINDA SANDIFER

A TOM DOHERTY ASSOCIATES BOOK
NEW YORK

RAVELED ENDS OF SKY

Copyright © 1998 by Linda Sandifer

This book is printed on acid-free paper.

A Forge Book
Published by Tom Doherty Associates, Inc.
175 Fifth Avenue
New York, NY 10010

Forge® is a registered trademark of Tom Doherty
Associates, Inc.

Library of Congress Cataloging-in-Publication Data

Sandifer, Linda.
    Raveled ends of sky / Linda Sandifer. —1st ed.
        p.   cm.
    "A Tom Doherty Associates book."
    ISBN 0-312-86378-0 (alk. paper)
    I. Title
PS3569.A5165R3 1998
813'.54—dc21   98-22369
                                                     CIP

First Edition: December 1998

Printed in the United States of America

0 9 8 7 6 5 4 3 2 1

To the women who have led the way

"Eastward I go only by force, but westward I go free."

Henry David Thoreau

FOREWORD

The Westward movement of the 1800s has seldom been portrayed in books and films from the viewpoint of the unmarried woman. Even those stories written about married women tend to lean toward the misconsensus that women in general undertook the overland journey because they had no choice, and that every step of the way was a torturous affront to their delicate sensibilities.

In writing *Raveled Ends of Sky,* I wanted to dispel that myth. I wanted to show that although there were women who did not want to go West, there were just as many who were an active part in the decision to emigrate.

In 1849, Catherine Haun wrote of her journey west with her husband: "It was a period of National hard times and we being financially involved in our business . . . longed to go to the new El Dorado and 'pick up' gold enough with which to return and pay off our debts. . . . Full of energy and enthusiasm of youth, the prospects of so hazardous an undertaking had no terror for us, indeed, as we had been married but a few months, it appealed to us as a romantic wedding tour."

In 1852, Lydia Allen Rudd traveled to Oregon with her husband. In her words, "We were leaving all signs of civilised life for the present. But with good courage and not one sigh of regret I mounted my pony and rode slowly on."

Raveled Ends of Sky hinged, to a large degree, on the motivations that drove my lead protagonist, Nancy Maguire, and her widowed friend, Lottie England, to join the Joseph Ballinger Chiles company in 1843. Chiles's company was only the second wagon train ever to undertake the overland journey to the Mexican province of California. The first wagon train to attempt the perilous journey had been in 1841, and unsuccessful. No wagon road existed across the Great Basin or the mighty barrier of the Sierra Nevada Mountains. The pioneers on that first journey were forced to abandon their wagons at the Sierras and walk the remaining distance, weak with starvation, to the California settlements on the coast.

In those early days, maps still did not exist, save those drawn on scraps of paper, or etched into the soil by some trapper's stick as he squatted near a fire before an anxious audience and tried to relate landmarks, water holes, and possible mountain passes. Chiles, and a few of the men who would be with him on his 1843 expedition to California, had made the journey in 1841. They had returned by horseback to Missouri in 1842. Although they still had not discovered the wagon road over the Sierras during that first expedition, they at least had a better idea of the best route south from Fort Hall and across the Great Basin. Finding a wagon road was the one thing Chiles wanted to accomplish more than anything.

Historical records are not consistent, but there appear to have been approximately six women and five children traveling with the Chiles company, including two unmarried women. One would automatically ask why those women agreed, or chose, to leave the relative comfort and safety of their homes to undertake a perilous journey to a foreign land where no wagon road had yet been discovered, and where rumors of revolutions and wars passed over the land with the regularity of the sun.

It has been said that people went West for three reasons: to get something, to get away from something, and just to get there. A study of the Westward movement reveals that men, at least, were usually motivated by financial difficulties, health problems of a family member, free land, business opportunities, or the call to be missionaries to the Indians. The discovery of gold in California and other areas lured thousands.

The women's characterizations in this book were crucial to the story's plausibility. "Gentle tamers" would not embark upon such a treacherous journey without men to protect them. Instead, the story called for highly independent women. Women who were driven by the desire for adventure and freedom from the restrictions placed on them by Eastern society.

For a while I entertained the notion that a single woman would have to be "forced" to embark upon such a dangerous journey alone. She would have to be running from something—a disastrous love affair, family problems, poverty, or scandal. But after numerous excerpts from women's diaries of the overland journey, I seldom found those things to be motivators for those women who journeyed westward, at least in the beginning.

Recently married nineteen-year-old Miriam A. Thompson Tuller set out for Oregon in 1845. "I was possessed with a spirit of adventure," she wrote, "and a desire to see what was new and strange."

Single woman Elizabeth Wood, traveling to Oregon in 1851, said, "I have a great desire to see Oregon . . . the beautiful scenery of plain and mountains, and . . . the wild animals and the Indians, and natural curiosities in abundance."

Many books about the overland journey end when that distant shore is reached, but the journey itself was only the beginning for the emigrants. For those in this book, who journey to California, getting settled in a foreign land where "gringos" were not welcome was as much of a challenge as the journey itself. As Eliza Gregson wrote of those difficult years before California became a possession of the United States, "We few women were very uneasy about this time for we did not [know] whether we were widows or not."

The reasons women went West were many and varied. But those unmarried women who set out alone—possibly more so than those who went with the protection of husbands and families—were possessed of the spirit of adventure that was fundamental in opening and taming new lands. They were stubborn and defiant, strong-willed and resourceful. They stepped out bravely into the unknown, risking their lives for a dream they could have no other way but by their own doing.

In Nancy Maguire and Lottie England I have tried to portray two single women who exemplified the courageous indomitability of the whole. Women who had nothing to lose by going West, and everything to gain. Women who possessed the tenacity and the fortitude to blaze the trails upon which an entire nation would follow.

ONE

The Americans

"If hell lay to the west,
Americans would cross heaven to get there."
Anonymous

1

May, 1843
Independence, Missouri

"I feel it my obligation to tell you, Miss Maguire, 'cause I ain't no liar, no sirree. I ain't one of those shysterin' horse traders what's taken up business in this town for the sole purpose of hoodwinkin' innocent emigrants. I'll tell you true, or my name ain't Abbot Moses. That little mare will sure 'nuf get you to California, but she ain't lady broke and I won't lie about it. No sirree."

Abbot Moses, the squinty-eyed hostler, came up for air, but not for long. "And I don't reckon she's ever had a sidesaddle on her neither," he continued, " 'cause no woman in her right mind would attempt to ride her. But I won't swear to her not ever having had a sidesaddle on her. It would be presumptuous for me to do that. I reckon *some*body might have cinched one on her at one time or another. But it weren't that farmer I bought her off of 'cause she plumb had too much spit and vinegar for that knucklehead. 'Course now, if I do say so myself, he was a poor hand with a horse anyway. Couldn't even make his old plow horse walk a straight line in last year's furrow."

The sunlight filtered in through cracks in the walls and the roof of the old livery barn that smelled strongly of moldy hay, wet horse blankets, manure, and oiled leather. Dust motes circled and drifted aimlessly down through the shafts of light. The latter shone on the mare's dark bay coat, causing it to gleam as if she'd been groomed for hours. Her short back, flared nostrils, and the proud thrust of her head attested to some Arabian blood, although Nancy Maguire suspected she had more Morgan in her than anything. She was small, probably only fourteen hands, and she watched Nancy with alert, wary eyes, her ears pricked forward to catch every little sound. She snorted at the smell of Nancy's gloved hand on her nose, but then reached her head out to try for a second sniff.

"Is she mean?" Nancy inquired. "Does she bite, kick?"

"No, sirree," Abbot Moses said without reservation. "No temper to speak of, but she acts like she's dancin' on hot coals most o' the time. Just needs to be rode. She likes to run. Had her out to a full gallop one day outside of town. If you're rider enough to stay with her, I guarantee there ain't no Injun pony 'round that can even come close to catching her—or *you* if you're on her back. And that might be a powerful consideration, where you're headed."

A flock of fork-tailed swallows rushed into the barn's loft, fluttering about and making squeaky, warbling exchanges among themselves. One landed in the straw and a piece of it fell down onto the mare's back. She felt even that faint stirring against her hair and flicked her tail in an attempt to remove it.

"Does she buck?" Nancy asked again, brushing aside a stray wisp of golden brown hair that had fallen from beneath her black beaver riding hat.

This time Abbot Moses hesitated and rolled a wad of tobacco around in his mouth before sending it streaming into the vacant stall across from the mare. "Wall now, she might. But she mostly just wants to run. She just likes her freedom. Likes to be goin'. It sounds plumb crazy I know, but it seems to me that she just likes the wind in her face."

Nancy suddenly smiled and stroked the mare's velvety nose. If what the old man said was true, then she and the mare were kindred spirits. "I think the two of us will get along fine, Mr. Moses. Just fine. But you'll have to lower your price ten dollars since you can't guarantee that she won't buck."

"Why, Miss Maguire," the hostler's tone was clearly indignant. "No horse is foolproof. If you were raised up 'round 'em, like you said you were, you'd know that."

Nancy laughed. She *had* been raised on a horse farm, and if it was one thing she knew, it was good horseflesh. Her father bred both saddle horses and draft horses, and everything Moses said was absolutely true. There were no foolproof horses. But she also knew the tactics that horse traders used back in Amherst, Massachusetts—and everywhere else, for that matter. She wasn't above using them now in order to get this horse.

"How many offers have you had for this mare, Mr. Moses?" she continued doggedly. "How many more do you think you'll get? She is clearly too spirited for just anybody."

He hem-hawed again. "Wall now . . . I don't rightly remember how many offers I've had, but horses—good *or* bad—are gettin' scarce as hen's teeth in this town, and somebody will come along willin' to pay the full price."

"And how soon before she eats up the ten-dollar difference in hay? Maybe she already has."

He kicked at a tuft of straw with a worn-out boot and rubbed his grizzled beard with a hand that curved as if perpetually gripping a pitchfork handle. "Dang it, Miss Maguire. You drive a hard bargain. All right, I'll let you have her for your price, but don't come runnin' back here wantin' me to *re*fund your money if she dumps you on your fool head."

"Don't worry, Mr. Moses. I won't."

"Ain't you gonna ride her before layin' your dollars down?"

Nancy considered it for only a moment. She could tell by the mare's confirmation that she would ride smooth, and that she could run fast. The question was, of course, whether she would try to buck, and if she did, whether Nancy could stop her. Nancy was a good rider, but her father's horses had been expertly broken and trained so that none of them bucked.

"I've found nothing else in this town but scags, Mr. Moses. Few alternatives await me."

Moses nodded, agreeing wholeheartedly. "Damned place is picked clean to the bone. Never seen so many people and critters headin' West in my born days. By God, it looks like a stampede a-comin' down on us. Worst part is, now that it's started, there prob'ly ain't gonna be no end in sight."

"You could very well be right, Mr. Moses. Now, I don't want to get caught in the stampede, so could you please tell me where I might find Colonel Joseph Ballinger Chiles? I understand he's heading up the company bound for California."

"By golly, if you ain't as spirited as that mare." He shook his head in utter bemusement, lifting his ratty hat and reseating it on his head. "Goin' to California alone. A fine, genteel lady like you. Good upbringing. I swear, I ain't never heard of such a thing. I'd say that maybe you've already been dumped on your head a time or two."

Nancy had heard similar remarks, by scores of people, too many times over the past six months to be offended by his. She knew he was curious about why she was going to California alone, and he was hoping she'd tell him, but she had decided that it was best to let people wonder, to let them think up their own deep, dark motivations for her insanity. They never understood the truth anyway.

Her laughter trilled up into the barn's high loft. "Well," she prodded. "Do you know where I can find Colonel Chiles?"

He shook his head again. "Crazy, I swear. He's up the street, and just outside of town about a mile. His wagon got bogged in the mud and broke an axle and he's been out there tryin' to fix it. Uncommonly wet spring. I'm beginning to wonder if we all ought to think about building arks. Anyway, Chiles had to come to town and buy a new axle. I hear that him and that friend of his, Billy Baldridge, are fixin' to load up machinery for a mill they're going to build in California. How they ever plan to get a load like that over those Sierra Nevada Mountains is beyond me. Heard those mountains reach right up to heaven, and so danged cold at the top that the snow never melts. Why, there ain't even been a road found over 'em from what I hear."

"I'm sure someone will find one eventually, Mr. Moses. Where there is a will, there's a way."

He sent another stream of tobacco juice into the straw. "That's the problem with you young people. You're always sure of things you don't know nothin' about. But maybe being crazy is a prerequisite for goin' to California." He eyed her skeptically again. "Sure 'ppears to be a common trait amongst you wayfarers. Anyhow, I reckon Chiles is still out there. He's tall and got a head full of red hair. You can probably catch him if you hurry."

The mare pranced sideways against the current of traffic moving down the muddy street. Wagons of every sort pulled by horses, mules, or oxen flowed on either side of her. The constant cracking of whips, of profanities, groaning wheels, clanking chains, and "gees" and "haws" to oxen teams resounded from every direction. A cacophony of music from the saloons mingled with the delighted screams of children at play, and with the yipping and barking of hundreds of dogs, and bawling cattle intended for the trail. To add an ominous quality to the mayhem, low rolls of distant thunder threatened more rain to the already soggy landscape. Nancy skirted around one wagon broken down in the street. While the husband fixed it, the wife stood anxiously by, clutching two small children to her legs. "Don't you two be gettin' out in front of those freight wagons now," she warned them. "I'm tellin' you, those big wheels will squash you flat as a June bug 'neath your daddy's boot."

More wagons could be seen beyond the edge of town, coming in on muddy back roads to make their rendezvous up and down the river. They came from the east and the north and the south, like the rush of wind before a hurricane.

Beyond the many encampments outside Independence and Westport, beyond these "jumping-off" places to the frontier, lay the unknown, the unexplored. Out there, too, beyond the Kansas and Missouri rivers, lay the promise of adventure, freedom and excitement, and the hope of a prosperous future free of disease and illness. The people came for the same reason that Nancy had, and although they were all strangers, she felt a sort of kinship with each and every one of them.

The mare suddenly shied sideways, nearly unseating Nancy. A quartet of squealing pigs darted frantically under the mare's belly. Behind them came their screaming owner, waving a carving knife that looked sharp enough, and long enough, to take their heads off with one mighty swipe. "If you damn-blasted shoats don't get back to your pen in about two shakes, I can *guarantee* you'll be tenderloin by nightfall!"

Nancy sensed that the mare not only danced to the noise and confusion, but to the energy permeating from every human being and animal. There was no mistaking the smell of haste. The mare's nostrils flared, absorbing it into her fiery senses, enjoying the titillation of being part of the melee.

Nancy's arms began to ache from trying to make the mare walk a straight line. Her occasional shrill whinny at nothing in particular rattled her sleek sides and shook Nancy perched atop her sidesaddle. It was the saddle she'd been given as a girl of twelve. She'd brought it on the journey in its own special trunk along with her tack, saddle soaps, liniments, and grooming tools.

Nancy had been in Independence for a week now, and talk was that no single group of people had yet to amass in such numbers here on the edge of the frontier, preparing to jump off the edge of civilization into the wild, untamed regions of uncertainty. The numbers had increased in just the past week and the newspapers were saying that there had to be at least a thousand people preparing to head across the prairie toward what they considered their "manifest destiny." Someone had dubbed the movement the Great Migration, and the name had stuck.

Many emigrants were just now arriving in town. Nancy saw their hurried steps, their worried expressions, as they rushed to get to the rendezvous sites, or to the supply stores before everything was gone. Likewise, merchants scrambled to keep their shelves stocked. Many storekeepers were taking advantage of the situation and raising prices ridiculously high merely because they knew they could get it.

Not all the confusion and din could be attributed to eager emigrants either. Shaggy Indian ponies suggested hundreds of Indians from various tribes were in town. Trappers had gathered here to get supplies before heading back into the mountains for the summer. Most would join the emigrant trains and act as guides or advisors. Freighters still came and went on the Santa Fe Trail. Soldiers from the outposts sauntered up and down the streets. John C. Frémont had a group headed out on another exploratory, map-making expedition for the government.

Kanza Indians in dirty, ragged blankets begged food from storekeepers, restaurateurs, and even emigrant women who had set up camp on the edges of town. One such redskin saw her and called out, "I do war dance for you, white lady! One dollar. Just one dollar!" But Nancy suspected that like many of the Indians who had succeeded in acquiring money, he would just spend it on whiskey, not food for his family. On every block there was at least one Indian staggering down the boardwalks in a drunken stupor, or lying collapsed against a store front with liquor jug in hand.

In contrast, the Shawnees and Wyandots strode proudly through town wearing fine calicoes and other "white man" fripperies, while the Sac and Fox Indians, sporting shaved heads and painted faces, managed to move with a wide berth along boardwalks and through stores.

Disreputable men in dirty buckskins, vagrants, outlaws, and footloose soldiers—armed to the teeth with every weapon conceivable to man—lounged on the boardwalks and around the saloons. They eyed Nancy as she rode past, casting out lewd remarks and wolf whistles, which she pretended she did not hear above the noise of the street. Still she shivered, knowing that the prairie was not the greatest danger, but rather these men. Back in Amherst, she had heard of the untamed, raw frontier, but these crude and oftentimes violent men had been the first shadow cast over the glow of her great adventure. Her father had warned her about them. As a matter of fact, he had warned her so many times that she had wearied of his lectures on the subject and often closed her ears to them. But his words rang loud and clear now.

"There are men out there who will not care one whit that you are a lady, Nancy. They'll be all the more drawn to you because of your breeding. Some men are evil, and they derive perverse pleasure from hurting weaker or kinder people. Please, I cannot dissuade you enough, Daughter. Give up this foolish notion."

Nancy could see now that her father had not exaggerated. Her sequestered life had indeed left her naive to what lay beyond her sheltered home of Amherst.

She had been shocked by the reality of the frontier nearly the moment she'd stepped from the stage and been accosted by a drunken soldier. If her grandfather had not had the foresight to buy her a double-action Allen Pepperbox pocket pistol, and coached her until she had become proficient at firing it, there is no telling what might have become of her. The six-shot, multibarreled pistol was actually too large to carry in her pocket. To accommodate its five-inch length, she and her grandfather had fashioned a lightweight leather shoulder holster that fit quite nicely under her traveling cloak.

She remembered the incident much too vividly. The soldier had grabbed her around the waist and pulled her against him, his mouth too close and his breath reeking of some vile alcoholic concoction. "How about a little entertainment, pretty lady?"

Nancy had reached inside her cloak for the revolver and rammed it hard into his ribs. "Would a bullet in your heart be the kind of entertainment you are seeking, sir?"

He had backed off immediately, offering a profusion of apologies.

Nancy had reacted out of pure fear and did not know yet if she could have actually pulled the trigger. She was just thankful that she hadn't had to. Afterwards, her hands had shaken so badly she had barely been able to return the pepperbox to its holster.

She had not been without the pepperbox since except when in the safety of her room at Eleanor Townsend's boardinghouse.

Nancy was a little nervous about riding out away from town alone, hoping none of these men watching her would take a notion to follow her. But even once out of town, there were enough emigrants on the road to discourage anyone from bothering her in broad daylight.

The mare wanted to run, but Nancy was unable to give her rein until they came upon a broad, sloping hill bright with spring grass and not as rain-saturated as the roads and meadows. Here, at last, Nancy leaned forward and loosened the rein. She made a little noise between her teeth. It was all the mare needed. With one bound she was off, galloping up the hill, kicking divots of mud out behind her. A few came up and slapped Nancy on the back, but she barely noticed as she enjoyed the rush of the spring air in her face. Emigrants on the road gawked, but she flew past them, their surprised faces little more than a blur. A few waved. But Nancy, with her hands full of rein, could not return their greeting with anything more than a broad grin.

At the crest of the hill, Nancy slowed the mare to a trot and finally a walk. Laughing, she patted the mare's neck. "Moses was right. You run like the wind."

She took a deep breath of the fresh spring air, thinking she would never forget the purity of it, or the exhilaration surging through her at this moment. For the first time in her twenty-six years of life, she was free. And it was a wonderful feeling. Regardless of what awaited her in the wilderness, it could not possibly resemble the empty, restricted, and tiresome life she had lived as a spinster in Amherst.

She sighed, never wanting the moment to end, and wishing that her grandfather could be here with her to enjoy it. Of all the members of her family, only he had truly understood the restless yearnings driving her. Flynn Maguire, tall and white-haired, had come to America from Ireland. Being a man, he had been able to follow his heart's yearnings with no recrimination from his family. If anything, they had welcomed him gone. It was one less mouth they'd had to feed.

"There was a hunger in my heart," he had confided in his thick Irish brogue. "Something that left me pained, frustrated, fer shoor. No matter what I did, it couldn't be satisfied. I'd go down and stand on old Ireland's shore and think I wanted to go o'er that ocean to see what was on the other side. I'd get a feelin' inside so powerful and so painful it would swell and nearly choke me, like a tremendous wave comin' down o'er me. It would consume my soul, and I'd feel beset upon as if by a pack of she-devils, but it was nothin' more than the wanderlust ragin' to be satisfied. And because I was the youngest son of a poor family, there wasn't much to hold me.

"So, one day, not even knowin' what I'd do if and when I reached that distant shore, I got aboard a ship and sailed. Oh, the feelin', Nancy. Nothin' can compare before nor since. It was like I'd been turned out o' bondage, it was."

Nancy had listened, enraptured, knowing exactly the feeling.

"There's those of us who can't ever fully shake that desire to be movin' forever onward," he had continued. "We need new challenges and a fresh dream forever on the horizon. Even at my age, I feel the need pullin' at me. Why, if I was a young man again, I'd head West, I would. I'd be out there with the trappers and the Indians and the explorers.

"But I can tell y' somethin', Nancy. Adventures come, and adventures go, and when y' look back, y'll see that the biggest adventure of all is the little things life has to offer. The things most people take for granted. Things like sunshine on y'r face, rain and a cold wind beatin' at y'r back. The kiss of the sweetheart that makes y'r heart sink to y'r toes and then back up. The little things, Granddaughter. Don't e'er forget it."

"You've never regretted leaving Ireland, have you, Grandpa?"

"When m' parents died and I was not there, I regretted it. I knew when I left, I'd prob'ly ne'er see them again, but young people always think time goes slower than it does. Then there were the times when m' stomach was empty and the only thing m' pockets held were me cold hands. But, after a time, the sun came out again."

"Then I'll always wait for the sunshine."

He had ruffled her hair with his big, gnarled hand. "Remember one thing, Nancy. No matter what happens, the past is the past, and the only way to go is forward. There's no returnin' to what y' left behind except the parts y've kept in y'r heart for safekeeping. Travel lightly, lass. Ride a swift horse. And never, never ever, look back."

Her announcement to go to the Mexican province of California and raise horses had nearly given her mother heart failure. Her father had gone into a fit, telling her he absolutely forbid such irresponsible behavior. Her brothers and sisters had rolled their eyes, sneered, and figured it was insanity that would pass.

Her family might have thought she had arrived at the decision hastily, but it had been five years in the making. The most difficult part had been the decision to leave her grandfather. While the others had ranted and raved that she couldn't possibly do such an insane thing and live to tell the tale, her grandfather had sat quietly with tears pooling in his eyes. Discreetly, he'd wiped them away and smiled up at her. "A safe journey to y', Nancy. May y' find y'r pot o' gold at the end o' the rainbow. My only regret is that I'm too old to go with y'."

Thunder rolled overhead again, jarring Nancy from the memory and forcing her to consider the possibility of rain. Seeing the clouds rising up again on the horizon was disappointing. It had been a cold, late spring with more rain than usual, and it was already apparent that the emigrants wouldn't get away as early as they wanted to. But the grass was slowly pushing its way up through the sodden soil. The countryside was undergoing a metamorphosis from brown to green. In a week or two, the grass should be abundant enough on the prairie to supply ample forage for the livestock, and then the wagons could move out.

In the meadow below, Nancy spotted the broken wagon and three men struggling to get the old axle out of the mud. She heard her heart pounding in her ears now, felt her chest grow tight with apprehension. "God, I've heard Colonel Chiles is a charitable man," she whispered. "Please let it be so." Then she took a deep breath to steady herself and nudged the mare forward.

2

Down on his knees in the mud, the redheaded Missourian was pounding on the old axle with a sledge hammer and punctuating each blow with a profanity. The axle, from all appearances, was winning the battle. Chiles, being absolutely embroiled in the task, was not as yet aware of Nancy's presence.

She had been taught that ladies should be offended by such language, but Nancy had the unladylike urge to laugh outright. The poor man, who was probably about six or seven years older than herself, and fairly handsome, was obviously at the end of his wits and patience. In her opinion, he deserved sympathy, not scorn.

On either side of him, his two companions, with muscles bulging through their cotton shirts, were using levers to hold the wagon up off the muddy ground so Chiles could get the old axle out of the way. The wagon had been pulled off the busy thoroughfare, but it was still bogged down in a sizeable puddle of mire.

"Hell, J.B.," the tallest man said. "What seems to be the problem down there? I don't know how much longer me and Billy can hold this damned thing up."

"Goddamned if I know, Hart," came Chiles's response, along with another clang of the hammer. "Trade places with me and you see if you can get the blasted thing to do what it's supposed to do."

"It clearly ain't going to go easy," the shortest man of the three announced, the one who had been called Billy. Nancy assumed he was William Baldridge, the millwright known around town as one of Chiles's best friends. She had no idea who the other man was.

"Maybe you should block the wagon up, gentlemen," Nancy suggested, rather boldly. "Then all three of you could manhandle the axle without fear of being pinned beneath the wagon."

The ear-shattering clang of the hammer suddenly ceased, but not the ringing reverberation. Seemingly oblivious to the mud, Chiles sat back on his heels and squinted up at Nancy, as if looking at her through the blinding sunlight instead of beneath the grayness of a heavy sky.

A smile cracked his frown, and he leaped to his full gangly height of six-foot-four. "I declare, men! Let the wagon rest. We've got a most lovely visitor who apparently knows something of wagon mechanics." He pulled a rag from his back pocket and took to wiping the grime and mud off his hands while sauntering toward her, where she still sat atop her mare. By the time he got there, he was stuffing the rag back in his pocket.

"Joseph Chiles at your service, Miss—?"

"Maguire," Nancy supplied, leaning slightly forward to offer her hand. "Miss Nancy Maguire."

His hand engulfed hers. "Miss Maguire. My pleasure." His grin widened a good inch from ear to ear. "This wagon has given us so much trouble we've considered torching it. And you are absolutely right. We should have blocked it first, but we were hoping for a quick fix. You would think we'd know by now that short cuts are seldom to be had."

The other two men lowered the wagon back into the mire. Baldridge took a position next to Chiles with his hands thrust into his front pockets. The other man, dark-haired and quite strikingly handsome, remained near the wagon. He struck a careless pose, leaning against the wagon wheel and folding his arms over a broad chest.

"What brings you out from town?" Colonel Chiles was saying. "Taking your mare for a run?"

The mare had finally settled down and was only shifting a bit now, but every nerve in Nancy's body was on end. This was the moment that would decide her future. Now that she was here, face to face with Colonel Chiles, her confidence teetered. But she affected a casual air, and dove into her request like a confident swimmer plunging into water. "Actually,

I'm here because I want to go to California with your company, Colonel Chiles. I intend to make it my home."

If a mule had kicked Chiles in the solar plexus with both hind feet, he couldn't have been more shocked. So was Baldridge. But the man leaning against the wagon wheel merely tried to suppress an amused grin, and shifted his weight to the other leg as if settling into a more comfortable position in which to enjoy the proceedings.

Few people, and fewer women, had made the overland journey to California. Most emigrants were presently taking the safer, more traveled road to Oregon country, following in the wake of mountain men, trappers, and missionaries. Those Americans now residing in California had gone via Cape Horn, or by way of the Santa Fe Trail and through southern California.

The overland migration of families had started officially two years ago when John Bidwell and John Bartleson, along with Joseph Chiles, had led a party to California. The thirty-odd members of their party, mostly single men and one woman and her baby, had not succeeded in finding a wagon road over the Sierra Nevadas as they had hoped. Starving, they had been forced to dump their wagons and most of their belongings, kill their mules for food, and walk over the mountains with winter nipping at their heels.

According to the gossip at Eleanor Townsend's boardinghouse, Joseph B. Chiles had been undaunted by the hardships of the journey. He and a dozen of the original 1841 group had returned by horseback last fall to try again. His intent was to settle in California himself, and to find that wagon road and open the passage to American emigrants. He had seen potential in California and had brought back with him John Bidwell's journal, which had been published in the Independence newspaper, encouraging more settlers to come. Nancy had ignored the rumors that the Californians did not welcome "gringos." She intended to be one of Chiles's company.

It was a good minute before Chiles managed to collect himself. He was no longer looking at her as if she were a lady out for a ride on a warm spring day, but rather as a potential candidate for his overland company. His bushy brows drew together and from beneath them his blue eyes searched for her mettle, along with her motivation. He wouldn't find either in her appearance; in her black riding habit, in the carefully coiffed, golden brown hair beneath her jaunty hat, or in the expensive, polished sidesaddle. But she hoped he would find it in her square shoulders; her tall, strong frame; the determined lift to her chin; and in the steady, unswerving, and daring green eyes she'd inherited from Flynn Maguire.

At last, Chiles cleared his throat and found his voice. "Am I to assume that you mean to travel alone, Miss Maguire?"

"Perhaps there's no significant comparison, Colonel Chiles, but I've come all the way from Massachusetts alone, and I intend to take the remainder of the journey in similar fashion."

Nancy said the words with a smile, hoping to make the declaration sound calm and unaffected, but despite her efforts she heard the trace of desperate defiance in her tone and hoped Chiles and his friends had not. She was more than desperate. She was frightened, so frightened that her great adventure—or her great folly, as her father had called it—would end here on the edge of the frontier, and she would be forced to return to Massachusetts, humbled and humiliated.

Colonel Chiles lifted his gangly arm and scratched his hatless head, then dragged his long fingers through hair that needed cutting as desperately as she needed to be accepted into his company. "I hope you'll not mistake my questions for nosiness, Miss Maguire," he said, "but I would need to know more about you before I could decide whether to let you come along. For one thing, we're traveling with mules, so people with oxen would not be able to keep up."

"I intend to take nothing more than two mules to carry my supplies and belongings, Colonel Chiles. And I'll be riding my mare."

His lips compressed into a contemplative line. "I see you've thought this through. But my first and foremost concern is for your safety on the trip as well as after we arrive in California. Do you have someone waiting for you there? A fiancé? Your father or a brother, perhaps? Otherwise, it could be a treacherous existence for a woman alone. Pardon me for making this observation, and I hope it won't offend you, but you don't exactly look the sort of woman who is accustomed to physical labor."

Nancy had heard the questions and concerns dozens of times from friends, families, and complete strangers she had met on the journey thus far. "I wish to acquire land for raising horses, and cattle, of course. My father is a horse breeder so I feel I have sufficient knowledge to succeed in such an enterprise. As for the cattle, I am admittedly not as well versed in what it takes to raise them, but I intend to hire vaqueros who will assist me with the work and from whom I can learn. You might also be interested to know that I've taught school, so I am not completely without skills that could be useful to an American settlement. I believe my knowledge and abilities far outweigh any possible burdens created by my gender."

She had left him with no argument, or a weak one at best, as she had intended to do. Still he was reluctant. "I suppose you know you will have to pledge your allegiance to Mexico, become a citizen of the country in order to obtain land?"

"I've kept abreast of the political scene. Everyone who's heading West believes that California will eventually be annexed into the United States. But in the meantime—yes, I'm willing to become a Mexican citizen."

"It's quite unexpected for a single woman to want to make such a journey without family in attendance, Miss Maguire," he persisted doubtfully. "And to engage in such a physical occupation as ranching. . . ."

"Precisely why I've chosen California, sir," she put in. "Eastern society would more than likely frown on an enterprising woman. Pardon me for being so bold as to say that I honestly believe a good number of men here in the states would not do business with a female horse breeder. But I hear the Californians are considerably less judgmental about what their women do."

Chiles acknowledged her point, then continued on his own train of thought. "We do have a single woman going with us, Miss Maguire, but she will be traveling with her sister and brother-in-law. I certainly wouldn't argue to the point that we'd love to see you grace California with your beauty and talents, but I cannot caution you enough of the dangers in getting to her golden shores. And there are many things you'll have to be able to do; shoot a rifle for your own protection, build a fire, pitch your tent, swim your animals across rivers, cook over a campfire, pack your mules without assistance. Although I'm sure the men might be willing to help you, each person is responsible for himself. Each person has his own duties and obligations."

His words weren't a rejection, but neither were they an acceptance. Despite her brave stance, Nancy began to see the cord that had held all her hopes and dreams together begin to unravel. How could she ever prove to him that she was strong, despite her genteel upbringing, and that she could suffer the hardships and difficulties of the journey? That she actually looked forward to the challenge? Or was it fruitless to try and convince someone of such a thing?

She looked at the wagon they were fixing. "Is that the wagon that will carry your mill to California, Colonel?"

Surprised by the change in subject, he glanced at the wagon and back at her. "Why, yes, it is. If we ever get it back together."

"I hear that no wagon road has been found over the Sierras. How do you plan to get it into California? Some are calling it your folly, Colonel Chiles, saying that you're foolish to be trying something that hasn't been done before."

He clearly didn't like being the object of people's speculations about his ability, but the spark of irritation her comment had incited guttered out almost as quickly as it had flared. "All right, Miss Maguire, I see your point. But I still find this request of yours incredibly hard to swallow. Pardon me for asking, but are you a spy for the government or something? I honestly cannot see what would possess a single woman to do such a thing."

For the first time since they'd started talking, it was Nancy's turn to be amused. "Do you interrogate all emigrants so thoroughly, Colonel? Or only single women?"

His smile bantered politely with hers. "I figure a man ought to know all those things."

"And do they?" Her eyes teased.

"Well, not always," he admitted. "Some don't know which end of the horse eats hay." ·

"I can assure you, I do. And what I don't know, I'm willing to learn. If I had a relative who wanted to go West, believe me, I would not be forced to go alone. But sometimes you can't wait for others to help you fulfill your dreams—whether you're a man, or a woman."

Chiles rubbed his chin thoughtfully. "I would highly recommend against you going alone, Miss Maguire. What if you were to become ill? Injured?" He shook his head, still not convinced despite her sturdy argument. "You may not know it, but I'm a family man. I had a wife who died a few years back, and I have four children I've left with relatives because they're too young to take with me. Women and children will be my biggest concern on this trip. I don't want to take them out there to see them die. I know the dangers that lie beyond—I've been to California and back. As captain of the company, it's my duty to make sure those who join up with me will be able to take care of themselves and not put an undue burden on the others. It's not going to be a pleasure ride."

The man leaning against the wagon wheel spoke up. "Why are you so all-fired concerned, J.B.? Miss Maguire will be married before she ever gets to California anyway, then she'll have a husband to look out after her."

Nancy refused to let his comment annoy her, as she was sure he had intended it to do. "I'm not looking for a husband to take care of me, Mr.—?"

The man pushed away from the wagon wheel and sauntered forward, extending his hand. "Daniels, ma'am. Hart Daniels at your service. And didn't you know that it's when you aren't looking for something that you generally always find it?"

His hand closed around hers, calloused, powerful, and as hot as if he'd had it stretched out next to a fire. She was shocked to admit she quite liked the strong, masculine texture of it, which was a pleasant contrast to the cold, effeminate hands belonging to the endless string of fops that had come courting over the past ten years.

Nancy politely eased her hand from his, realizing he would have held onto hers longer than propriety deemed respectable. A flirtatious glow in his brilliant blue eyes toyed with her, unsettled her, and warmed her from head to toe. "I'm not going to California to be tied to a husband, Mr. Daniels," she said evenly, managing a tolerant smile. "My horse ranch is my own endeavor, and I intend to be in charge of how it is developed."

Amusement curved his lips. Like all the others who had learned of her plans, she suspected he thought she didn't have the slightest idea what she was getting into. He probably thought she would crumble in the face of hardship and danger. Just the same, a spark in his eyes suggested he was curious to see if she could prove them all wrong.

His words proved her intuitions correct. "I say we should let Miss Maguire test her strength against nature if she's so inclined to do so," he said. "She looks strong and healthy to me. Who are we to tell her no? If she can find a traveling companion, I see no reason why she shouldn't be allowed to come along."

Nancy was surprised by Daniels's support, as was Chiles, but the latter brightened, apparently liking the idea of her finding a traveling companion, which suggested that he really would like to see her come along after all.

"That sounds like a good idea, Hart," Chiles said with new enthusiasm. "She can inquire out at the rendezvous and see if she can find someone who will let her travel with them, in exchange for her help with the cooking and possibly the care of children." He turned to Nancy. "The company is gathering out at Fitzhugh's Mill, about twelve miles from here. But you really shouldn't go out there alone, what with all the low-lives crawling all over this place."

Nancy released a frustrated sigh at yet another roadblock the man was placing in front of her, but she'd barely cleared her lungs of it when Daniels spoke again. "I'll escort her out there tomorrow, J.B. I've got to go out anyway and see how things are shaping up. That is, if she doesn't mind my company."

The inflection in his voice drew her eyes to his again. While he waited for her answer, she had the feeling again that he wanted to see her succeed. She didn't know if she would mind his company or not, but offers of assistance were so few, she was certainly in no position to refuse his. "I'll meet you at five in the morning at Abbot Moses's livery," she said, with hope surging anew.

"Make it six," he said easily. "My rooster doesn't crow that early."

3

Nancy closed the door to her room at Eleanor Townsend's boarding-house and sank wearily into the green brocade armchair. With tired arms, she removed hat pins and hat, discarding both on the nearby rosewood table. Leaning forward, she shook her hair free and massaged her sore scalp, wondering how she was ever going to get to California if she couldn't even get out of Missouri.

Searching for a traveling companion, or a family, out at the rendezvous had been fruitless. She had thought it would be relatively easy to find someone who would welcome an extra set of helping hands. Hart Daniels had gone along with her, introducing her and explaining her situation. More than once she had wondered why he was going out of his way to help her. When she'd finally asked him point-blank, he had merely said, "There was an old trapper who taught me how to survive when I first went into the Rocky Mountains ten years ago to explore. No tellin' what would have happened to me if he hadn't given me some guidance. Just call it passing along a favor."

Nancy had felt that restless energy again, inside herself and inside the men and children bustling about in camp. But she had gone away disturbed by the women who had worn glum or tired expressions as they'd gone about the business of preparing a meal over wind-blown campfires. They clearly hadn't shared their family's enthusiasm for the journey. They were here only because their husbands were, and she sensed they'd had no say in the decision to go West. It didn't seem fair that they had no pro-nouncement of their own destinies.

There had been Miriam Waite, mother of eight children—all boys—and pregnant with her ninth. She had nearly begged her husband to let Nancy travel with them, to help her with the cooking and washing and the care of the younger children. But her husband had scrutinized Nancy from head to toe and impudently stated his opinion. "She's nothing but a rich Eastern blueblood. You'll be waiting on her instead of the other way around. Why a woman like her would even want to go overland in the first place makes me suspicious of her character."

"But Arthur—"

"The wagons are overloaded as it is, Miriam."

"Surely we could find room for a few more things," the woman had uselessly argued. "And she said she'd buy her own supplies. We wouldn't be feeding her. I could really use the help."

"I've spoken, Miriam."

Hart had taken Nancy by the arm and moved her on to the next fam-ily, but not before slicing Arthur Waite down to size with a look that was as deadly as a poisoned Indian arrow.

The second woman, Lucille Royal, had glared contemptuously at Nancy, Hart, and the entire congregation as if they were no more than an infestation of rodents. "It wasn't my choice to come out here," she had de-clared with powerful bitterness. "We had us a nice home in Indiana, but my husband kept listening to those tall tales about California and Oregon as if they were both Paradise. If it's anything like what I can see from here, then it's nothing to leave home for. If you aren't running from the law or a man, then you're plain stupid to be here."

Nancy had politely excused herself, feeling the woman's eyes stabbing her retreat with a peculiar triumphant glow at having driven her away and given her a piece of her mind in the process. Apparently Lucille Royal had no need for friends.

A young pregnant woman, barely eighteen years old, had also tried to convince her husband to accept Nancy's help and company. Nancy had recognized Garnet Stillman's fear and uncertainty and the desperate need for someone besides her stoic husband to talk to. But Ethan Stillman had said, "I've got my hands full, Garnet. All I need is some fancy East-ern woman to look out after, too. She probably can't even saddle her own horse."

After another hour of inquiring, Nancy had found no one who was willing to let her join their party. The women had mostly been kind, and would have tried to find a way to help her, but the men were more adamant, fearing she would be more hindrance than help. Even hauling her own provisions on her mules hadn't made a difference. They didn't want another person to "look out after."

Nancy's thoughts inadvertently strayed to Hart Daniels. On the entire trek out to Fitzhugh's Mill and back they had exchanged the standard, polite inquiries about each other. She had learned that he was from Tennessee, the youngest son of six.

"I left my parents' farm at the age of eighteen," he said. "I had a hankering to head into the Rockies, do some trapping and exploring. When I got restless again, I came back to Missouri and took a job as a freighter on the Santa Fe Trail. Two years ago I joined J.B. to go to California. I liked it so well out there that I figured it would be a good place to settle so I applied for citizenship with the Mexican government. Maybe by the time I get back there, they'll have approved it. I'll be acting as a scout on this trip so J.B. can concentrate on being the wagonmaster."

After riding with Hart for a short distance and seeing that his eyes were always searching the horizons, never missing a thing, Nancy came to understand why he had been entrusted with such an important position as scout.

He hadn't inquired into her personal life too deeply, although more than once Nancy had sensed his curiosity about the *real* reason she was headed for California. But an unspoken code of etiquette existed here on the edge of the frontier, and a person was careful what he asked of another person's past. Seeing the rough nature of the town and its inhabitants, Nancy understood his reticence, suspecting that this was a place where people came who had secrets they would just as soon take to the grave.

She had discovered Hart's teasing nature. Once, with his blue eyes flashing devilishly, he'd said, "You never did tell J.B. if you were a spy. I reckon a woman out in California could find out all sorts of things about the strength of the Mexican army and the sentiment of the Californios if she was careful how she went about it."

Nancy laughed. "I keep up on politics, Mr. Daniels, but that's as far as my involvement goes. However, I'm beginning to think that people would accept political intrigue much quicker than they would the simple truth, which is that I came seeking adventure. To see the world, like yourself. A nasty tonic for most people to swallow, coming from a single woman."

Hart Daniels had sobered, looking far down the road as if he saw well beyond its reaches and into that place where dreams lay hidden. "The need for freedom and adventure is in the blood, Miss Maguire. For some of us it's so powerful that it abolishes all fear. There are those of us who can't be happy to sit and wonder what's out there beyond our front gates, or to wait for others to tell us. We have to know. We have to see it for ourselves. So we get in our ships and we sail, or we get up on our horses and we ride. And sometimes, we just toss our pack on our back and start walking. But nobody understands that fever except another inflicted with it."

They had ridden in silence after that for several miles. It hadn't been an uncomfortable silence. Camaraderie had come between them, and even though they didn't know much about each other, they seemed to know all that was necessary.

A knock at the door startled Nancy and scattered her musings. She hadn't heard anyone coming down the hall. Thinking it was probably Mrs. Townsend, she was surprised to see a stranger—a rough but striking woman of about thirty-six, wearing her long, wavy brown hair loose and partially covered by a man's hat. A young boy, of about six, with close-cropped sandy hair, stood directly in front of her, held there by the woman's hands on his shoulders. In a glance, Nancy took in the coarseness of the woman's brown jacket and skirt, and the boy's linsey-woolsey shirt poking out the sides of a pair of serviceable overalls.

"Eleanor told me which room was yours, Miss Maguire," the woman said in a drawl that many of the people from these parts affected. "My name's Lottie England, and this here's my boy, Josh. We were sent by Hart Daniels. He said you needed a traveling companion to California. Well, I'm wantin' to go there myself, so I figured maybe we could talk."

The woman's eyes reminded Nancy of a blue-violet summer sky when the heat is oppressive and the only breeze that can be found is man-made. But those eyes sparkled with friendliness and a definite hint of mischievousness. They also took up the larger share of a small, narrow face that was, in itself, almost lost in the lion's ruff of hair. Her big, eager grin, revealing small, pearly teeth, reached out and grabbed Nancy as well as any handshake could have done, and Nancy felt as if she'd just been drawn into an embrace of sisterly warmth.

Surprised by the unexpected turn of events, Nancy pulled the door wider. "Please, come in. I was just . . . thinking about what I was going to do. I could fix some tea, if you'd like. I'll go down to the kitchen and get some hot water if you wouldn't mind the wait."

Lottie England stepped into the room, giving her surroundings only a cursory glance. Small in stature—barely five-foot-two—she nonetheless exuded strength, independence, and complete confidence in herself. "A cup of hot tea sounds as if it would just about hit the spot, but I've known Eleanor for years and I'm sure she wouldn't mind accommodatin' us with a tray." She turned to her boy, "Josh, run down to the kitchen and see if Eleanor will fix us some tea. Then you can bring it up. But be careful not to drop it. Her cups and teapot are china, and she'd sure 'nuf skin your hide and nail it to the woodshed wall if you was to break something."

Josh nodded obediently and took flight out the door. Freckle-faced and tanned, the boy looked the sort to prefer the outdoors where he could run wild and get into all sorts of mischief.

Nancy offered Lottie England one of the two chairs in the room, then seated herself in the other. "So Hart Daniels told you I was looking for a traveling companion?"

Lottie England's unique combination of femininity and ruggedness was immediately fascinating to Nancy, who had never seen anyone quite like her before. The woman seemed oblivious to fashion, dressing in a manner that served her own purposes and possibly a yen for comfort.

She removed her wool jacket, a serviceable man's coat, and draped it on the back of the chair. A cream-colored, loose-fitting muslin blouse, collarless and without darts or tucks, covered her full bosom. The blouse buttoned up the front and at the cuffs, and was set off by a heavy brown belt cinched at her extremely small waist. Nancy would bet she wore no corset, and was delighted by the prospect of making friends with such a nonconformist.

She didn't remove her hat, but pushed it to the back of her head with the tip of her finger the way Nancy had seen most of the men in Independence do when they settled down for a meal, a smoke, or a drink.

Lottie England didn't follow convention as far as her hair was concerned either. She wore it loose, not in the unbecoming current style which was to part it down the middle and pull it severely over the ears and back to the nape in a tight bun. Instead, Lottie's hair appeared to be pulled back at the top and sides and held in place with a barrette or pins hidden beneath the hat. The remainder fell down well past her shoulders in a wild array of natural curl that framed and softened her face.

"I've known Hart for years," Lottie said. "He used to work for my husband before the danged fool—my husband, not Hart—went and run off with a ten-cent Mexican whore in Santa Fe and the both of them got themselves scalped by Apaches while trying to get to California. Served 'em both right, I figure.

"Anyway, I've been ready to quit this damned place for years. I've been trying to keep my husband's freighting business going, and I've been making better money than he ever did, but it's doing nothing but making me as ornery and cantankerous as a tomcat that's got its tail caught in the barn door. There's other things to do and new things to be found. A body has to keep reaching for new horizons or they just grow stale as week-old bread.

"I've heard it said there are three reasons a person heads West," she continued. "One, to get something. Two, to get away from something. And three, just to get there. I figure I've got all three reasons pushing at my back. So, I reckon it's time to move on, to see why that no-good, two-timin' sonofabitch and his ten-cent whore were so all-fired eager to see California.

"I see these emigrants coming and going and I just get antsy to be part of the excitement. There's more to this old world than Missouri and that damned, dusty Santa Fe Trail. 'Course, you know that, coming all the way from Massachusetts. Back East is one place I've never been, but I don't have a hankering to either. Guess I just know I wouldn't fit in with that crowd of fancy people. Now, you don't look the sort who'd be headin' to some wild place like California, but I know for a fact that a body can't judge another by appearances. My husband was about as handsome as a man could come, but he wasn't worth a Mexican peso.

"Anyway," Lottie England headed into a conclusion to her monologue, "when Hart stopped over at the house to tell me hello, we got to talking, and the next thing I know he's telling me all about you and what you're trying to do and I'm saying, 'Well, hell, I'll go with the Maguire woman, if she thinks she can tolerate me.' I got the mules and can trade my freight wagons in for something more suitable, and I hear you've got a fine saddle horse and a couple of mules, too."

Before Nancy could reply, Josh came through the open door, juggling a metal tray with china teapot, cups, creamer and sugar, fancy-handled spoons, and butter cookies. Lottie jumped up and rescued the china. "Bless Eleanor's heart. She never could resist a sweet. Here, Josh, why don't you take my cookies. I sure wouldn't be needin' them. My hips are startin' to look like they'd belong better on the rear end of a jackass than a woman."

"Oh, Ma, that ain't true. You eat them. Mrs. Townsend gave me a whole pocket full." He patted his pocket, then said, "Can I go now? Harry's outside on the step and I'm afraid one of those danged Injuns is gonna steal him and cook him up for supper."

Lottie nodded. "Sure, son. Run along. This is grown-up talk anyway."

The boy was out the door practically before Lottie had the words out of her mouth. She turned back to Nancy. "Harry's the boy's pup. He's just a stray mongrel Josh found wandering around town about a month ago. Poor thing was starving, probably left in town by some farmer that didn't want another mouth to feed. Either that or he was lollygagging and got left behind. He can't be more'n six months old. He and Josh are pretty attached."

Nancy had gathered the teapot and was filling Lottie's cup while listening to her dissertation. She'd been surprised by Lottie's candidness, but grateful for it, too. "Yes, I have a horse and two mules," she said, picking up the conversation. "Mr. Daniels must have told you a lot about me."

Lottie dumped two teaspoonsful of sugar in her tiny china cup and stirred. "Everything you told him, from the way it sounded—why you're going, what you plan to do. Pretty ambitious plans for a woman. I have to tell you, girl. Hart Daniels ain't easily impressed, but you sure 'nuf got him."

Nancy felt a blush rising in her cheeks. For some reason the subject of Hart Daniels tended to make her warm all over, as if she needed to go throw a window open. She kept remembering how his hands had felt around her waist when he'd assisted her from her sidesaddle out at Fitzhugh's Mill.

"He already knows where he wants to settle," she said to cover her thoughts. "Did he tell you?"

"Yes. He told me all about it. Said it was the prettiest place he'd ever laid eyes on. Right on some big river and in a beautiful little valley nestled among green rolling hills."

The two of them sipped their tea while the street noises slipped into the silence, but only for a moment. Then Lottie was rattling on again.

"If you figure we could travel together without strangling each other, I thought we could hire one of those single boys to ride herd on the remuda. I'll drive the wagon myself and you could spell me. I used to go with my husband—Major was his name—on some of the trips to Santa Fe and I would spell him on the driving. I could get more out of those mules than he ever could. You've got to like your animals, and Major hated anything that had to lift its tail to poop.

"So, what do you think? Should we show Colonel Chiles what two headstrong women can do? Why, we don't need any men to look out after us. I can tell you one thing, Major never looked out after me. I was the one always covering his sorry behind. Besides, I can probably drive a team better than half the emigrants stacked up out there along that river. Don't get me wrong, I'm not a braggart. I just know I can handle a team of mules."

Nancy didn't doubt it a bit. Her manner was as coarse as her homespun dress, and cuss words rolled off her tongue as if they were right at home there. Her hands were as rough and dark as pine bark, but she was honest, sincere, and savvy, and Nancy knew she could trust her. What was just as good, if not better, was that Lottie England seemed to be able to see Nancy's true character, too, and wasn't afraid to head West with her.

"I've never driven a team of mules and a heavy wagon," Nancy said, warning her, "but I've driven buggies."

"I ain't worried about you, girl," Lottie replied confidently. "If you didn't have any courage, you wouldn't be here."

Excitement coursed through Nancy. "We can start packing tomorrow."

Lottie gulped her tea and stood up. "Figured we would. Now, my havin' the boy along isn't going to trouble you, is it?"

"Of course not. I taught school for a while so I'm accustomed to children."

"You're a teacher? Well, hell. That was one thing Hart didn't mention. He seemed more intrigued by your ranching plans." She moved to the door and hesitated. "Can I offer you a word of advice, without you gettin' mad at me?"

"I could probably use it," Nancy replied, good-naturedly.

"Well, out here, you don't want people to know you've got money. There's those who'll kill you for nothin' more than a silver dollar. So I recommend you get shed of those fancy clothes."

Nancy extended her hand and the older woman shook it heartily. "You're the only person who hasn't asked me if I was out here to find a husband, Mrs. England. So I have a feeling we're going to get along just fine."

Lottie grinned. "Yes, ma'am, Miss Maguire. You're absolutely right about that one."

4

Hart Daniels saw Joseph Chiles stalking down the boardwalk from a block away. At six-foot-four, even with a hat pulled down over his eyes and covering his brilliant red hair, it was hard not to notice the big, raw-boned Missourian. And hard not to see that he was piqued. Perturbed. Maybe even downright pissed.

J.B. seldom got out-and-out irate, but he definitely had a burr under his blanket today. And Hart would bet the two most important things he owned—his boots and his saddle horse—that he knew exactly what could be blamed for his friend's sour mood.

He returned his attention to the task at hand, trimming his buckskin gelding's tail.

"I surely do hope you're happy with yourself, Hart Daniels," Joseph Chiles proclaimed while still twenty feet away. "By God, if you weren't my friend, I'd take you down and whup your skinny ass."

People up and down the boardwalk turned at the comment. A few loitering nearby with nothing better to do made it a point to saunter closer so they wouldn't miss anything that might be fodder for gossip. J.B. saw them and told them to go mind their own damned business. He clearly wasn't joking, so they scattered, leaving the street to him and Hart.

Hart picked up another strand of his horse's tail and expertly slid his knife along its length in a razoring motion. J.B. stopped in front of him, leaning forward as if trying to hold his gangly body up against an imaginary wind. "It wasn't hard at all to see why you did it. A man wouldn't even have to have good eyesight."

"Did what, J.B.?" Hart asked innocently, knowing darn good and well why his friend was in a lather.

"Why you went and found a traveling companion for that Maguire woman. You could have kept your nose out of it. But for the love of God, did it have to be *another* woman? I'm going to place you in full responsibility for those two females. Something goes wrong that they can't fix—like a broken axle—and *you've* got the detail."

Hart studied his horse's tail, deciding where it needed a little more trimming. "Don't be so hard on those women, J.B. You know Lottie England is a better hand with mules than most of those emigrants you've got signed up. Why, you might even be concerned that she'll show you up." He saw J.B. bluster, getting ready to explode. "As for broken wheels and axles and things of an accidental nature, isn't it customary for everyone to pitch in and help each other, regardless of gender? I mean, we're not going to leave anybody behind if their wheel falls off. We're going to stop the whole train and help the poor bastard."

Chiles's glare would have seared the hair off a ten-year-old bull moose. "I'd wager every mule I own that you've got your eye on that Maguire woman."

Hart razored away and the pile of horse hair on the ground grew. "The only reason I can see why that would bother you, J.B., is if you've got your eye on her, too."

J.B. snorted. "Don't be ridiculous."

"You've got to admit she's a pretty one. And she's mature. So many of these single women running around are so young they require bottle feeding."

"She's pretty danged determined if you ask me. She doesn't want a man standing in her way. If you're toying with getting serious over her, you'd better think twice. She'd run all over a man worse'n a stampede of buffalo."

"Not if she had a man with some backbone, and one that would give her the rein she needs. You see, there's a certain balance involved with a woman like her. But, then, I can clearly see you don't understand her temperament."

"And you do?"

"Yeah, I think I do."

"She's set in her ways, Hart. It would be damn near impossible to tame her, as old as she is."

"Why would you want to tame her? That would take all the fun out of it." Finished with the horse's tail, Hart slid his knife into the scabbard at his hip. "California isn't a place for weak women, and I've got a hankering for a pretty woman to come home to every night. It's a lonely country out there, pal. And me and Miss Nancy Maguire are after the same thing. We might as well go after it together."

"I think you were so smitten with her that you didn't hear a danged thing she said. She *said* she didn't want a husband tying her down."

"Oh, I know. But she didn't really mean it."

J.B. squinted, clearly confused. "What about that woman you've been half-assed courtin' over in St. Louis? I know you went over there and saw her a few weeks back."

Hart shrugged. "I thought I was in love, but when I went to St. Louis, all ready to propose, I suddenly couldn't see her in California with me on that piece of land. I realized we were heading in two different directions, wanting different things from life.

"My old grandma used to grouse about men allowing their tallywhackers—she always called them tallywhackers—to do their thinking. At the sake of being self-defamatory, I admit she was right. She used to say, 'Ask yourself where your pain is, boy—in your heart or your old tallywhacker.' Well, there in St. Louis, it hit me that I didn't have any pain in either place."

"So you're going to court the Maguire woman with intent?" J.B. was skeptical.

"Isn't that the only way to court? There's nothing to be gained otherwise, and it's not my nature to take advantage of a good woman. You know that."

"Yeah, you're so pure and all. What if she tells you to head on down the pike?"

Hart grinned. "How could she possibly resist my charm and wit?"

"That woman could resist anything she set her mind to resist. Why, you never know, underneath those fancy clothes she might be even tougher than Lottie England."

"Don't be so hard on her, J.B. She's human. As for Lottie, she sheds tears the same as everybody else. I've seen it. You wouldn't believe how it broke her up when her husband ran out on her. Oh, she didn't show that face to the world, but she loved that man more than she had the good sense to."

Chiles had calmed down. He threw an arm up on the buckskin's hip and leaned against him. He looked at his heavy work boot and kicked at the pile of coarse black tail hair on the ground. "I wish Polly was still alive. God, I miss her, Hart." His voice cracked and he swallowed convulsively. "I went out to see the children the other day. We had a good long visit. You don't know how hard it was for me to tell them they were just too young to come with me and would be better off with their aunt. But I'm going to come back for them. I made them a promise, and if the Indians or Mexicans don't get me, I'm going to stand by it."

"Maybe you ought to get married again yourself, J.B.," Hart said softly, watching the agony his friend was still going through over the loss of his wife. "It's been seven years since Polly died."

Chiles shook his head. "I've thought about it, but I'm not a man to take a wife just for the sake of taking a wife. I had something special with Polly. She was my first love, and I still love her. It hurts just thinking about her and the times we shared together, knowing they're over and never will be again. I don't know if I'll ever be able to feel that way for another woman."

Hart stood with his hands in his back pockets. If he and J.B. hadn't been so close, the personal confession might have been uncomfortable for them both. But they were good friends who understood each other, and neither was afraid of emotion. "Maybe you won't feel exactly the same way, but you could love another woman, if you let yourself."

The Missourian said nothing.

"You can't fault me for wanting what you and Polly had, can you, J.B.?"

Chiles stared at the ground for a full minute then finally shook his head. "No. But I still think you're a crazy damned fool to go courtin' that Maguire woman. She's a heartbreaker if I ever saw one. I'll bet she's left a string of broken hearts all the way from here to Massachusetts."

Hart laughed and slapped his friend on the back. "What do you say we head over to Miss Lily's Restaurant and discuss our two female additions over a plate of fresh steak? I haven't eaten since breakfast and from the way my stomach's been carrying on, I think my big guts are eatin' my little guts."

Defeated, Chiles shook his head. "It's comforting to know that there are some things in life that never change."

"If you aren't a sight for sore eyes, girl. Breaking rules and raising eyebrows." Lottie England pushed herself away from the wagon wheel she'd been leaning against. Latching her thumbs in the brown belt that circled her small waist, she took a wide stance on the edge of the busy street just as Nancy pulled her mare to a stop a few yards away.

"I took your advice," Nancy said, self-consciously raising a hand to the brown hat she wore. "I just purchased it over at Holcomb's General Store, along with some cloth to make some serviceable skirts and waists for the journey. I've already commissioned Eleanor to do the sewing. So, what do you think of the hat? Do I look utterly ridiculous?"

With her hands on her hips, Lottie sauntered closer. "Needs to come down over your eyes a bit more. You look like a tinhorn with it stuck up there on your hairline."

Nancy tugged on the brim, bringing the hat down onto her forehead just above her eyebrows. "How's that?"

"Yes, right there," Lottie approved. "Now, you look like you've got a handle on the world."

"I think it's a little big," Nancy admitted, "but it was the only one that would come close to fitting. Mr. Holcomb wasn't any help. He let me know that *ladies* didn't wear men's hats."

"You shoulda told the old goat it was for somebody else."

Nancy grinned slyly. "Well, I did. I told him it was for you."

Lottie's laughter spiked out into the street only to be swallowed by the bawl of a cow running frantically through the wagons looking for her wayward calf. "And I suppose he told you I was corrupting you?"

"He said we'd probably both be wearing pants next and smoking cigars."

"The part about the pants ain't a bad idea, but we'd best let the men get used to seein' us in their hats first. Trust me, girl. You'll never trade that hat in for no sunbonnet. Damned things are like blinders. No, if bonnets were such great inventions, men would be wearing them, you can be sure of that. Now, I reckon we'd best get down to serious business. Word is out that Colonel Chiles is pulling out in five days. And we've got a sight to do if we intend on being with him."

✿   ✿   ✿

Lottie pulled the wagon and team of mules up in front of Eleanor
Townsend's boardinghouse. Nancy was waiting in a rocker on the front
porch. "I was beginning to think you'd gone on to California without
me." Nancy trotted down the steps to meet her. "Did you have problems
getting a buyer for your freight wagons?"

"No, but I did have trouble getting that damn farmer to let go of this
farm wagon." Lottie handed herself to the ground using the front wheel.
"The old turd demanded twice what this thing was worth—*new*. But
come here and look her over. She'll get us to California without breaking up."

The wagon's box was nine feet long by four feet wide with sides and
end boards two feet high. "It'll carry a ton or more," Lottie assured
Nancy. "It's made of the best wood, too. Elm for the hubs; oak for the
spokes; beech for the felloes; ash for the framework; poplar for the box.
And there's even a false bottom divided into compartments. If there's
something we won't be using until we get to California, we can store it in
there out of the way."

Nancy was duly impressed as Lottie pointed out the excellent condition of the running gear, the tire irons, tongue, axles, and wheels. After
Lottie had explained all the wagon's parts to her, she went to work mend-
ing harnesses and Nancy and Josh accepted the messy job of filling up the
tar buckets.

Financially secure with the sale of her husband's inventory and heavy
freight wagons, Lottie had decided they should keep fifteen mules, including Nancy's two, for the trip and for collateral in getting established
in California. "We'll use four or six to pull the wagon, depending on the
terrain," she explained to Nancy. "The rest of them will serve as replace-
ments. They can run with the company's remuda on the journey but we'll
have to lead them out to Fitzhugh's Mill. You can lead two behind Lady
Rae. Josh can ride one and lead one. The rest we'll tie in strings behind
the wagon, which I'll be driving."

It took all three of them to stretch the double thickness of canvas over
the wagon bows and get it pulled tautly down so the wind wouldn't tear
it off. Then they assembled their provisions and supplies in Lottie's three-
room house, which she had sold for a handsome profit to a young couple
who would move in as soon as she was out.

After four days of preparation, they were ready to load their belongings and supplies. Lottie's freighting experience left her with a knack for knowing the best way to load for easy accessibility and fit. There were blankets, a tent, two rifles, three pistols, a shotgun, powder, lead, knives, an ax, hammer, shovel, saw, gimlet, hatchet, two of Major's saddles, extra harness leather, scissors and other sewing supplies, ropes, staples, wax, twine, shoe leather, beeswax, soap, candles, liniment, herbs, medicines, two lanterns, silverware, dishes, pots, a Dutch oven, a washbasin, and scores of other essential items. In the jockey box, they put in kingbolts, linchpins, extra chain, more rope.

"You'd best get yourself an oilskin raincoat," Lottie advised Nancy, "and a warm overcoat and sturdy shoes in case you end up walking. Now, I don't mean to try and read the tea leaves, girl, but remember what happened to Bidwell's bunch goin' over those mountains in '41." The brunette also saw fit to throw in a few of Major's cotton duck trousers and flannel shirts. "Just in case."

The food took up a good portion of the space: sacks of flour, salt, sugar, coffee, dried fruit, cornmeal. They brought some sacks of beans, too, for the times when they would be stopping long enough to cook them. They brought bacon and dried beef and a few delicacies: pickles, vinegar, tea, jams, cheese, and eggs packed in buckets of oats. The perishables wouldn't last long, but they could enjoy them for the first week or two of the trip.

After several farewells from people who knew them, Nancy swung onto her mare, whom she'd named Lady Rae, and Lottie climbed up on the left-wheel mule, settling astride on a heavy saddle pad she'd arranged over the harness gear.

At Nancy's wide-eyed look of surprise, Lottie just grinned. "This is the way mule skinners do it, girl. Sure, I could sit on that piece of board they call a wagon seat, but that damned contraption rocks and sways and jounces and bounces and will shove your spine right up through the top of your head in no time at all. It makes worse sores on your precious derriere than riding astride ever could, and it'll plumb wear you out, too." She straightened her skirt, pulling it down over her tall boots. Taking up the single rein, which she called a jerk line, she added. "If the men—or the women—don't like it, they can just turn their heads the other way."

Nancy grinned and shook her head. "I think Holcomb was right. You *will* be in pants next."

"Maybe so, but I won't be smokin' no cigars. Those are about the nastiest damned things that were ever invented. Major took to smokin' 'em when he found out how bad I hated 'em. That bum, he did it just to annoy me."

Josh, riding one of his Pa's saddles, and with Harry bouncing alongside, reined his mule up next to his mother's. Lottie expertly threaded the jerk line through her gloved hands. Despite the traffic jam down main street, Lottie and Nancy turned their share of heads as they moved out of town. Nancy didn't like the looks of some of the men loitering on the boardwalks, watching them leave without male escorts. By now, more people than not knew the two of them were heading to California with Chiles, and knew they were going to Fitzhugh's Mill, twelve miles away.

Lottie seemed to read her mind. "Don't worry, girl, I have a reputation in this town, and they know they'd better not fool with me if they don't want their heads blown off. Since they've been watching us pack, they saw me put the shotgun inside the wagon by the seat. People been talkin' 'bout you and that pepperbox, too. But the first lesson to survival out here is to know what's going on around you. Keep alert and always keep your eyes moving, your ears peeled, and your senses honed. Watch out for men who might be following you, waiting for the right moment to seize upon bad intentions. They may think we're nothin' but silly women, but we must never let them be right."

They made good time on the road to Fitzhugh's Mill. The sun they'd had for the past few days had dried things out and the mules were fresh, pulling the loaded wagon with ease. Nearly four hours out, and just a mile from their destination, the women could no longer ignore the black thunderhead moving rapidly toward them from the west.

"I was hopin' it would go around us," Lottie said, "but it looks like it's gonna hit us head-on. I think we'd best try to get a little more out of these mules and see how fast we can make that last mile."

She'd no sooner said the words than the first drops of cold rain, driven by a blustery wind, hit Nancy in the face. She pulled her hat down tighter on her forehead to keep the wind from tearing it from her head. Lady Rae pranced nervously now, sensing the nearness of the impending storm and the charge of electricity in the air. The energy of it seemed transmitted to her and absorbed. The mules leaned into their harnesses and forged onward, merely flicking their ears at the drops of rain, the rolls of thunder, and the occasional sound of Lottie's voice urging them on.

"Damn," Lottie mumbled. "It's gonna get us, ain't it? Josh, I think you'd best get in the wagon. Give me your mules. I think I can lead them and still work the jerk line."

Josh bounced along on his mule's back, in the saddle that was way too big for him. He couldn't even use the stirrups because they couldn't be shortened enough for his legs. "It ain't much farther now, Ma. I see the other wagons just ahead." He kicked his mule into a trot, moving it out ahead of the others, ignoring his mother. The mule he led obligingly followed.

"That danged boy." Lottie feigned exasperation, but there was pride in her voice just the same. "He needs a father's hand to pepper his skinny behind now and again. He never listens to me."

Nancy watched the boy, looking smaller than ever against the ominous clouds lumbering overhead. "It's an adventure for him, Lottie. He doesn't want to miss any of it."

"Sorta like you?"

"I guess you could say that."

Lottie cocked an eyebrow. "Have you ever had to sleep in a wet bed, Miss Nancy Maguire?"

Nancy's laughter rippled out, low and sultry like the clouds. "No, but I have a feeling I'm going to get the opportunity."

Lottie shook her head and chuckled. "I haven't figured you out yet, girl, but I think you're about as crazy as a horse that's gotten into a patch of locoweed."

A ferocious gust of wind nearly knocked Nancy from the saddle. She grabbed for her hat and caught it just before it went sailing. "Here comes the rain, Lottie!" she shouted above the roar of the wind. "You'd better put the whip to those mules!"

5

Fitzhugh's Mill

Their approach had been spotted some time ago, and people from the other encampments sauntered out to see who the new arrivals were. Arthur Waite followed alongside their wagon, shouting questions up at Josh.

"We're going to California, mister," the boy responded freely and proudly. "Ain't interested in Oregon."

"Where's your pa, boy?"

"Dead. But my ma and me don't need him anyhow."

The boy's last words were swallowed in a rush of wind and flying dirt and twigs. With it came a sudden and fierce downpour, soaking the mules to the skin almost instantly, and pouring off the brim of Nancy's hat onto her oilskin.

Someone shouted from the encampment, and she looked up to see Hart and Colonel Chiles motioning for Lottie to drive her wagon around to an opening in the small circle of seven wagons. "Pull up between these two wagons," Hart hollered above the din of the rain. "We'll help you un-hitch. Nancy, ride on inside the enclosure, and you and Josh get down off those animals before you get struck by lightning!"

Inside the wagon circle were tents and a few saddle horses. The rest of the animals were outside the enclosure, some picketed, others left to graze and wander, but the rains had brought them in closer, huddled to-gether in the brush and trees for protection. The air was strong with

smoke from the campfires that had suddenly been extinguished by the
rain. By the time Lottie had maneuvered the wagon between the others,
the rain had even cleared the air of smoke, driving it hard into the
ground.

Lightning cracked overhead and plunged to the ground in a jagged
white blade. Thirty yards away, an old elm tree popped and burst open,
filling Nancy's nostrils with the scent of sulfur. Beneath her hat, her hair
prickled. Lady Rae danced sideways, snorting and liking none of it.

Nancy leaped to the ground. Hart was there to hold the mare's bridle and to help Nancy get her gear off. Some other men rushed to assist
with the mules. In minutes, they had the harnesses off and had turned the
mules loose, along with the strings of extra mules. All made haste to join
the other animals in the trees. Josh's mule and Nancy's mare were held
back inside the circle of the wagons so they could be easily caught and
used to round up the other animals when it was time to pull out.

Nancy felt an arm at her waist and looked up into Hart's rain-splashed
face. His eyes were half-closed against the onslaught and he held his
head cocked so his hat would break the force of the wind from his face.
"The three of you come on into my tent. We'll worry about setting yours
up after this rain quits."

A conical bivouac, Hart's tent greatly resembled an Indian tipi. The
oiled canvas had been secured around a circle of lightweight poles, giving the interior a circumference of about ten feet. A small fire burned in
the center, and kept a pot of coffee warm. Once inside, everyone shed
their wet coats and Hart handed a blanket to the women and Josh. The
other men rushed back to their own tents but Chiles joined them, folding his tall frame double to get through the tent's small opening.

Hart poured coffee and even handed a cup to Josh, who wrapped his
little boy's hands around it and sipped it like a man.

Outside, the rain pelted the tent's oiled canvas and the wind pushed
the sides inward, but Hart had a good location behind a band of bushes
that helped break the force of the storm. Some rain came in through the
opening at the top of the tent, but not enough to do more than spatter the
piece of gutta-percha spread over the ground.

"You ladies made it in the nick of time," Chiles said, taking his wet hat
off and setting it aside. "The prairie can use this rain, but it's surely de-
laying our departure more than I would like to see it. I hate to say it, but
we're going to have to leave in a couple of days regardless, or we won't

make California before the snows. We're going to be pressing our luck now as it is."

Lottie scrutinized Chiles with great interest, sizing him up, but with no indication of approval or disapproval. She thrust her hand toward him. "I'm Lottie England, Colonel. This here's my boy, Josh."

Chiles's big hand closed around Lottie's, swallowing it. "Pleasure to meet you, Mrs. England. Josh. Hart tells me you were married to Major England and took over his freighting business after he died."

"Yes, sir. But he didn't just die. He got hisself scalped while trying to cross Apache country on his way to California. And, as long as we're exchanging hearsay, I hear tell you were with the Bidwell–Bartleson bunch that went over to California two years ago this spring. But I hear you still don't have a wagon route figured out over those Sierras."

"No, ma'am," he said without apology. "But we fully intend to find one. Billy Baldridge and I have a sawmill we want to get into the country, and we sure can't pack it on our backs over those mountains." Chiles reached over and ruffled Josh's hair. "You're certainly a brave boy to be going to California. A good hand with that mule you were riding, too."

"I'm gonna get me a horse when I get to California," Josh said confidently. "But I guess that mule's okay for now. Sometimes he doesn't want to do what I say, but he usually comes around eventually. I named him Uriah."

"Uriah? Now, there's a fancy name I don't believe I've heard on a mule before."

Josh shrugged. "I figured it was better than Jackass. That's what my ma calls him."

Chiles's hearty laughter boomed loudly in the small tent. "I had my doubts at first about your mother and Miss Maguire coming on this journey. I figured they needed a man to look out after them, but I see they've got one that nobody told me about. You're all going to be a welcome addition to our company."

"I hope so, Mr. Chiles," Josh said with maturity beyond his years, " 'cause we didn't come along to be no hindrance."

"There's something I'd like to know," Lottie cut in. "Not that it's going to make much difference at this point. But are me and Nancy going to be able get us some land of our own in California, or do those damned Mexicans have some law saying we have to have husbands?"

Chiles sobered. "Juan Bautista Alvarado was governor when he granted John Sutter eleven square leagues, over forty-eight thousand acres of land for his colonization purposes. As far as I know, he placed no limitations on what Sutter could do with the land. I suspect he saw it as a way to further his own ends, for there has been a constant power struggle in California for years now.

"As for John Sutter. He's a visionary who desperately wants to build his own colony, his own empire. I would wager that he wouldn't care whether the people who do the colonizing are men or women. If he's like most Americans in California, he would welcome white women with open arms. Besides, you two will be married before long anyway. Probably marry some rich, handsome Californio."

Lottie grinned. "So you think you know our motivations for this crazy trip, do you, Colonel? Well, don't be jumping to no conclusions. The only good thing my husband ever did for me was to die and leave me his freighting business. I ain't hankerin' to get hitched again. I get along fine by myself."

Nancy had followed the political situation in California as closely as anyone could, but there was still something she had never been able to fathom. "Why was Alvarado so agreeable to Sutter's plans for American colonization? Couldn't he see the possible ramifications of too many foreigners moving into his country?"

"The Californios are not concerned about a new government taking over, Miss Maguire. If anything, they would welcome it if it would help them get what they can't from Mexico. And the sentiment seems to lean toward American rule over that of British, Russian, or French. But for the most part, they're mainly concerned with their own private power struggles. Alvarado wanted to diminish his uncle's power, Mariano Vallejo, in the northern part of the province. He figured Sutter, being nearby in Sacramento Valley, would steal some of that power. He also wanted to keep the American trappers out, and he wanted the Indians domesticated. So he used the American settlers to achieve all his goals.

"He was able to oust Governor Nicolas Guitiérrez about five years ago by employing a bunch of American ex-trappers," Chiles continued. "Their rifle power, and their willingness to fight, was just what he needed to elevate his own authority and status. But neither lasted, of course, when Mexico sent Manuel Micheltorena to take his place."

"From what I hear, California might have belonged to the United States already if Commodore Jones hadn't made a fool of himself last fall," Lottie put in. "The Mexican government was actually negotiating with President Tyler for the sale of California, or at least for the port of Yerba Bueno."

"I suppose you couldn't blame Jones for his actions," Chiles said, not quick to criticize. "Like a lot of Americans, he was afraid Britain would try to claim California. The British have been saying for years that any nation could put up its flag in California. And Mexico, being in the political mess that it is, wouldn't put up much of a fight. I believe it's inevitable that someone will do just that, and soon. The province is so neglected and unprotected by military power that it's a prime target for anyone who wants to make a move."

"What happened with Jones?" Nancy was curious.

"Jones's orders from the Secretary of the Navy were to protect American interests in California," Hart responded. "He had his ship anchored at Callao, off the coast of Peru, so he could watch the movements of the British Pacific squadron. He got a message saying that the United States and Mexico were at war and that Mexico had handed California over to England in payment of some debts. Supposedly, he also received word that British ships were departing under sealed orders with a secret destination.

"Jones was afraid of their intentions and rushed for the California coast and planted the American flag at Monterey Bay, claiming a peaceful occupation of the country by the United States. But he should have read the newspapers first because the very next day he found out that there was no war, and Mexico had made no deals with England. Suffice it to say, he removed the flag, and himself. And he wasted no time doing it."

"Didn't the Californios protest?" Nancy found the entire scenario hard to believe.

"The Californios didn't take it seriously. They even invited him to a dance, which he attended before leaving. But government officials in Mexico City *weren't* amused at all, and Tyler's attempts at negotiations for the peaceful annexation of California to the United States collapsed like a sail without wind."

"Maybe for now, but it's far from over," Lottie prognosticated. "The United States has made it clear that they will protect the interests of American settlers in California, and as long as they do, settlers will continue to go there. I personally ain't hankerin' to be under British rule, or under those Russians who are still roaming along the coast, that's for sure. So we Americans had dang well better make sure it's us that takes control."

"There are plenty in both the political and private arenas who would agree with you," Hart replied.

"I tend to believe that Frémont must be one of those looking to further his career and his political power," Lottie continued. "Talk is that he's going out to collect information on the political situation for the government, under the guise of another exploratory and map-making expedition. Others say they think he might even be preparing his men to lead a rebellion."

"If he is, then I sincerely doubt it's by orders of the President," Chiles said. "Frémont has his own grandiose ideas and has a reputation of overstepping his bounds. But the American settlers going to California believe that California is for the taking and that they can acquire it the way they did Texas seven years ago, and possibly with less bloodshed. The English don't seem that interested in colonization, or possibly locking horns with the Americans again. Frémont knows a ripe piece of fruit when he sees one."

A brilliant flash of lightning lit the interior of the tent and ricocheted off a ribbon of water slipping past Hart's leg, winding and curving across the gutta-percha to the opposite side. He pushed himself to his knees. "Guess I'd better go dig a trench around this tent or it'll be under water before morning. This storm looks like it'll last all night. Lottie, I think you and Josh and Miss Maguire had better stay here in my tent. I'll throw my blankets down in J.B.'s tent."

Chiles nodded agreeably, preparing to leave with Hart. "Pray for some drier weather, ladies," he said as he clamped his wet hat down over his head and backed out of the tent. "We really need to shove off, but if this keeps up, I'm afraid it'll be in rowboats instead of wagons."

6

Nancy didn't try to sleep. She lay awake listening to the wind and the rain buffeting the tent. She listened to the thunder roll and to the nervous neighs and brays of the horses and mules. But mostly, she listened to her thoughts.

She heard men's voices carrying on the wind, between thunder claps. Mostly she couldn't understand the words, but once she deciphered, "This storm will have 'em all strung to hell and gone by morning." And a resounding, "Yeah, and then we'll have to try and wrest them from the thievin' Indians."

She listened to Josh breathing heavily in a child's sleep. But she sensed Lottie, too, was listening.

She didn't pray like Chiles had asked her to do. She was too busy smelling the rain and the wet earth, and watching the eerie tremors of lightning undulating across the sky and across the thin walls of Hart's tent. And she was too busy remembering the last conversation she'd had with her father.

"I want to go some place where I don't have to present my pedigree to be accepted," she had said. "Where I can be in charge of my life, and where it doesn't matter that I don't have a husband—or where everyone isn't trying to find me one. Be happy for me, Daddy, the way Grandpa is. Wish me well. Don't make my departure more difficult."

"More difficult?" he'd countered. "It would seem that you are most anxious to be free of our company, Nancy. Understand how we feel. It's likely we'll never see you again. What can you hope to accomplish in a place like California? Surely you're not thinking you can find a *decent* husband from that rough frontier lot? Better to stay here, a spinster, among family and gentility."

"My God, Daddy! Why must our society define a woman's worth, or her success in life, by how well she marries—or whether she marries at all?"

"This is absolute insanity, Nancy. Your mother and I raised you to be more sensible."

"If I married today, tomorrow my life would not show an appreciable change. It's the change I'm seeking. Besides, I'm tired of being sensible."

"Do you know what he said to me?" Nancy whispered aloud.

"Who?" Lottie whispered back.

"My father."

"What did he say?"

"He said, and I quote, 'You're a twenty-six-year-old spinster, Nancy. You've got no business crossing the continent to a foreign territory, especially one that is a hotbed of revolution. Only outlaws, whores, and adventurers go West. You'll get yourself scalped by Indians or murdered by Mexicans. As a matter of fact, I daresay you'll never even make it to Missouri. Some thug will knock you in the head and steal all your money. Probably violate you, too."

"He's just worried about you, girl."

"I know, and I posted him and my mother a letter before we left Independence."

"Don't tell me you're homesick already?"

Nancy closed her eyes, focusing on the hardness of the ground beneath her hips and how it differed so much from her soft, clean bed back in Amherst. Yet, she did not miss that bed. There was a loneliness about it, while there was a solidness about the earth, an incentive to get up and move on, to accomplish *something*.

"Darn it, Lottie. I'm going to miss him," Nancy admitted, wiping at tears that sprang unexpectedly to her eyes. "The worst of it is, I know I'll never see any of them again."

"You never know what the future will bring," Lottie soothed. " 'Never' is real final, and nothing in life is final except death. He might have been upset with you, and tried every tactic known to man to keep you from going, but once you get to California in one piece, he'll forgive you."

Nancy waited for another long roll of thunder to rumble away before speaking again. Then, "Are you afraid, Lottie? Afraid of what lies ahead?"

Understanding and kinship passed between them there in the fire-lit semidarkness. It was something Nancy had never felt with her own two sisters, Charity and Millicent, and certainly with none of the women whom she had called her friends.

"Of course, I'm frightened, girl. Scared half out of my wits if I was to stop and put some real thought to it. But my greatest fear is to die, never having lived. Like you, I'm running headlong into life, and nothing is going to make me go back now. I'd say I've come quite a way for a Texas orphan."

Nancy was silent for a minute. "I didn't know you were an orphan, Lottie. How did you survive on your own?"

Lottie chuckled. "I wasn't completely orphaned until my mother died when I was thirteen. We never did know what killed her; it seemed she just got sick, was in a terrible amount of pain, and slowly started deteriorating, as if something was eating her up from the inside. I had some brothers, but they were older and took off, leaving me to my own devices. We lived in Texas, and I found work around the ranches and farms. Some of the neighbors were charitable. I did whatever anybody would hire me to do. Except whorin'. I never did that."

"What about your father?"

"He went out one day to gather a herd of wild horses and he never came back. We never found a trace of him. I reckon the Indians got him. I was only about nine at the time."

"When did you meet Major?"

"Oh, when I was about your age, I guess. I'd had some beaus before Major, but none of them fell in love with me hard enough to put a ring on my finger. Respectable men are looking for women like you, Nancy." She grinned at her from across the fire. "They want women with class and money. I had neither."

"I don't believe all men are so shallow, Lottie. Major must have loved you."

Lottie was quiet for a minute. "I guess maybe he did, for a while. Leastwise, until he got bored with married life and having to work for a living. He preferred gambling and getting money any other easy way that it could be had. He liked to horse trade. He wasn't much good for anything, not really. I don't know why he turned my head the way he did. Probably because he was handsome. I'd never seen a man as handsome as him. But we clashed a lot because I'm a worker, and he wasn't."

Nancy was ashamed to have whined about the problems she'd faced in Amherst. Her life had been privileged compared to Lottie's. There were those who would be grateful to have had the luxuries she had taken for granted. It was no wonder most of the people she'd met had thought she was insane for leaving the comforts her father provided her with for possible poverty in the West.

"There I've gone and depressed you, girl. Guess that's why I don't talk about myself overly much. But things will be good out in California." Her chuckle was soft but rang with a sultry quality. "I plan to pluck my food off trees. Pitch a tent to keep the sun out, take siestas in the afternoon like the Mexicans, and dance the fandango at night with young, good-looking men. Only the young ones, mind you. I plan to live like there's no tomorrow, because out here, there might not be."

A ripple of lightning briefly lit the tent, long enough for Nancy to see Lottie's dreamlike smile. But Nancy couldn't picture Lottie sitting beneath fig trees and being content with it for more than an hour or two. However, she could certainly visualize her dancing the fandango with young, good-looking men.

"We made quite an entrance today, didn't we?" Lottie said, her thoughts shifting. "You looked right smart on that little mare. You had some of those old boys bending over and picking up their eyeballs when you came riding into camp."

Nancy chuckled. "Why, thank you. My mother would be very pleased to hear that. Back in Amherst, we girls were always taught to make the best entrance we could." She pulled the blanket up under her chin, feeling satisfied. "You made a good show of handling the mules, too."

"Yep, we raised quite a stir, and I reckon we'll hear all about it come mornin'."

"What do you mean?"

"Oh, the ripples from the rock we just dropped are gonna go all the way out to the edges of the pond, I'm afraid. Come morning, you'll see."

◦　◦　◦

"I don't believe our request should be taken so lightly Colonel Chiles. There's a number of us who don't want those two women joining the company. I say let them join the Oregon train that's pulling out today."

At first, Nancy thought the words had been part of a dream, but as sleep cleared from her head, she realized they were not.

"What the hell—" Lottie tossed her blankets aside and sat up. "Do you suppose that pompous jackass means us?"

Nancy exited her blankets and was pulling on her boots. "He means us."

"Then come on. He's going to get my boot shoved so far up his fanny he won't be able to swallow." Lottie threw back the tent flap and bolted out of the tent with Nancy right on her heels. The rain had ceased, but in the predawn the clouds hung low and a mist rose up from the land.

"These women can—and will—take care of themselves," Colonel Chiles was saying. "Mrs. England freighted goods to Santa Fe with her husband for years. I would stake my life that she can handle a team better than you yourself, Mr. Waite."

Lottie swaggered up next to Chiles with her hands on her hips. "I can drive circles around you, Waite. Do you want me to prove it?"

Arthur Waite, Miriam's husband, not expecting direct confrontation by the hot-headed brunette, was stunned into temporary silence. Not so the woman at his side. She stepped forward, meeting Lottie nose to nose.

"My name is Lucille Royal, and Arthur Waite isn't telling all of it. We have other concerns about you two." Her haughty perusal took in both Nancy and Lottie. "I've been talking to some of the other women and we don't want no whores on this wagon train trying to bed our husbands and talk them against us."

Nancy was so shocked by the accusation, she could not even speak. Not so Lottie whose tongue was never tied. Her face had gone as bright red as a Mexican chili. Noticing a crowd had gathered, and fearing a scene, Nancy stepped closer to Lottie, hoping to calm her.

"Lottie, let it go."

"She called us whores," Lottie said, her voice rising indignantly. "Are we going to stand for that?"

"There are ways to solve this, Lottie."

"Yes, and I can think of several, but strangulation with my bare hands is one that appeals the most."

Lucille Royal appeared as fiery and belligerent as Lottie and held her ground. Even so, Nancy figured she and Lottie could take her.

Suddenly she almost burst out laughing. Here it was her first day out and she was contemplating hand-to-hand combat, with another woman no less. Good heavens, what would they think back in Amherst?

Nancy stepped between the two of them, pushed them apart, and held them there at arm's length. "We are not harlots, Mrs. Royal," she said diplomatically. "Nor do we intend to leave this contingency. If you are worried about your husband's fidelity, then I suggest the root of the problem lies in your own relationship with him."

"How dare you suggest—"

"You suggested it yourself," Nancy continued levelly. "Now, *I* would suggest that you return to your family and your breakfast. Worry about how you'll get your own wagon to California, and let Mrs. England and I concern ourselves with ours."

"What do single women want with going to California anyway? There's only one thing out there that would appeal. Men. I'll bet you're planning to open up a brothel."

Nancy lifted her eyes to the faces of the other women standing on the sidelines, hoping to gauge their sentiments. She had met most of them when she'd been looking for a traveling companion. She was relieved to see no animosity among them, only curiosity at the confrontation and, on a couple of faces, unconcealed amusement. Apparently sensing a need for interference, one stepped forward.

"My name is Elizabeth Yount," she said. "I'm single and I'm here with my sister, Frances Vines, and her husband. I don't know who Mrs. Royal is including in her survey, but I think it's wonderful to have Miss Maguire and Mrs. England join the company. I suspect we'll all have a good time on the trail, as well as in California."

A murmur of agreement rippled through the remaining women, six by count.

Lucille Royal stood her ground. "I still say no decent woman would leave the security and comforts of her home to head across a godforsaken wilderness infested with savages. The only reason any of us women are going is because our men want it."

"Then I feel sorry for your men," Nancy said in a softer voice that ran with pity. "And I feel sorry for you."

Lucille Royal lifted her chin belligerently. But seeing she would get no support from the others, she whirled on her heel and returned to her wagon, rattling the bows as she ungracefully climbed inside.

"You're making a mistake letting these women come along, Colonel," Arthur Waite insisted, not so easily chased away as Lucille had been. "You'll end up doing everything for them or having one of us do it. Why, already they've taken over Daniels's tent. He may be fool enough to allow that, but I can tell you, I won't lift a finger to help them."

Hart stood with his rifle planted, butt to the ground in front of him. A glimmer in his eyes warned that he had reached the end of his patience. "I would have offered my tent to anyone who had arrived in the middle of that rainstorm, Waite. Probably even you. Now, Mrs. England and Miss Maguire are going to California. If you don't like it, then I suggest you join the Oregon company yourself. And take Mrs. Royal, if she's a mind to go."

"You're only thirty men strong, Daniels," Waite snickered. "You need every man you can get. Me included."

"Don't overestimate your importance, Waite. Every company needs at least one man they can sacrifice to the Indians."

Hart sauntered off and the others followed, leaving Waite to ponder the foolishness of his tongue.

Hundreds of yards of white canvas gleamed brightly in the morning sun. Raindrops from the thunderstorm beaded on the pristine shrouds and sparkled like diamonds in the sunlight. Stretched tautly over the bows of some one hundred and fifty farm wagons, the new canvas concealed bits and pieces of lives left behind, and harbored the shining hope for new and brighter futures in the western wilderness beyond.

The Oregon-bound wagons uncoiled from their circles and, one by one, company by company, joined the line that stretched out onto the Santa Fe Trail. As the mules struggled through the new mud left by last night's rain, the wagon bows bounced from side to side. The canvas tops swayed with the motion and, from a distance, the train resembled a long white scarf rippling in the faintest of breezes.

On either side of the wagons, drovers trailed the cattle and other livestock. Dogs barked, causing confusion and trouble with the livestock. Children skipped alongside the wagons, excited to be moving at last. Men, walking next to their oxen, cracked whips, and their constant commanding barks of "haw" echoed up and down the line. A few women walked, but most stayed in the wagons because of the heavy mud.

The fifty-three members of the California company gathered on the hills near their camp and watched the Oregon company's departure with growing anxiety. The half-breed, Charles McIntosh, finally said what was on everybody's mind. "It's getting late in the season, Colonel. Way late. Maybe we ought not wait any longer ourselves."

Chiles acknowledged the concern. "I know it's getting late, but if we leave too early and the grass isn't sufficient, we'll pay for it when our animals drop off, maybe die. They've got to have strength for the last half of the journey, which is going to be the hardest."

"There won't be any grass anyhow." Lucille Royal pushed her tall, skinny frame to the front of the group, confronting Chiles with her hands on her hips in a belligerent stance. "Those Oregonians must have five thousand head of livestock among them. Do you honestly think a blade of grass within a mile of the trail will be left standing after they pass through? If you ask me, we *should* have left *before* they did, not after.

"You're a damned fool, Chiles," she continued, "for filling men's heads with fancy ideas and pretty pictures of some foreign country that would be better off left to the Mexicans. We've heard about those mountains we're going to have to cross—bigger mountains than any of us can even comprehend—and you without even knowing how to get us over them. Oh, don't think I'm stupid. I've been listening to the talk. You don't *have* a trail, do you? Admit it."

Chiles sauntered over to her, positioning himself directly in front of her, staring her down with his keen blue eyes. His typical joviality faded. "I've never kept it a secret, Mrs. Royal. Everybody in this company knows what he or she faces on this journey."

Billy Baldridge stepped up next to his friend. "You are free to stay behind, Mrs. Royal, if you question the Colonel's decision."

She ignored both of them, as if they were senseless birds twittering in the trees overhead. She turned to the others, pleading, "We should never be heading out this late in the season. Why don't you all listen to me! We'll pay for this insanity with our lives."

Brenham Royal, who had been standing by with his face growing increasingly red from embarrassment, moved self-consciously forward and took his wife by the arm. "Lucille, please. We've discussed this. Don't be getting everybody upset."

Lucille jerked free of his hand and vented her fears and frustrations on him. "I'm no fool, even if you are, Brenham. I can see what's going to happen to us. Here we are the last ones getting away. Already we're running out of time." She glanced to the west as if she could see Death painted on the distant horizon.

Chiles tried to ease the silence and Brenham's obvious discomfort over the scene his wife was making. "If it will make you feel any better, Mrs. Royal," he said, "I can assure you that our mules will travel much faster than the oxen, and we'll catch up to the Oregon companies before they reach the South Platte. We will more than likely overtake most of their companies. I know mules, and you have my guarantee on that."

Lucille lifted her chin arrogantly. Her small, thin mouth compressed into a tighter sneer. "I suppose it takes a jackass to know one."

Haughtily, she gathered her skirts and stalked to her wagon, climbing ungracefully up over the wheel and disappearing to the privacy inside. It seemed to be a favorite method of hers to end a conversation.

"I'm sorry," Brenham mumbled to Chiles. "She's just—" he halted at a loss to explain her behavior, as if he didn't quite understand it himself.

"Don't worry about it," Chiles said. "But you might want to seriously question whether your move to California is wise, considering the way your wife feels about it."

Brenham's chin came up and with it a stubborn jut to his jaw. "This is one time she won't tell me what to do. By God, I'm going. I already told her she didn't have to come if she didn't want to. Now, if you'll excuse me, I've got some harness to mend."

The group broke up, returning to camp and final preparations. Only Nancy, Hart, Baldridge, and Lottie remained. Billy Baldridge sauntered over to Chiles and flung a brotherly arm over his shoulders. "What say we recruit that woman to the Sioux or Potawatomi?"

"What makes you think either of them would want her?"

"She's got about the same contemptible temperament. I figure she'd fit right in."

Chiles shook his head glumly and blew a breath out between his teeth. "That woman's only asset is her husband. I just wonder how much trouble she and that Arthur Waite are going to cause us."

"A bunch, my friend. You can be sure of that."

❉   ❉   ❉

The rifle blast brought Nancy from a deep sleep at four o'clock in the morning two days later. She sat up, pushing her hair back from her face. Lottie was already up and on her knees in the middle of her blankets trying to tie her unruly locks into a knot on top of her head. Hairpins lay scattered on her blanket; a few protruded from between clamped lips. She removed one from the latter location and pushed it into the bun.

"God, I never thought morning would come," she said in a low tone, glancing at Josh who had slept on through the rifle blast. "I spent all night with the cramps. You know, female trouble. What a time to get it— the first day out. I hope I didn't wake you, what with having to rummage around in my bag for laudanum and personals, and then going outside and all."

She glanced at Nancy apologetically. Nancy pulled a blanket around her shoulders to chase away the early morning chill. Even in the dim light, she noticed the dark circles under Lottie's eyes from lack of sleep.

"No, you didn't wake me." She rotated her shoulders, trying to ease the stiffness that came from sleeping on the hard ground.

"I hate this time of the month," Lottie said. "I always get to hurtin' so bad and bleedin' so much I lose all my energy and strength. Guess I'm headin' into the change. Leastwise, that's what a doctor over in St. Louis told me. Told me if I wanted any more babies, I'd better get it done in the next five years. 'Course, I told him I had Josh and no husband, so I wouldn't be gettin' anymore since I wasn't interested in burdening myself with another pig-headed man."

Nancy was surprised but warmed by Lottie's candidness, and glad to have a friend with whom she could share even the most intimate concerns. Her own mother had been squeamish to discuss personal matters such as menses, and said no more than was absolutely necessary. Like pregnancy and sexual intercourse, it was a taboo subject. "I don't have such problems, although my oldest sister was put to bed once a month and given laudanum for the pain. If you need anything, Lottie, please don't hesitate to ask."

Lottie gathered up two more pins from the blanket and pushed them into the bun. The coiffure completed, she lifted her eyes to Nancy's. A moment of silent understanding passed between them, then Lottie reached over and touched Nancy's hand. "You're gold, girl. Genuine gold. Now, I reckon I'd best get those mules rounded up and hitched up. How about you fixin' breakfast and breakin' down the tent?

"Won't you need help rounding up the mules?"

"No, I think Josh and I can do it. We don't want to be the last ones ready so we'll have to split the duties, Nancy."

Lottie reached over and gently shook her son. "Come on, son," she said in a tender voice reserved only for the boy. "It's time to get up. The wagons will be rolling out real soon. I'm gonna need your help gettin' the wagon ready."

Josh sat up, pushing the sleep from his eyes, but it didn't take long as the prospect of the journey, starting at last, erased the last of his dreams. "My gosh! We'd better get crackin'. I'm gonna prove to that Waite guy, and that danged old Royal woman, that we don't need no man. The two of them's gonna eat those words before this trip is over."

7

May 20, 1843
The Santa Fe Trail

All up and down the line whips cracked, drivers filled the air with profanities and strident commands. Wood creaked, chains rattled, wheels groaned beneath the weight of their loads made more burdensome by the clogging mud of the trail.

Chiles sat astride one of his big, black Missouri mules watching the wagons pull out. He had placed Billy Baldridge, driving the mill machinery, in second position. Nancy and Lottie had been given the lead. The decision was immediately questioned by Arthur Waite who had been assigned to eighth position. "Those women were the last to join this company, Captain, and it's only fair to the rest of us that they be the last in line. I'm beginning to think there's some personal interest going on behind our backs."

Chiles's blue eyes flared at the insinuation. "It is my every intention to rotate the wagons so that each person will get the lead one day in eight. The positions have nothing to do with who joined first, or last. I put Mrs. England in the lead today because her mules have been down the Santa Fe Trail a good many more times than yours have. *And* it could just be that I'll keep them in the lead a day or two until I feel we have all the knots worked out of this string. Now, is that answer sufficient enough for you, Arthur, or do you think you'll be staying right here where you're at?"

Waite glared up at the big captain. "It's sufficient for now, Chiles, but I'll be counting."

"Oh, I trust you will, just in case I lose tally."

The remuda of horses and mules was being driven by two Kentucky boys, barely twenty years old, named Torey Porter and Thane Lewis. The few cattle being brought were driven by their owners, or members of the owner's family. Other men riding horseback, stretched out along either side of the wagons, acted as outriders. The Indians in this region were usually not hostile to whites, but occasionally engaged in battle with each other. It was the job of the scout to ride a considerable distance ahead of the wagon train and keep an eye out for anything that might mean trouble. Hart was not always alone in this job. One or two of the other men usually went along with him.

Spirits lifted at finally getting away and most tried not to think about how late in the season it was, rationalizing that because it had been a late spring, they were likely to have a late fall and winter, too.

They made good time down the Santa Fe Trail despite the mud sucking at the wagon wheels. As soon as things were lined out good, Chiles, John Gantt, Pierson Reading, and Samuel Hensley left the contingency to hunt for fresh meat.

Nancy had taken a position next to Lottie's wagon, trying to get her eager mare to walk docilely alongside the left-wheel mule, a feat made more difficult when the men rode away on a lope. The effort to hold her back was beginning to wear on Nancy's arms and shoulders, leaving her muscles tired and aching.

"Go on and let that mare run, girl," Lottie said. "Don't feel like you have to stick by my side all the way to California. Why don't you ride on up the hill to where Hart is. A good run will take the fidget and fuss out of that mare. And I don't think Hart would mind the company."

Nancy was more than happy to oblige. Something about the broad-shouldered scout had drawn her gaze hundreds of times already this morning. She enjoyed watching the easy way he sat his saddle, as if born to it. He had switched from his regular cotton shirt and vest and had attired himself in a soft buckskin shirt with fringe along the sleeves and across the upper chest. The line of the shirt seemed to broaden his chest even more, intensifying his rugged masculinity. Nancy had known no men quite like Hart, Chiles, and the others. Daring, bold, and not fully polished, they were gentlemen just the same, and their half-wild nature allowed her own to flourish.

She only had to loosen the reins and nudge the mare with her heel, and the horse was off, flying past Billy Baldridge's wagon and a few of the riders who were out in the lead. She caught glimpses of the men's smiles as she raced past. Laughter bubbled up in her throat and she waved to them. To her surprise, several of them joined in, and a race ensued to the top of the hill. She tossed a look over her shoulder and saw them leaned out over their horses' necks in a full gallop, trying to catch her fleet-footed mare, hooting and hollering as they encouraged their horses to go faster. But the mare effortlessly stayed ahead, never breaking her stride and coming out on the crest of the knoll as the winner.

Nancy pulled her to a dancing stop. Within seconds the others thundered in around her and Hart.

"She beat you boys good," Hart said, grinning, and if Nancy wasn't mistaken, he sounded proud of it.

"She had a head start," James Williams said good-naturedly. "We'll have to try it again sometime. A real race."

"I would be delighted, gentlemen," Nancy replied.

"I doubt it would have mattered," Hart added. "That mare never did hit her top speed."

"I've never seen anything that could run that fast in my life," put in the other Williams boy, John.

Nancy patted the mare's neck. "The old man at the livery said there was no Indian pony around that could come close to catching her."

"Speaking of Indians"—Hart nonchalantly folded his forearms over his saddle horn—"it looks like we're about to have some company from a party of Shawnee."

Everyone visibly stiffened. Smiles vanished. Eyes searched and saw the party of ten or twelve braves heading straight down an open meadow and toward them. The men reached for their guns, but Hart's right arm shot out in a refraining motion. He had seemed relaxed before. But Nancy saw it had only been an illusion. Hart Daniels was always ready.

"I recognize the leader," he said. "It's Blue Talon. From the way he's riding, he recognizes me, too. Knowing Blue Talon, though, he's probably been watching us since we pulled out."

Surprisingly, Nancy's mare stood stalk still, watching the approach of the Shawnee as if mesmerized by their strangely beautiful but savage appearance, as Nancy herself was. Fear pumped through her veins as her father's words darted into her mind, but Hart had nudged his buckskin and moved a few feet out in front of her and the men to await the Shawnees' arrival.

Nancy had exercised wariness of all the people she had come into contact with since leaving Amherst, but had found that those who frightened her the most were not the Indians but the white renegades. These Shawnees held only fascination for her, and she openly scrutinized their bronzed, half-naked bodies and their beautiful costumes and plumage. And they scrutinized her back. She supposed white women were as much objects of curiosity and awe as the savages were to them. Seeing so much exposed brown male flesh was probably the greatest fascination of all. These young Indians all possessed lean, muscled bodies, held stiff and straight in proud carriage. Many whites criticized their naked savagery, but Nancy found it rather captivating.

Hart offered his hand to Blue Talon, who pumped it vigorously in the white man's way of greeting. A big smile revealed strong white teeth. "When I see it is you, Daniels," Blue Talon said, "I come right away. We leave soon for summer hunt. We have Bread Dance tonight. You come as my guests." His eyes strayed to Nancy. "Bring woman. Maybe she trade horse."

Hart smiled, giving a slight shake to his head. "I don't think so, Blue Talon. She has to have it to ride to California. It's a good mare and Miss Maguire wants to keep it to start her horse farm in California."

"I have heard of this California," Blue Talon said. "It is over the Great Mountains."

"Yes. We travel until the first winter moon, maybe the second."

Blue Talon eyed Nancy and her horse covetously, making Nancy uneasy. "Everyone go to California, even Captain Frémont."

"Frémont?"

Blue Talon nodded. "His men are not far from here, at Elm Grove."

"That's where we were planning on putting down for the night."

"Bring everyone to the Bread Dance, Daniels. Big fun. We go now." Blue Talon lifted his arm in farewell and rode away, followed by the others. Apparently he didn't expect Hart to turn down the invitation.

"What exactly is the purpose of a Bread Dance?" Nancy inquired while watching the Indians recede from sight.

Hart folded his arms over his saddle horn. "It's a big festival of thanksgiving that the Shawnee hold in the spring before planting their crops.

They thank God for everything good they've ever received, then they ask him to give them a fruitful season, successful hunts, and they pray for the general welfare of the people. They also honor the younger generation of boys with bread because it will be their duty to carry on the traditions of the people."

"I hope you intend on going because I want to go with you."

Hart smiled sardonically. "You're not afraid of Blue Talon and his bunch? They sure liked the looks of your horse. If you won't trade it, they might try to sneak into camp and steal it. Maybe steal you, too, for that matter."

"It didn't appear to me that he had intentions of lifting our scalps," she said lightly, thinking how much she liked the warm, teasing look in Hart's eyes. "Unless I'm terribly bad at judging character."

Hart chuckled. "No, you seem as adept at that as you are at racing. Blue Talon is a friend, but he's still an Indian, so don't underestimate what he might do. They don't look at stealing as offensive, but rather as an accomplishment, a coup. I met Blue Talon a few years ago. When I came into Independence from Santa Fe, and was half sick with a fever, some ruffians tried to rob and kill me. Blue Talon and his braves stepped in and made short work of them. I can assure you, he'll entertain us handsomely tonight. But if you've got some trinkets you're not too attached to, I'd advise you to bring them along for trading purposes. The men like tobacco so I'll see if I can get a few pigtails for you to take along."

As Blue Talon had said, Captain John Charles Frémont had made an encampment at Elm Grove. But to everyone's surprise, Thomas Fitzpatrick, famed guide and mountain man, was also there, striding out to greet them as if he had been looking forward to their arrival.

The small company pulled to a stop in front of Frémont's camp tent. Colonel Chiles stepped from his mule and Fitzpatrick grabbed his hand and pumped it in a two-handed shake. "J.B. So you're at it again. I see you're still recruiting the ladies." His eyes lifted to Nancy and Lottie, whose wagon was directly in front of him. "And some beautiful, very accomplished ones at that."

He seemed most enthralled by Lottie as she sat where she had all day on the left-wheel mule. Chiles took a moment to introduce them, since they were clearly of interest to Fitzpatrick and close enough to do so.

Fitzpatrick hurried over to tip his hat and shake their hands, holding onto Lottie's a bit longer than necessary.

"My pleasure, ladies," Fitzpatrick gushed. "I don't believe I have ever had the opportunity to meet such brave and beautiful women."

Lottie couldn't resist a mischievous quip. "And it's likely you never will again."

Fitzpatrick hooted with delight and finally released her hand. He turned back to Chiles, throwing an arm over his shoulder. "Tell me, J.B., how did your previous trip with Bidwell and Bartleson fare? I was afraid you'd all gotten lost and scalped."

J.B. removed his hat and ran a hand through his red hair. "Nope, still got it. It wasn't too bad, considering. Let me set up my encampment and we'll talk."

Chiles directed the wagons to a spot about a hundred yards away from Frémont's camp and into a loose circle. A few horses were kept inside the corral; mules were hobbled outside the corral and some tethered to wagon wheels so they wouldn't wander. Nancy was particularly worried about Lady Rae. She figured she would sleep tonight with one hand on her mare's lead rope and one eye open.

While Lottie and Josh tended to the mules, Nancy proceeded to put up the tent. Before she'd seen Hart's bivouac, she hadn't had the slightest idea how to prepare a shelter from the oiled canvas she had purchased in Independence. But she had paid careful attention to the tipi construction of Hart's and had copied its form on consecutive nights. Lottie had been too busy with the mules to help her, but she had managed, albeit clumsily. Tonight was the fourth night of sleeping on the ground, and the third of her putting the tent up. She found she was getting quicker and more adept.

During the two days at Fitzhugh's Mill, she had collected long, straight poles from dry timber. For traveling, she had constructed some dual "slings" out of rope, putting them on either end of one side of the wagon, above the wheels. It was easy then to slide the poles into the slings during the day and remove them at night to build the tent.

The biggest problem she had confronted was starting a fire. Lottie had helped her on previous nights but tonight she really wanted to see if she could do it by herself before Lottie got back. A breeze from the nearby band of trees kept snuffing out her progress. Her patience was thinning and her desperation growing. Not only was she wasting the precious, phosphorus matches she'd bought in Independence, but she feared she would still not have the fire started by the time Lottie returned. And she knew she certainly would not be able to start one with powder and spark!

She glanced up and saw Fitzpatrick talking to Lottie, having apparently waylaid her on her return from the stream to water the mules. It would buy her a little time.

"Having trouble, Miss Maguire?"

Nancy swung around to see Hart smiling down at her. "I didn't hear your approach, Mr. Daniels."

He gave her that charming, flirtatious grin she was coming to anticipate. "Scouts are supposed to be quiet, ma'am." He squatted next to her, taking over the task. "The key to a fire is the right tinder. Good, dry tinder. Then graduate it up to the larger kindling and finally your bigger pieces of wood."

From his pocket he removed something that looked like a wad of gray hair. "You find an old dead tree and peel it off in these fine strings. Or if no trees are available, dry grass left from last winter is good, or strip the bark and dry leaves from bushes."

Shortly, almost miraculously, and with the strike of only one match, he had a healthy fire going. He leaned back on his heels and occasionally added another piece of tinder or a stick to the growing blaze.

"Thank you, Mr. Daniels," she said. "Would you like to join Lottie and me for supper?"

"I have never been known to turn down a meal cooked by a woman. I would be obliged, ma'am."

Nancy looked away from his bright, blue eyes that occasionally probed deeper than what she was comfortable with. If she wasn't mistaken, Hart Daniels liked her. But a man like him—so wild and free. What would he want from a woman? And more pertinent, what did *she* want from *him?*

"I must admit that I'm not a very good cook myself," she said. "We always had a cook, but I would go in and watch her prepare all sorts of incredible dishes and she would let me help her." She smiled, remembering her life back on her father's estate. "However, preparing something over a campfire is definitely a test of what skills I do have."

"Lottie can give you pointers. She's cooked over more campfires than she has stoves. God, she did try to make a go of it with that worthless

Major." He shook his head. "Lottie wasted a lot of good years on that man. Maybe now she can get on with her life. Find a man who will truly cherish her. Fitzpatrick is taken with her, but he isn't what she needs."

"You seem to care a great deal for Lottie."

"Well, we're pretty good friends. She says I'm the little brother she never had. And I guess she's sort of like a big sister to me."

Their conversation ended when Arthur Waite halted his mule in front of them. "I told you you'd be doin' for these women, Daniels."

Hart slowly pushed to his feet, tall and threatening. The look in his eyes matched his stance. "*You* clearly don't believe in helping women, Waite." Hart glanced over to where Miriam Waite was struggling with her own fire and listening to her teenage boys haranguing on her because they were hungry. The oldest was saying, "Are we gonna get fed sometime tonight, Ma, or are we gonna have to wait until next week before you git that fire goin'?"

Miriam didn't reply, keeping her head down in the same air of subservience she gave her husband. Her movements became visibly more agitated, jerky.

"Women have their jobs. Men have theirs," Waite replied.

"I see you've taught that same philosophy to your boys. I truly pity the women they marry."

"Mind your own business, Daniels."

"My sentiments exactly, Waite. Now, what were you doing? Oh, yeah, watering your mules. Why not get on with it?"

Waite scowled but left with no further adieu. Hart waited until he was a distance away before turning to Nancy, who had also risen to her feet. He replaced the frown with a smile and touched the brim of his hat. "I'll be looking forward to supper, ma'am. Just give me a whistle."

Nancy grinned. "I'm afraid whistling, along with fire building, is one of those things I never learned to do."

"Oh, it's easy. It's all in the way you pucker your lips, sort of like kissing." At that he winked at her and sauntered off, turning once to call over his shoulder. "Ride with me tomorrow, and I'll teach you."

8

The steady thump of drumbeats, and the flickering glow of numerous fires in the woods beyond, told Nancy that the Shawnee encampment was drawing near. Light was gone from the depths of the forests, and dusk sank deeply into the hollows. The return trip to camp would have to be taken by moonlight.

A few clouds were building again, but the members of the California Company were willing to risk getting wet in order to see the wonders of the Bread Dance. There were ten of them in all: Hart, Nancy, Elizabeth Yount, Torey Porter, Thane Lewis, Charles McIntosh, and the four Williams boys. Nancy had wanted Lottie to join them, but she still wasn't feeling very well, and had said she was going to collapse as soon as she got Josh to bed. Some of the other women had wanted to come, but their family's needs had come first.

"Now, remember what I told you," Hart reiterated to everyone. "When an Indian wants to swap, he will point to the article he wants, then he'll tap his left forefinger twice with his right forefinger. When he wants you to *give* him something, he'll point to the object he wants and make a motion to his chest, or hold the object to his chest. If you can remember that, it'll keep you out of a lot of trouble and keep the Indians happy."

In groups, the Shawnees had gathered in a large meadow. They had constructed a "stage" by placing logs around the perimeter of the area, which people were using as benches. Among those people were emigrants from the Oregon company, as well as their own Arthur Waite and Ethan Stillman, the latter being married to the young pregnant woman, Garnet. Both were staggering about with bottles in hand, aggressively and disgustingly making lewd overtures to the young Indian women. To Nancy's amazement, most of the women didn't seem to mind.

"I didn't know your invitation extended to Arthur Waite," Nancy said to Hart, her contempt for Waite clearly ringing in her voice.

Hart didn't care for Waite anymore than most of them did. "It didn't," he replied tightly. "But it's hard to keep secrets in a company the size of ours."

Blue Talon had seen their arrival and strode across the encampment to greet them. "I am glad you came, Daniels." His keen brown eyes took in Nancy and then Elizabeth, but finally settled on Nancy. A sly smile curved his rather broad, flat lips. "Is your woman ready to trade her horse?"

Hart had warned Nancy to be prepared for Blue Talon's attempts to get Lady Rae, and she had come prepared with trade goods that Hart had recommended. But she was not prepared for Blue Talon's assumption that she was Hart's woman. Her gaze shot to Hart's, but he merely smiled with amusement. If she wasn't mistaken, it seemed he liked the idea and possibly even encouraged Blue Talon to believe it. She decided it would be pointless to try and persuade the Shawnee otherwise. She also knew it would be wise to let Hart answer the question that had been directed to him, not her.

"As I said before, Blue Talon," Hart replied, "Miss Maguire must have the mare to get to California. But she is honored that you think so highly of her animal. She has a small gift she would like to give you since she regretfully cannot make you a trade for the horse."

Hart had warned Nancy that it might come to this, but she didn't think it would be before they had even had a chance to alight from their horses. Still, the time had come. Hart dismounted and helped her from her sidesaddle. The matter of her first trade had her a bit jittery, but not so much so that she didn't notice the heat of Hart's hands at her waist and their pleasant, lingering imprint as she turned to her saddlebags.

Inside, she found the braided tobacco, or pigtails, that Hart had acquired for her. She removed one and held it out to Blue Talon. "This is very fine tobacco, I am told."

Blue Talon's brown hand closed around the pigtail, and his eyes gleamed brightly with satisfaction. "I have something very special for you, too, Ma-gwire. Come."

They were ushered to a position of prominence on thick, sleek buffalo robes that had been spread out on the grass in front of the stage ground. Blue Talon slipped away and returned a few minutes later with a fine, beaded belt which he proudly presented to Nancy.

Thousands of beads, in the colors of the rainbow, formed an intricate design over the entire length of the belt. Graceful leather ties dangled from the ends to hold the belt together at the wearer's waist. "It is one of the most beautiful things I have ever seen, Blue Talon," Nancy said sincerely. "Thank you very much."

"You wear, Ma-gwire." He pointed at her with his forefinger. "Your dress, too plain."

Nancy chuckled and stood up, pulling the belt around the waist of the dove gray dress she was wearing, pleased that it fit quite nicely.

Blue Talon's effervescent smile broadened. "Is very pretty. Now, we eat and dance."

Strutting in his proud peacock way, he lowered himself to a position on the other side of Hart, sitting cross-legged. He gave a signal and the festivities began.

The exquisite, semiclothed bodies of the Shawnee gave new meaning to the word redskin as they prepared for their dances in the light of the fires. There were too many of them to count, but Nancy estimated about a hundred.

Beyond the fires were the Indians' cornfields, where tender green stalks were just now sprouting, along with those of beans and squash. Surrounding the fields were clusters of crudely built log buildings, both indications that this was a permanent settlement of the Shawnee.

The drumbeats changed and the dancing began. The men moved away from the sidelines into a single file and onto center stage, lifting their arms and legs in ordered, graceful movements. The monotonous accompaniment on the drum was being conducted by an ancient man with a pockmarked face and rheumy eyes that suggested he might have slipped into a trancelike state brought on by his own music. The steady rhythm of his drumbeats occasionally grew more intense and were joined by a yowl that resonated wildly above the dancers' voices like the song of a demon.

Beyond the stage, darkness inked down over the thick stands of trees, broken only by more fires that lit the movements of smaller groups of people, carousing about. Nancy could make out much mischief among the young men and women who were slipping into the darkness to hide their sexual indiscretions. But the primitive music, if one wanted to call it music, did contain a very erotic beat that left one feeling quite wanton. She herself became highly aware of Hart's knee and shoulder touching hers. Occasionally, he would lean close to make comments, or jokes. Aside from the food, which was questionable in taste and appearance, she could not remember when she had so thoroughly enjoyed herself or been in the presence of such pleasant, stimulating company.

The drumming and dancing seldom ceased as different groups and combinations of groups took their turn entertaining. After a couple of hours, the spectators began getting up and moving about. Nancy and Elizabeth were the only white women present and found themselves the objects of much Shawnee interest and behind-the-hand conversations by the native women. As she and Elizabeth left their seats, accompanied by Hart, Charles McIntosh, and Blue Talon, many of the women came forward and shyly fingered their clothing, enthralled by the strange material and design. If any spoke English, it was very broken and only a word or two.

Soon Nancy found herself in the middle of a group of women who proceeded to show her beautifully crafted moccasins, buckskin dresses, leggings, necklaces, bracelets, medicine pouches, beaded and quilled belts, sashes, and bags, even bows and arrows and tobacco pipes. Many were making the signs of trade Hart had told her about. Nancy turned to Elizabeth for possible advice, but saw that she, too, was surrounded by women. Hart and the other men were similarly engaged.

The men had picketed Nancy's horse some distance away by the trees and all the items she'd brought for trade were in the saddlebags. She motioned for the women to follow her. With some of the younger ones giggling, they gathered their goods and stayed on her heels. She took the items from the saddlebags and laid them out on the grass. It was not as light here and only the red glow of a small fire nearby lit the trading floor, nature's grass.

The Indian women, seeing what she had, moved in closer, shoulder to shoulder, keenly examining the items. They blocked what little light there was and were soon pulling things out of each other's hands and holding them up to the light. Nancy, fearing the women might think she was giving the things away, or worse, might start fighting over them, held up a hand to indicate to the women that she wished them to be quiet and to back away. She was nervous about dealing with these strange people, but she saw quickly that they were intelligent and canny, and she wouldn't be surprised if they were sharp enough to smell fear. She was careful to act as if they were no different than any other people she had known. And in many ways they weren't. She tried to look upon them with the same re-gard as business people, store owners, out to get the most money for their merchandise. She also sensed they would be eager to take advantage of her if she didn't display assertiveness.

She held up the items, one by one, letting each woman get a closer look. Even though she couldn't speak their language, she spoke to them in short sentences, using words that many of them were able to under-stand. But the words didn't really matter. They were only interested in the goods. Some of the things were so alien to them that Nancy had to demonstrate their use, such as the tiny bottle of perfume she had decided she wouldn't need in California. One woman thought it was something to drink and Nancy had caught her just in the nick of time before she had poured it down her throat.

After each item was inspected, the trading began, the bolder women making their offers first. One by one, Nancy traded everything she had brought. For a necklace and matching earbobs, she had acquired a lovely pair of beaded moccasins lined with soft gray rabbit fur. For three lace-trimmed hankies, with her initials embroidered in the corner, she found herself in the possession of a fringed bag of finely tanned white leather. For an old corset, she got a "shawl" made of several fox pelts sewn to-gether, tails attached. She traded off a pair of blue satin slippers for a pair of beaded leather gloves sporting eight-inch fringe on fancy gauntlets. For the hat that matched her riding habit, she acquired a necklace made of bear claws.

Nancy sat back on her heels and watched the women mosey back to the dance, chattering in their native tongue, showing off their new pos-sessions with smiles and laughter and silliness. She ran a hand over the fine leather goods now belonging to her, and thinking that women every-where must have a special fondness for soft things against their skin—whether leather, fur, or silk—and for pretty baubles to dress up their hair, wrists, and throats.

Hearing rocks crunch beneath boot heels, Nancy looked up expecting to see Hart or Elizabeth, but saw Arthur Waite instead stumbling out of the trees a few yards away, buttoning up his trousers. Behind him staggered his drunken companion, Ethan Stillman, an arm over the shoulder of a buxom young Indian woman who couldn't have been more than sixteen. His other hand was molded to her breast. She giggled and took Stillman by the hand, dragging him back into the woods.

Nancy would have hidden, not wanting the men to know she'd witnessed their unfaithfulness to their wives, but she was in plain view and, as misfortune would have it, Arthur saw her and pulled himself up short. He had the look of someone who would turn tail and run, but seeing that she was alone, he skulked along the edge of the trees toward her, staying in the shadows.

She expected a verbal confrontation, but was completely unprepared when he grabbed her wrist and twisted it back in a painful vice. His breath, reeking of whiskey, nearly knocked her over.

"Now, you listen, you highfalutin' blueblood. You'd damn well better keep your mouth shut about what you saw, you hear? If my wife gets wind of this, I'll know she heard it from you, and I'll come after you."

Furious that he would accost her and threaten her, Nancy didn't think of her safety. Angrily, she tried to wrench free of his bruising grip, to no avail, and realized she had committed the worst folly of the frontier. She had left her weapons back at camp.

"Why should I care what you and Ethan Stillman do?" she said evenly. "But I feel truly sorry for your wives, carrying your babies and thinking you're being faithful."

He twisted her wrist back farther. "We ain't doing no harm with these Indian sluts. It's 'cause of those babies our women are carryin' that we're out here. A man can't go for months without relief. But you probably don't understand what I'm saying, do you? I'll bet a spinster like you has never had a man 'tween your legs, have you?"

She shivered at the evil intent that slithered into his eyes, then suddenly a shadow loomed over them. He was jerked away from her as if a huge monster had plucked him up from the sky. A half dozen Indians converged on him. A fist cracked bone and he doubled over. A knee to his chin sent him flying backward into a pile of brush. Blue Talon grabbed him by the shirtfront and hauled him back out of the brush and to his feet. A knife had appeared from the leather sheath at the Shawnee's lean waist and was now pressed against the pulse point in Arthur's throat.

"Daniels's woman," Blue Talon warned with a deadly tone. "You no touch. Daniels kill you. *Quick*. Blue Talon kill you, quicker."

Nancy felt hands at her waist and was turned into Hart's arms. "Are you all right?"

With a hand that had suddenly begun to shake, reminding her that she wasn't invincible, she pushed a stray tendril of hair out of her eyes. "I'm fine. It seems our fellow emigrant has a few secrets he wants to keep."

"I should have stayed closer to you, especially after the women left, but I couldn't get away from the buck who was trying to con me out of my hat. Come on. It's time we headed back to camp anyway."

Blue Talon hauled Arthur to his horse and told him in no uncertain terms to leave the Shawnee encampment and not to return. The dance was still going strong, but Hart said the Indians could, and would, continue on through the night. "We've got to get back or we won't get any sleep at all. And J.B. won't cut us any slack. He'll pull out tomorrow morning same time as always."

He helped Nancy bundle up her trade goods. Blue Talon, afraid Waite might seek revenge by ambushing them on the way back to camp, rode along with them, bringing several of his braves for added security. He reined his pony to a stop when the emigrants' fires could be seen winking in the darkness.

"It is my wish that you will have a safe trip to California, my friend," he said to Hart, shaking Hart's hand in the white man way. "Be on guard for the Pawnee. They need no reason to kill." To Nancy he said, "It has been my honor to meet you, Ma-gwire. I will remember your green eyes and fine horse."

Before Nancy could respond, he had spun his horse around and was galloping away, followed by the thundering hooves of his companions' horses. Their own party continued on to their encampment, but Hart pulled his horse to a halt in the shadow of some trees. "Bring your horse over here, Nancy. We'll walk a spell."

She was apprehensive about the dark band of trees that could easily conceal deadly foes. But Hart seemed unconcerned, so she nudged the mare into the shadows next to his buckskin.

He stepped from the saddle. Circling her waist with his hands, he lifted her from her sidesaddle and to the ground. Gathering her hands in his, he said. "I was thinking that I might be too busy tomorrow to teach you how to whistle, and thought you might like the first lesson now."

Slowly he lifted the hat from her head then drew her into his arms. Sensing a change was about to take place in their relationship, Nancy's heart gathered momentum to the speed of a locomotive racing out of control down a mountain.

"Whistling is all in the way you pucker your lips, Nancy." He tilted his head close to hers; his mouth was only inches away. "Let me show you."

Her knees nearly buckled as she gripped his biceps, powerful and bulging beneath her hands. "Hart—"

Before she could say more, his lips closed over hers. All resistance slipped away. Nothing was more right than to be with him, in his arms. Desire she had never known before exploded inside her, shooting all the way to her toes. Dear God! This was what her grandfather had spoken of.

Then much too soon he dragged his lips from hers and to her neck, where the sweet fire lingered, and where his breath came in erratic puffs against her sensitive flesh. He clung to her and she to him, both amazed now at the fire that had sprung so easily to life between them.

"I thought you were going to give me a lesson on whistling," she murmured.

He gently placed her hat back on her head, adjusted it and readjusted it until it was at just the right, jaunty angle. A mischievous smile pushed back the edges of his seriousness. "That *was* the first lesson, Nancy. You see, whistling is all in how you pucker your lips. But seeing how well you do it, I don't believe you'll have any problem at all with lesson number two."

"Then I'll be looking forward to it . . . whenever you can find the time."

"I'll *make* the time. You can be sure of that."

9

Nancy slipped quietly back into the tent, guided only by the fire at its opening.

"Don't worry about waking me," came Lottie's whisper. "I can't sleep anyway." She sat up and reached for something. In the next moment, the firelight glinted off her bottle of laudanum as she lifted it to her lips.

"Are you still in pain?" Nancy whispered, glancing at Josh but seeing that he was sleeping soundly.

Lottie nodded. "It lasts a few days. Riding the mule all day didn't help. How was the Bread Dance?"

Nancy began plucking pins from her hair and dropping them onto her blankets. It was Hart's kiss that held the stronger memory. "I enjoyed it immensely. Tomorrow I'll show you all the wonderful things I got in trade from the Shawnee women."

"You must have had a good time, girl. You're wearing a high blush, and something tells me it isn't caused from the heat of the fire. Hart wouldn't have something to do with it, would he?"

Nancy smiled and gathered her heavy wool shawl around her shoulders. "Maybe."

Lottie grinned and took another swig of the laudanum. "I thought as much."

As Nancy watched her friend recork the bottle, the pleasant memories of the evening were overshadowed by a gnawing concern. "Are you going to be all right, Lottie?" she asked softly, afraid that her interference on such a delicate subject might not be appreciated. "I don't mean to sound like a mother hen, but you could get addicted to that medication if you're not careful. I had an aunt who took it constantly for headaches until it got to where she took it even when she didn't have a headache."

Lottie shrugged her shoulders and slipped the bottle under her pillow. "I reckon I already am addicted to it, at least once a month. I couldn't get by without it when these stomach cramps hit me. I'd be down rolling and bawling and throwing up if I didn't have it. But I know the dangers, and the rest of the time I force myself to stay away from it. Like you, I've seen women take it just to keep their minds dulled so they wouldn't have to face a life they didn't want to live. People like Miriam who find themselves in situations they can't get out of.

"I'm surprised that poor woman hasn't resorted to something drastic before now. I hear tell that bastard she's married to hauled off and slapped her right across the face first thing this morning. 'Course, nobody noticed the bruise since she kept her sunbonnet on all day, but Frances told me about it. Frances was so mad she was ready to kill old Waite herself."

"Why did he hit her?" Nancy was shocked that a man would be so cruel to his own wife. And yet, remembering how Waite had behaved at the Bread Dance, she was beginning to understand his true nature.

"Apparently she sat down to rest for a minute and dozed off," Lottie explained. "He got his ass out of bed just in time to see the bacon burning in the pan. I swear, somebody ought to kill him."

Nancy shared with Lottie what had taken place out at the Bread Dance and what Waite had done to her. "He doesn't know how close he came to ending his journey right there. Blue Talon wasn't playing games."

"Somebody will kill him before it's over," Lottie said matter-of-factly. "His kind won't last long out here."

Nancy watched Lottie settle back down beneath her blankets. She changed into her nightgown and slid beneath her own, thinking again of Hart and his kiss and wondering where a relationship with him could possibly go. Wondering where she *wanted* it to go.

Worry for Lottie stayed embedded in Nancy's mind, too. She had heard of women hemorrhaging. What if it happened to her friend?

"I can drive those mules for you tomorrow, Lottie, if you'll show me how," she offered. "I need to learn sooner or later, and you could use the rest."

It was a minute before Lottie replied, as if she were weighing the pros and cons of allowing an amateur to take up the jerk line. "You'll have to sit astride, girl. Is that gonna bother you?"

Nancy chuckled. "I used to do it all the time when nobody was looking. But my mother caught me once and passed out right in the middle of the yard. The servants had to bring her around with smelling salts. No, it won't bother me."

Lottie's lips curved into an amused grin. "I should have known better than to ask."

The Oregon Trail

The rain began the next afternoon, coming straight down in an unrelenting torrent and transforming the trail into a quagmire. It worsened when they reached the turnoff to the Kansas River that had been, a few years ago, little more than a faint trace where a few trappers and brave missionaries had dared to take wagons into the Rocky Mountains. Now it was coined the Oregon Trail, and here their troubles began.

In the wake of the Oregon company's one hundred and fifty wagons, the muddy trail wound like a black viper across the undulating hills. It had no base at all, and with the heavy traffic that had gone before, it was rutted much worse than the Santa Fe Trail had been. The wagons often times became so bogged down in the mud that they had to be unloaded, or risk broken axletrees, before the mules could pull them out.

Nancy had been doing quite well with the mules, but turned them over to Lottie's more experienced hand. On the third day, it appeared as if the low-hanging, slow-moving clouds had stalled right over the wagon trains. A cold mist hung down in the vales and penetrated the bands of dark, rain-soaked trees.

Arthur Waite, who was in lead that day, stalled the entire train for over two hours when his mules laid down in the mud and refused to go any farther. Chiles was forced to hook some of his spare mules in front of Waite's and literally drag the sullen animals out of the mire. Chiles called for Lottie, who was seventh in line, to put her mules in the lead. Accustomed to any condition that could be thrown at them, her sturdy Spanish mules leaned deep into their harnesses with no objection and competently led the wagons. Arthur Waite boiled with rage to think a woman had shown him up.

Each day offered a new crisis, and the rainy, muddy conditions seemed to aggravate each and every one. A runaway team resulted in an overturned wagon that careened over the steep banks of the Wakarusa River. Sacks of coffee, flour, and sugar were grabbed by the swift current and lost. The young men who owned the wagon had been so discouraged by the loss that they had decided to head back to Independence. Chiles, knowing their manpower could be crucial in getting his company to California, convinced them to stay on by giving them some of his own supplies.

Chiles had been careful to screen the people he had allowed in his company, taking only those who had had experience with horses and mules, but night watch was a new experience for most of them. Some fell asleep and let the livestock wander off, which resulted in lost time in the morning. Some, never having been away from the safety of cities, thought that everything in the bushes was an Indian. One man shot at a shadow and found he'd killed a skunk. It could have just as easily been one of the emigrants out relieving himself. Chiles had given a lecture the young man would not soon forget.

Wolves moved in too close to the encampments at night, and their eyes could be seen gleaming frightfully close from the darkness. Their howls upset people and animals alike. Women and children didn't dare leave the wagons. Horses and mules squealed and broke tether lines. Dogs howled in fear, and some took off in response to the call of the wild, only to be killed by the wolves. A pack of six big grays took down one of Brenham Royal's mules, which Arthur Waite, on night guard, had allowed to wander off too far from the others. Royal had threatened to kill Waite and had lit into him with his fists. Lucille had gone into hysterics over that—and everything else—and now stayed in the wagon for such extended periods of time that some of the women were beginning to worry that her bladder would break.

Rubber sheets and enameled or oiled canvas was brought out and transformed into raincoats by those who didn't own the real thing. Women and children were forced into the cramped wagons as protection from the rain and as a reprieve from slogging through the mud and water that was often over their shoe tongues. The sky's dismal offering began to show on everyone's face, and tempers were soon strung as tight as banjo strings. Men spouted off profanities and didn't apologize for it. Children cried. Women cried. Dogs trailed along, muddy and wet, ears drooping and with sad expressions that suggested they truly wondered what craziness had invaded the minds of their people.

Lottie summed it up best. "If I'd wanted to drown, I'd have jumped into the Big Muddy!"

A week into the journey the company passed a freshly dug grave. Chiseled words on a crude stone marker told them a young boy had been buried there. Because the emigrants were afraid he might have had a contagious disease, Hart and McIntosh rode to the Oregon camp and brought word back that the boy had fallen from a wagon and been run over.

The next day they passed another grave. This one belonging to a young man who had accidentally shot himself.

When Nancy had envisioned her great adventure, it had always been with the sun shining. But, despite the rain, she rode her mare every day, determined to face the elements just as the men had to do—and Lottie, too, who sat astride her mule and asked no one in particular, at least a dozen times a day, why in the hell she'd ever left Independence.

"It really wasn't such a bad place after all," she muttered time and again.

Nancy learned that only patience and perseverance, and a few profanities, got a tent up in the rain with the wind whipping it unmercifully in her face. On some nights, not even the gutta-percha on the ground, or the trench she and Lottie dug around the tent, would keep the rain out of their beds. Like the other women, they retreated to the crowded wagon at night and put in restless hours with aching muscles, too tired and miserable to sleep. At least Josh had taken to sharing Hart's tent, which gave them a modicum of privacy and a little more room. Hart somehow always managed to pitch his tent with no problem, something that Nancy began to observe with definite envy and more than a little annoyance.

Fires were nearly impossible to start and keep lit. Again, Hart was one of the few men who seemed to be able to accomplish getting a shelter up and a fire going. People tried to copy his technique but most had little success. Occasionally he got a fire going for someone else, but they could seldom keep the rain or wind from putting it out. With no fire, meals were lacking. Men griped because they couldn't get a cup of hot coffee.

Most of the emigrants contented themselves with dried meat, hardtack, and a few of the luxuries, like pickles, fresh apples, and cheese, all of which would be gone too soon.

Nancy occasionally wondered if God had gone back on his word and was planning another forty days and forty nights of rain. Chiles jokingly commented that maybe they would have to convert the wagons to arks. No one was amused.

Since Elm Grove, John C. Frémont and his men had traveled quite closely with the California company. At first, no one minded Frémont and the manpower his group offered. The union, however, lasted only a few days.

It came about that Chiles and Hart, who were doing most of the hunting for both companies, came back to camp one evening with some wild turkeys and two deer. Frémont boldly claimed the hindquarters of the deer—the best meat—leaving Chiles's party with only the front quarters. Chiles was normally a good-natured person who tended to take things in stride, but he clearly didn't care for John C. Frémont's arrogance and he told him so, without mincing words.

"You are the biggest ass I have ever encountered, John. I'll give you your fair share of this kill. Mind you, I said 'fair' share. And come tomorrow morning you can gather up your men, forge your own way— since you are supposedly such a skilled pathfinder—and you can kill your own damned meat."

"You, sir, are a fool who will regret the parting of our ways," Frémont had countered.

"Then let the regretting begin."

There were some in the company who thought Chiles might kill Frémont right then and there, and possibly the only thing that saved him was that Frémont must have sensed it, too, and stalked back to the protection of his camp and his men.

"For two bits, I'd shoot that pompous sonofabitch," Chiles had muttered, as the cocky captain marched away, "but, unfortunately, he isn't worth the bullet."

At least they weren't troubled by Indians who were, for the most part, friendly throughout this region. If any warring went on, it was between the Pawnees and other tribes of the area.

The way to the Kansas River crossing was over an interminable number of low hills and swells, undulating like green ocean waves, seemingly tumbling into sky and eternity. Once past the Wakarusa, they followed the southern bank of the Kansas River, staying out away from the timber for easier traveling.

The company at last found organization within itself, and each individual began to fall into a routine that worked well for themselves and in accordance with the others.

A few miles from the Kansas crossing, the sky cleared and the sun came out. Spirits lifted and the company nooned in a little grove of trees. The forests had thinned since leaving Independence but could still be found in protected folds of the hills and along the waterways.

Nancy and Lottie, like the others, spread their gutta-percha sheets or painted canvas tarps over the damp ground, wiped them dry and covered them with blankets, then settled into a noon-day feast of bread, cheese wedges, pickles, dried beef, and fruit. A few of the women, Lottie included, had boiled several dozen eggs before departure and placed them in cans of oats to keep them fresh and cool. The cool weather had helped, too. Some people had brought chickens along, and milk cows, but the chickens were so upset from being jounced about in their cages strapped to the wagons that most of them had already quit laying. Inevitably they would sizzle in frying pans before journey's end.

Everyone settled near the trees, but not in the shade. They were chilled and damp and chose to sit out in the open, soaking up the warmth of the sunshine. Hart, shadowed by Josh, joined Nancy and Lottie. The men talked about the problems of the journey. The women usually didn't voice their opinions on such matters, except for Lucille Royal, who always had to inform the men of how they should be doing things.

"She should have married Arthur Waite," Nancy whispered to Lottie. "They're a good pair."

Lottie poured salt liberally onto her boiled egg and whispered back. "Or been hung alongside him from the same limb. He certainly has a problem with women who assume something other than a servant's role."

Because of the rain, the women had had very little opportunity to socialize. After the meal, the men departed to hitch up the teams again for the afternoon trek to the Kansas River. The women pulled in closer together and a lively conversation ensued along with rounds of questions as they took the first steps in finally getting to know each other.

Frances Vines said that she and her sister, Elizabeth, were going to California to reunite with their father, a trapper named George Yount who had gone into the Rocky Mountains eighteen years before and whom they had not seen since.

"Our father asked Colonel Chiles to escort us to California on his return trip," Frances supplied.

"That's quite a responsibility for Colonel Chiles to assume," Miriam Waite replied. "But, then, he's a good man in my estimation."

"He's a stupid one in mine," Lucille Royal put in smugly.

Mrs. Martin, always flanked by her three lovely daughters—Mary, Arzelia, and Martha—pleasantly continued as if Lucille had not made her brash remark. "Yes, Chiles is a noble man, Miriam. A friend to all. I have complete confidence in his ability."

"Then that just goes to show that you're as stupid as he is." Lucille stood up, pushing reddish-gold wisps of hair from eyes that darted nervously over the wilderness surrounding them. "Every one of you would follow the fool right through the gates of hell. Look around you. This is hell, and the devil's warriors—those savage redskins—could come screaming over one of those rises any second and kill us all. This is no place for women. At least not for *ladies.*" On the latter, she shot insolent glances at Lottie and Nancy.

"Nobody promised this journey would be a pleasure ride," Lottie reminded her with blunt honesty. "There are inconveniences and hardships we'll all have to accept until it's over. Don't think it's easy on the men either. If we can't do our share without complaining, then we should go back before it's too late."

"You'd like me to do that, wouldn't you?"

"I'd give your husband a whole team of mules if you'd do that. Yes, ma'am, I surely would."

Frances chuckled and rose to her feet, amused by the friction that was always between Lottie and Lucille. "This may not be a habitat hospitable to ladies, but, frankly, my bladder doesn't care, nor is it as durable as yours, Lucille. But I doubt that even you can hold it all the way to California. So, lady or not, I'm going to mosey down to that big clump of bushes. If anyone would care to come along, we could offer each other some protection from roaming children and men with wandering eyes. And those men of Frémont's can't be far away. There are a few of those who give more cause for concern than the redskins."

Except for Lucille, all the ladies rose, seeing it as probably their last opportunity to tend to private matters before the night encampment hours away. They started off across the meadow for the intended strip of bushes and trees. Frances turned back to Lucille. "Aren't you going to join us, Lucille? You haven't been out of your wagon all morning."

Lucille lifted her chin in a defiant gesture they were all beginning to tire of. "I shall not humiliate myself by turning such a private function into a community affair. This journey into the wilderness is going to turn us all into barbarians. We'll be no better than those heathen Indians, squatting in the bushes. They're probably lurking over there right now, just waiting to kill the whole foolish lot of you. I have a chamber pot in my wagon and I will continue to use it."

"You should be applauded your ingenuity," Lottie replied facetiously. "As for the rest of us, we'll stay far back from your wagon when Brenham heads it uphill, just in case you don't have your pot tied down."

Lucille's face turned as red as Colonel Chiles's hair and she took a step toward Lottie with her fists clenched. "Why you Santa Fe whore—"

Nancy bolted forward, thrusting herself between the two of them. "This isn't necessary, Lucille."

"Tell it to that bitch. She's the one who started it. Who asked your opinion anyway?" Lucille turned on Nancy with a vengeance almost more hateful than she had Lottie. "You sit out here on your blanket like you're on a picnic, and you ride up and down the line all day on your fancy horse, flirting with the men. You're as bad as she is, riding that mule like a man and acting as if this journey is a pleasure ride, a lark. I won't even mention how you continually use your feminine wiles to get the men to do your heavy work for you. You say you don't want a husband, but we can all see what's going on between you and that scout. You'd take the first one that asked you. Arthur Waite was right when he said you two shouldn't have been allowed to join this company."

Nancy hadn't prepared herself for a personal attack, but she was not one to back down to it either. "I have not coerced any man into helping me," she hotly denied. "Nor flirted with any of them. If they have assisted me and Lottie at all, it was because they chose to."

Lucille's two daughters appeared on either side of her, each taking one of her arms. "Come on, Mama," suggested Elise, her oldest child, a pretty fourteen-year-old girl with wheat-colored hair. "Let's just us three walk down the creek a little farther. Nobody's asking you to do something you don't feel comfortable with."

The girls physically dragged their mother away from the confrontation then headed her to a point more distant from the wagon train than where the other women were going. "Is it safe to get so far away?" Lucille could be heard saying. "What if some savages, or wolves, are laying wait in those bushes? That fool Chiles should have let Frémont have that deer meat. We could have used their rifle power in case of an Indian attack . . ."

Lottie relaxed, but her brown eyes followed Lucille and her daughters, who were both much more likable than their mother and who had apparently acquired their father's more compassionate nature. "If the Indians don't kill that woman, I might."

Frances laughed, her eyes twinkling. "She certainly tests the limits of one's good nature, doesn't she?"

Garnet Stillman, who seldom said anything, suddenly grabbed her protruding stomach and released a sharp cry of pain. The women simultaneously rushed to her, asking if she was all right and suggesting that she sit down again.

"You've been slogging through mud all morning," Miriam said, mildly scolding her as a mother would a daughter. "Why don't you ride in the wagon this afternoon and give yourself a break."

" 'Cause the wagon's . . . rougher," Garnet replied, riding out the pain with clenched teeth and closed eyes. "The road is so rutted, it rattles my teeth, not to mention what it does to the rest of me. I begged Ethan not to come, to wait until next year."

"When did men ever listen to women?" Miriam's face darkened for a moment before she added. "How long before your baby is due, child?"

Garnet finally released the breath she'd been holding and opened her cornflower blue eyes, dark with fear. "Not for six weeks or so."

Miriam put an arm over Garnet's shoulder. Her sympathy and concern for the girl was clearly written on a face whose prettiness was lost behind sadness and fatigue. "Don't worry. We'll help you. And I heard someone mention that Dr. Whitman was with the Oregon company. They're not so far ahead of us that we couldn't get him if we need him."

"I don't know what to do," Garnet admitted meekly, looking very much like a child herself. "I don't know what to expect. I wish my mother was here." Her voice cracked and her eyes teared. "It frightens me out here. It's so . . . vast. I can't comprehend its beginning or its end. It's like the sky turned upside down. No matter where you stand or how far you travel, how far you look, there's no end to it. I don't want to be out here alone, having my baby out here alone."

Miriam tried to soothe her fears. "I've midwifed. Delivered over thirty babies and given birth to eight of my own. I'll be here to help you."

"And I brought a good supply of herbs to cure whatever ails you," Frances offered. "I had a neighbor, an old woman, who was an expert on the healing quality of plants, and she taught me everything she could before she died."

Miriam's lips thinned to a tight, angry line. Her tone was suddenly harsh and bitter. "Have you got anything to keep women from having babies in the first place?"

By now they were all aware of her husband's verbal and physical abuse, and how he and the boys seldom lifted a finger to do anything to help her. Practically every one of them had secretly wondered whether she would be strong enough to even make it to California. She couldn't have been forty, but her actions and the age in her eyes gave the impression that she was well past it.

Frances nodded and, like an old friend, hooked arms with the older woman and started strolling across the meadow. "Certainly. There are ways, Miriam, and none of which you should be ashamed of using. Come along. I'll tell you everything I know on the subject."

10

The company paused on the bluffs overlooking the Kansas River, their first major crossing. Despite the muddy trail and the rain, they were still full of spirit and energy. It helped that the sun had come out again, shining through a partly cloudy sky. It brightened the verdant valley below, bringing it alive with spring's new grass and wildflowers, and with crops of corn, beans, squash, and pumpkins planted by the Kanza Indians.

Oregon companies were camped on both sides of the river. The ones who hadn't crossed yet were waiting for the river to recede. The California company would have to wait, too.

Each side of the river supported one or two permanent Kanzan villages. Their dwellings were made of dirt piled over poles and limbs, resembling giant molehills. Grass grew on some of the abodes, causing them to blend somewhat into their surroundings, but if the wind was coming from the wrong direction, the "houses" released a stench that forced the emigrants to camp upwind.

But the friendly Kanzas could not be avoided. Already they were leaving their huts and their crops and coming out to meet the California company, to help them as they had the Oregon companies before them, and to strike up trades.

Nancy had noticed before that the Kanza men were, for the most part, tall, straight, and handsome. They walked with shoulders pulled back and heads lifted in a proud way. Most wore nothing but breechcloths, showing strong, brown, muscular legs. Others opted for leggings and maybe a blanket over their wide, square shoulders. The most fascinating thing about the men, however, was the way they shaved their heads, leaving a strip down the center that resembled the roached mane of a horse. In this "rooster comb" they attached all sorts of feathers and geegaws. The women, by contrast, or like nature's feathered friends, were very plain, leaving all the adornments and bright plumage to their male counterparts.

Next to the first Kanzan village there was also a cluster of white man's buildings: a Methodist mission, a trading house, and a smithy. Damaged wagons could be fixed before getting any farther into the journey. Supplies that had been lost, or items that had been forgotten, could now be restored, providing the huge Oregon contingency hadn't cleared off the shelves.

While riding with Hart, Nancy had been quite surprised by all the crops the Indians were raising. "They seem to be learning quite well from the white man's teachings, aren't they?"

"I suppose you could say that the government has managed to civilize these tribes quite successfully," Hart agreed, "insofar as an Indian can be civilized. The government has taught them how to grow crops. And the government has given them pigs and cattle, and has put fences around the livestock to keep them from straying and being killed by other tribes less agreeable to civilization. That works quite well, until winter sets in. Then the Indians lose the entire concept of the program. They pull up the fences, make bonfires out of them, and put the pigs and cattle on spits. The next year, the government starts all over again."

Chiles and Hart led the way down off the bluffs to the river, finding a suitable encampment for their small wagon train. If they could get through the night without rain, the river might recede enough that they could cross safely in the morning. As June drew frighteningly near, Chiles didn't want any more delays. They simply didn't have the time to waste.

Nancy watched the colonel occasionally glancing toward the West and detected an unspoken urgency motivating him. But if he worried about what lay beyond on those distant horizons, he did not transfer that worry to his contingency. He always moved through the company with a smile and a joke, or a teasing remark.

That evening, the friendly Kanzas invaded the encampment, wandering about the wagons as if each were a veritable storehouse of trade potential. Others hunkered down next to fires and joked and chatted with the emigrants. A few of the men tried to start up games of gambling. Nancy was amazed at how well they spoke English. She was also amazed that, on closer inspection, many of them were crawling with vermin. Not wanting to bring lice into the wagon, she and Lottie had no desire to do any trading this time, but one young brave who particularly liked baking powder biscuits gave them a handsome hunting knife in exchange for a dozen biscuits and a cup of honey.

Lottie inspected the knife and scabbard for lice then strapped it around her narrow waist. "I wonder how many scalps he's taken with this thing?" she said out loud, holding it up so the firelight glistened off the wickedly sharp blade. "The guards had better not fall asleep tonight or we could lose every horse and mule we own to that smiling, thievin' bunch of savages. Old Biscuit-Lover particularly likes your mare. I think he sort of likes you, too. Or else he just appreciates the way you make biscuits."

Nancy's eyes widened. "He does? How do you know?"

"Saw him eyeing you both pretty good. He'll try to sneak back here tonight and steal that horse. Maybe you, too."

"Maybe I'd better have the knife, Lottie."

Her friend chuckled, unsheathing it. "Sure. Just sleep light and don't use it on the wrong man."

Nancy did more than sleep light. She didn't sleep at all. She heard every crack of a twig, every cough, every whisper in the night. She counted the hoots of an owl that had decided to perch in a big tree over their encampment, as if keeping his own night vigil. After fifty hoots she tossed her covers back and left the tent, pulling her wool shawl over her shoulders.

A few stars shone through a broken cloud cover, leaving hope for sunshine tomorrow. Lady Rae was still securely tied to the wagon wheel, as were the mules. Many people had left their mules inside the encampment tonight, knowing the Kanzas would be leaving on their summer hunts soon and would not hesitate to steal what horses they could. The sentries had been doubled inside the camp, and tripled outside the camp to watch the main body of livestock. They alternated every two hours, but Nancy wondered if anyone was sleeping tonight. She saw the men moving about with their rifles in hand. One had heard her and sauntered over. As he came closer she recognized Hart.

"I nearly mistook you for an Indian," he whispered. "That is, until you stepped out of the shadows. The moonlight makes your hair look like spun gold."

Self-consciously she lifted a hand to her hair, aware of the seductive quality of his words. One corner of the shawl slipped off her shoulder, but a warmth grew inside her that chased away the night's chill.

"I couldn't sleep," she said softly. "There's an owl out here who likes listening to himself." Her gaze lifted to the leafy dark crowns of the trees in search of the noisy culprit. "I also heard a noise like someone crying."

Hart's brow furrowed. "Be careful of what you think you hear, Nancy. Indians might use any tactic to lure an unsuspecting person away from safety."

Nancy studied the roughly hewn angles of his face, the strong jaw and pronounced cheekbones. He had an extraordinary sixth sense, as if every nerve and fiber of his body contained some supernatural power of insight. He always seemed to know something was going to happen before it did. Had he known the owl would keep her awake, and that she would come out here in the darkness to talk to him? Had he guessed that part of her insomnia had been due to thoughts of him, and his kiss that still lingered in her mind?

"The Stillman wagon is right over there," she said. "Maybe it's Garnet I heard crying. Ethan's out on guard duty and she's alone. She's so young and frightened, Hart. I think the poor girl is frightened of her own shadow. But I don't envy her having her first child out here in the wilderness."

"No, but she isn't the first. Nor will she be the last."

"Perhaps I should check on her."

She started to turn away, but he caught her hand, and pulled her into the shadows away from watching eyes. As if they moved in time to the steps of a dance, they simultaneously turned into each other's arms. "Don't run away, Nancy," he whispered. "I know of a magic potion that might very well make you sleep better."

Her curves molded naturally to the hard contours of his body. His muscular strength lit the sparks of passion no other man had ever been able to stir. Where she had always felt an urgency to flee from the advances of other suitors, she now faced the exciting desire to meet Hart's lovemaking head-on. Her senses came alive; her skin tingled beneath the heated imprint of his fingers on her back, and wherever else his body came into contact with hers. His nearness fulfilled romantic dreams that she had known as a young woman, but had begun to believe were only grounded in fairy-tale fantasy.

Her shawl fell from her shoulders. Only his arm circling her waist kept it from cascading all the way to the ground. He propped the rifle up against the trunk of a tree, and with both arms free pulled her closer. He hesitated a moment, searching her eyes for approval or disapproval. Seeing the former, his kiss claimed her boldly, parting her lips with deeper and thorough possession, sampling the warmth of her inner honey with the light, flicking play of his tongue over hers. A scorching fire like none she had felt before sprang from the embers that had lain dormant for too many years while waiting for this moment, this man. Nancy wanted him with a desire that was all at once shameful and wonderful. Passion was summoned and questioned. All physical and mental restraint was challenged.

But too soon, or so it seemed, Hart released her. After a moment spent collecting himself, the flirting smile returned to his lips. "I'll be a guard every night if the rewards are so sweet." His whisper was as soft as powder snow, and she could barely hear it above the blood pulsing wildly through her veins.

"I should let you get back to work. The company is depending on you to protect them." She said the words, but her true desire was to stop time so that the two of them could stay here forever in this secluded place where the world could not intrude.

"At this moment, I regret the responsibility." His voice still held a thick, erotic timbre but moved on with a teasing inflection. "You should warn a man beforehand of the pleasantly debilitating quality of your kisses."

She smiled, finding it easy to banter with him. "You are not without fault yourself, sir."

An invisible force more powerful than common sense drew them together again. Hart showered more kisses across her lips, her eyelids, her throat, and up along her neck and into her hair. She slid her hands around his shoulders and gripped his sinewed back for support. She clung to the pleasure he offered. Her fingers glided into the silky, dark hair that curled at his collar, and she branded his throat and jaw with her own eager kisses, tasting the pleasantly salty texture of his skin on her lips and tongue.

He mounted his last ounce of willpower and set himself away from her, staggering like a dizzy, drunken man. But he wasn't alone in his intoxication. Nancy had to grip a nearby tree trunk to steady herself.

"You'd better go back to your tent," he whispered raggedly. "Before I forget that you're a lady and do something we'll both regret tomorrow."

"I'm beginning to see that being a lady is a most disagreeable burden to bear."

Her comment drew his smile. "Be careful how you tempt me, Miss Maguire." He turned to go, hefting the rifle in his strong hand again. "But do keep me in your thoughts."

"You came offering a potion for sleep," she quipped. "How can it be effective if I am to lie awake thinking of you?"

Again, he reached across the distance separating them, across the darkness, and stroked the length of her cheek with the back of his hand. "Perhaps I wasn't completely honest about the true nature of my potion. When you go back to bed, Nancy, think about being my wife, because as I see it, we were meant to be together."

Nancy stopped breathing. Time stopped, too. When she at last gulped for a deep breath of air to keep from fainting dead away, she wondered if she had possibly misinterpreted his words. "We hardly know each other, Hart. How could you possibly want to . . . marry me?"

A slow dance of devilment began in his eyes. "You came out here to get away from convention. And I'm not a conventional man. You know as well as I do that when a person waits for something to come to him, he'll die in a rocking chair, still waiting. I don't care that we only met a couple of weeks ago. I knew from the first moment you came riding up on that hellion of a mare, perched up there a little too cocky in your fancy riding habit, that you were the woman I wanted by my side in California. We have the same dream, Nancy. Why not build it together?"

She felt as if she had a mouthful of flour, trying to swallow it down without water and digest it all at once. "But I didn't plan to marry. I didn't come out here looking for a husband."

"Plans can be changed, if one so desires." Hart swung the barrel of his rifle up to his shoulder. "And like I said earlier, it's when you're not looking for something that you will generally always find it."

The starlight caught the reckless gleam in his eyes. She understood it; understood him. An invisible hand seemed to push at her back, urging her to rush into his arms again and say yes. But common sense and willpower kept her where she was.

"I don't want to settle down," she said, more as a reminder to herself than as a declaration to him.

"Who said anything about settling down?" His low-throated chuckle drifted across the short distance, seemingly like a caress in the wake of one of his tumultuous kisses. He touched the brim of his hat in a courtly manner. "Don't be afraid of me, Nancy. I'll never take away your freedom."

Nancy stood rooted to the spot, watching him stroll back into the center of the encampment as if nothing had happened. As if he hadn't left her with a tangle of emotions and questions and possibilities that might very well steal her sleep for weeks to come. He had thrown her into the center of a whirling tornado. She had come out here knowing exactly what she wanted to do. She had plotted and planned for years. He had littered that direct course with sweet roadblocks of caresses and kisses and promises of sexual bliss. Was it love they felt for each other? Or did he just want a woman to take care of him in California? To warm his bed? Wash his socks? Cook his meals? Help him build his ranch? Everyone knew there weren't many English women in California. Was he just looking for a wife, and was he willing to settle for the first likely candidate?

Pondering her new and completely unexpected dilemma, Nancy moved quietly to Garnet's wagon.

11

Nancy paused just outside Garnet's wagon, listening for the sound she thought she had heard before. Shortly it came, a sniff and then soft, muffled sobs.

"Garnet?" she whispered. "It's Nancy. Are you all right?"

A heavy silence followed and Nancy visualized the startled girl, holding her breath and trying to collect herself. She heard the rustling of blankets being tossed aside. "Yes, I'm fine, Nancy. Is something wrong?" She pulled back the canvas hanging down over the back of the wagon and met Nancy's concerned eyes just briefly before lowering her own in obvious embarrassment while wiping away a stray tear.

"I was wondering the same about you, Garnet."

"I've been upset," she admitted. "I'm sorry I woke you up with my bawling."

"You didn't wake me," Nancy replied with a kindly smile. "There's an old hoot owl in the trees out here somewhere and he's the one to blame."

"I heard him, too, but I don't mind. A noise like that is constant and sure, and it helps me so I don't feel so alone. It's when it stops that I get scared and imagine Indians lurking outside the wagon, just ready to dive inside screaming with their tomahawks a-flying." Garnet glanced past Nancy, as if to make sure no one else, like those Indians, was within earshot. "I shouldn't be a sissy, but coming out here frightens me. I just know I'm going to die. I feel it deep inside."

"Life is never a sure thing," Nancy said. "Even back East. Look at the people who die of cholera, typhoid, and numerous other ills and accidents."

"I know, but I look out across the vast emptiness of this land and it's as if Death is out there just over the next hill, waiting for me."

"Everything will be all right. It's natural for a person to be afraid of the unknown."

Garnet looked embarrassed by her confession. "As long as you can't sleep we might as well visit. Will you come inside? It's crowded, but we can sit on the edge of the bed."

Nancy climbed into the wagon and found a place on the narrow little bed Ethan had fixed for him and his young wife. Some of the emigrants slept in their wagons every night, but Nancy preferred the roominess of the tent. The only advantage the wagon had was that it was high and dry, as long as it didn't rain so much that the canvas leaked. Most people had so many things stacked in their wagons that there was little or no room for sleeping. Large families had brought two wagons. In those instances, one of the wagons could be used for women and children to ride and sleep in; the other for the supplies. It required an extra driver, however, so some of the married men who didn't have sons or brothers would hire a single man to drive the extra wagon.

"I've wanted to talk to you, Nancy," Garnet said. "But there never seems to be a good time. And when we're with the others . . . well, I try to be part of the conversations, but nobody ever seems to hear my comments."

"Don't underestimate your influence, Garnet."

She shrugged. "Well, no one acknowledges what I say. I get to where I don't bother putting in my two cents' worth because I figure nobody really cares."

"Only the self-centered people don't care."

Garnet looked away wistfully as if she might cry again. "I've been wanting to tell you it wasn't my idea to turn you down when you came looking for someone to travel with. Ethan was just afraid he'd have to do for you. You looked so sophisticated, so regal, that day you rode out to camp in your lovely riding habit and matching beaver hat. I can see now that you're not the helpless person everyone thought you would be."

Nancy wasn't offended, just annoyed that the worth and intent of a person was too often determined by appearance and background.

"You've certainly had tongues wagging," Garnet continued, looking brighter.

Nancy was amused. "I have?"

The young woman's wide smile brightened her face. She self-consciously brushed a stray strand of blond hair from her wet cheek, then ran two fingers daintily over her face to dry it. "People are saying that you aren't what they expected you to be. That you get right in and do your share. You've gained their respect, Nancy. Both you and Lottie have. The men are all envious of the way she can handle those mules."

"Yes, she has a special touch with them."

"I would have liked having you join us." Now that Garnet had been given the opportunity to talk, it was as if the floodgates to her mind had been opened. "I think men sometimes don't understand a woman's need to have other women to talk to. And I can talk to you. Mainly because you listen. You're not like that nasty Lucille Royal who only wants to listen to herself complain. I see you and Lottie laughing and having a good time. You two seem to have so much fun."

"It's hard *not* to when Lottie's around." Nancy laughed.

"I envy you both your freedom," Garnet said wistfully again. "You don't have anybody else you have to please. I guess I didn't know what marriage was all about. If I had, I would have stayed single. I wanted a baby, but . . . I didn't know getting one would involve such an . . . unpleasant and . . . humiliating act. The only good thing about being with child is that Ethan leaves me alone at night. I like being held and caressed, but I don't like the other. He seldom touches me but what he doesn't want to . . . you know . . . do it all.

"I guess I shouldn't be talking to you about such things, what with you still being single. It's just that you're older than I am so I assume you probably know about it anyway. Have you ever . . . you know . . . been with a man? —Oh, I'm sorry I shouldn't have asked that. It's none of my business."

Regardless of her hasty apology, Garnet was looking at her with those wide, eager eyes, still wanting the answer to her question if Nancy would be so bold as to offer it.

"No," Nancy said softly, not caring to discuss such personal matters. "I haven't."

Satisfied with the answer, Garnet plunged into her diatribe again.

"I've tried to enjoy it, Nancy. I really have. Ethan says he loves me, but still I just don't like that part. You're lucky you don't have a man pawing at you every night when you go to bed and you're tired and want nothing but to sleep. Stay single, Nancy. Hart's a nice man, and I can tell you like each other, but he won't be any different. It's just the way men are from what I can gather. I guess some women don't mind the marriage bed. And whores *like* doing that revolting thing with men. But I don't see how anybody could. Not even for money.

"Don't misunderstand me, Nancy," she hastened on. "I want my baby. I want that land in California, and a nice house. I couldn't have those things without Ethan. He's a good man and a good worker. He'd do anything for me. I wouldn't have anything right now if I hadn't married him. Our family was so poor. I saw a way to get away from that so I took it. Ethan was a lot older than me—eighteen years—but he isn't too bad looking. Then here you come along, showing me that I could have done if all by myself if I'd been brave. Just brave. Instead, I prostituted myself to stay alive."

Tears swelled in the girl's eyes again. Nancy suddenly wished she had stayed in her tent and listened to the hoot owl. What he'd had to say had been considerably less disturbing. Was coupling really as awful as Garnet said it was? She'd heard other women say they didn't like it. She remembered the way she, too, had been repulsed by the touch of most of the men she'd been courted by. But tonight, she had wanted nothing more than to get as close to Hart as she could. It had been her body's natural response to his touch.

And the image of Ethan Stillman and Arthur Waite dallying with the Indian women in the woods returned to taunt her. Here was poor Garnet torturing herself. If she only knew of his infidelity. It made her wonder if men could be trusted at all. Would she be foolish to consider marriage to Hart? Foolish to share the control of her destiny with him? Or maybe relinquish control altogether?

"Everything will work out," she said firmly, as much to assure herself as Garnet. "Your husband loves you very much."

A deep sadness entered Garnet's eyes. "Yes, I know."

The wide banks of the Kansas River barely contained the swollen stream, but still the current appeared relatively slow and not terribly treacherous.

The river was three or four hundred feet across, but only about fifty of those feet required the animals to swim.

The ferry, consisting of two scows and measuring twenty feet long by five feet wide, belonged to two enterprising Kanza Indians who charged a toll of one dollar per wagon. The scows were solid, but the crossing, especially with the river so high, looked to Nancy to be precarious at best.

Most of the emigrants were able to afford the ferry and made the trip across the river with no mishaps, although the Oregon company hadn't been quite so lucky. Several of their wagons had carried too much weight and had capsized the ferry.

Other emigrants, with caulked wagon beds, boated across. Livestock swam, along with some men who attempted to keep a semblance of order about the animals. The Indians camping near the river were extremely accommodating and offered to swim the livestock across in exchange for a little money or food.

Nancy and Lottie watched as the two Kanzas attached ropes to their wagon and expertly hauled it onto the ferry and blocked the wheels.

"Are you sure you can get it over without one of us going with you?" Lottie said to the Indian. "We need to help swim the mules across."

"No worry," the spokesman of the two Indians replied in stilted English. "Yesterday we tip wagon in water, but it too heavy. We tell man to take things off, but he call us stupid Indians." A sly smile pulled his full, dark lips tightly against his big teeth. "But he the stupid one. You ladies, no worry. We get your wagon across very good. If we don't, we ask no money."

"I guess that's fair enough," Lottie quipped derisively. Looking apprehensive, she swung onto the mule she was going to ride across. For this dangerous undertaking, Nancy had let Lottie talk her into borrowing one of Major's saddles. To her surprise, only Lucille Royal and Arthur Waite had made rude remarks about it. Everyone else seemed accustomed to her and Lottie's unconventional undertakings.

Giving one last look at the Indians preparing to shove off, they directed their mounts back to the milling herd of horses and mules and cattle that the men were preparing to swim across.

"I hope we're not making a mistake by not going with that wagon," Lottie said, glancing one more time over her shoulder and seeing the ferry moving slowly now into deeper water. "But I'll be damned if I'm going to give Arthur Waite any reason at all to see us behave like typical women and say we're not carrying our load."

"I don't believe there is any fear of that." Nancy chuckled as she gripped the mare's sides with both legs. Astride riding was considerably different from aside, but better in many ways. She was confident she could have taken the river on her sidesaddle, though. She'd been practically born on it and had jumped at her father's hunts on the estate since she'd been a young girl of ten. But riding astride had eased Lottie's mind, and perhaps it was wise to listen to a voice of experience in alien matters such as crossing swollen rivers.

"Can you swim?" Lottie asked suddenly, her brow furrowing as she looked out across the muddy water.

"Indeed. We had a small lake on our estate and we swam every day during the summer. It was one of my father's passions and he taught all of us children. I can still remember my mother's look of horror when I would peel out of my clothes and dive in wearing nothing but my personals. But I could outswim my brothers. I was like a fish."

Lottie smiled sardonically. "I imagine your mother is going to be able to throw away her smelling salts now that you're gone."

"I suspect she already has."

"Well, girl, I'm glad you can swim because I can't. But if I come unseated I can damn sure hang onto this mule's tail and let him carry me to the other side. Josh is the one I'm worried about. He can't swim either, but he's such a stubborn little cuss he's not going to miss out on any of the excitement."

For the first time, Nancy saw fear in Lottie's eyes. Not for herself, but for her boy. The child was her world. He meant everything to her. One night while they'd been talking in the tent, she'd told Nancy that Josh was the main reason she had come West. She wanted to help him get a start. She figured she'd get the land and then turn it over to him when he was a man.

"I'll keep an eye on him."

They brought their mounts alongside Hart's. Josh was with him, having become his shadow, but Hart didn't seem to mind. He had the patience of Job with the boy.

"We're going to help swim our mules," Lottie announced.

"It's not necessary, Lottie," Hart argued. "There are plenty of men here who can handle it. You go on with your wagon."

" 'fraid not. It's halfway across the river. No, sir, we won't be accused of shirking our duties."

Seeing everyone in position and all the livestock bunched, Chiles lifted a hand and motioned for the drovers to begin crowding the animals into the water. Some men planned to literally swim the river without the aid of a mount. There were several single men as well as Brenham Royal, who looked too frail to accomplish the task. The way his clothes hung so loose on his small frame, it was hard to tell if he had meat on his bones, let alone muscle.

Nancy might be able to swim, but she'd never pushed a reluctant herd of four-legged creatures across a swollen river. She watched the men and followed their lead, removing her hat and waving it, and yipping and hooting at the poor frightened creatures when the occasion called for it. Many of the riders' horses balked and refused to plunge into the deep water. Torey Porter was bucked off for his persistence and landed three feet out in the river. He came up swearing and threatening to shoot his horse that had promptly dove into the water without him and headed across with the others.

Nancy's mare, usually of an excitable nature, hesitated only briefly to sniff the water's edge and test her footing. Then, as if afraid she'd be left behind, she took a few cautious steps and plunged in up to her belly, striking out alongside the mules. Nancy saw Lottie on the other side of the herd. Her voice carried over the ruckus, coloring the sky a deeper shade of blue. Lottie knew all the profanities and she was very adept at using them. Nancy just smiled, glad she'd found such a true and honest friend.

The men whistled through their teeth, swore and waved their hats. The Indians who had offered to help were wonderfully strong swimmers and were doing an excellent job of getting the bawling and braying animals across. It amazed Nancy how the men in the water were able to keep the animals from plowing over the top of them. She glanced up once and saw their wagon being pulled in close to the opposite shore. She waved at Lottie from across the milling, lunging herd, then suddenly the bottom went out from under her horse.

She gasped, grabbing for the saddle horn, as the cold water flowed up over her saddle to her waist. The mare was swimming now, and it was all

Nancy could do to stay astride as the deep water buoyed her up out of the saddle and pushed her feet out of the stirrups. She forgot about the livestock and concentrated on hanging on, thankful for the big saddle horn on Major's Mexican saddle. She wasn't afraid of the water, but she was afraid of getting into the middle of the swimming livestock. And her vanity was enough that she wanted a successful crossing to save face in front of Arthur Waite and a few of the other men who had been watching her and Lottie closely the entire trip to see if they would fail.

It seemed an eternity before the ground came up under the mare's feet and Nancy was able to slip back firmly into the high-backed saddle. She pulled a deep breath of relief and focused once again on keeping the livestock together as they emerged from the river.

But a shout from behind made Nancy turn in the saddle. She saw several men pointing and hollering, but their words were lost to the raucous bray of a mule. Then she heard Lottie screaming.

"My God, he's drowning! Somebody help him!"

12

Nancy shot back around in the saddle, fully expecting to see Josh. Instead, it was Brenham Royal in the middle of the river, struggling to keep his head above water. The last of the horses and mules were all around him now, plowing over the top of him, pushing him down on their way to the opposite shore. He tried grabbing tails and manes but to no avail.

With no hesitation, Nancy turned her mare back into the river. A horn from the Martins' milk cow slipped between her lower leg and the saddle fender, nearly yanking her from the saddle before she managed to pull her leg up out of the stirrup.

She urged the mare alongside Brenham Royal, forcing the other animals to veer out of her way. If she left the saddle she would be in the same vulnerable position as Brenham was, but she also knew her mare's instincts were to find the shore and solid ground.

As the mare swam steadily closer to the flailing man, Nancy leaned down, holding out her arm. "Grab my hand, Mr. Royal! Come on, or we'll both go down! Do it. Now!"

Her hand closed around his, but his weight nearly dragged her from the saddle. She couldn't hold onto him and keep her seat, too. The mare was searching for solid ground and wanted to stay with the herd. She circled in the water and headed back the way she'd come despite Nancy's efforts to stop her. Nancy was forced to release Brenham or be pulled over the back of the saddle.

"Grab my stirrup!" Nancy pulled her foot free of it as she grabbed the reins with both hands again to control the mare. "I can't hold onto you. You've got to help yourself, Brenham! Get the stirrup."

Brenham sank again, but instinctively reached out and found the stirrup. His strength and breath were nearly gone. Seeing his grip loosening, Nancy gave the mare her head at last and let her swim for shore.

Several men had seen the situation and had dove their horses back into the water to lend assistance, but Brenham was visibly weakening. If she lost him, he could very well be swept downstream before the men could reach him. A few seconds later, his eyes rolled back in his head, his hand fell away from the stirrup, and he started to roll with the water under the mare's belly.

Seeing no alternative, Nancy slid out of the saddle and into the water. Circling Brenham around the chest with one arm, she tried to keep herself afloat with the other. Her skirts weighed her down and tangled around her legs. Suddenly she feared she had made a deadly mistake. She was a good swimmer, but not when encumbered by yards of wet cotton. She reached for the nearest thing, her horse, but all she caught was the mare's wet, black tail. Desperately she clung to it. Brenham's weight was too much. Knowing she couldn't maintain the tentative grip for much longer, she twisted her arm so the long, coarse hair would wind around her hand and wrist and help to hold her.

It seemed an eternity before the mare found solid footing. Almost simultaneously, the men were there, leaping into the water from their horses' backs. With Brenham's weight taken by the men, Nancy gripped Lady Rae's tail with both hands. The mare lunged up out of the water and scrambled onto the wet bank, dragging Nancy with her.

Onlookers rushed forward to lend further assistance. Frances Vines and Mrs. Martin draped Nancy between them and gently lowered her to a sitting position on the sandy shores of the Kansas while she caught her breath. A few minutes later, Hart was there, leaping down from his horse and dropping to his knees next to her.

"You damn near scared me into the next life, Nancy," he said through ragged breaths and with water dripping from his clothes. "That was a crazy stunt you pulled. You could have been killed."

Nancy heard the anger in his voice but saw the fear in his eyes, and something else, too. Something that warmed her to the soul and made her heart hum with joy. He had asked her to be his wife but had said nothing of love. Now, if she wasn't mistaken, she saw it as clearly as the midday sun.

He watched worriedly as she caught her breath. "I didn't think about it at the time," she finally managed between gasps. "He was in trouble and I was closer to him than anyone else. How is he?" She couldn't see him for the crowd that had gathered around him. Lucille was hysterical, screaming that he was dead, and Lottie was telling her to be quiet and get control of herself. His oldest daughter was trying to help him and to calm her mother. The youngest daughter was quietly crying.

"They're trying to revive him from the looks of things," Frances replied. "He went unconscious before you dragged him out of there. Took in too much water, I expect. God, you're a brave one, Nancy. I swear . . ." Tears welled up in Frances's eyes as emotion overcame her. She hugged Nancy's shoulders then turned away. "I'll take care of your horse."

The crowd around Brenham broke up, leaving him lying on the ground, weak and dazed but alive. Lucille pushed a few of the remaining people aside and fell dramatically to her knees next to him. She grabbed him by the shirt collar as if she'd like to shake him.

"You're nothing but a damned fool, Brenham Royal! What if you'd died and left me out here alone? Then what would I do? You with your stupid idea to come out here in the first place." This time she did shake him. "I didn't want to come and you knew it! It would be a damn dirty trick if you went and got yourself killed."

"Don't use profanities, Lucille," Brenham managed weakly. "Please."

"I'll swear if I damn well feel like swearing and you won't tell me not to! That's one thing you have no control over. What difference does it make anyway? You've brought me to a land of savages and heathen white people. I see as I have no choice but to become one of them, or perish."

Brenham finally got up on one elbow. Still breathing hard, he took hold of her shoulder, ignoring the death grip her hands had on his shirt front. "Help me to the wagon. I need some dry clothes."

"Is that all you can think about? Dry clothes? You don't care about me or how I feel! If you did, you wouldn't have dragged me out here against my will."

He was to his knees now, looking even thinner than usual with his wet clothes clinging to his bony frame. "We can talk about this later, Lucille. This is not the place."

He finally got his feet under him and swayed unsteadily as he started for the wagon. She was right on his heels, followed by their worried daughters. "All you care about is yourself and your own stupid dreams. Well, what about mine! You're a selfish man, Brenham Royal, and I don't know why I ever married you."

He stopped so suddenly she collided with his back. Staggering, he turned, and the fire in his eyes suggested he would like nothing better than to put his hands around her throat and shut her up once and for all.

"I don't know why I *asked* you to marry me, Lucille," he lashed out at her with a vehemence that shocked everyone. "I must have been blind, crazy, and just plain stupid. The only good thing that ever came out of our union was our daughters. Now, I'm going to say this once, Lucille, and only once. You can stay with me, or you can find your way back to Independence and make it on your own. I'm sure you can hire someone to escort you there. But I take the wagon and the girls. Here's your chance to do whatever it is you think me and the girls have been keeping you from doing. You always wanted to go to New Orleans. Well, there's nothing to hold you back. The door's open. You can leave anytime. But I'm going to California, and you can go to . . . to hell!"

He stalked off to their wagon. Lucille stared after him, apparently quite speechless for the first time in her life. The crowd decided the fight was over and dispersed to tend to their duties and the chore of getting the wagons underway. Chiles said they would try to make a few miles before setting up camp for the night.

Lottie sauntered over and joined Hart and Nancy. "I'll be damned. Old Royal has some piss and vinegar after all. Maybe now that stupid woman will open her eyes and see what a good man she's got. Although, God knows, he's wasted on her."

Chiles had promised that his mule train would overtake the slower oxen trains of the Oregonians. Shortly after crossing the Kansas River, his promise held true. Everyone's fears about the late start eased somewhat, and skeptics like Lucille Royal and Arthur Waite were temporarily silenced—until the rain started again.

The prairie stretched before them now, offering little shelter from the hostile whims of Mother Nature. If they were lucky, their backs were to the cold wind and driving rains. They lost precious time at swollen streams and had to build rafts, using ropes and poles to propel them to opposite shores.

The Red Vermillion, a dark and narrow river, twisted through thick stands of trees that hugged its banks and hung out over its murky waters. It marked the boundary between the lands of the Pawnees and the Pottawatomies. Beyond the Red, they crossed its tributary, Rock Creek, and entered the valley of the Black Vermillion, or Big Vermillion.

They had days when they were lucky to make five miles. Children were confined to wagons again, increasing the degree of whine and screech until Frances contended that someone should invent a lubricant that would silence children as effectively as tar silenced squeaking wagon wheels.

They tried in vain to dry out their muddy, soaked shoes and boots, and tried hard not to think of the comforts of the homes they had left behind. Again they dug trenches around tents, went sleepless in their wet beds, struggled with fires and were shown by Hart and the half-breed McIntosh how to build them in trenches for better protection and to get more heat out of them. Wood was at a premium. To keep from going far afield for it, they oftentimes used last year's dried grass.

Colonel Chiles patiently called it an unusually wet spring. Lottie called it Hell. Everyone agreed with Lottie.

They stayed on high ground as much as possible, not just to keep out of the soggy lowlands but to keep an eye out for Indians, particularly the hostile Pawnees. But the only Indians they came into contact with were a party of Kanza warriors, bloody and bandaged. They were returning home from a buffalo hunt and had been attacked by Pawnees. They warned the emigrants to be on guard against the "bad" Pawnees, particularly groups of young braves looking to take their first scalps. They would be riding alone without a chief or older warriors to temper their actions.

The California company was now some two hundred miles from the Missouri line. Life on the trail, living in cramped wagons and rickety tents had long since lost any romanticism it might have held in the beginning.

Delicacies and perishables were gone. They had seen no buffalo, but the hunters had brought down antelope, turkeys, and other small game. One evening they ate turtle soup, grateful for anything hot to drive away the chill. They mostly ate sowbelly and biscuits, the latter cooked in Dutch ovens, the former in a frying pan over the fire—if the rain wasn't pouring into it. For breakfast it was more sowbelly and maybe some flap-jacks. And coffee, of course. Always coffee.

Occasionally the sun shone, heating the wet ground until they found themselves traveling through a green and steamy, surrealistic world of mythological proportions. Grass grew almost visibly when the sun came out, and fields of wildflowers unfolded on the high, rolling prairie.

Despite its high waters, they crossed the dank and odorous Black Ver-million, as well as Mosquito Creek, without mishap. They made their way to the Big Blue and the crossing at the confluence of Alcove Spring Creek.

The rains had the Big Blue running swift and deep. Even Alcove Spring Creek was estimated at ten feet. The spring lay on the edge of a level prairie and was ringed with many large, old trees. Hackberries, elms, sycamores, and oaks skirted the banks of the river. Here, the clouds rolled away completely and the sun came out, hotter than necessary. They crossed the river with no incident, then set up camp on the other side, deciding to take a day, or possibly two, to dry out.

The Blue offered freshwater clams for their pots, and men and women alike went into the woods and collected wild berries. With full stomachs and contented minds, they sat around their fires enjoying the perfumed scent of wildflowers and the sharp, pungent odor of wood smoke.

There were a number of musicians in the company and they brought out their Jew's harps, banjos, and guitars. Hart joined in with his har-monica, and Chiles on his fiddle, to play a medley of tunes that took them well into the night. The lively notes of instruments and the hardy male voices in song drowned out the croaking of the frogs and the chirrup of the crickets. Weariness slipped away and everyone danced. Laughter, like wind slipping through wind chimes, drifted through the encamp-ment and filtered back into the trees.

Several times, Hart left the group to partner up with Nancy. Through Virginia reels and square dances, Nancy found herself twirled from man to man. The single men vied for dances with the women, too, regardless of the latter's age or marital status. Even the young girls were welcome in the dancing.

After two hours of steady dancing, Nancy found herself in Hart's arms for a waltz, but to her surprise, he waltzed her right away from the oth-ers and into the shadows behind the wagons. A few noticed and hollered for him to bring her back, but he just grinned from ear to ear and kept going.

Laughing, they collapsed shoulder to shoulder against a giant old sycamore to catch their breath.

"They're going to miss your harmonica," Nancy said, leaning her head back against the rough bark. "You're very good at it. How did you learn to play?"

"Oh, from my Grandpa. He taught me when I was just a boy and I wanted to be as good as him so I practiced all the time."

"What about your parents, Hart? How did they feel about you leaving Missouri and going off by yourself into the wilderness at the age of eighteen?"

"My people have always been pioneers. My ancestors go back to the Colonies and were among those who forged a way over the Appalachians. They settled in Kentucky, but generation after generation, son after son, brother after brother, they just kept moving westward right up to the edge of the frontier, wherever it happened to be at any given time. When my turn came, I followed the tradition. Not out of obligation or some duty to the tradition, but because it was in my blood."

"It's so different with women. You don't know how lucky you are to be free to do anything you want to do."

He dropped the harmonica into his pocket and turned to her, placing a hand on either side of her head against the big, old sycamore. "I know how lucky I am right now to be the man standing here with you."

As easily as playing a tune on his harmonica, he kissed her. She tilted her head back as his lips left hers to explore the sensitive curve of her neck. She slid her arms around his slender waist and drew his hips closer to her own.

Suddenly a yell rose up from the encampment and the music stopped. Hart grabbed Nancy's hand and they raced back to camp, expecting a Pawnee attack. Instead, they found Garnet collapsed near one of the fires with Ethan trying to gather her into his arms.

"What's happened?" Hart demanded, seeing Chiles race off toward the horses.

"She's going into labor," Miriam said, taking charge. "The Colonel is going for Dr. Whitman."

Hart released Nancy's hand and headed across the encampment after Chiles. "Thane, Torey, Charlie! Come on! We'd better go with him in case he runs into Pawnees!"

13

A twig cracked just yards away and Nancy stiffened, flattening herself against the tree where just an hour before she had stood with Hart. Expecting to see an Indian, or a wolf, she nearly collapsed with relief when Lottie stepped out of the brush along the river. Lottie was just as surprised to see her.

"God Almighty," the sassy brunette said, picking her way through the brush. "A body can't even find a bush to pee behind that ain't already occupied. Although from the pensiveness in your eyes, I'm inclined to think you aren't out here to tend to such mundane matters."

Nancy removed her hand from her thumping heart. "Just biding time until Garnet has her baby."

As if on cue, they heard another of the young woman's tortured screams coming from the encampment.

"It could be hours, girl," Lottie said in the silence following the heartwrenching sound. "First babies are always slow coming into the world. I was in labor twelve hours with Josh. 'Course, I didn't scream like Garnet." She glanced worriedly in the direction of the encampment, and Nancy sensed that Lottie predicted something wrong.

Nancy pulled her shawl closer around her shoulders. "I wish Hart and the others would come back. They've been gone an awfully long time."

"Don't worry about him. He can smell Indians, which, due to the sanitary habits of most of them, isn't hard to do."

"He asked me to marry him," Nancy said with a sigh, leaning her head back against the tree. "I didn't give him an answer."

Lottie didn't seem surprised. "You'll never find a better man."

Nancy looked into the darkness and spoke in a troubled voice. "I didn't come out here to marry. I came out here because I'd made up my mind I wasn't going to wait around for a man to give meaning to my life. I came seeking adventure and to pursue impossible dreams. And marriage—well, marriage just complicates everything."

"Do those things you were going to do anyway, but do them with him. A good marriage shouldn't complicate life. It should make it easier. It should set your heart free for true fulfillment. He must love you, or he wouldn't have asked you to marry him, but the biggest question is whether or not you love him."

Nancy settled to the ground, leaning back against the tree. She drew her knees up and circled them with her arms. "I look forward to being with him. I get a nervous and wild feeling inside when he comes around, and I want him to hold me and kiss me. I dream about him. I—"

Lottie chuckled. "That certainly sounds like love. So what's so complicated about it?"

Nancy sighed again, clearly confused by it all. "Because after all these years of being pressured to get married, I had finally put the idea of love and marriage out of my mind and decided it was never going to happen to me. I set my mind on another course. Hart says that a person generally finds what they want when they're not looking for it. I guess maybe he's right, because this has hit me broadside." She plucked up a stem of grass from between her boots and twirled it anxiously between her thumb and forefinger. "The land and the horse ranch are my dream, and I'd love to have Hart by my side, sharing it with me."

"But?"

"But I'm afraid he'll take it over, and I'll be left on the sidelines watching him do all the things I want to do while I tend to housework and babies."

"I don't believe Hart would be the sort to steal your thunder. Real love won't tie you down, girl. It'll set you free."

"Was it that way with Major?"

"Major?" An unladylike snort of disgust came from Lottie's nose. "Hell, no. Marriage to Major wasn't nothing but a trap, and believe me there were times when I came close to gnawing off my own leg to get out of it. I loved the bastard. I don't know why, but I did. Still, I knew it was wasted love. But then Josh came along, and I stuck it out because Major was his daddy, and I didn't think I should take him away from his daddy. Turned out that Major didn't give a shit about that boy."

"Then how do you know about love setting you free?"

"Well, I guess I don't. At least, not firsthand. But I saw it with my parents before my father disappeared.

"If Hart is wild about you, Nancy—and I think he is—you'd be a fool to walk away from something that will more than likely never come together again with that same brand of magic."

"What if I end up like Miriam or Lucille?"

"Miriam is abused because she lets Arthur control her. Lucille is contemptible because she *tries* to control Brenham. If you and Hart give each other respect and room to breathe, you'll be okay. And love is essential. Arthur and Lucille don't love their spouses."

A rustle in the brush drew their attention. They leaped to their feet, reaching for their weapons, and found themselves facing the gleaming topaz eyes of a timber wolf not twenty yards away.

"Shit," Lottie breathed, her fist clenching and unclenching on the hunting knife the Kanza Indian had given her. Simultaneously, Nancy waited with the Allen pepperbox in her palm. Then Garnet's scream shattered the stillness, and the wolf darted back into the darkness.

"Let's get the hell out of here," Lottie said.

Their arrival back at camp coincided with the arrival of Dr. Whitman, Hart, and the others. J.B. escorted Whitman to the Stillman wagon then everyone settled down to wait and to watch Ethan pace nervously back and forth, around and around the wagon and the fires. Miriam, because of her experience in such matters, had been requested by Dr. Whitman to assist. Some tried to sleep, but Garnet's tortured screams commingled with the ululant cries of the wolves with chilling and unsettling results.

The pack had started howling in earnest right after Nancy and Lottie's confrontation with the wolf. It sounded as if hundreds of them lay in wait just behind the perimeters of the camp, beyond the light cast by the fires. A glance into the dark woods, at the glowing yellow coals of their eyes, attested to their nearness as they watched and waited, and occasionally moved boldly closer.

Women and children, wide-eyed and frightened, huddled in their shelters and listened to the hideous cries and to their mens' assurances that the guards would keep the hungry packs away. The horses and mules shifted restlessly on their picket lines, stamping and pawing the ground. Their nervous movements concealed any sound of a possible approach from marauding Indians, and the guards moved about the camp alert against the dual threat.

Once, wearing a worried expression, Miriam left the wagon to get more of the water that Nancy and Lottie were keeping hot over the campfire. Pausing near the fire, Miriam's eyes darted to the heavy collar of trees lining the Blue, and at the wolves' eyes staring back from the darkness. "Damn them. It's like they smell her blood," she said angrily. "Like they're just waiting . . ."

Nancy shifted uneasily. "Waiting for what, Miriam?"

Miriam's eyes were as sober as anyone had ever seen them. "The baby's too early, Nancy. It's coming breech."

By morning, Nancy understood the full meaning behind that one word. Dr. Whitman emerged from the Stillman wagon and solemnly announced that the baby, a boy, had been born dead.

They buried the Stillman baby and moved on.

For ten days they traveled through the serene valley of the Little Blue. The plain stretched level for miles, and ahead and behind swayed the canvas tops of the wagons belonging to both the Oregon and California companies. The gentle Little Blue wound through sunny, rolling hills fringed with groves of oak, cottonwood, and long-leafed willows. Its waters carried catfish, suckers, and soft-shelled turtle, all of which tasted, unfortunately, like mud. In the valley, they had dry weather for the most part. Chiles's mule train made excellent time and began overtaking the slower, oxen-drawn trains of the Oregonians.

Nancy rode next to Hart when he wasn't out ahead of the train scouting for possible Indian trouble or hunting for game. Here there were signs of Indian summer camps. During this time of the year, they didn't carry the cumbersome skins for tents, but left tipis and shelters set up at various camping sites. There could be as many as one hundred tipis at each encampment.

At night, hundreds of campfires flickered in the darkness all up and down the river. At Walnut Creek, thousands of beetles, drawn to the light of the fires and lanterns, had kept all-night vigils of batting themselves on the tents and canvas roofs, making sleep nearly impossible for many of the emigrants.

Past that now, the night offered serene stillness, and Nancy inhaled it into the very center of her soul. One of her most favorite times was just before bedtime, after the nightly music had ended, the children were asleep, and the adults were finally settling down. She would take a few minutes to leave the tent, lean against the wagon wheel, and stare up at the stars. They filled a firmament bigger and broader than the one back home. Night after night she would return to the sight, but it was one she never tired of.

By day, she rode her mare through the tall grass that was the home of wildflowers of every kind: lupine, scarlet globe mallow, aloe, pale blue digitalis, larkspur.

They saw large herds of elk and antelope. Previous buffalo passings were evident in the chips littering the prairie, but they saw nothing of the beasts themselves. Because of the scarcity of wood now, the chips soon became the only fuel for the campfires without going far afield. The ladies lifted their noses in distaste at having to collect them, but all the women in the California company set about good-naturedly gathering them, making their fair share of ribald jokes when the men weren't around. All except Lucille, that is, who refused. Her strident voice carried over the encampment as she told Brenham what she thought of it.

"If you want something to eat, you can collect those disgusting 'chips' yourself and you can build the fire, too. I draw the line at this, I truly do. You and your stupid adventure have already pushed me to the limit of my sanity. I am a lady, Brenham, and you will not turn me into a workhorse."

Nobody gave Lucille sympathy except for Arthur Waite, which surprised everyone, considering the way he treated Miriam. He was seen on many occasions talking with her, calming her down, even helping her. His actions didn't go unnoticed by Miriam. She said nothing to Arthur or to anyone else, but the other women knew it was because she feared the back of his hand across her face again.

To the ladies' surprise the fires made of buffalo chips burned clean and put out good heat. Using their Dutch ovens and burying them in the hot coals, or even cooking in pans directly over the fire, meals came together quickly. On Sundays when they rested from traveling they took the opportunity to bake bread, pies, wash clothes and bathe in the rivers or creeks. The latter was usually done partially clothed for modesty's sake. On these days they had the time to roast the wild game brought back to camp and add wild onions or greens, and to cook up rice and beans that took too long to cook while on the trail.

As for Garnet, Dr. Whitman said her body was recuperating well from the childbirth. He had gone on ahead with the Oregonians, but the women could see that Garnet wasn't recuperating emotionally.

"She told me how much she wanted the baby," Elizabeth Yount said when the women had all gathered around the fire the night of Whitman's departure. "Whatever will she do now?"

Miriam's lips thinned to a bitter line. She pulled her shawl tighter around her shoulders and looked into the darkness beyond the wagons, at the wolves' eyes staring back. Always staring back. The light from the fires limned the hard set to her jaw and her own protruding stomach. "Why, she'll have another one. Those are the cold, hard facts of life, Elizabeth."

It was expected that Garnet wouldn't be back to her duties for awhile so the ladies took turns inviting Ethan to eat with them.

On the night it was Nancy and Lottie's turn to cook for the Stillmans, Lottie called Ethan over to the campfire while Nancy prepared a plate for Garnet.

"Don't reckon you can get her to eat anything," he said, putting a piece of venison stew in his mouth. "She refuses anything I give her. She's wastin' away right before my eyes. She refuses to look at me most times. When she does, it's with blank eyes. Sometimes I wonder if something didn't happen to her mind. She won't even let me touch her, comfort her. Blames me for the child's death. Says it wouldn't have come early if I would have waited until next year like she wanted to." He chewed silently then added, "I guess she was right. I keep telling her she'll have another baby, but that doesn't seem to make her any difference."

Nancy found it difficult to have much sympathy for Ethan, not after she'd seen him the night of the Bread Dance sneaking into the trees with that pretty Indian girl. He was thirty-six years old, married to a child, and he had no sensitivity whatsoever. He hadn't even shed a tear when the baby had been buried. The other men, Hart included, who had dug the grave and buried the child, had seemed more grievous than Stillman.

"Even cows get upset when they lose their calves," Lottie said bluntly, exasperated with his line of thinking. But he only stared at her blankly, not understanding at all how a woman could get attached to an unborn child and feel the loss just the same as if she'd had it in her arms for months or years.

Hart, who ate with them nearly every night, touched Nancy's hand as she turned to go to Garnet's wagon with the food. "Would you like me to go with you?"

In his eyes was all the understanding lacking in Stillman's. He, J.B., Torey and Thane had dug the grave for the baby back on the banks of the Big Blue. They had dug it deep to keep the wolves from disinterring the body, then they had lowered the tiny, blanket-wrapped body down into the cold, damp earth and gently put the rain-soaked earth back over it. Later, Nancy had found Hart alone in the darkness of the woods, sitting on a fallen log.

"What is it, Hart?" she had asked, running her hand comfortingly across his back. He had turned into her arms and held her for the longest time. Finally he had said, "Burying that baby was the hardest thing I ever did, Nancy. I don't ever want to do that again."

That moment had brought them closer, allowed Nancy to see into the heart of him and to know that men, like women, grieved and cried, even if the latter was not always done with a show of tears.

"I wouldn't mind some company," she said now.

Hart was to his feet in an instant, carrying the plate for her. When they reached the Stillman wagon, Nancy touched Hart's arm. "Wait just a minute for me. I'd like to pick a few flowers for Garnet."

She stepped over the wagon tongue into an undisturbed patch of grass and in just minutes had filled her fist with a colorful array of larkspur, scarlet mallow, and pale blue digitalis.

At Nancy's announcement that she had a plate of food for Garnet, the canvas at the back of the wagon was pulled back. Hart handed the plate of food up to her, which she took with a thank you, but it was Nancy's flowers that seemed to mean more.

"Could you use some company, Garnet?" Nancy asked. "It's been a while since we visited."

Garnet glanced suspiciously at Hart who immediately stepped away from the wagon, brushing his hand over Nancy's in a gesture of departure. "I'll talk to you later." He touched the brim of his hat toward Garnet, "I hope you're feeling better, Mrs. Stillman."

When he was gone, Garnet pulled the canvas aside but said nothing. Nancy hauled herself up into the wagon and settled herself on the edge of the narrow bed. Garnet sat next to her and made an attempt to eat a few bites although it was clear that she was not interested in food. With eyes as empty as the prairie sky, she stared at the plate, at the canvas walls of the wagon, at Nancy.

"Ethan says you haven't had much of an appetite," Nancy said, trying to sound cheerful.

As if on cue, Garnet set the plate aside where it balanced precariously on the edge of the bed. "The wolves are back there eating my baby. I wake up nights seeing them . . . tearing at my baby . . ."

"No, Garnet. Don't fret about that. The men dug the grave deep enough that it wouldn't be disturbed."

"I wish I'd died with my baby. My baby's back there, Nancy. Alone in the horrible wilderness. I'll never see him again. Never put flowers on his grave." She stared at the flowers in her hand. "I couldn't even get out of bed to put flowers on his grave. He was so tiny and now he's alone in that . . . that black, cold hole. I should have died with him. They could have buried him in my arms so he wouldn't be so alone."

Nancy put her arm around the young girl. "The other women and I put flowers on the grave for you, Garnet. Flowers of every kind and color."

"Why does God do this, Nancy? Why?"

Nancy pulled Garnet into her arms and tried to soothe her. She ran a hand over her golden hair, noticing that it was matted and probably hadn't been washed or combed since the baby had died.

"I don't want to go on, Nancy." Her voice was dull with a final note to it. "There is simply no reason."

"There's Ethan. You must go on for Ethan. He's very worried about you."

"I don't give a damn about Ethan. He doesn't love me and I don't love him. He just married me because he was getting on in years and decided he needed a wife. I just married him because I wanted to get away from home, from the poverty I grew up in. He was older and not bad looking, and I was stupid enough to think marriage would solve my problems. All I did was change one set of heartaches for another. And I know Ethan has had other women since we've been married."

"How do you know that?" Nancy asked cautiously.

"I know because I can smell them on him," she said bluntly.

Nancy held onto the secret about Ethan Stillman and Arthur Waite, and what they'd been doing the night of the Bread Dance, wondering again if keeping it to herself was the right thing to do.

"What about your dreams, Garnet? Your dreams of land and a fine house in California?"

"I've always been searching for something, Nancy. Something I've never found yet. And I used to think I wanted to find it before I died, but now I don't care. There just isn't any sense in it anymore."

"It's just because of the baby, Garnet. You'll start feeling better again. Mourning is normal, but it won't last forever. And one day you'll want to have another baby."

"He blames me. Did you know that? He blames me for the baby dying. He said I shouldn't have been dancing. But it was only a waltz, Nancy. He says I never wanted the baby because I don't love him, and that I did that intentionally so I would lose it. But if anybody is to blame it's him for bringing me out here so close to my time. I begged him to wait until next year."

"These things happen, Garnet, and nobody is to blame."

"He isn't ever going to touch me again, Nancy. Never."

Nancy said no more, just soothed her like she would a small child and wondered all the while if Garnet would ever shed tears for the baby. Keeping her grief inside the way she was could never help her come to terms with the loss.

She left the tent awhile later and sauntered back to the fire. Hart was the only one still there and had apparently been waiting for her. He rose to his feet and opened his arms to her. She welcomed his embrace, allowing him to hold and comfort her the way she had Garnet.

She pressed her cheek to the steady beat of his heart, wondering what she had ever done before she had known him, before she had felt his solid strength, his fiery kiss. He seemed to know her soul, her mind, practically better than she did herself. Garnet and Miriam might have told her she was lucky to be alone and single, but with each passing day she did not consider herself either. She was a part of Hart Daniels, in spirit, and she knew that if they separated now she would be like a ship set adrift on the ocean with no captain and no crew, left to wander aimlessly.

He kissed her forehead. "Is she going to be all right?"

"She's frighteningly morose, Hart, and she refuses to allow Ethan to comfort her." She went on to repeat what Garnet had told her. "I know she probably intended for that to be in confidence, Hart, but I can't shoulder such a burden alone."

He drew her down next to the fire with him and they sat on the fallen log, hand in hand, staring at the leaping flames that offered warmth against the chill that was threatening to settle into Nancy's soul. "There is nothing you can do, Nancy, but continue to give her your friendship."

She rested her head on his shoulder and laced her fingers through his. "I don't know what I would do if I lost you, Hart."

Surprised at the comment, he pulled back just a little and looked at her with twinkling eyes. "Did I hear what I just thought I heard?"

She merely nestled closer against his chest and lifted her eyes to the stars. "Have you ever seen such a beautiful sight?"

"No, I don't believe I have," he whispered. But he was looking at her, not at the stars.

14

July
The Platte River

At thirty-two-mile creek, the emigrants left the Kansas River watershed and set out across a waterless twenty-five mile stretch to the Platte River. Nancy thought it was a wild and lonely expanse of sky, grass, and wildflowers. By day, she wrote poetry in her head. By night, she transferred it to paper while watching the wolves that inched close to camp.

Muddy, and riddled with sandbars, the Platte River stretched wide but not overly deep. Very little timber lined the river's shores except on its islands, and then in the form of cottonwoods. Winged by bluffs, the river bottoms sprawled broad and flat, but the grasses that might have been luxuriant were eaten down to the dirt by the huge herds of buffalo whose trails crisscrossed the region and came down off the bluffs to the river's edge from all directions.

There were thousands of the creatures, maybe millions. Nancy believed they must number more than the stars in the sky. Their masses blackened the land, but they were easy pickings for the hunters and every night their prime humps cooked in the emigrants' kettles.

Despite the abundance of meat and the ease of the trail along the river's southern shore, Nancy never completely relaxed. She found it difficult to even join in with the dancing that went on practically every night.

One evening while Lottie and Josh were tacking buffalo hide to the mules' feet to protect them from the prickly pear that worked its way into their hooves, Lottie finally asked Nancy what was bothering her. "You're as nervous as a long-tailed cat in a roomful of rockers."

Nancy absently stirred a buffalo stew over the campfire while glancing uneasily up the river to where hundreds of other campfires glowed in the darkness. "Listen to them, Lottie. You can't see them but you can hear them. That deep-throated bellowing that comes back across the prairie like a husky whisper. It's unsettling."

"Well, at least the damned wolves are leaving us alone."

That much was true. Since they'd reached the Platte, the wolves could still be seen at practically any time of the day and night, but they had diverted their attention away from the emigrant trains and focused on taking their meals from the herds' young and weak.

In the days to follow, Nancy continued to watch the horizons for that unseen danger she could only sense. In contrast, Josh was never more relaxed riding next to Hart. The boy seemed to settle naturally into the wild nature of the land and proclaimed more than once, "I wouldn't mind being an Indian. Riding around on horseback and chasing buffalo all day would be a danged lot of fun!"

This was the prairie. A land of illimitable distances. A land that affected them all in a different way. It made some of them eager to get to the other side, to the coolness of the mountains and trees. For them it was just a wasteland that needed crossing. For others, it placed doubts on what lay ahead and cast shadows on dreams. Some even yearned to turn back, suddenly realizing just how far into the wilderness they had come, and just how much security they had left behind. And then there was Lucille Royal who feared the vastness even more than she feared the Indians and stayed hidden inside her wagon, safe behind her canvas walls.

But one day when the sun had reached the broiling point, so did Brenham. He pulled the wagon to a halt and tore open the canvas flap. "I'm tired of that stinking chamber pot of yours, Lucille! Just get out of the wagon and walk along with the other women. The wagon won't save you from Indians anyway if they decide to attack."

To which she replied, "I will divert my eyes from this hell you have brought me to, Brenham, in much the same manner I divert my eyes from your pathetic excuse of a body. Both are equally distasteful to a lady's sensibilities. As for the stench of my chamber pot—you should have thought of that before you dragged me out here to this treeless wasteland against my will."

The Chiles company moved swiftly during this time, overtaking the slower oxen-driven trains. Eighteen mule-driven wagons from the Oregon company joined up with Chiles, hoping to make better time. But the journey along the Platte was monotonous, nothing changed from day to day, least of all the suffocating dust filtering back along the trail from the hundreds of wagons in front of them, and from the herds of buffalo constantly stringing back and forth to the river. No one wanted the sort of rains they'd had through the first part of the journey to the Little Blue, but none argued that some clouds and a light shower wouldn't be a welcome respite from the intense heat that shimmered across the land.

It was Lottie who first hiked up her skirt, removed her stockings and waded into the shallow edge of the Platte. The other women watched in envy, imagining the deliciously cool water swirling around their legs and sweltering feet.

"Come on!" Lottie hollered. "Don't be priggish! This ain't no time for modesty!"

The Royal sisters, Elise and Beth, eagerly abandoned propriety and tossed aside shoes and stockings to plunge in with her.

"You girls get out of that water right now!" screamed Lucille. "I swear, Lottie England, you're going to burn in hell!"

"I'd rather burn in hell than play a harp in heaven with you."

Soon the men had come over to stand on the banks and watch the action, grinning and egging the women on while secretly hoping to see some bare female ankles and knees.

"This water party ain't reserved for women," Lottie goaded.

That was the only invitation needed. Billy Baldridge shed everything made of leather and dove in with a bucket in hand. Immediately he began scooping up water and throwing it on everyone on the bank. More buckets materialized and a water war was on. Everyone except Lucille and her crony Arthur Waite were in the water, dumping and scooping, splashing and shrieking. Even Harry the dog came in for a swim.

The prairie was no friend to womankind, and yet it had a special way of bonding them, of cementing friendships that would last beyond the trail and on into the remainder of their lives in the new country. The women turned to each other more often now because their menfolk had precious little time away from their own duties of taking care of animals and equipment. Except for Lucille, the ladies suffered through the stark terrain and its lack of foliage no taller than a grass blade. During those moments when they had to tend to bodily functions, they were forced to offer privacy to each other in the circle of their skirts.

Besides Lucille, Garnet was missing from the circle. She had barely left her wagon except to eat and relieve herself. She only ate because Ethan fixed the meals and set the plate in her hand.

"What do you make of her?" Lottie asked one night as she and Nancy were settling down for bed. "I can understand how she would feel losing the baby, but it seems there's something more there. Her eyes are so vacant. No emotion whatsoever. Not even grief."

Nancy contemplated the problem while she brushed her hair, having no wisdom on the subject to impart.

"She won't even respond to Ethan," Lottie continued. "Frances said today that she was beginning to wonder if Garnet isn't settling into quiet insanity."

Nancy told Lottie about what Garnet had said to her after the baby had died, and about the wolves tearing its body from the earth.

"Well, for her sake, I hope she gets a grip on it pretty soon," Lottie replied, "or she'll be sliding off right into the deep end and there won't be a damned thing any of us can do."

The conversation lulled. Lottie groped around in her bags and pulled out her bottle of laudanum. Outside, a low rumble and a brief flash of lightning warned of an approaching storm.

"Didn't you just get over your menses a couple of weeks ago?" Nancy asked worriedly, hoping not to sound too nosey.

Lottie took her swallow and recorked the bottle. "Yes, but the damn thing came back early. Oh, don't worry. The doctor over in St. Louis said it was natural for women to be irregular when they started going into menopause. Maybe I'll be rid of it entirely in a few years."

Yes, if you don't bleed to death in the meantime.

The tent was lit by another shudder of sheet lightning, followed a few seconds later by an ominous roll of thunder.

"That storm doesn't sound like it's going to miss us," Lottie said with a disapproving frown.

"I don't know what's worse. The rain or the dust those buffalo are continually kicking up."

Within a few minutes, the storm raced down on them with a

vengeance, building in intensity on a wind that threatened to pick up their tent and all the poles it was lashed down to. Hot, white blades of lightning plunged to the ground in short, quick, deadly strokes. Simultaneously the thunder boomed, sounding like cannon artillery and shaking the heavens and earth.

Outside, the frightened horses squealed with fear while the mules brayed pathetically. Both stamped and pawed at their tether lines and tried to pull themselves free of their restraints.

Then, as if the sky had opened, the rain came.

"Christ Almighty," Lottie said, scrambling for the tent opening. "I've got to get Josh."

"He'll be fine with Hart," Nancy tried to reassure her. "You shouldn't go out there."

"I know you take a lot of stock in that man, Nancy, but he ain't so talented as to turn lightning. It can strike me down just as easily in this tent as out there. Call it a mother's need to protect her young, but I want Josh with me."

Lottie started out of the tent when Nancy caught her arm. "Wait. Listen."

Lottie saw the concentrated look on Nancy's face. "What is it, girl?"

"Something. I don't know." She cocked her head, listening. "It's like the ground is trembling, rumbling."

"Jesus!" Lottie nearly exploded. "Come on! We've got to get the men up. This storm has put those buffalo on a stampede. If they're headin' this way they'll trample this camp into the dust!"

They darted across the campground. Lightning crackled all around them, splitting the black sky into ragged pieces. But before they could reach Hart's tent, his tent flap flew up and he bolted outside, hollering for Chiles and Baldridge to get their asses out of bed.

He saw Nancy and Lottie and ran to meet them. "Get Josh and get in your wagon! It's the safest place. Tell the others to do the same. I'll take a dozen men and we'll try to keep that herd from coming this way. They might not see the camp in the dark. The men we leave here had better get those fires built up high, and light every lantern in the company." His eyes met Nancy's for a brief moment. In his, she saw fear. She had begun to believe that Hart Daniels feared nothing, but he feared this, and because he did, her own heart leaped higher in her throat. "Do as I say, Nancy. Don't try anything heroic this time. Please."

"And what of you?"

"Don't worry about me."

Then he was gone. They watched as in the next few minutes the entire camp poured out of bed. Fires were stoked high and lanterns placed around the encampment in hopes the head runners of the stampede would see them and veer away. Hart and a dozen men threw saddles on their horses and headed out hell-bent to the west. Nancy wondered how they could find their way across a black prairie lit only by the purple-white flashes of lightning.

Another bolt shot to earth and hit a tree not far away on the river, splitting it wide open with a crack as loud as a rifle shot. Fear pounded through Nancy's veins as she and Lottie and Josh climbed into the wagon. She didn't like being in the wagon, unable to see or do anything. She hated this helplessness relegated to women, and decided she would rather be out in the dark helping in some way, seeing her death come to her instead of cowering beneath a canvas cover, waiting. She didn't see how the wagon would be much of a deterrent anyway to a rampaging mass of thousands of frightened buffalo running blindly through the night and being pushed by the sheer mass and force they created of themselves.

She glanced at Lottie who held Josh in her arms while the boy squirmed on her lap and kept saying, "I want to go help the men."

"Don't be a fool, son," Lottie said, mincing no words with him as she seldom did. "Those men will be lucky to get back here with their lives."

The three huddled together and listened to the rumbling in the ground growing louder, closer than the thunder in the sky. The ground shook now like an unending earthquake. The canvas over their heads shook. And Nancy's mind shouted one word over and over and over. *Hart. Hart. Hart.*

"He'll be all right," Lottie said quietly as if she had heard Nancy's silent fears. "There ain't nobody can ride better than Hart Daniels." She reached over and gripped Nancy's hand. "Don't worry, girl. He'll come back to you."

Through brief flashes of lightning, the men saw the buffalo pouring down over the bluffs like thick blackstrap molasses over a stack of buckwheat pancakes.

"They're headed straight for the goddamned wagons!" Chiles yelled, galloping alongside Hart.

"We've got to get in next to them and veer them west!" Hart shouted. "Head them to the river and then get the hell out of their way!"

The word was passed as the men shouted it to each other, never slowing their treacherous pace over the Platte River plain. With hearts in their throats, the men headed directly for the herd. Only the jagged strokes of lightning lit the darkness as they ran as blindly into the oncoming stampede as the stampede ran toward them. Each and every one of them prayed that their horses wouldn't stumble.

Some of the men rode to the left to come up on the side of the buffalo, hoping to bend them away from the wagons and to the river. To push them down the river plain in either direction would only jeopardize the other emigrant encampments. Riders coming too close to the rampaging herd for comfort, swung their horses around and moved in to lead the stampede, hoping the thundering mass would see them and follow. They waved arms and shouted, but their voices were lost to the thunder on the plains and the thunder in the sky.

Hart raced at the head of the herd. Up ahead he saw the black line of the Platte. A quarter of a mile more and they'd be there. Its sandy bottom could pull a horse and man down, so they had to steer away from it at the last possible minute. Too soon, and the buffalo might not follow them. Too late, and the massive herd would come down over the top of them in the water.

Hart shot a glance over his shoulder and saw the mass not far behind, following him and six other riders. To the right, only a half mile away, were the fires of the encampment. The men were supposed to be firing their guns to help steer the buffalo away, but he couldn't hear anything over the stampeding hooves behind him.

He leaned out farther over his horse's neck. The river loomed closer. Then suddenly the bottom fell out from under him.

The rumble in the ground ended abruptly. The throng of buffalo disappeared into the river and came out on the opposite side, successfully turned away. Except for the lingering rumble in the sky, an eerie silence settled down over the encampment.

Shortly the men returned from their dangerous run, but Nancy's hopes plummeted when she did not see the familiar figure of the man she loved astride his big gelding. She looked beyond the loose line of men, straining her eyes through the darkness for a glimpse of Hart. Panic began to swell inside her.

"There's somebody coming now," Lottie said next to her.

Nancy's heart fluttered with hope. Another horse was loping toward camp. Relieved, she took a step forward just as a bolt of lightning sent a flash of blue-white light over the prairie and made her stop in her tracks. She stared in disbelief, and in escalating terror, as the horse came closer.

It was Hart's buckskin. But it had returned with an empty saddle.

15

Nancy had not left Amherst to fall in love. And yet she had. Quickly, simply, and irrevocably. Hart Daniels had stolen into her life and into her heart to make her reassess her goals and what she had thought would be her purpose in life.

She tried to swallow back the fear circling her throat, threatening to strangle her. Surely God could not be so cruel as to bring her love at long last only to snatch it from her so prematurely?

Chiles reined his mule to a stop in front of the group and dismounted. He avoided Nancy's questioning eyes, but she didn't miss the grim shadow darkening his own.

"Where's Hart?" she heard herself say as if in a dream.

The colonel released a heavy sigh and finally looked at her with sorrow in his eyes. "We didn't see him, Nancy. Stillman is missing, too. We came back to get some lanterns."

"I'm going with you. He can't be too far away."

"I don't think that would be a good idea, Nancy."

She followed his solemn gaze and saw Thane and Torey tying tarpaulins and short-handled shovels to their saddles. Something lurched inside her and turned over with a sickening fear.

"You don't expect to find them alive, do you?"

J.B. looked at the ground, then out across the prairie. Nancy had never seen the optimistic leader so void of hope. "No," he replied. "I really don't. And what we find will more than likely be something you won't want to see."

"He could still be alive," she insisted stubbornly. "Maybe he just fell off his horse and . . ."

Chiles's eyes were so full of sympathy she wanted to take her fists and pound him on the chest, scream at him, and tell him it wasn't true. Hart wasn't dead. Instead, she turned stiffly away, feeling the eyes of everyone on her, following her with pity.

The search party left camp leading no spare horses, another indication that they didn't expect to find either man alive. Denial, tainted with fear, nearly suffocated her. Lottie tried to get her to come to the campfire and have a cup of coffee or tea while they waited, but Nancy was too nervous and restless to sit still. Frances, Elizabeth, and Miriam came over to offer support and encouragement, but their eyes said they had already resigned themselves to the worst. If he'd gone down in front of that raging mass, there would be nothing left of him.

Nancy pushed her loose hair back off her shoulders. She needed to keep busy. She couldn't sit and wait, and she couldn't bare the knowing look in everyone's eyes. "I haven't seen Garnet," she said. "Somebody needs to tell her about Ethan. I'll do it."

No one tried to stop her.

At Garnet's wagon, Nancy told the young woman what had happened, but Garnet merely stared blankly at Nancy then rolled back onto her bed, giving Nancy a cold shoulder.

Dismayed by the girl's indifferent attitude, Nancy rejoined Lottie.

"I don't understand her," Nancy said. "I know she doesn't love him, but you'd think she would feel something. *Any*thing. It's as if she's separated herself from the world so that nothing can ever hurt her again."

"Hart ain't dead! He ain't!" Josh, who had been listening, shot to his feet and tossed the stick he'd been whittling into the fire. Then he ran off and disappeared out behind the wagons, more than likely to cry without anybody seeing him.

"That boys looks up to Hart like a big brother, or a father," Lottie said, watching him go. "He loves him about as much as you do, Nancy. I'm sure glad Hart had the good sense to walk away from that woman he had back in St. Louis."

Nancy stiffened. "Hart didn't mention another woman."

Lottie chuckled. "Of course he wouldn't talk to you about her. He met her about five years ago. He used to go see her when he'd come back to Independence from his various adventures. He went this time, too, thinking about asking her to go to California with him. But he came back alone, saying he wondered why he had ever been interested in her.

"But I guess he figured it out, because a few days ago he said that God must have been protecting him from making the biggest mistake of his life. He couldn't see around the bend and see you coming, he said, but God could. And God knew you were the woman he was truly destined to love and share the rest of his life with."

"Then he can't be dead, can he?"

Lottie squeezed her hand. "No, girl, not if God has anything to do with it."

Nancy kept her eyes pinned on the lanterns bobbing in the distant darkness, as if their movements alone might signal the news she desperately needed to hear. For the first night since they had come upon the great buffalo herds, the night sounds were clear without the beasts' throaty murmurings in the background to muffle them. It was as if their wild run had left them too exhausted to grumble. She wondered now if the unease she had sensed upon arriving at the Platte had been some sort of premonition to this horrible moment.

Finally she closed her eyes and prayed that it was not so. She prayed for what seemed hours and hours.

Then suddenly Josh's strident yell jerked her to her feet.

"There he is! I told you all he wasn't dead! Ain't nothing can kill Hart. Nothing!" He tore from the encampment, jumping over wagon tongues and racing into the darkness beyond. The storm was completely gone now and the prairie calm. The stars in the half-sky cast enough light to illuminate the lone figure limping toward camp.

Lottie and Nancy had come to their feet, along with everyone else in camp.

"It's him," Nancy said, nearly collapsing beneath the heady wave of relief that rushed over her.

She released the intense grip she'd had on Lottie's forearm and ran after Josh, lifting her skirts to her knees. The men who had stayed behind to protect the encampment were not far behind her. She stopped short of Hart in a moment of hesitation to assure herself that he was all right, and that she wasn't hallucinating. Then she threw herself into his arms and buried herself in his wonderful embrace. Tears of relief poured down her cheeks. And she knew in that moment, without the shadow of a doubt, that she would marry him if ever he asked again.

Colonel Chiles and the search party found Ethan Stillman's body, or what was left of it. Garnet accepted the news with a strange, unemotional calm. She returned to her wagon, not even asking where they had buried him, only saying that it wasn't necessary for them to gather at the grave for prayer.

Nancy stayed with Hart until morning, tending to a bad cut he'd received on his leg and another on his head, which had rendered him unconscious for over an hour. Apparently when his horse had hit a low spot and gone down, the efforts of the other riders to veer the buffalo to the left had been successful and had been all that had saved his life. The stampeding herd had missed him by only a hundred feet. But a rock had gashed his leg and something else, maybe the buckskin's hoof, had sliced into his head.

Because no one had gotten any sleep, the group stayed in camp and didn't pull out until the following morning. Garnet Stillman didn't object when young Torey Porter offered to hitch up her team and drive it. For the first time since her baby's death, she came out of the wagon and sat up on the wagon seat, with Torey. If Nancy wasn't mistaken, a new light shone in the girl's eyes. It was as if she was suddenly seeing the world through a beautifully colored prism.

The North Platte cut its winding passage through a maze of broken hills and ended in the precipitous declivity known as Ash Hollow. The springs here were cold and good. Ash trees and cedar trees shaded their campgrounds, and the sweet scent of wildflowers flowed on the gentle breeze.

The wagons were lowered down the steep hills by ropes. No mishaps occurred, and the company moved on to Fort Laramie, past the austere and lonely wonders of Courthouse Rock and Chimney Rock, past the castlelike Scotts Bluff and innumerable, imposing red sandstone cliffs, over steep and sloping terrain that required great skill in maneuvering wagons and teams from crashing into ravines or turning onto their sides. Women and children left the wagons and walked, feeling safer on solid ground.

Dust poured from the wagon wheels and drifted up into the still July air that shimmered with miragelike heat over the persistent prairie. Not a breath of air stirred the wild grass. The women found some reprieve by going into deep ravines, protected by several of the men, to gather chokecherries and currants that grew in those places in great abundance.

At Fort Laramie they were able to rest for a few days. The fort had been constructed in a narrow valley of grassy hills next to the left bank of the Laramie River. Made of adobe bricks, the walls of the fort were six feet thick and fifteen feet high and enclosed an area approximately one hundred fifty feet square.

Inside the walls of the fort, every accommodation was available. There was a trading house, shops for the repair of wagons and harnesses, quarters for those who stayed there, and warehouses for storage of everything from food to furs. And a blacksmith shop.

Everything here was four times more costly than it had been back in Independence, which Lucille proclaimed was "highway robbery." But the emigrants had no choice but to pay the price, and the merchandisers at the fort knew it. Good wagons, if they could be had, ran from four to thirty dollars. Mules ranged from a hundred to one hundred fifty. Flour was a dollar a pint, or forty dollars a barrel. Sugar ran one and a half times that. Dried buffalo meat could not be had for any price. The fort was also running low on supplies since the huge Oregon company had, for the most part, passed through already, leaving the California company picking scraps.

Still the reprieve from the trail had put everyone in good spirits. Feasting and dancing went on every night. One night some Oglala Sioux near the Fort invited the emigrants to a buffalo and dog dance where the men danced around holding a buffalo head and its attached hide over their heads, bellowing and shaking their own heads in imitation of the mighty prairie lords. The exact meaning of the dance was never made clear to the emigrants, but most considered the savage dance a mesmerizing and delightful experience. Even Garnet seemed to enjoy the dance and didn't seem to be reminded that Ethan had died beneath the hooves of thousands of the beasts. She sat next to Torey, just as if they were still on the wagon seat, and watched the dancing with a smile in her cornflower blue eyes. Frances found the girl's behavior eerie. "It's almost as if she's exorcised Ethan completely from her mind."

The second night at the fort, Miriam gave birth to her ninth baby boy, which she named Laramie, even though Arthur said he hated it and would name the boy something else.

While Miriam had been in labor, Nancy had seen Arthur slip out into the darkness behind the wagons. Nancy had shortly seen the fleeting shadow of a woman in a full skirt and a shawl over her head following him. Nancy's first impression was that the woman was Lucille Royal, but that had to be an illusion since Lucille would never venture out of her wagon at night for fear of being scalped. Nancy shrugged it off, deciding it was probably another Indian girl Waite had seduced.

The baby's first cries didn't bring Arthur, but they drew Garnet away from the dancers. Almost as if in a trance, she left Torey's side and followed the sound. Nancy and the other women stepped aside so she could enter the tent and see the baby. They all feared the sight of the baby might be too much for her to bear, and would set her back into that dark world she had escaped to after her own child's death. But to everyone's surprise she asked if she could help take care of the baby. Miriam, so overworked, was more than grateful for the offer of assistance.

Garnet settled onto the ground next to Miriam's blankets. With the baby bundled and in her arms, she began to rock back and forth, singing a lullaby that filtered out softly into the night in stark contrast to the Oglala drumbeats in the distance.

August

The trail out of Fort Laramie circuitously followed the North Platte, bypassing ravines, steep sidling hills, and boulders bigger than houses. This time of year, the Laramie Mountains appeared dry and thirsty, the pines and cedars on their distant slopes looked black, desperately needing rain. But rain didn't come, and Colonel Chiles said the next moisture this country was likely to see would be snow.

They hadn't been on a trail any rougher. As they followed the river toward the Red Buttes, the road became littered with belongings dumped out by the advance party of Oregonians in their attempt to lighten their load up the steep grade. Lady Rae smartly sidestepped barrels, cooking stoves, rocking chairs, trunks, anvils and other tools, clothing, and even the grave of an unknown woman from the Oregon company who had died in childbirth.

Some of their own company had to leave behind some baggage as well. The most heartfelt loss was Miriam's china dishes. She begged her husband not to discard them. "They don't weigh enough to make any difference, Arthur," she pleaded. "Please find something else. I'll walk up the mountain and carry the baby, just don't throw out my dishes. They were my grandmother's. You know that, Arthur."

He paid her no mind, just gathered up the crate and heaved it out with a vengeance and a shattering of glass, as if it were more than dishes he was getting rid of. It was worse than a slap in her face, and left a bruise bigger than any he'd inflicted on her body thus far.

All the women turned away in anger, wishing they could take him down and give him a good lashing. All except for Lucille, that is, who smugly made the comment that, "It served the stupid bitch right."

The dishes were like the loose rock on a cliff, and they sent Miriam skidding over the edge. With tears streaming down her cheeks and a roaring blaze of hatred in her eyes, she took baby Laramie and got down from the wagon. "You didn't have to break my dishes! I'd have rather seen those poor Indian women use them for *hats* than to have you break them!"

"Get back up in the wagon, woman."

"You will not tell me what to do ever again, Arthur Waite. I shall walk the rest of the way to California before I'll sit by you on that wagon seat. Furthermore, if you ever so much as touch me again, in any way, I will put poison in your food."

"My God, woman, they're only dishes." But there was genuine fear in his eyes, for Arthur Waite liked his food.

"They were *my* dishes. My grandmother's dishes, and you had no right. No right whatsoever."

"You're behaving like this because those England and Maguire women have influenced you with their rebellious ways. I knew they shouldn't have been allowed to bring their corruption into this company."

Miriam didn't waste breath on rebuttal. She turned on her heel, leaving him with his mouth gaping, and wondering if his next meal would be his last.

The period of recuperation they'd had at Fort Laramie had helped lagging spirits, but the journey into the mountains and into a wilderness, more bitter and hostile than the prairie, had everyone on edge. The journey itself, the endless travel, dirt, repetition of meals, lack of privacy, and poor beds began to fray even the toughest nerves. And it was easier to fray the nerves of those who didn't want to be here.

Three days after Miriam threatened to poison Arthur, the men unhitched the teams for nooning in a shady spot by a creek. But when they started to hitch up again, Brenham Royal found himself staring down the barrel of his own shotgun. Lucille was on the trigger end, standing wide with her heels dug deep into the dirt. And she said she wasn't taking another step.

16

"We are going back to Fort Laramie, Brenham," Lucille said, allowing no argument. "We will join up with some fur traders there and return to Independence. I have seen enough of your insane folly."

Brenham was sufficiently afraid of how bad the crack in her mind was that he didn't dare risk putting all his weight on it for fear it would snap in two and take him down with it. And of course no one else was about to step into the middle of it either.

"Come on now, Lucille," Brenham said cautiously, moistening lips that had suddenly gone dry. "Don't be unreasonable. Things will be much better in California, and you're holding up the entire company."

"I'm not stopping anybody from going on. They can go to hell if it so pleases them."

Chiles made one attempt to help out. "You can't get back alone, Mrs. Royal. You might not see Indians out here, but they see you, and they will not miss the opportunity to assault a lone wagon."

"You keep your nose out of it, Chiles. *You* are the fool who caused us to be here in the first place. I ought to shoot you."

Nancy, who had been standing on the sidelines, was overcome with blinding fury. While Lucille had her eyes trained on J.B., Nancy marched up behind her, stepped around her, and jerked the shotgun from her unsuspecting grip.

"We will not tolerate your little temper tantrums, Lucille Royal," she snapped, as if talking to a school bully. "Return to your wagon where you can show your royal butt to your chamber pot because the rest of us are getting damned tired of seeing it."

Lucille's shock took a moment to overcome, but she quickly saved face the best she could. "You won't tell me what to do, you high-society bitch."

"Oh, I won't?" Nancy pointed the shotgun at Lucille's heart.

Fear flashed across the woman's face but was quickly replaced with a sneer. "You don't have the nerve to shoot me."

"Don't I? I had the nerve to save your husband from drowning. I had the nerve to come out here without a man to protect me. Pulling this little old trigger would actually be one of the easiest things I've done so far, and one of the more pleasurable, so don't bet your life that I don't have the nerve."

"Brenham"—Lucille's fearful eyes darted from Nancy to her husband and back—"for heaven's sake, take the gun away from this madwoman."

"Why should I? She isn't bothering me none."

Finding herself on the short end of the stick, Lucille tried attacking Nancy again with the viciousness of her tongue. "You will regret you ever crossed my path."

"Let me assure you, I already do."

Having been completely outwitted, Lucille stalked back to her wagon and disappeared inside. Nancy returned the shotgun to Brenham, and the wagon train proceeded on.

The sun had barely cropped the western peaks when a handful of riders, Indians and white trappers, rode into camp from the west, led by the famous mountain man, Joseph Reddiford Walker. Their packhorses were loaded down with furs and they were headed for Fort Laramie.

Both Walker and Chiles were surprised to see each other. Acquaintances from Missouri, it had been many years since they'd talked. After introductions, hand-shaking, and backslapping, they settled down around the campfire to get caught up on what had happened in the past ten years.

Joe Walker, forty-seven years old now, was a noted mountain man who ten years before had been part of the Bonneville party of American fur trappers' expedition engaged in forging a trail to the Great Salt Lake.

From there, Walker had led the men west to Mary's River, south to Carson Sink, and on into California over Mono Pass. On the return trip the following year, he had discovered another pass at the southern end of the Sierra Nevada, which was duly dubbed Walker Pass.

As the fires burned down, many of emigrants retired to bed, but Nancy and Lottie remained to listen to the men discuss the best possible route into California.

"I hear you and your group nearly perished two years ago," Walker said, sipping at a cup of coffee. "I hope you're not planning on trying to get wagons over those mountains again, J.B. I don't think you'll have any better success than you did then."

Chiles nodded. "You're right about '41. We barely made it to John Marsh's ranch with our lives. But we headed over in the wrong place, ran into all sorts of problems. Can a person get wagons over Walker Pass?"

"I wouldn't advise it, but I can draw you a map to show you how to find it."

Everyone cleared back and Walker proceeded to draw a map in the dirt, carefully explaining each line, landmarks, details that would be invaluable to Chiles on this, his second try. "But you're a few weeks later than what you should be, J.B.," Walker said. "I know I don't need to tell you that, but you'd better head south. Don't risk getting caught in the higher mountains."

"What we need is a guide, Joe," Chiles said earnestly. "What would you need to come with us? Show us the way across the desert and to Walker Pass. We don't have time to wander around, searching."

"No, you certainly don't," Walker acknowledged. "But you've been over those mountains before, J.B. I really don't have much over on you. And you know a hell of a lot more about wagon travel than I do."

"But you know where Walker Pass is," Chiles countered, "and I could spend precious days, maybe weeks, searching for it."

"You still can't get wagons over it."

"We'll cross that bridge when we come to it. Will you do it, Joe?"

Joe Walker was silent as he studied his map in the dirt, balanced there on his haunches and the balls of his moccasined feet. "I've got to get these furs to Fort Laramie, but I suppose I could catch up with you. I'd need at least three hundred dollars to do it, J.B. You got that kind of money?"

Joseph Ballinger Chiles nodded without a moment's hesitation.

Joe Walker gave it another moment of consideration then finally put out his hand. Colonel Chiles shook it. "It's a deal. I'll catch up with you before you reach Fort Hall. But there's something else you should know."

"Well, what is it?" Chiles prodded.

"Some of those Californians are getting nervous about all the Americans coming into the province. The sentiment towards the increasing number of emigrants isn't good. They're saying that they'll fight to hold California, and the Americans living there could likely get killed."

Chiles sighed heavily. "So we've heard, but it's too late to turn back now, Joe. And none of us hanker going to Oregon. We'll have to deal with that issue when we get there."

"I just figured you ought to be aware of the climate you're heading into. Not everywhere in California is warm."

Despite the last disquieting news from Walker, Chiles was happy to have the mountain man as their guide past Fort Hall and into the Sierras. With high spirits, they set out along the Platte and onto the Sweetwater, making good time.

The August heat was intense, but the nights were cold and the mornings crisp. One morning, Nancy caught Hart staring off toward the west, his nostrils flared like a horse that smells something on the wind.

"What is it, Hart?" she asked worriedly, pouring him a cup of coffee. She feared Indians, or maybe another buffalo stampede.

He turned back to her and ran a hand along her cheek. "Nothing really. I just smell winter not far away. There will be no time to waste from here on out. We've got to make it to the Sierra Nevadas before the snow does."

A party of buffalo killers and beaver skinners had, some fifteen or twenty years before, stopped here and celebrated the Fourth of July. With buffalo grease and gunpowder they had painted their names on the gigantic lump of granite and named it Independence Rock. Since then, hundreds of other names, dates, even messages, had been painted or inscribed on the surface. And this day, Hart Daniels and Nancy Maguire added theirs.

With others from both the California company and the Oregon companies—the latter of which were now stretched out both in front and behind the Chiles party—they climbed to the top of the rock. It rose some six or seven hundred feet above the broad and bleak plain where buffalo grazed along the meandering Sweetwater River. It was a land of naked granite rocks, scrub brush, rattlesnakes, jackrabbits, antelope, and Sioux. The latter, unlike the former, kept themselves well hidden.

The wind whipped at Nancy's skirt, flattening it against her legs and stomach. Hart held a hand to his hat to keep the wind from snatching it away. But Nancy removed hers, allowing the wind to run through her hair with rough fingers that tore strands from their pins and even sent the pins flying to be lost forever.

Nancy breathed in the wild spirit of the land, its latent danger, its harsh loneliness. She breathed in its emptiness, and allowed it to fill her heart and soul with its strength, its power, its perserverance for survival against a temperamental, and sometimes cruel, Mother Nature. She maintained a healthy fear and respect for this land and of those who lived here, both man and animal, who never conquered it but merely coexisted. And, for all the harshness of the land, she envied the freedom of the wind and the inhabitants. She knew, at that moment, on this exact spot, that this was possibly the culmination of every reason she had come West. To feel the freedom infiltrating her soul, and to feel both freedom and soul become one with the land, the sky, and the earth. To belong to something. To understand the meaning of life, and of creation. Somehow it all came together in that one glorious moment atop Independence Rock.

Hart's arms circled her as he stepped up behind her, pulling her into his embrace. Her laughter escaped into the wind and went with it, wherever it might go.

"It's beautiful, Hart. So very, very beautiful."

"Some call it hostile."

"It's not gentle," she conceded. "But I hold it no ill regard."

She turned into his arms and ignored the others on the massive rock, soaking up the panorama below. A few tried to draw the scene before them while the wind whipped their papers, their clothes, and their hair every which way.

"Marry me, Nancy," Hart whispered next to her lips. "Here. Now. Marry me."

The question sobered her for a moment, but then suddenly she laughed, joyously and free. She wondered where her laughter would go, and if some Indian or some old trapper a hundred miles away might, in a day or two, hear its echo and wonder . . .

Her heart had never been so light. Her head never more clear. Her dreams never more defined. She looked deep into his blue eyes and saw his love, felt it in his anxious body and in his tender touch. She felt a part of him, and they were both a part of the land. This wild, wonderful land.

"Yes, Hart. I will marry you. Here, and now. There's a preacher with the Oregon company. We'll send someone to fetch him."

Later, Nancy was to think how ironic it was that she had relinquished her single status atop a rock called Independence. And yet, nestled in Hart's arms in the privacy of his tent that night, she thought she had never felt so unfettered. She had stood there in her riding clothes with a bunch of wildflowers in her hand, the wind whipping her hair. She had thought that if she could have planned her wedding, it couldn't have been more perfect.

There had been a dance afterward that had gone on into the night. She had changed into the one nice dress she'd brought along. Hart, too, had changed into clean black trousers, a white shirt, and a gray cotton vest. She and Hart had led the dancing.

The camp was quiet now. The fiddles and banjos had been put away. People snored or whispered quietly in their tents and wagons. The sounds of this lonely land, beyond the fragile protection of the canvas, filtered past the snorting and stamping of the horses and mules, past Laramie crying to be fed, past one of the Martin girls giggling while her mother tried to convince her it was time to sleep.

"My only regret on this day," Nancy whispered against Hart's chest, "is that my family could not be here to share our joy."

Hart kissed the top of her head, her forehead, then continued scattering kisses over her closed eyelids, the bridge of her nose, and along the soft contours of her cheeks. "I'd like you to meet my family some day, too."

He pulled her closer in a fierce embrace, as if suddenly the kissing was not sufficient. "I've dreamed of this moment since first we met, Nancy. I can hardly believe it's real."

Nancy had thought she might be frightened of this night when at long last she became a man's wife, but being with Hart was more natural than being alone. Garnet's discouraging words had drifted occasionally through her mind, trying to give her second thoughts, but they had been weak whispers easily banished in the face of true love.

"You were right, Hart," she whispered, tracing his cheek with her finger.

"About what?"

"That I wouldn't make it to California alone."

"Let's just say I had plans even then for your future—with me. You don't know how strong the punch was to my senses when you came riding up to the wagon that day. I swear, just the sight of you sent me reeling. I had never seen anyone more beautiful, more appealing. And I knew. I just knew what I had to do."

He sat up and brought her with him. Hart had built the fire outside the tent tonight, and they closed the tent flap to it so they could have privacy. Its orange glow gave just enough light through the canvas that they could see each other, but no one could see them from the outside.

He kissed her lips again passionately while his hands drifted to the buttons up the back of her dress and, one by one, released them until the cloth could easily be slipped off her shoulders. In this same fashion they undressed each other.

Nancy thought Hart's body rivaled the fortresses of granite that shaped this wild land. Yet, for all the strength and hardness of him, there was exquisite tenderness in his hands and lips, and in his heart. When he touched her, everything inside her quaked and yearned and responded in the way a budding young rose responds to water and warmth, opening to its full beauty.

There was no refuting the rightness of lying with him, lifting her legs around his slender hips and pulling his hardness deep inside her, knowing him and having him know her. The preacher had said, "This love you feel now as you say your vows is only the beginning and only a fraction of what it will be ten or twenty years from now. Each year you are together, it will grow until it is as strong and solid as a mighty oak with great branches that spread out over time and generations."

So it was. Hart took her to a pinnacle of light and height like none she could have dreamed in her wildest imaginings. And she brought him with her. They cleaved as man and wife and clutched the cries of their ecstasy in their throats so all the camp wouldn't hear. But the little sounds of pleasure slipped out into the darkness of the empty land, onto sleeping ears that would not remember come morning. But they would know. For all the joy and fulfillment that went with the union of Nancy Maguire and Hart Daniels would, come morning, be as bright and shining as the sun of the new day.

17

September

Thunder rumbled across the Bear River Valley; profanities roared. Mules balked and brayed. Horses whirled and bucked. Axles creaked and groaned. Ropes frayed and snapped. Opinions rampaged. Tempers flared. Accidents flourished.

During a crossing of the Sweetwater, a team belonging to one of the Oregonians who had joined up with Chiles back on the Platte had spooked and stampeded, overturning the wagon and nearly trapping the driver beneath it. Alacrity and youth had been all that had saved him from drowning.

At the soda springs, another Oregon-bound team had also stampeded. This time the driver had been tossed from the wagon seat, leaving his wife and a child screaming from inside the wagon as the mules took the wagon up the side of a steep hill where it promptly overturned. Both wife and child had been killed.

One man from the Oregon company had fallen from his horse and been dragged for a considerable distance before he could be rescued. His leg was in bad shape, although not broken. His back had been raw from the rocks and brush, and Dr. Whitman had been called onto the scene again.

Outside Fort Bridger, the Cheyenne had snuck into camp and stolen a dozen horses. The men had had a two-day delay going after them and stealing them back.

Now, Lucille Royal refused to get out of her wagon again so it could be lowered down a steep embankment. With raveling patience, Colonel Chiles had informed Brenham that if he couldn't convince Lucille to leave the wagon by the time their turn came to lower the wagon down the hill, then they would just have to leave them behind.

"I'll get her out," Brenham had said. "Either dead or alive."

Sixteen wagons had been successfully lowered down the hill so far. They'd traveled over a thousand miles since leaving Independence and were still only about halfway to their journey's end if they went south through Walker's Pass. If they could find a pass over the Sierras, they could cut five hundred miles off the distance. Joe Walker had caught up with them as he had promised, and had told them that what they'd left behind was nothing compared to what was yet to come.

"How much more can we take?" Lucille had cried. "How can it get any worse?"

But the women weren't the only ones who were tired. So were the men, and their tempers and their patience were dangerously close to the breaking point. A shortage of supplies and meat was becoming evident. Chiles had wanted to stop at Fort Bridger for ten to fifteen days, kill buffalo, and make meat for the rest of the journey. But the best buffalo country was behind them now, and they found no buffalo around the fort. They stayed only two days and then moved on, straying from the Oregon Trail in hopes of finding some game undisturbed by the emigrants who had already passed. Occasionally they brought back a deer or an antelope, even an elk or a bear, but it was never enough to fill stomachs and have any left over with which to make jerky for the remainder of the journey.

They had finally headed north into the Bear River Valley and returned to the established trail. They were behind schedule. *Too* far behind. Talk around the campfires was that, two years ago, the Bartleson–Bidwell party had already been well past the Great Salt Lake by this time of year. With growing fears and anxieties came short fuses.

Nancy was probably one of the few who had passed the last three hundred miles in a state of bliss. She'd ridden next to Hart all day, every day, and had made love in his arms every night. She hardly noticed that food supplies were getting low, for love seemed to sustain her. Lottie told her she glowed.

But Nancy worried about one thing. She worried about what would happen to Lottie when they reached California. Lottie had brushed away her concerns. "I'm going to get me that land just like I said I would, Nancy. I know we talked about maybe homesteading together, but I never did figure you would last long out in this country."

"Well, thank you kindly for your faith in me," Nancy quipped playfully.

"I didn't mean that you weren't tough enough to survive, for Pete's sake. I meant that you'd find a man even though you said you weren't looking."

"What about you, Lottie?" Nancy searched the brunette's eyes for a telltale flicker of truth. "Do you ever want another man?"

Lottie's gaze had scoured the horizons, as if the answers were out there somewhere, and finally she had found one. "I'm searchin' for something that I can't quite put a name to. Maybe it's love. Maybe it's just peace with myself and the world around me. Contentment, you know. Satisfaction with the way things are. Love would be fine to have, but from my experience, I can't help but fear that it would never end up being what it was in the beginning. And, like it was with Major, I'd be left with nothing but raveled ends of sky."

Nancy thought of those words now, for some crazy reason, as she nervously watched the men begin to lower her and Lottie's wagon down the nearly perpendicular incline on a bevy of ropes. Even though she was married now and shared Hart's tent, she and Lottie were still a team. She had left her personal belongings and her share of the supplies in her and Lottie's wagon, and she still traded Lottie off on driving.

The back wheels of the wagon were locked with a chain that had been attached to the body of the wagon, then secured to a tree with a system of pulleys to regulate the speed of the descent. If the chains weren't secured properly, and the wagons started rolling, the men and teams wouldn't be able to hold it.

The mules had been unhitched, and Lottie stood at the top of the hill, holding them, with the help of Hart and J.B. The mountains rose up around them like a courtesan's corseted breasts, leaving little room in the valley between for anything but the course of the river. The Oregon companies that had already passed had smoothed the edge off the banks with shovels, and the hundreds of hooves and wagon wheels had helped to wear down the lip. Deep ruts helped somewhat to keep the wagons on course. Still, if the wagon got away from the men, it would take the natural course down the hill that led directly to the river.

Nancy had helped Lottie chain their wagon's wheels. Lottie had been confident in her work and was mildly insulted when Colonel Chiles had come around to inspect it.

"Don't you think a woman knows how to do such things, J.B.?"

Chiles had merely grinned, checked the tightness of the chains again, and said, "I'm a man who leaves very little to chance, Miss Lottie."

"Oh, really? And what would you call this expedition of yours if not chancy?"

He shrugged his big shoulders nonchalantly. "A calculated risk."

Lottie's robust laughter still echoed in Nancy's ears as she stood by, watching the front wheels of their wagon dip precariously over the lip of the ridge, sink into the ruts of the previous wagons and begin the inch by inch descent to the bottom.

Josh rode his mule over next to Nancy and dismounted. His dog, Harry, was at his heels, as usual. For a moment, they stood in silent camaraderie watching the slow progress. Back behind them, Arthur Waite was unhitching Brenham Royal's team, and the mules were acting up, not liking Waite any better than anybody else did.

Waite, who seemed to go out of his way to help Lucille, had taken over while Brenham had left the position to try and persuade his wife to get out of the wagon long enough to get it down the hill. They were next in line, behind Lottie and Nancy's wagon, and would miss that position if they weren't ready to go. From the looks of things, Brenham might be forced to bodily remove Lucille from the wagon to accomplish his objective.

Meanwhile, Waite's strident voice carried out across the quiet valley, making it difficult for the men lowering Nancy and Lottie's wagon to concentrate and relay their commands to each other.

"I offered to unhitch that team for Mr. Royal," Josh said, "but Ma told me I'd better leave it up to one of the men. 'Course, she wouldn't have said that, I reckon, if she'd known Waite would be the one to end up doing it. That surprised us all since he's never one for lifting a finger to help anybody. But look at him. Why, I can handle a mule team better than he can, and I'm just a kid! That team of mules was fine until he got hold of them. He's got them dancing around like the wolves were after their haunches. There's going to be trouble if he doesn't get them under control, or if one of the other men doesn't take over."

Mules seemed to instinctively trust Lottie and did her bidding without balking. Arthur Waite, on the other hand, had the opposite effect on any animal he came into contact with. He somehow even managed to make enemies with the dogs, and they growled every time he came around. One dog had bit him through his boot, doing no damage, but he'd shot it with his pistol, creating another enemy of the dog's owner.

Another string of foul expletives burst from Waite's mouth, followed by a chorus of men barking instructions, orders, and more profanities. As Josh had predicted, Brenham Royal's mules had gone into a conniption fit, unsettling the other mules. Lottie, holding her team on the ridge, suddenly had her hands full and Royal's mules started crowding into hers.

"We've got to keep them steady," Lottie warned Waite, amazingly keeping from panic when panic was all around her. "Calm down, and they will, too."

"Get those damned mules under control, Waite!" Chiles yelled from his position. "Hart! McIntosh! Get over there fast. If those mules run and hit those ropes, we'll lose the wagon!"

Nancy's heart leaped into her throat. Dropping Lady Rae's reins, she ran to help Lottie. But before Hart and the others could reach Waite, and before she herself had gone more than a few yards, the mules broke away and stampeded right into the ropes. Men yelled and cussed, barking useless commands and cuss words as the ropes were yanked from their grips and went spinning through the pulleys and into the air. The freed wagon careened down the hill on its front wheels, jumping the ruts. The locked back wheels jerked it around and it flipped to its side, rolling over and over to the river. Bows broke. Wood sprang off it and flew into the air. It hit the water upside-down.

Immediately the swift current grabbed the sacks and wooden boxes and crates, bedding and loose clothing, anything that would float. Nancy raced after it, digging her boot heels into the loose dirt as she raced down the hill. Still, she was barely able to keep her footing on the steep slope and slipped back onto her fanny numerous times, bruising it on rocks. Josh was right behind her. They both knew that if they didn't get the supplies out of the water quickly, everything would be ruined.

Without regard for even her leather boots, Nancy dove into the water feet first. She was joined by nearly every man in the company who had a free hand. They spread out up and down the river, trying to catch anything that had pulled free of the broken wagon and torn canvas and had begun to float away. The heavier items sank with the wagon or were trapped beneath its weight. Soon a human line was formed, using women and children to pass the contents of the wagon from the river to dry ground.

The mules that had caused the accident were apprehended. Lucille, having seen what had happened to Lottie and Nancy's wagon, gave Brenham no further argument and exited her wagon. Despite being the cause of the disaster, Arthur Waite didn't appear the least contrite. Wearing a look that appeared almost smug, he sauntered back to his wagon to await his own turn down the hill.

The thin pages of the old Bible were soaked. The ink that had once recorded the births, marriages, and deaths of Nancy's ancestors in beautiful flowing cursive, now ran together in illegible scrawls and black, spidery blots. Nancy gently laid the Bible on the blanket. Next to it, she spread her eight precious daguerreotypes, all but ruined. Her family had had the daguerreotypes made up just last year, for it was a new process of portraiture that had only recently been invented.

The fire would dry the pages of the Bible, and even the daguerreotypes, but they had suffered irreparable damage. She fought back tears while staring down at the one that had reflected her grandfather's image.

A shadow fell over her. She looked up into Arthur Waite's sneering half-smile. "Serves you right," he said in a voice that wouldn't carry to the other emigrants who were busily making their camps. "You and that England woman needed some comeuppance for thinking you could come out here alone with no men."

Something tightened inside Nancy, like a guitar string stretched to the limits of its durability. She rose to her feet, feeling murderous. Waite took a step back, sensing it.

"You did this intentionally, didn't you?"

He gripped his insolence. "What if I did? You can't prove it."

She saw through his bravado to the flicker of fear in his eyes. Fear of her. And her fists clenched while it was all she could do to keep from

wrapping her fingers around his scrawny, chickenlike neck and squeezing with every ounce of her strength until either his life, or her rage,
were gone.

"I don't need to prove it, Waite. Out here, law doesn't matter. Order
doesn't matter. I can damn well do what I see fit to do, and if I see fit to
blow your ugly face off your head, I can do it and nobody would fault me."

He took another step back, startled by her threat. He forced a smile,
but Nancy thought she saw it quiver just a bit. "You haven't got the guts,
woman. You're impotent. As impotent as all the rest of your kind. It's a
long way to California, Mrs. Daniels. Accidents *will* happen."

He tipped his hat mockingly, but he walked away quickly, glancing
back frequently like a man who has a vicious cur dogging his trail.

Nancy's arms were shaking at her sides as she fought the desire to
pull her pepperbox from its holster and show him just how impotent
she was. But she couldn't kill a man in cold blood. This was a harsh land
that made for harsh people. Gentility had no place here. But you didn't
kill someone, even if he might deserve it. Only God could make that
judgment.

She sat back down and took a deep breath to calm herself.

Returning her attention to the Bible, she fingered the pages. They
would dry eventually, but they would never return to their original shape,
and she wished she had paid more attention to the names and dates so
she could have written them down somewhere else.

A hand on her shoulder startled her again. Thinking Waite had returned, she whirled, ready to lash out. But it was Hart.

He lowered himself to his haunches next to her. "What did
Waite want?"

"To offer his condolences," she said snidely.

Hart glanced down at the Bible, the ruined daguerreotypes. He
pulled her into his arms. His silent understanding was more comforting
than words could have been, and it was also her undoing. The torrent of
tears she'd been holding back broke free.

"I didn't bring very much with me, Hart," she sobbed against his
chest. "Just a few clothes, and . . . and these." Helplessly she waved the
daguerreotype of her grandfather. "I wanted to pass them down to . . . to
our children."

"You still can. And when you do, you can tell them the story of this
day, of your journey overland to California. If I know anything of human

nature, they will cherish these things all the more as evidence of the sorrows and struggles in holding onto them."

He comforted her in his arms until Lottie and J.B. came over to join them.

"Are you going to be all right?" Lottie's brow furrowed with concern.

Nancy wiped her tears and managed a smile. "We're alive. The mules are alive. That's all that matters."

J.B. sipped at a cup of coffee he'd brought along with him. "Lottie and I inspected your wagon pretty good, Nancy, and we decided that with some repairs it'll probably limp into Fort Hall. But I suggest you get another one before going on to California."

"And I told him there was no point in it," Lottie put in. "Joe Walker says we aren't going to get those wagons over the Sierras anyway. No, if you agree with me, we'll just pack the mules. But I do hope to hell there are some supplies left at Fort Hall, or we could be in serious trouble."

18

Joe Walker squatted next to the fire, prodding it with a green willow stick while working up to what was on his mind. "I'm sorry to have to take such a hard-nosed stance, J.B., but I can't, in good faith and good conscience, head out across the desert without a better supply of meat. As you well know, there isn't much but jackrabbits and rattlesnakes along the Mary's River."

Hart, Chiles, and a dozen men sat around the campfire, discussing the scarcity of supplies at Fort Hall. The Oregon companies that had gone ahead had left no meat, flour, sugar, or rice. Captain Richard Grant, the Hudson Bay's representative in charge of the post, had cattle grazing nearby but refused to sell any at any price. They all understood his circumstance. Those at the fort needed something to live on, too. But it left the California emigrants, and those other Oregon-bound companies coming behind them, in a desperate situation.

Chiles ran a hand through his shank of red hair. "I appreciate your honesty, Joe. I wouldn't ask you to take these women and children across that barren wasteland without a decent supply of meat. But we can starve to death just as easily sitting out the winter here at the fort as we can in forging on."

Julius Martin stood up, taking agitated steps back and forth behind the circle of men. "Grant has supplies. You all saw them in his storehouse. Maybe he just needs some persuasion to sell. I have three daughters and a wife, and I can tell you I will do whatever is necessary to keep them from starving to death."

One of the Oregon men, who had joined Chiles's company, spoke up. "Martin's right. I say we force Grant to sell us what he has. He can't just leave us out here to die. Besides, he'll be getting more provisions before winter."

"You don't know that for sure," Hart put in, trying to stay calm. "Anything could happen to prevent a wagonload of supplies from coming in. It could get lost in a river, stolen by Indians, delayed in snows over South Pass."

"I know your biggest concern is for your family, Julius, as it should be," J.B. said, standing up. "But don't be thinking of doing something rash. You could get yourself killed and others, too. I'll talk to Grant again. I'll see just how much money it'll take to make him part with a few of those cattle."

Colonel Chiles, Billy Baldridge, Hart, Pierson Reading, and Samuel Hensley left to talk to Captain Grant at the fort. They returned a few hours later with four head of cattle, and clearly not the best four of the herd. When asked how much Chiles had had to pay to get Grant to sell, all he would say was, "Too much."

Joe Walker was still apprehensive. Even though most of the Oregonians who had traveled with them from the Platte would not be turning off with them to California, the meat from the four cattle still wouldn't last nearly long enough, especially when all of their other provisions were low.

"It isn't enough, J.B.," Walker said to Chiles and Hart in private. "You know it, and I know it. The others know it, too."

Chiles nodded grimly. "There's only one thing I can see to do then, Joe. We'll have to split the company for the good of everyone."

At Walker's agreement, Chiles gathered everyone together to make the announcement. He mounted his black mule and rode into the center of the encampment. The emigrants left their chores to gather around him. "You are all aware of the situation concerning our food supplies," he began. "In lieu of that, I have made the decision to split the company. Joe Walker will take the wagons with the women, children, most of the men, and all of the meat. I'll take a small group of volunteers with me on horseback, and we'll head to Fort Boise to see if we can find more supplies."

Chiles went on to say that it was his intention to swing around the

Sierras and come into the Sacramento Valley from the north. From Sutter's Fort, he would then gather more supplies and either send Samuel Hensley over the mountains to meet them at Carson Sink, or—if the snows had already settled heavily in the Sierras—he would make his way south to meet them at Walker Pass. There was only one glitch in this plan that he didn't mention.

"That territory you're planning on heading into is unexplored, J.B.," Hart said later when they were alone. "And being farther north, more susceptible to early snows. God, man, you don't know where in the hell you'll end up. Do you really think you can do Joe Walker and the rest of the company any good? You've got something else in mind, don't you?"

Chiles was reluctant with his response, but Hart would accept nothing but the full truth. "All right, maybe I do. I want to find a pass for wagons over the Sierras, and it's unlikely Walker will find it. He'll have his hands full just getting everybody to the settlements before they starve to death. You know I don't like separating the company like this, Hart, but Joe can do everything I can, and more. Plus, if we find a passage, we can ride hard and fast to Sutter's Fort and meet the company with supplies at Carson Sink."

"You can get your ass in a sling too. You might find your wagon pass over the Sierras. Or you may not get over those mountains at all. I felt a chill this morning in the air that smelled an awful lot like snow."

"It's early, Hart. Even if we get snow, it won't stick."

Hart just shook his head. "This isn't Missouri, J.B. Damn it, but you are a hard-headed man! And I wish I was going with you, just to keep you out of trouble, but I won't leave Nancy."

"And I wouldn't ask you to. But I will ask you to look out after Lottie."

Hart nodded, understanding the look in J.B.'s eyes. "Don't worry. I know you're a little partial to her."

There was no dancing that night in camp. There was fear. Food was running out. Time was running out. And J.B. Chiles had abandoned them. Only Garnet Stillman seemed unafraid. She used her time by gathering up all of Ethan's clothing and personal belongings and handing them out to anybody who wanted them.

"Chiles has looked out after his own hide," Lucille Royal said smartly to the circle of women gathered together watching Garnet. "He drags us out here on promises then leaves us behind."

"You're so full of shit I'm surprised it's not choking off your wind," Lottie readily responded. "I'd say that if you really don't want to go to California, then head that wagon of yours to Oregon tomorrow. This is the fork in the road, lady, and I, for one, wouldn't mind seeing you take it."

Lucille held her ground. "You're just upset because you thought Colonel Chiles had the eye for you."

Lottie shook her head in disgust. "Colonel Chiles has more sense in his little finger than you have in your entire head, Lucille. He's a friend. Nothing more."

Nancy didn't want to believe what Lucille said about J.B. either. Chiles had too much integrity to walk off and leave them and never look back. His intentions had never been anything but honorable where his company was concerned.

"He left so there would be more food for you and your daughters, Lucille," she countered.

But inside, Nancy was secretly ashamed of the roiling thoughts. Had J.B. known they would never get over the Sierras at this late date? Did he know that for lack of food they might not even get across the desert country to the south? He had been across the desert two times before. He knew what was ahead. Was that why he was going another way? Had he run from the responsibility and the burden that would be on his shoulders if they all perished? Was he really looking out for himself, as Lucille said? Walker didn't seem upset to have been left in charge, but Walker owed them no allegiance either. Who was to say they might not wake up one morning and find him gone, too?

She tried to calm her fears, not mentioning any of it to Hart that night in their tent. She made love to him and held him, wondering in a peculiar calm how many more nights they would have together. But Hart had been over this wasteland numerous times as well. He knew how to survive and he would, to the best of his ability, see that the rest of them did, too. And Billy Baldridge would be staying with them, still toting the heavy machinery for the sawmill. The chances of getting it over the Sierras without a wagon pass, however, looked very bleak indeed. The mountains they'd crossed had been difficult enough, and everyone said they were insignificant compared to what lay ahead.

She had to think of the future, of a home, land, of the baby she hoped to some day carry in her womb. She touched her flat stomach, wondering if Hart's seed had already begun to grow. She pressed closer to him, thinking in those moments that she loved him more with each new day. She had felt that special something between them from the very beginning, but had been stubbornly determined to go it alone. She could see now how idealistic her ideas had been. And how foolish.

"What are you thinking, Nancy?" Hart whispered, pulling her closer.

She put the distressing thoughts aside, and nestled down into his love. She listened to the steady thump of his heart, and warmed herself with his life. Oh, but life was frail and precious, and should never be taken for granted, nor squandered. That was a lesson she'd learned very well on this journey.

"I was thinking that I should have married you sooner."

He chuckled and pulled her closer. "Amen to that. You most certainly should have. About ten years ago, but the waiting makes it all that much sweeter." He kissed her lips, then murmured, "I love you, Mrs. Daniels. We spent a good many years and a lot of traveling to find each other, didn't we? But nothing will come between us now. And don't worry. Hensley *will* meet us at Carson Sink with supplies, just like J.B. promised."

His words faded away into the darkness. After a few moments she felt him drift away into contented sleep. She ran a hand over his head of dark hair and pressed a kiss as soft as a rose petal to his throat, feeling the sweet stab of day-old stubble. She thought about tomorrow and California and what Joe Walker had said. And she hoped above hope that Hart was right.

A series of crashing noises interspersed with two strident voices—one male and one female—brought Hart and Nancy awake to the gray predawn of the next day.

"What in the world?" Nancy sat up, reaching for her clothes. "What's going on?"

Hart pulled on his pants. "Sounds like Brenham and Lucille having another argument."

"I swear, I don't think anybody would fault him a bit if he broke that chamber pot over that woman's head—without emptying it. She's the most contemptible person I believe I've ever known, outside of Arthur Waite, that is."

Dressed haphazardly, and pulling on coats against the chilly morning air, they joined the others to see what was causing the ruckus.

"You can't do this, Lucille," Brenham was saying, his face as red as a poker left in the fire.

"I don't see you stopping me, you spineless toad." With that she tossed Brenham's shotgun out the back of the wagon. It hit a box of spilled clothes—his—and made a cracking sound of wood against wood. Brenham raced to gather the precious firearm and inspect it for damage.

"I'm taking this wagon to Oregon and you won't stop me," she announced. Next came a hatchet, a hammer, and a box of shotgun shells. The last scattered and disappeared into the sagebrush.

"You've completely lost your mind." Brenham stared at her in utter disbelief. "How do you think you can drive a wagon all the way to Oregon when you don't even know how to hitch up a team?"

She threw out a sledgehammer that tumbled end over end and smacked Brenham in the shin. Then she stood in the wagon with her hands on her hips, satisfied as she watched him dance around on one leg, cursing in pain. But it was a male voice that answered Brenham's question.

"She won't have to drive, Brenham." Arthur Waite sauntered forward and placed himself in front of the wagon. "Because I'm going to drive for her."

A gasp rose from the group of women. The men waited for the next boot to fall.

Arthur's beady eyes sought out Miriam, and found her among the women. Perhaps she was too stunned to say anything, but she seemed as unmoved by the declaration as the other onlookers. He spoke in a voice loud enough for everyone to hear, and his tone was clearly meant to humiliate her, as if this public speech wouldn't be adequate enough.

"I'm leaving you, Miriam," he declared arrogantly. "And I'm taking all the boys except the two youngest—and the baby, of course. I could say I'm sorry to be doing this, but I'm not. I've tolerated your insolence for seventeen years. Maybe now you'll realize all the mistakes you made that drove me away."

It was quite amazing how easily the matter was settled. There were no arguments. Brenham simply didn't seem to care that Lucille was leaving. If anything, he acted greatly relieved, muttering that, "Arthur can sit and smell the stench of your infernal chamber pot now. Good riddance to you both." And nobody knew for sure if he meant her and the chamber pot, or her and Arthur.

Brenham proceeded to gather up the belongings Lucille had dumped in the sagebrush. But when Lucille tried to gather up her two daughters, she found to her surprise that the girls refused to go with her. They took a position on either side of their father and made their own declarations of independence.

"I won't go with that nasty, ugly Mr. Waite," Elise said.

"And his nasty, ugly boys," Beth added. "We're going with Papa. Besides, he doesn't cuss us the way you do."

Humiliated that her children would choose Brenham over her, Lucille covered her shock by tossing her head indignantly. "This is the gratitude I get for birthing you and raising you? Well, suit yourself. You'll regret it one of these days."

Arthur took one of the two wagons he and Miriam had left Independence with, leaving her the worst of the two. The oldest boy would drive it, as he had been doing. Waite also took all the tools, extra parts, gears, harnesses, etc. Miriam stood by and said nothing as Arthur and Lucille and the six boys headed out in a hurry to catch up with the Oregon company camped upriver. Brenham stood in the sagebrush with his belongings piled around him and no wagon to put them in.

Miriam seemed the first to see a solution to his problem. "You might as well put that stuff of yours in my wagon, Brenham. Ain't nothin' left in there now anyway."

Clearly relieved for a solution to his dilemma, Brenham brightened. "I can drive the wagon for you, Miriam. I wouldn't know what to do if I wasn't up on the seat behind a team."

"That's a fair trade-off. Let's get it done then."

The wagons pulled out from Fort Hall right after seven o'clock on September 17, feeling the nip of fall in the air as they followed the left bank of the mighty Snake River.

The California company, now turned over to Joe Walker, watched J.B. Chiles ride on ahead with thirteen men, including Pierson Reading,

Samuel Hensley, and the four Williams brothers. With them went twenty-six horses and mules and lean provisions for ten days.

Walker and the remainder of the men, some two dozen, were left to get the women and children and livestock to the Sierras, and hopefully over them. Walker had never traveled with wagons before, but intended on taking them through the same route he had followed back in 1833.

Lottie and Nancy hadn't bought another wagon at Fort Hall. What provisions and possessions they had salvaged from the Bear River incident had been loaded on the mules. Each, including Josh, rode and led a string. Nancy had had to switch permanently to one of Major's saddles, for it was easier to lead the mules while riding astride than aside. Her sidesaddle was safely harbored in Garnet's wagon now that the young woman didn't have Ethan's belongings to "take up space," as she had said.

Torey Porter was clearly smitten with Garnet and still driving her wagon. He was out first thing each morning, hitching up her team. Many wondered if a relationship might be developing between them, but Garnet seemed interested only in Miriam's baby whom she took care of constantly and handed over to Miriam only when the child cried for his mother's breast. Miriam didn't seem to notice, much less resent the growing attachment between Garnet and baby Laramie. She seemed glad to be relieved of rearing one more child.

The California Trail

They left the Oregon Trail at Calder Creek and headed south. The Oregonians who had joined them on the Platte left their company to proceed on to Oregon. They were a small contingency once again, and, this time, blazing trail. They were not following the course taken by the Bidwell–Bartleson company of 1841. The latter had bypassed Fort Hall, turning south toward the Great Salt Lake from the soda springs on Bear River. It had not proved to be a good trail either, and the company had nearly perished trying to get across that wasteland between the Great Salt Lake and Mary's River.

From Calder Creek they crossed to the Raft River Valley and followed it southward to Goose Creek and Thousand Springs Creek. For a hundred miles, they struggled over three mountain divides on a treacherous trappers' trail not at all suitable for wagon travel. Day after day they scaled the frightening faces of inhospitable mountains, and descended their terrifying backsides. As many as sixteen mules, and every man on ropes, was often necessary to keep the wagons from crashing down the mountainsides. The scouts rode far ahead, sometimes being gone for two or three days at a time searching for a better route, but it seemed the only way around the mountains was through them.

The first snow brought an eerie hush to the land, and to the emigrants. Their numbers were small and the land illimitable and fearsome. They were so close to their destination, yet so far away. Their supplies ran disturbingly low, and all they saw for food were a few jackrabbits and sage grouse. The wagons were breaking down more frequently; the animals were tired, their feet sore; the grass was dry and sparse. And the snow, so early in the year, brought a fear too deep to voice.

But the snow didn't last. It was gone by the next morning and the warm autumn sun followed them to the head of Mary's River. At nooning, while all gathered about talking and resting, uplifting their spirits over the new milestone they had met, Miriam suddenly began to laugh. She laughed until tears streamed down her face. She laughed until she was doubled over. She laughed until she was down rolling in the middle of the pungent sage, in the middle of this godforsaken wilderness. She laughed until everyone thought she had gone mad.

When at last she lay still, out of breath and flat on her back looking up at the cobalt sky, she said, "Lucille Royal was a bigger fool than I thought."

19

October

The Mary's River switchbacked through the sterile, sagebrush plain worse than a sullen, gray sidewinder through a cactus patch. Only willows lined the Mary's banks, along with some wild currant bushes. But the berries were gone, harvested by the birds. And by the Digger Indians who ran naked and hungry through this bleak country, and whose fires flickered at night from the vastness like thousands of orange, watching eyes.

The smoke from the fires often left a haze over the barren valleys if there was no breeze to push it onward. It drifted into the immense, cloudless sky, smudging it a coppery hue. The sun shone through the haze like a giant ball of fire. Along with the smoke, the incessant dust filled the emigrants' lungs and covered their faces and hair and clothes in its fine, white powder. At first there was good grass in the valleys along the river, but there were no buffalo. No herds of elk or deer. Only small isolated bands of antelope, some jackrabbits, sage hens, sandhill cranes, and wolves that crouched near their encampments at night, envisioning solid meals in the form of their mules and horses and children.

The ubiquitous sagebrush plains lent themselves to mirages in the heat of late afternoon as the small party rolled ever westward toward dreams that had themselves become made of a delusionary substance. The end of this tiresome journey came closer each day as another twenty or thirty miles was put behind them. They hoped with the appearance of each new mountain range, thrust up like steeples from the flat desert floor, that they were witnessing the mighty wall of the Sierra Nevada. But each time a new range serrated the distant sky, Walker disappointed them with a negative shake of his head. Journey's end soon faded into a tireless horizon of snow-capped cordilleras, marching one after another until the final horizon became forever just beyond reach.

"We get up every morning to the same scene," Josh said, shaking his head with discouragement. "And we go to bed still looking at it. I feel like I'm in one of those dreams where you run and run but you never get anywhere." There was no singing and dancing at night by the campfires now, and very little conversation. Each individual found his thoughts moving inward, dwelling on what he had left behind, and wondering if the loss, the hardship, and the emptiness in his gut and in his heart could be fully negated by the golden fruits said to be waiting in California. Hunger began to gnaw like a rat trying to get out of a cage, and each and every one seriously began to doubt whether he would survive at all.

And then, one day, it was there—the Sierra Nevada. The culmination of a seemingly endless journey. From the distance, the mountains looked deceptively similar to those the emigrants had already crossed, but Walker reminded them that it was a hundred miles across those mountains, straight up and straight down, day after day, mile after treacherous mile, through heavy pine forest, deadly ravines, sheer cliffs, and snow. And they were still many days and many miles away from the mountains themselves. But the sight of the Sierra Nevada gave new hope to the California company. Just on the other side of that sheer granite wall was their destination. A little farther, and their ordeal would be over.

They headed onward across alkali flats where the grass shimmered in the temperate, October sunshine like salt crystals. Where, when they looked behind them, they could not see a trace of a wagon wheel or a horse's hoof print.

For nearly four hundred miles, that felt like four thousand, they had skirted the Mary's River. Now, toward its end, it disintegrated into a series of stagnant ponds, increasingly alkali to the taste. They came to boiling springs rimmed with salt and sulphur and tainted with more alkali. Even the grass was white with it.

"Whatever you do," Walker cautioned, "don't let your animals eat the grass or drink the water from these ponds."

Most of the time the animals refused to anyway, but the next morning they found one of Brenham's mules in the middle of a pond, dead.

"It's all my fault!" Beth started to cry. "I was the one who tied him up. Daddy told me to make sure the rope was good and tight—"

Brenham enfolded his youngest daughter in his arms. "It'll be all right, Beth. Things like this happen to all of us no matter how careful we think we're being. He'll supply a few days of meat to the company so his death is not a complete loss."

"I don't want to eat him! He was my favorite."

"God would want you to eat him so you can live to get to California."

"No, I won't eat him! He was my friend, and I killed him!"

That night under the stars, after Beth had finally cried herself to sleep, Lottie propped her hands beneath her head and lamented to everybody within earshot that, "This is the deadest goddamn chunk of earth I've ever laid eyes on. It *would* have to be right on the way to California."

"It's not the worst there is," Walker's deep voice came back from the dark.

"And I suppose you're going to show us something worse come morning."

Walker's only response was a baritone laugh.

"I think there's an austere beauty about this place," Nancy ventured.

"I swear, girl, you'd find something pretty about a dried-up horse biscuit," Lottie proclaimed. "But I do admire your optimism."

Nancy couldn't argue that this land was bleak, but she thought it spectacular at night when the cold moon cast a white, surrealistic glow onto the ragged mountain peaks towering over the broad, flat basin. It could have been another planet far out in the black reaches of space where the stars shone so close and clear that they, too, were beyond reality. But she wouldn't say that. No, she'd be the laughingstock of the company for sure if she started waxing poetic.

The California company had exchanged the intense heat of summer for the cold nights of late fall. Fires were made of dry willows and sagebrush and stoked high. The emigrants didn't worry about attracting the attention of the Indians, for the Indians had known all along that they were there. A few were always seen, following at a curious but safe distance. Sometimes they ran right up to the wagons on their fleet, bare feet and offered friendly greetings. Their nakedness mortified the women and made the children giggle before their mothers could hide their young, curious eyes.

"Don't be misled by their friendliness," Walker had warned. "They're looking to see what we have so they can sneak into our camp after dark and steal it. Make your weapons visible so they'll know the firepower they will face if they try anything."

The Indians always wanted to trade, and they offered dried meat and roots, and pouches made of furs and leathers. But the meat looked to be gopher. It was questionable as to whether the roots were even edible, and the pouches were virtually useless to the emigrants.

No trading was conducted, but Walker appeased the Diggers by occasionally giving them a little bread. The emigrants had very few provisions left with which to barter. They were subsisting on bread and what game could be killed. Hart and Charles McIntosh went out each day to hunt. Nancy worried that the hungry Diggers would ambush the two men, kill them with their crude weapons, and eat their horses. But each night Hart came back to her. Most times, he and McIntosh had bagged something, even if it was only a few sage hens.

By the time they reached the Carson Sink in late October, where the Mary's River vanished into the ground, Nancy was beginning to suspect her pregnancy. She had gone fifteen days past menses and was beginning to feel a queasiness in her stomach. That the provisions were getting low didn't help. The meat didn't settle well on her stomach unless it was dried, and she threw it up most of the time. Bread wasn't any better, possibly worse, for it came up as globby chunks of yeasty matter. She could not drink coffee nor suffer its smell. She sought unleavened bread and hot tea, but oftentimes even that could not be digested.

It became evident here, too, that getting over the mountains would be next to impossible, even if J.B. and his men had somehow found a pass to the north. New snow crowned the distant peaks. In a few weeks, winter would settle in. Those emigrants from the East or the South who did not understand these western lands argued that it was early yet, and it was worth a try to at least "look around a bit."

"We can manage a little snow," Brenham said stubbornly.

"A little snow, yes," Hart had countered. "But that's all you boys have seen compared to what will fall in these mountains in a few weeks. It piles deep, up to twenty feet or more. Once there, it won't melt until spring. The animals even leave for lower pastures. There's nothing to eat, men, unless you think you can subsist off pine needles and bark."

The argument ended. Instead, the small group kept looking toward the solid granite outcropping, hoping to see Samuel Hensley come riding down toward them with provisions and information about a pass, perhaps one like the South Pass which had taken them easily over the spine of the Rockies. But there was no sign of Hensley.

Hart and Walker and some of the other men formed a circle around one of the campfires that night. The women had put the children to bed with their rations of meat and bread. Worry etched its lines in all their faces as they joined the men.

"Chiles has probably gotten himself lost," Bartlett Vines, Frances's husband said.

"Or killed by Indians," Julius Martin put in. "That country he headed into past Fort Boise was virtually unexplored."

"Or he just plain abandoned us," Torey added.

"I've known J.B. for years," Billy Baldridge countered angrily. "He'll try his damnedest to get here. He isn't a man to go back on his word. If he isn't here, it's because he's run into problems. You can say he ran out on us, but he knew if they all stayed we'd have run out of food long before now."

"We don't have time to spare, but we ought to give him at least a few more days to meet the rendezvous," Hart said.

Thane spoke up. "A few of us men could head into the mountains and see if we could find a pass."

Walker rubbed the knotted muscles in the back of his neck. "I've told you all what you're facing by heading into those mountains this time of year, and I won't jeopardize the lives of the women and children. We're going to have to head south now, one way or the other. The alternate plan if Hensley missed this rendezvous was for Chiles to have a man meet us at Four Creeks on the other side of Walker Pass. We've got to stick to our plan."

"But we're nearly out of food," Thane argued, getting up to pace around the group. "Maybe a few of us could try to get over and come back with some supplies. I don't see how we'll last going all the way south with no provisions. And the hunting around here sure isn't anything to write home about."

"It's foolhardy to keep splitting up, Thane," Lottie said. "There ain't many of us now and we need to stick together. We all knew it might come down to this when we left Missouri. If we have to, we'll eat the damned mules and walk. There ain't nothin' wrong with any of our legs, except for Nancy who's sick. We need to keep that in mind and take the easier course for her sake. And we need to listen to Walker and Hart and the others who've been in those mountains. I don't know much about snow, but if it's gonna get past my boot tops, I'm willing to stay clear of it."

November

They waited at the Sink for eight days to give Hensley a chance to meet the rendezvous. When he didn't show, they pulled out, heading south into a desert country worse than that which they had just traversed. Here the sand was deep, pulling at wheels and hooves. The heat wasn't bad being early November, but the dust billowed up around the emigrants in the still, dead air, clogging their throats and noses and forcing them to cover all but their eyes with bandanas. The only sounds across this alkali waste-land were those of the harness chains clinking, the snapping of whips when mules wanted to lay down and die, the strained cursing of mule-skinners whose throats were raw from the dry heat and lack of water. And the hungry cries of baby Laramie.

The fact that they had rested their teams for eight days, fattening them on the grass around the Sink, helped tremendously in getting across a waterless stretch of forty miles to the first river that flowed out of the Sierras. In two days' time they connected with another river flowing east-ward, and later a lake, which they named after Walker.

It was all Nancy could do to stay in the saddle across this forty-mile desert. The dust choked her and aggravated her nausea. She began to vomit and grew weaker by the mile.

Hart turned the scouting over to McIntosh and rode next to Nancy. "Let me make a place in one of the wagons so you can lie down," he coaxed.

She gripped the saddle horn and tried to swallow down another wave of nausea. "There isn't room, Hart. I couldn't ask anyone to leave their personal belongings behind when we've come so far."

Walker, having also joined them to check on her condition, rode alongside them. "I haven't wanted to say this, but only the necessaries will be with us when this journey is over. Leaving them here instead of a hundred miles from here won't make any difference."

Nancy held firm. "I won't be the reason any of these ladies has to lose something precious. Besides, riding in a wagon over this terrain would be harder than riding horseback."

"At least ride in my saddle in front of me," Hart said. "I'm afraid you're going to pass out, Nancy."

Finally she conceded. But while she leaned back against Hart's chest and dozed in the security of his arms, a peculiar fear pervaded her and she wondered if she might get so weak that she would simply die. She had always been physically and mentally strong, and prided herself in that, but she felt both capacities greatly deteriorating with each new day. The vomiting came more frequently and stayed longer until there was no respite from it even in the middle of the night. This sickness was out of her control; there was absolutely nothing she could do to diminish it.

She willed herself to keep going, although it became an agonizing ordeal just to hold her head up. She relished the nights when she could lie on her blankets in the tent and give into the weariness and the weakness, and sink into peaceful inertia. But there was danger in that too, because she found it increasingly more difficult to rise in the morning.

That night at Walker Lake, Nancy crept outside the tent, being forced to empty the contents of her stomach into the scrub brush. From her tent, she went to the edge of the water and repeatedly splashed it over her heated face. Her head was tight and achy, her body shaky from the lack of food and the constant vomiting. She leaned back into the dry grass that bordered the lake and stared up at the stars in the desert sky. It was cold, and she pulled her shawl closer, wishing she'd worn her coat.

The men had managed to shoot two ducks that were flying off the lake, but there hadn't been enough meat to go around so they had given it to the children and Miriam. Miriam hadn't wanted to take it, but since she was nursing the baby, everyone had insisted. They had tried to give some to Nancy, too, but she refused, knowing she would be unable to keep it down and felt it would be better put to use if it went into someone else's stomach.

Now she placed a hand to her abdomen. It was flat and gave no indication of the life growing inside. Wouldn't it be ironic, even cruel, if God were to end her life just when she had found love and a future worth pursuing?

A rustle in the grass made her sit up with a start, but she immediately relaxed when she saw Hart. His presence always buoyed her spirit, and she managed a weak smile for him. He settled down behind her and enveloped her in the security of his embrace.

"I woke up and found you gone," he whispered, brushing her damp hair from her forehead. "You had me worried."

"I'm sorry. I was . . . sick again, and I didn't want to keep you from your sleep."

"You need to find something to help you stop vomiting, Nancy," he said worriedly. "You haven't kept anything down for days now. You can't go on without nutrition. Hasn't that raspberry leaf tea that Frances gave you been doing any good?"

Nancy swallowed hard against another wave of nausea. She somehow felt she had failed Hart by being so sick. She hated weakness in any person and now she was facing it in herself. She had always prided herself on being so strong. What was wrong with her anyway? Pregnancy shouldn't be debilitating. "No," she replied in answer to his question. "My stomach rejects it as quickly as everything else. But maybe it's just all the dust and the traveling."

Hart held her tighter, and she felt his fear as if it were as tangible as his strong arms around her. He who was always in control, and so much a master over the ills of man and nature, was as helpless as she. This child they had created frightened him. Her illness frightened him.

"Talk to Frances again tomorrow, will you?" He slid his hands down over her shoulders and put his cheek to hers. "See if there's some other herb that will help you. You need your strength, Nancy. I don't want anything to happen to either you or the baby, and, believe me, the worst of this journey is not over yet."

December

They continued south through a valley hemmed in by desolately bare mountains to the east, and the towering Sierras to the west. Beyond Walker Lake a definite route became harder to discern. Wagon travel became nearly impossible as they picked their way around hot springs and cruel upheavals of black basaltic rock. Grass was nearly nonexistent. The animals weakened dramatically.

The emigrants were not much better off themselves. The cries of the children came more frequently; their parents' desperation bleaker.

Josh endured better than most. If anything, the boy thrived on the adversity. He met the challenge of survival head on, relished it, and looked for ways to conquer it. He spent every day catching grasshoppers in a glass jar, and frogs at the streams. At the end of the day he fried the grasshoppers and frog legs and shared them with Harry, who was little more than a rack of bones. Nobody fought Josh for his unique meals. More than once they ate rattlesnake meat and drank brackish water. Starvation marched close beside them now, but most refused to dwell on just how close.

They started killing the mules, one by one. After the third, Nancy called Hart to her side that night in their tent and gripped his hand with all her strength. Her eyes were sunken and dull, the skin around them dark and bruised looking. Her cheekbones protruded. The bones in her hands stood out. Even her beautiful hair had lost its luster. Hart silently feared she was dying right before his eyes, but there was nothing to be had to alleviate her body's incompatibility to the baby growing inside.

"If I die, don't let them kill Lady Rae. At least not until the end, the very end, after all the mules are gone." She took his hand in hers, squeezing his fingers with a desperate sort of strength. Her eyes beseeched him, sought his unequivocal promise.

"You're not going to die."

"Promise me, Hart."

He fell into the depths of her eyes, thinking he wouldn't be able to bear life without her. "I promise."

At Owens Lake they abandoned the wagons. They carried so few provisions now that it seemed senseless to struggle along with the wagons any longer, putting undue burden on the emaciated animals.

Billy was possibly the hardest hit by this decision. Reluctantly he cached his sawmill machinery, burying it in the sandy soil. "I got so close," he said. "There was no goddamned point in hauling it all this way."

"You can come back for it," Hart suggested, feeling for the man's loss.

Billy just cast the Sierras a contemptuous glare, shook his head, and never mentioned the machinery again.

The women and children, the remaining provisions, and all essentials were loaded on the mules. Hart made a litter for Nancy, pulling it behind his buckskin.

Peaks towered over them, half veiled in clouds and tipped with snow. But the snow seemed the only living thing, if one wanted to consider it an entity. This dry, treeless, and forlorn slash of country was not the California of their dreams.

"It's beautiful up north, Nancy," Hart promised, holding her close in his arms that night and trying desperately to give her enough hope and encouragement that she would fight for life. "There's a hill that overlooks the Cosumnes River. It's about the prettiest view you ever saw, and, if you like it, we'll build the house there."

Nancy smiled weakly and ran a finger along his cheek before her arm dropped to her side and her eyes closed again. "Are there trees?"

"Oh, yes. Plenty of trees."

"Then I'm sure I'll love it, Hart."

Later that night, while Nancy slept in a rare moment of peace, Hart went quietly to Lottie's tent, needing someone to talk to about Nancy's condition. Thankfully she was awake and willing to listen. Josh was asleep and Hart settled himself at the foot of the boy's blankets.

"You don't look like you're holding up too well, Hart."

He ran a shaky hand through his hair. "I'm scared, Lottie. So damned scared. I'm afraid she's going to die, and there's not a thing I can do to stop it. I should have waited until we got to California to marry her, but I never dreamed . . ."

Lottie touched his hand in friendship and understanding. "Some women can't handle pregnancy very well, Hart. Others never get sick. I've seen women like Nancy. They're strong women otherwise, but the change their bodies go through during pregnancy is violent. Most of the time, though, this sickness eases at the third or fourth month."

Hart shook his head, all hope gone. "She won't last that long, Lottie. She's starving to death right before my eyes. She might have a chance if I had her in a home, in bed with somebody tending to her. But hell, we've got five hundred miles left to go!"

Lottie took a deep breath and released it, knowing full well how bad the situation was, but she didn't want to think about anything happening to Nancy, who had been an honest and true friend. A woman who had never, not for a moment, judged her by her rough ways and lack of Eastern etiquette.

"She's tough, Hart. She'll make it. Besides, she's got a lot to live for, and she'll fight."

Moisture sparkled in his eyes. "If she dies, it's my fault . . . for putting that baby inside of her."

Lottie was dismayed. "Don't be silly, Hart. All you did was love her. Now, you get on back there with her. Keep making her drink the tea. Maybe some of it will stay down."

So Hart returned to Nancy's side and, once again, curved his body close to hers. He wanted his vibrant Nancy back. The woman who had ridden, laughing, next to him over the prairies, making dreams and seeing far into the distance and the future with wonder and excitement in her eyes.

It was sometime later, as he lay praying, that he felt a warm wetness soaking through his pants leg. He sat up, moving slightly so the fire's glow lit the blankets they lay upon. Peering through the darkness, he saw the dark splotch against the gray bedding. Panic leaped into the pit of his stomach and rose, tightening like eagle's claws around his heart and throat. He placed a finger to the wetness, and simultaneously his nostrils were stung by a familiar, metallic smell. The smell of blood. Nancy's blood.

20

While Hart ran to get help, Nancy lay in silent shock in the darkness of their tent. Only the flickering light of the fire kept the world in focus while she felt the heavy gush of warm wetness between her legs, coating her nightclothes and the blankets, and leaving her to wonder how many minutes or hours she had before death summoned her. She had left Amherst expecting to be scalped or drowned or starved to death, but bleeding to death had never been on her list of possibilities. How ironic, after worrying that hemorrhaging might be Lottie's fate, to have it be her own.

Frances and Miriam arrived with Lottie. Before long, Garnet and Elizabeth were there, too, trying to calm her fears, and offering what assistance and support they could.

"You're not dying. You're miscarrying," Miriam told her. "Now, don't worry. You'll be all right." But something in the older woman's eyes—or maybe it was the way she looked away when she said that last—suggested that she wasn't at all certain.

What Nancy was to remember later about that night was not the bleeding or the fear of dying, but the women. Her friends. And how they had all bustled about, cleaning up her clothes and bedding and preparing pads to catch the blood. How they'd made tea and broth and encouraged her to eat. She remembered Lottie spoon-feeding her and saying, "Come on, girl. I wouldn't have found the nerve to come out here if you hadn't found yours first. So you remember that and don't leave me to face California alone."

"That's right," Miriam had reiterated. "Your courage and passion for life is what gave the rest of us the strength to go on when we didn't see no point in taking another step."

And there had been Garnet, saying very little and staying out of the way by positioning herself next to Nancy, holding her hand, smoothing her hair back from her face, crooning soothing words as if she were a child, and all the while understanding fully her pain and her loss. All the girl ever actually said was, "You're the only one who has ever really listened to me, Nancy. Maybe I never had much of anything important to say, but I do know that it's better to lose the baby now than later . . ."

The bleeding had slowed, seemingly of its own volition, after the expelling of the tiny fetus. But Frances had told Joe Walker, in an uncompromising voice, that he and the men had better go hunting and bide their time because Nancy could *not* be moved. Her voice had carried across the camp and past the thin walls of Nancy's tent, "We've been in this godforsaken wilderness for so long, a few more days won't mean diddle."

At the end of four days, Nancy felt stronger and the bleeding had diminished dramatically. Hart ducked into the tent to check her progress, as he had a hundred times a day. He had worried and doted over her, and done everything the women had told him to do, and everything he could think to do that might make things easier for her. Mostly, he had been there with his loving eyes, caressing touch, and encouraging kisses. This time he carried a mug of soup in one hand, and a cup of hot tea in the other.

"Time to eat," he announced, settling down next to her.

She brushed a limp strand of hair away from her cheek. "It smells wonderful. Do I dare ask what it is?"

His smile made her so thankful she was alive that she reached her hand out and touched it. In turn, he kissed her fingertips. "Yours is jackrabbit soup," he said, when she had lowered her hand back to her side. "The meat cooking over the spit outside is horse meat." He saw the flash of alarm in her eyes and hastened to calm her fears. "It was a wild horse, Nancy. There are so many of them in this country that it won't hurt for us to eat a few. We got into a herd of them yesterday. The one we killed was an old mare that was lame. The wolves would have taken her down anyway."

Nancy nodded, knowing that it was better to eat one of the wild horses, than one of their own. "I'm sorry to hold everybody up," she said, voicing a regret that had been on her mind from the beginning of her ordeal. "We really need to be getting on."

"We're in no hurry. It's not like we're trying to outrun the snow this far south. We're on Walker Pass. From here on, it'll be all downhill—so to speak," he added with a grin meant to lighten her mood.

"We may not be running from the snow, Hart, but we're running from starvation."

"We're doing all right," he insisted, not telling her that horse and mule meat was about all there was left. Their other supplies—flour, sugar, salt—were depleted. "Now, come on. Eat this soup while it's still hot."

He helped her sit up against a stack of bedding and placed the bowl in her hands because she was strong enough now to feed herself. He talked to her while she ate but didn't tell her how many times he'd thanked God for sparing her.

When she finished the soup, she drank the tea, then she nestled down close against him. He kissed her forehead and the tip of her nose. Then suddenly his arms tightened around her and a rush of emotion overcame him. "You scared me, Nancy," he said in a choked whisper. "You scared me so damned bad. I was afraid I was going to lose you. I can see now how selfish I was to encourage you to come along, but I fell in love with you from the moment I saw you, and I wanted you with me, come what may. I made you suffer by . . . by getting you with child."

Nancy pulled back, dismayed by his words. "Hart Daniels, don't ever say such a foolish thing." She ran her hand alongside his clenched jaw. "*Our* baby didn't get there by your doing alone."

He buried his face in her neck, attempting to get a grip on his emotions. "I know, but I should have waited until we got to California before making you my wife. When I think that carrying this child could have killed you . . ."

She ran soothing fingers along his face and through his dark hair. "How could either of us have known? I'll be fine now, Hart. And everything else will be fine, too. I came out here wanting to live—to *really* live. To experience things I couldn't have back home. I've accomplished that, and I'll never regret one second of it. You are a part of that, and I don't want you to regret any of it either."

Tenderly, he placed his hands on either side of her face while his eyes searched hers, probing deeply into her soul. "I could never regret one moment of life spent with you," he whispered. "Never, my love. Never."

December
Sutter's Fort

"Riders comin' in, Captain Sutter."

John Augustus Sutter looked up from his diary at the young messenger, Frayne Nye, standing in the doorway. Setting his pen carefully on a blotter and closing his book, Sutter pushed his chair back and rose. With very precise movements, he tugged his vest down to his waist and reached for his overcoat.

"Can you tell who it is?" he patiently asked, thinking that Nye should have offered the information without being prompted to do so.

"Appears to be Colonel Chiles and his men, sir. They're comin' back alone."

Sutter's head snapped up, his eyebrows shot together. "Oh, that is not good."

He finished pulling on his coat as he left his office and trotted down one side of the double-approach stairs that hugged the main building's outside wall. He was waiting in the courtyard when guards swung the big wooden gates wide for Chiles's entry. Looking extremely disheartened from the ride to Four Creeks and back, Chiles and his four men dismounted.

"You did not find them?" Sutter asked, fearing the worst.

Chiles shook his head, his eyes revealing the dismal weariness from months on the trail. "No. We couldn't even pick up their trail. We waited for days and then I rode to Walker Pass. They should have been there. Unless they never made it that far." He shook his head, beside himself with worry. "They were a small party, undermanned. Anything could have happened. Indians. Starvation. I shouldn't have left them back in Fort Hall."

"Don't blame yourself, Colonel," Sutter tried to ease the Missourian's distress. "You would have been there sooner had you not run into so many obstacles yourself coming from Fort Boise. But don't worry. It's easy to miss trails in a country as big as California. Walker, Daniels, McIntosh—all of them know how to survive. The women and children are in good hands, wherever they are."

"Yes," Chiles nodded bleakly. "Wherever they are. What if the damned Mexicans have taken them prisoner for being in the country without passports?"

"Then we shall find out and demand their release. I am very well acquainted with Governor Micheltorena, and I am sure that if that is their fate, I can remedy the situation."

If they haven't been lined up in front of a firing squad, Chiles wanted to say.

"They will find their way here," Sutter said confidently. "Now, you and your men need to rest and eat. From my calculations you have been on that mule for eight months."

Chiles managed a wan smile. "Your calculations are correct."

One of Sutter's Indians, acting more as slaves than employees, took the tired animals to be fed and brushed down. Chiles and his three men followed Sutter to the dining room. Sutter, always a cordial host and gentleman, tried again to ease Chiles's fears by striking up a light conversation. Chiles tried to reciprocate, although he was bone tired and too worried to completely block out his concerns for his friends.

He and his thirteen men had run into their share of troubles as soon as they'd arrived at Fort Boise. The commander of the post, Francis Payette, had had very little food, but had decided that sending them out with nothing was inhuman so he had given them enough for fifteen days. He had then drawn them a map that would take them about halfway to the Sacramento Valley, following the Malheur River. But they had been forced to leave its deep-chasmed ravine frequently in order to make passage. The savages along the river were hostile, and had dogged their steps, coming close to their camp at night and stealing whenever the opportunity arose.

They'd headed into the Sierras, continually dogged by snowstorms, bitter cold, driving winter winds, and starvation for both them and their animals. The country was so rough that the animals, their hooves badly torn from the rocks, could barely make the steep grades, and the men had been forced to walk and lead the discouraged, exhausted creatures.

They had arrived at Sutter's Fort too late for Hensley to head eastward over the Sierra to Carson Sink. The snow in the mountains was too deep by then, and he had been advised against it. Chiles had immediately set about collecting provisions to head south to the Four Creeks rendezvous. But he had either not arrived soon enough again, or hadn't waited long enough. It gnawed at him that Walker and the others might have been later than expected getting to the pass due to unforeseen hardships like those his own party had experienced.

Over wine, Joseph Chiles thought about Lottie England, Nancy Maguire Daniels, and the other women. Never had he met such outstanding, persevering women. He should have been there for them. They had been his responsibility and he had failed them. Had his dreams of being the first to discover a wagon road over the Sierras blinded him? He had justified splitting the party up because of lack of food—and it had seemed necessary at the time—but deep down inside could he have been driven by a stronger force? He had known they couldn't make the Sierras in time to find a suitable pass for wagons, so he had grown restless, turned the plodding wagons over to Walker—and set out to explore. He'd left his friend, Billy, to get the sawmill machinery over the mountains, the sawmill that had been *his* idea. He'd jeopardized the lives of his men, and that of those good women, for a taste of glory. An elusive, insipid taste of glory.

December 25th
Salinas River Valley

Hart helped Nancy from the litter and assisted her the few feet to the blanket spread out beneath the grove of trees. His eyes were still shadowed with worry for her, as they had been for the past week since they'd been on the trail again.

She removed her hat, and he automatically smoothed a stray strand of hair from off her forehead. The way the back of his hand lingered, she knew he was really checking to make sure a fever had not developed.

He hadn't wanted her to travel so soon after the loss of the baby, but hunger had finally forced them to continue down out of the southern mountains, north to the San Joaquin River and then across the valley toward the coastal range. Walker had headed them toward the Californio settlements and to the headwaters of the Salinas River where he knew the game was more plentiful, rather than head up the San Joaquin valley in their present, weakened state to Sutter's Fort that still lay two hundred fifty miles to the north.

While Sutter could give passports, most of the single men chose to go to Monterey and acquire them there. Most were anxious, too, for some female companionship and a taste of liquor, although they wouldn't say so in front of the ladies. Thane had had a starved look in his eyes that didn't come from an empty stomach when he had said, "I'd like to get in on one of those fandangos I've heard about and do a little foot-stomping with some pretty Californio girls."

Walker had been right about the game available in the coastal mountains. The men had already bagged a deer, several turkeys, and McIntosh had even brought down a mountain sheep. They were bustling about now, setting up camp and building campfires.

"I'm going to take care of the horses," Hart said. "Don't try to do anything, Nancy. Just lie down and rest."

"I really should help," she argued, knowing full well that she didn't feel up to it yet. "The other women are going to tire of tending to me."

"Nonsense. They want you well as much as I do. Now, no arguments." He rose but she caught his hand and drew him back down to her side.

"Do you know what day this is, Hart?"

He shook his head. "I guess I've lost track."

"Well, I haven't. I've been marking it down in my journal. Today is Christmas. Our first Christmas together, and I have absolutely nothing to give you."

"And I have nothing to give you, except my love." He held her face gently in his hands and caressed it with a slow, circular stroke of his thumbs.

"Love is fitting for our first Christmas. Still . . ." She faded off with obvious yearning for a gift to give.

He kissed away her further attempt to rue the destitution of their situation.

"Hey, Hart!" Billy Baldridge hollered good-naturedly. "You'd better quit that before you make the rest of us jealous. Come and tend to your horses."

Grinning, Hart kissed Nancy one last time then left her to keep from being accused of shirking his duties.

As she watched the others bustle about the encampment with new vitality, she told herself that she would just rest for a minute and then get up and help in some way. But she fell asleep. When she awoke two hours later it was to the smell of venison, turkey, and mountain sheep cooking on spits over hot coals, and to a gaggle of childish laughter as Josh and Harry chased the girls around the encampment. The women spoke in the liveliest tones she'd heard since leaving Fort Hall, and they moved with lightness in their steps despite their worn shoes and ragged clothes.

Brenham hollered for the children not to get too far away. "There could be bears out there," he warned. "Or Indians."

But his threat didn't slow the children who had found new life and new hope with all the fresh water they could drink and with the smell of something besides mule or horse meat wafting through the air. Soon they were chanting, "No bears out tonight. Daddy shot them all last night. No bears out tonight . . ."

Shortly Josh metamorphosed into a bear, and the girls' screams reached a shrill, ear-piercing pitch as they scrambled to escape him.

The women gathered the food onto what plates had survived the journey and filled everyone's tin cup with cold, sparkling water; there was no coffee or tea left. Everyone gathered around the fires, sitting close in, facing each other, as if from across tables covered with fine linen and sparkling china.

Joe Walker lifted his tin cup. "Since this is Christmas, let's all make a toast." A round of hearty agreement went up among the trail-weary group. Joe continued in a solemn voice. "I would like to toast all of you for sticking with me and persevering when I'm sure you were beginning to think I'd never get you here."

One by one, the group had their turn at making a toast. Some voices were soft, some bold and loud.

"A toast to Colonel Chiles. I hope him and the other boys are still alive and that they found that dang-blasted wagon pass."

"A toast to the future."

"A toast to life."

"A toast to this here food. By God, it was a long time coming."

"A toast to those pretty Californian girls, waiting breathlessly all these years for this handsome Yankee boy to arrive."

"A toast to the perseverance of Brenham's ex-wife. If she had gone back to Independence like she'd wanted to do, I would never have found mine."

"A *salute* to my ex-wife. I never thought she would do it, but I never gave up hope."

"A toast to Major, the no-good bum. If he hadn't been scalped, I wouldn't be here right now among some of the finest friends I've ever known."

"A toast to my mule, Uriah. I'm sure glad he didn't give out gettin' here, 'cause I don't think I could have eaten him."

"A toast to my parents back in Missouri. I wish they were here so they could meet my wife, Nancy."

Silence fell over the group as Hart's eyes lifted to Nancy's, filled with unconcealed love.

The last one to make a toast, Nancy slowly lifted her cup. Meeting Hart's gaze as if the two of them were the only ones present, she concluded, "A toast to California. May she always be as beautiful as she is tonight."

TWO

The Californios

*"He may fight you on the field, but in his family,
you may dance with his daughters,
and he will himself wake the waltzing string."*

Walter Colton

21

January, 1844

The white adobes of Monterey, with their red clay tile roofs, dotted the wooded hillsides and lay carelessly scattered along the edge of the beach. With a somnolent quality, they overlooked the storm-tossed, winter bay. The uncobbled streets were empty; silent. The village's inhabitants—sailors, soldiers, Californios, and a few adventurers of numerous nationalities—were all sequestered away in homes or in oceanfront bordellos and cantinas, finding refuge from the cold wind that whipped up whitecaps and pushed the waves onto the white sand with a pounding roar.

Trading vessels, with their sails pulled in tightly to their masts, crowded the half-moon harbor and cluttered the lower horizon. The rays of the noonday sun, giving the illusion of warmth, glinted over seagulls' wings in flashes of silver. And far out to the north, the sky ran gray into the gray sea and disappeared.

The crashing sound of the ocean reached up the hill to the second-story balcony of Thomas and Rachel Larkin's house. A number of the Walker party had been invited to stay with the Larkins upon their arrival in Monterey a week ago. From her vantage point on the balcony, Nancy could see the Royal girls and Frances's daughters playing with Josh and Harry down on the expansive lawn surrounding the Larkin house. The men, waiting to be called for dinner, had gathered on the veranda below the balcony to smoke and talk. Their voices drifted up to her now, quite audible.

"Why not just take the province with a little gun power and get the matter settled once and for all so we can get on with our business," Pierson Reading heatedly proclaimed. "We wouldn't even have to involve Washington."

Thomas O. Larkin gave Reading's opinion his patient consideration and then proceeded to explain his own. "The Americans are greatly outnumbered here, Pierson. Although acquisition might be accomplished by a cleverly planned coup, I would strongly advise against doing anything not orchestrated by Washington. An ill-conceived or hasty plan might jeopardize the lives of the Americans living here.

"As you might know," Larkin continued, punctuating his words with gesticulations, "Governor Manuel Micheltorena has an army of three hundred unpaid Mexican prisoners who were granted freedom by promising service to their country as soldiers. These *cholos* are a most disreputable lot, I can assure you. But Mexico sent them believing that with their show of power, Micheltorena could gain control, once and for all, over the wayward and indifferent colony of Californios. *Except* that from the very beginning Micheltorena had no control over his new 'army.' They immediately squelched any success he might have had by quickly earning the people's contempt for themselves as well as the governor. Their initial march from San Diego to Monterey was little more than a rampage of rape and plunder, sparing few Californios in their path."

The men listened with rapt attention as Larkin, the most knowledgeable on the matter, filled them in on more details. "The Californios are more than weary of this sort of governmental 'attention.' Most of them, from the sentiments I've heard, want California to be an independent republic. They would probably not mind if the province were even purchased by the United States, but would probably prefer being merely a protectorate of the United States. However, if the Americans come in and try to *seize* the country from the Californios, then that is an entirely different matter. One of integrity. And the Americans would likely feel the backlash of such an attempt.

"We would all be wise to watch the political struggles taking place here in California itself. The struggles for power among the Californios who consider this land theirs, not Mexico's, not the United States', nor any other foreign government's. But *theirs*—they who were born and raised here. The Californios are the ones you should watch, for they have the most to gain, or the most to lose, in the final outcome of the struggle over their homeland.

"You and other Americans wanting to make your homes here are anxious to bring this matter to a head, but let me assure you, I've been working on the peaceful annexation of California for years now, along with the President of the United States. I feel war can be avoided. The political leaders here in the province—such as they are—could, in my opinion, be easily convinced to declare their independence from Mexico and seek annexation with the United States. All without bloodshed.

"A diplomatic conclusion could be arrived at, and I've sent numerous reports to Washington stating this belief. I've also sent reports keeping the President informed of every political murmur that occurs on this side of the continent. We just need to bide our time and independence will be inevitable." Larkin concluded with a distinctive air of confidence.

"But the United States must move to keep Britain from stealing California out from under our noses," Pierson Reading persisted. "From what I'm led to believe, most Californios want freedom from Mexico but don't care *who* takes over, as long as they are allowed to continue living as they've always done. They could just as easily side with Britain."

"What of those Californios who maintain allegiance to Mexico?" Hart inserted. "A lot of them are uneasy about us Americans coming into their country. What's to say their complacency won't change when they start feeling threatened by more of us taking land and seeking positions of power in the Mexican government?"

"It's conceivable that they could join Micheltorena's army and put up a fight, or even form their own rebellion," Larkin responded. "That's why I firmly believe that we Americans must not take this matter into our own hands, but wait for the President's plan to unfold."

Nancy moved around to the other side of the balcony, not caring to hear any more of the discussion. She had come here with the hope, and the belief, that the Mexican government would sell the province to the United States, or that somehow American rule would triumph over all others. She didn't like to consider that bureaucratic bungling, or interference by overzealous Americans like Reading, might destroy all possibilities of such an outcome. Things had looked much simpler and brighter on the other side of the continent when not faced with the disturbing reality of so many variables.

It was too unsettling to think of war when all she wanted to do was get on with her life here in California with Hart. No, she much preferred the ocean's roar, over a half mile away, to the annoying discussion of politics that had prevailed nearly nonstop among men and women alike ever since they had arrived here. She had crossed a continent to get here, nearly died in the pursuit of her dream, and technically the journey was not over yet. She and Hart had over a hundred fifty miles yet to go before they would reach the land where Hart had said he wanted to settle. She was anxious to start on the plans they had made for their new home and future together. She felt fully recuperated and was anxious to begin.

From her position on the balcony, she was able to see this new world for miles in every direction. From the ocean before them, to the pine-covered coastal mountains curving around them in the shape of a crescent moon. It was young and beautiful, uncluttered, unharmed by man, untamed. And it was everything she had hoped it would be.

Granted, Monterey was only a smattering of buildings, a veritable handful of people compared to what she'd left in the east. But it was the center of California's social, business, and governmental world, and its quaint adobes maintained a charming dignity, grace, and beauty all their own.

She sensed that for all its serenity, things would never be dull here in California. It was quiet today, perhaps because of the cold breeze coming in off the ocean, but she had already seen one bullfight in the plaza since their arrival and had sat in on a fandango. Music could always be heard in the background; distant or close, lively or low, or sometimes only the single, soft strum of a guitar accompanying the forlorn mood of a lonely Californio.

The Californios were a people who enjoyed their good times. Their dances and festivals, their celebrations of birthdays and weddings—and anything else that warranted an excuse for celebration. And it was not unusual for their celebrations to last for days. There was a law against selling liquor here, but from what Nancy could see, the law didn't stop anyone from drinking it.

They were a friendly people, and, for the most part, seemed to readily accept the Americans. Thomas Larkin, even though not a citizen of Mexico, had been here twelve years and was a friend to all. In his store, he sold products which had been brought in on the Boston ships. He traded in flour, produce, soap, even sea otter skins. He had a flour mill, and also dealt in lumber and shingles—the latter two products being something that the Americans preferred more than the Californios.

The Larkin's two-story home, a lovely combination of adobe and redwood lumber, and of eastern and southern architectural design, was the focal point for newcomers from both America and Europe. It had become the unofficial American embassy in California. And Larkin, the unofficial American ambassador.

Most of the Californios, except the rich *hacendados,* made do with one-room adobes that were little more than dirt floor shelters. It was not unusual to see women who had twenty children. They would pile into these dwellings at night to sleep shoulder to shoulder for warmth, especially in the winter. Oftentimes, they even made room for guests or relatives. No one seemed to mind the conditions. If they could eat and sing and dance, all else was inconsequential, even the fleas that were so numerous as to practically carry them off.

But this talk of rebellion and war . . . well . . .

Nancy didn't like to think that her father's premonitory advice might come true. When a continent had lain between her and her dreams, it had been easy to convince herself that nothing so dramatic as war would ever actually happen.

Footsteps, light and feminine, indicating the approach of a woman, drew Nancy's attention to the door that led back into the house. In another moment it opened.

"Well, hell, girl. There you are." Lottie grinned, stepping out onto the balcony to join her. "I've been to hell and back looking for you. Thought you'd like to know we got word from J.B."

"Then he's alive? Thank God. I was so worried he and his men hadn't made it through."

"They damned near didn't," Lottie replied. "They ran into a lot of snow and cold. Like us, they nearly starved to death. They arrived in about the same condition as we did."

"So it was too late for Hensley to even think about going over the mountains and meeting us at the Sink?"

Lottie nodded. "He and his men arrived at Sutter's Fort in November. They re-outfitted and set out to meet the Four Creek rendezvous."

"They apparently didn't find the wagon pass they were searching for?"

"No, and I imagine J.B. is pretty disappointed about that. It was sort of a dream for him to be the one to discover it. Anyway, he told the dispatcher that since we were fine he was gonna head to Catacula and start settling in on some land up there. Reckon we won't get to see the danged redhead for a while now."

Nancy knew Lottie well enough to detect the note of disappointment in her voice as she spread her hands over the white balcony rail. Lottie had always claimed she wasn't the right woman for J.B. Chiles, but she liked him anyway and was clearly disappointed that she wouldn't be seeing him any time soon.

"I guess I shouldn't be surprised," Lottie continued. "It's time for all of us to go our separate ways. Frances and Elizabeth will be heading up north to see their father. Brenham Royal and his daughters are wanting to claim some land somewhere up around Sutter's Fort, away from the Californio settlements. And Miriam sure surprised us all the other night by saying that she was going to start up a bakery and expand into a restaurant here in Monterey if all goes well. Maybe even open up a boardinghouse or a hotel."

"I didn't figure her to be so enterprising."

"Since that no-good husband of hers abandoned her, she's a different woman," Lottie put in. "Why, she looks ten years younger despite the hardships of the journey. I'm surprised that Garnet is staying with her, though. The way Torey Porter stuck with her on the trip, I figured those two would get married."

"Poor Torey," Nancy said, shaking her head. "He's completely in love with her, but Garnet isn't ready for another man. I'm not sure she ever will be. She insinuated to me once that she didn't care for the intimacies of marriage."

"Well, at least with Garnet staying on to take care of the baby and the two boys, Miriam will be free to handle her business. I think she's about had it with child rearing anyway and wouldn't mind turning it over to somebody else."

"It was good of Larkin to offer to finance her." They stood in a moment of quiet thought and camaraderie, then Lottie said, "I think I've found some definite direction, too."

The tone of her voice brought Nancy's guard up. She pulled her eyes from the ocean and to the dark gaze of her friend. "I hope you haven't changed your mind about settling near Hart and me."

"Oh, I'd still like to settle near the two of you, all right. But I've been talking to Brenham, and in the course of our talk we came to the conclusion that if we partnered in a ranching operation we would both benefit. Now, I know that Hart has offered to help me get a place set up, but he's going to be busy enough tending to his own matters."

Nancy had to close her gaping mouth. She couldn't believe what she was hearing. "Lottie, are you sure that's a good idea? A woman partnering with a man—"

"Now, don't go jumping to conclusions, girl." Lottie flashed her an amused smile. "It isn't like I'm going to jump into bed with the old boy. He isn't my type, and I'd be surprised if I was his. 'Course, him bein' a man and used to that stingy old Lucille, he'd probably accept any reasonable offer. But I'm not goin' to be offering. No, it'll be strictly business."

"What if one of you wants to get married someday?"

"To each other?" The idea was clearly ludicrous to Lottie.

"Actually, I meant to somebody other than each other."

"You know, girl, I didn't think you could be undone, but I think I just succeeded in doing it."

Nancy tried to collect herself. "Well, I *am* surprised. I just have my doubts how it will work out. People are bound to think the worst, Lottie."

"Nancy, when have I ever given a damn what people thought? And the only ones who'll think the worst don't know me anyway. If this will benefit both me and Brenham, even if only for a year or two, then it's served its purpose. We'll make us up some rules and regulations. A bona fide partnership agreement.

"He needs a woman to help with the girls and the woman-stuff. And I'm tough, but there are some back-breaking things I'd rather leave to a man. I'm getting old enough that I don't feel I have to prove myself anymore, the way I did when I was younger. God gave men muscles for a reason, and women ought to let them use them.

"If it doesn't work out, we can either kill each other or just divide the silverware. But Brenham's not a greedy or vicious man, and I know he'll be reasonable even if we decide to quit the partnership after a time. It's a start, and we'll just go from there and take each new step as it comes."

Nancy just kept shaking her head in disbelief.

"Another fact of the matter is this, Nancy," Lottie continued, not to be deterred. "I want to be away from the Californio settlements, out there with you and Hart. But I don't want to be a burden to the two of you. And, out there, a body has to build everything from scratch. There aren't any ranches already set up for a person to just buy. If I was alone, sure I could hire help, but it would just be easier to have a man like Brenham to handle that sort of thing."

Nancy sighed, meeting Lottie's gaze. "I sort of left you in a pickle, didn't I?"

"What do you mean?"

"Well, you and I talked about doing something together. Helping each other. Being partners, you know. Then I went and got married. I feel like I let you down."

Lottie threw her arm over Nancy's shoulder and gave her a sisterly hug. "Don't be silly! I wouldn't have it any other way. Besides, I knew you wouldn't last long as a single woman. The men would be clamoring around you like bees around honey, even if you thought you had such great plans to go it alone. No, you and I came out here together but with separate intentions, and now it's time to follow those intentions. First thing tomorrow morning, we'll head over to talk to the governor and see what can be done about making ourselves legal in this country."

22

Governor Manuel Micheltorena, a slender, brown-haired man, rose from his desk with the piece of parchment paper in hand. He held it carefully, as if the ink, months old now, were still wet.

"In the year of your absence from California, Señor Daniels," he said, "your petition for Mexican citizenship has been reviewed and approved. I present you with this certificate of naturalization bearing both my signature and that of Secretary Manuel Jimeno of the Department of California. You are now a Mexican citizen and eligible to apply for the land you are seeking between the Cosumnes and Mokelumne rivers. As soon as you have determined the boundaries, return here with a map and description."

For Hart, the certificate was merely a formality. He was not a Mexican and never would be. He was an American, loyal to the United States, and he would support all American efforts to annex California into the Union. Of course, Micheltorena did not need to know that.

He shook the governor's hand, then Micheltorena addressed Nancy, Lottie, and Brenham Royal. "I will give your petitions for citizenship top priority, señors, señoras." He smiled at Lottie with discerning eyes and tight lips. "I am glad that Señor Royal has agreed to form a liaison with you. A woman should have a man to protect her, but I am sure you will not be alone for long. A woman as beautiful as you are will soon have another husband. Perhaps Señor Royal himself."

Brenham squirmed uncomfortably as color crept up his neck and into his cheeks, but Micheltorena didn't notice. His gaze was riveted to Lottie.

Lottie sensed the governor approved of her, perhaps too much, although she couldn't fathom why. The trip had taken its toll on her. Her face was sunburned, her hands chapped and red. Her dress—the only good one she'd brought—hung from a reed-thin frame that had been more curvaceous at the onset of this adventure. She had never been considered a beautiful woman anyway. But she gave him her warmest smile. She hadn't known if she would run into trouble with the Mexican land laws, being a woman, but Micheltorena had been most agreeable to her wishes.

"We will sign the petitions and dispatch them to Sutter's Fort within a few weeks," Micheltorena was saying, speaking of the citizenship papers. Then returning his attention to Hart, he continued, "Please encourage your other traveling companions to apply for citizenship, Señor Daniels. There are many Americanos staking claims to lands, particularly in the northern part of the province. But the law passed three years ago allows land only to Mexican citizens, so we will inevitably be forced to remove any illegals if a Mexican citizen, either by birth or naturalization, should petition for the same land." He flashed Hart another diplomatic smile. "And we don't want to take anything away from someone after they have put months, possibly years, into improvements."

"I will pass along your advice, Governor."

Micheltorena shook hands with the men. Then, in turn, bent over Nancy and Lottie's gloved hands, lifting each to his lips in a brief and polite gesture. "It has been my pleasure to meet you, señoras. I did not believe California could be made more beautiful, but your presence has made it so. If there is anything—anything at all—that you need, remember I am your humble servant."

Governor Manuel Micheltorena walked to his window and watched the departure of the Americanos, particularly that of the fiery England woman with her heavy mane of wavy, dark brown hair. He couldn't help but envision her naked and in his bed. Ah, but she was one to excite a man's soul. She was thin from the journey, but despite the weariness in her eyes from the months on a hard trail, there was much fire there still.

She was most beautiful indeed, perhaps not in a classic way, but there was something about her that intrigued him. An innate strength perhaps, or a wisdom that told him she would be a match for any man. And that, unfortunately, she would also be able to see all his flaws and insecurities as well.

"Such a pity," he muttered and settled heavily back into his chair. This Indian-infested wilderness was a place he had not wanted to come to. Always in his dreams he was back in Mexico City.

Still, it unsettled him each time he gave Mexican citizenship to an Americano, even one as lovely as Señora England. He still considered why that fool Juan Bautista Alvarado had given Sutter a land grant for colonization when he'd been governor. Alvarado had done it for power and strength. He had had a perverse idea that the Americanos here in California would side with him against his enemies.

Alvarado had foolishly promised land to the Americanos, including that hombre Isaac Graham and his compadres, but then Alvarado had made the mistake of not fulfilling those promises. It was something the Americanos had not forgotten, and they had immediately lost their faith and their trust in the Mexican government.

As for Micheltorena, he was suspicious of Americanos and didn't like to ask for their help. He did not know their inherent nature well enough to trust them. He *did* know they placed much importance on the ownership of land, and they were not afraid to fight to obtain it.

But what was to be gained by the presence of such reckless and uncouth foreigners even if they were good in battle? Nothing, that he could see. Those coming over the past two years were educated and had money, and were, therefore, powerful and dangerous. He wouldn't be surprised if this last group of settlers had been sent by the United States government to spy and plot the overthrow of California. Would they stop there? Or would they go all the way to Mexico City?

With all the other power struggles in the province, he did not relish this added burden of the Americano emigrants. The Californios accepted and respected the merchant Larkin, who had never applied for citizenship. They listened to him and went to him when they needed capital for their ventures. He extended credit and sometimes even cash. He was wise in trade matters, and enterprising in business. He was a stabilizing force here in Monterey. The people, Americanos and Californios alike, gravitated around him and his big hacienda on the hill. That troubled

Micheltorena somewhat. More than once he wondered what sort of plotting against him and Mexico went on up there in that house. Larkin gave lip service to Mexico, but hadn't he come here solely because he saw there was money to be made from this isolated arm of civilization?

Yet, for all his musings about the powerful and influential Larkin, it was people like Hart Daniels and Brenham Royal who troubled him as much, if not more. People like those two wanted land. The land was the country. And once the land was in their hands . . .

He heaved a sigh and stared at his copy of Daniels's citizenship papers. Two years ago, he and his army of three hundred had been sent by Mexico and had easily ousted that fool Alvarado. Intuition told him that the Americanos would not be as easy to drive back over the Sierra Nevadas if it came to war. Then there were those Californios, like Mariano Vallejo of Sonoma, who nonchalantly commented that it was inevitable that the province of California, too far from Mexico and inadequately protected, would someday succumb to the rulership of another country. Vallejo and others merely shrugged and too easily assumed that the future ruler would be the United States. They didn't seem to care or to mind. One wondered if they even encouraged it.

Through the open window, Micheltorena listened to the sea waves lapping at the shore, and at the seagulls squawking as they scavenged for food along the coast. There were the sounds of the boats creaking in their moorings, of the longshoremen shouting, dropping crates carelessly on the docks, and occasionally even laughing as they unloaded goods from the big foreign trade vessels. All such familiar sounds.

But there was a different smell to the wind today as it skipped through his open window and ruffled the Americanos' petitions for citizenship, lifting one completely and flipping it to the floor. As he reached automatically to gather it back up, he wondered what it was that the wind carried to his sensitive nostrils. It was not the usual smells from the sea.

Another deep sigh shallowed his chest. Maybe it was all those damned Americanos tainting the place with their incorrigible energy and Yankee ideas.

Or maybe it was just the approach of an incoming storm.

23

May

The mud glided over the adobe bricks like warm butter over hot bread. Nancy hummed while she plastered the walls of the little *cabaña,* and stood back occasionally to survey her handiwork.

She and Hart had had help building it. Thane and Torey had hired on as permanent ranch hands, and John Sutter had let them hire a dozen male Miwok Indians from the fort, along with their families, because he'd had more people there than he could take care of.

The men had worked for weeks mixing mud and dried grass, pouring it into wooden molds, then spreading the dried bricks out onto the ground to sunbake them for at least an additional two weeks. The bricks had then been mortared around the house's timber framework, the adobe roof had been thatched, and the window openings covered with grass mats woven by the Indian women.

Nancy knew her family in Amherst would not have understood her pride in the small two-room adobe. By Eastern standards, it would have been considered crude at best, but she had helped build the little house with her own hands and she loved it, finding that being inside it brought a very special peace to her heart.

"Is there a lady in here who could use some male companionship?"

Nancy turned at the sound of Hart's voice and flashed him a welcome smile. "I swear, Hart, you're getting as silent as those Indians. I didn't even hear you."

Hart found a wall that was dry and leaned against it. He removed his hat and ran a hand through hair that was matted with sweat. "You just didn't hear me because you were singing."

She blushed. "I was *not* singing. I was humming. You know I can't carry a tune in a bucket with a lid on it!"

"Actually, you have a very lovely voice. You ought to just let it flow. Nobody around here would mind."

Nancy scooped up another handful of mud and smeared it on the wall. "I'm afraid I still remember all too well my mother telling me not to try to sing because I would only embarrass myself if someone outside the family heard me. Wouldn't she get the vapors if she saw me now with mud up to my elbows?"

"Didn't she allow you to make mud pies either?"

"My mother could barely tolerate jam on my fingers. Actually, I wasn't allowed to do much of anything back in Amherst except dream. Don't misunderstand me. I love my mother, but the two of us were certainly not cut from the same cloth." She picked up the trowel and worked the plaster into a smooth layer over the bricks. "Only my Grandfather could truly appreciate the challenges and the raw beauty of this land. I think that if he were younger, he would be on a ship right now sailing around the Horn."

"Funny you should mention your grandfather. Thane and Torey just got back from Sutter's Fort and they brought this letter—" Hart reached into his shirt pocket and pulled out an envelope.

Nancy nearly jumped straight up. "A letter!" She doused her hands in the bucket of water and slap-dried them on the nearby towel. Hart was laughing as she eagerly snatched the letter from his hand and tore open the seal.

"Oh, Hart! I finally got a letter, and it's from Grandpa! Dated last October." Her eyes raced across the lines, devouring the news from home. Then suddenly she sat down on a stool and began to cry.

Hart dropped to a squatting position in front of her and placed his hands on her knees. "What is it, Nancy? What's happened?"

"Oh, nothing. It's so silly of me to get sentimental over a letter. It's just that he writes the way he talks. I can hear his brogue in the words. God, I really do miss him."

Hart breathed a sigh of relief that the news wasn't bad. He put an arm over her shoulder. "Well, what does he say? Don't keep your old husband in the dark."

Nancy swiped at the tears. "He says, 'Dearest Granddaughter. I am hopin' by now that you have found the end o' the rainbow, and y're pot o' gold. We have not received word from you as I write this, but we are trustin' that y'r journey went faster than the mail.

" 'We're fine here. Millicent is in the family way again, due in February. Charity and her husband are thinking about moving to New York City. Y'r brothers and father are hard at work trying to expand the profits of the horse farm. Y'r dear mother has been in good health and active, as always, in the various societies she belongs to. Nothing has changed appreciably here, only on the political scene. We listen for news of California constantly and worry about your well-being. I trust your mother will fill you in better when she writes.

" 'Y' know that if I could, dear one, I would be there with you, sharing in y'r ev'ry adventure. I'm sure you are having much more excitement there than I am here . . .' "

Nancy finished reading the two-page letter then carefully folded it back up. "Millicent must have given birth shortly after we arrived in Monterey. I wonder if it was a boy or a girl."

Hart saw the wistfulness enter her eyes as she thought about the loss of her own child. He slid his arm around her. "He'll tell you in the next letter, I'm sure."

They discussed her news for a few minutes more. Hart guiltily admitted that he should write to his own family as soon as he found time, then he excused himself to get back to work.

For Nancy, it was more difficult to focus on the plastering. A dozen times that afternoon she took the letter out, needing to see the words that enabled her to see her grandfather's face as clearly as if he were standing right next to her. But the letter brought a pain too deep to mention to Hart.

"Why haven't you written, Mother?" she murmured to the empty room. "Are you still angry with me for leaving? Surely you would have posted a letter before Grandfather? I've written you letters. A dozen, at least."

That night, by the light of a coal oil lamp, and while Hart slept, Nancy once again gathered her pen and wrote to the only person in Amherst who seemed to care.

My Dearest Grandfather,

Hart and I have a ranch that we have named Rancho Vallecito, meaning little valley. It sprawls between the Cosumnes River and the north fork of the Mokelumne. It rolls up over the oak-studded foothills to the edge of the snow-tipped Sierra Nevadas, then tumbles back down toward the long and broad San Joaquin Valley. In all, nearly thirty thousand acres. We are a day's ride from Sutter's Fort to the northwest, and a day's ride to Lottie's ranch south of here.

There is so much to do to build our ranch that there is never time to be lonely or bored. Yet it is very peaceful and quiet here. At night the only sounds are the owls and the nightbirds, and occasionally the mournful wails of coyotes and wolves. During the daytime, I find it enjoyable to listen to the lilting discussions of the Indians who work for us. I am learning some of their language, as well as Spanish. They speak both. But don't worry, the Indians are loyal and hard-working and not to be feared. I am constantly warmed by their honesty and sense of humor.

You would love it here in California, Grandfather. It is indeed the pot of gold at the end of the rainbow . . .

The weeks that followed were filled with the clearing of land for grain crops, a vegetable garden, and a fruit orchard. Seeds and fruit seedlings were brought from Monterey, along with six young vaqueros and a housekeeper named Magdalena Renteria. Magdalena's family included her widowed daughter, Carmelita, and her seventeen-year-old son, Osvaldo. Magdalena and Carmelita would do the housework, cooking, and sewing. Osvaldo, an experienced vaquero, had been hired to break horses for the ranch's remuda.

They were back from Monterey only a week when Hart announced that he would be leaving again. "I need to get busy and start rounding up stock for the ranch, Nancy. We'll be heading into the San Joaquin Valley to get the longhorns."

Thousands of longhorn cattle roamed the province. They were wild and combative, had no owners and no brands. They proliferated faster than the Californios themselves. A man could get his herd with nothing more than some hard work, a good horse, and a free-flowing lariat. Nancy admired her husband for going out to capture the beasts, but she wasn't looking forward to being left alone on the ranch with only four hired hands and the Indians who would be working the fields.

"I'd love to go with you, Hart. It's been awhile since we slept beneath the stars."

He laughed and pulled her into his arms. "I thought the overland journey would have cured you from ever wanting to sleep on the ground again."

"I'm always ready for a new experience. If you'll give me a few minutes, I'll get my things together."

He frowned and sighed deeply. "Someone needs to stay here, Nancy. Someone in authority. And don't worry. The Indians recognize you as their *patróna*. They'll respect your wishes and obey your orders. They'll protect you, too, if the need arises."

Reluctantly Nancy gave into his wishes, knowing that everything he said was true. They had put too much into their ranch to leave it attended only by hired help.

The next morning, the sun slumbered just below the horizon, painting the clear eastern sky with vivid strokes of red and gold. In that quiet calm before daybreak, Nancy watched Hart swing into the saddle. The four vaqueros who were going with him were already mounted and waiting a few yards away.

Hart leaned down from the saddle and placed his hand on her cheek. "I won't be gone longer than three weeks. We'll get only what the five of us can manage without too much difficulty. We'll be making forays like this all summer until I have the stock I need."

Nancy pulled her thin shawl a little tighter around her shoulders, not from the cold, but from the security it seemed to offer. She and Hart had been together now for a year, never without each other for even one night since they'd married, but she sensed that the demands of the ranch would now keep them frequently apart. Already her bed felt empty, and her heart thumped anxiously for his return. How could she have gotten so dependent on him when she had set out for California so utterly independent?

He took her hand in his. "Just one word of caution, Nancy. I know how you like to ride, but don't go too far from the ranch alone. There are still some bands of renegade Indians that can't be trusted."

She laughed. "You've told me that a million times, Hart."

"I know, I know. But if you want to ride, or if you have to go to Sutter's

Fort for anything, take the men. Oh, and don't be going out to help catch wild horses with Antonio and Osvaldo. I know you'd love to, but it's too dangerous. I'll take you with me some time when I get back. Okay?"

Nancy wondered why it was that men always felt it was their duty to protect women, as if women were completely helpless and without any common sense whatsoever. When would they learn that they couldn't keep women neatly confined to ease their own minds?

"I've got more than enough to do around here to keep me busy," she gave him the answer she knew he wanted to hear. "I've got to water those fruit trees every day, work on the garden. I won't have time to chase wild horses."

He leaned down from the saddle and kissed her farewell. His horse danced away from her, anxious to be gone, even if he was not. The ruby glow in the east had given way to the first sharp rays of morning sunlight. He gathered his reins and wheeled his horse. Nancy shielded her eyes against the sun and watched him ride away.

"Antonio and I will go after some horses this morning, Señora Daniels," Osvaldo said a few minutes later.

Nancy forced her eyes away from her departing husband and her mind away from the empty hole his absence was already opening up inside of her. She banished the thoughts of the dangers he might face in getting the longhorns home. There were dangers everywhere, and one could not cripple oneself by worrying about them.

She turned to the young vaquero who had addressed her so politely in a thick Spanish accent. "That's an excellent idea, Osvaldo. Saddle the gray gelding for me, *por favor*. I'll be going with you."

24

July

"This digging post holes is man's work, Señora Daniels. I do not understand why you don't leave it for the men." Magdalena Renteria shook her graying head. "I am afraid you will faint in this heat. Here, have some cold water I have brought from the well."

Nancy pushed her hat to the back of her head and shifted her shovel to her left hand. She circled the tall glass with a hand gloved in leather and poured the cold water down a parched throat, not realizing until the moment that she had been so thirsty.

When she was working, she could too easily slip into a state of mind that blocked the awareness of pain, fatigue, or discomfort. She would just work and think of things. Of her grandfather, her parents and siblings, of Amherst, of the overland journey, and the women who had gone their separate ways. She would think of Hart, gone away for more cattle, and wonder when he would be home. Wonder if he was all right. She would look at Rancho Vallecito and consider the months of grueling labor put in so far to make it the dream they had both envisioned. But those months had been full of hope and enthusiasm. Never had she felt so alive, with such a strong purpose. She enjoyed work. Digging post holes for another horse corral was rewarding, needed to be done, and it was something she could do. It was also something she would never have been able to do back East.

She almost laughed, thinking of her appearance and how shocked those at home would be. Here she stood in her man's hat, a red bandana around her throat to absorb the sweat, an old white shirt of Hart's opened nearly down to her bosom to let in any breeze that might stir. No corset. She had been tempted to discard her skirt for a pair of Hart's pants, too, but had, instead, made a skirt that went up above her ankles so it wouldn't tangle in her boots as she dug the post holes. She had fashioned loops at the waistband and strung one of Hart's leather belts through it. And she'd bought a pair of leather gloves from an Indian trader. They were small gloves, made for a woman's small hands. They hadn't been for sale. His squaw had been wearing them, and Nancy had asked if he had a similar pair he would sell.

The Indian trader had said something to the squaw, who had reluctantly taken the gloves off and handed them to Nancy. "She sell. Make another pair."

"I don't want to take her gloves," Nancy had objected.

"You take. She make more."

He had insisted and traded them to her for a chocolate cake and two loaves of bread that Magdalena had baked just that morning.

"I would like another pair made of goatskin for riding," Nancy had said, "but for hard work, I would like a pair or two made of deer hide. And maybe a pair with some leather fringes on the gauntlets for fancy occasions."

The Indian had nodded eagerly. "Squaw make. But she slow. When you need?"

"Whenever she can make two or three more pairs."

He nodded. "When moon comes again. We come back with more gloves."

The Indian couple had been true to their word and had returned every month with more gloves for her and others on the ranch.

Nancy swirled the last bit of water in the glass and looked out across her land, drinking in its beauty as greedily as she did the cold water. It was good land for cattle, for raising hay and grain and vegetable crops. Here, the wild horses ran free, and game was plentiful. Here, her life was full.

Magdalena shook her head again. "You don't need to do this, señora. Señor Hart will do it when he returns."

Nancy handed the glass back to Magdalena and looked wistfully across the valley. "I *would* rather be chasing wild horses—"

Magdalena rolled her eyes. *"Es una loca.* You are lucky you weren't killed that other time. Señor Hart would not have approved, had you ever told him," she concluded on an accusatory note.

Nancy laughed, knowing it would be hopeless to make short, stocky Magdalena, who hated horses and looked like a barrel when perched on one, to ever understand the pure exhilaration she had felt while racing full gallop across the hills and valleys in pursuit of the wild horses, to ride with the wind if only for a moment. And she had empathized with the wild horses when, dusty and tired, she had helped funnel them into the big blind corral at the end of the valley.

She wiped the sweat off her brow with her bandana and remembered the ground flying away beneath Lady Rae's dainty hooves. She longed for the feel of speed in her face.

"I may have a husband, but that isn't going to stop me from doing what I came out here to do. Besides, Maggie, I don't mind working. You ought to know that by now."

"Sí, but understand? No, never. And I wish you wouldn't call me Maggie. It does not suit me, you know?"

Nancy's grin only widened. She enjoyed teasing the Mexican woman who was probably in her mid-fifties. Magdalena pretended to be annoyed, but she really didn't mind. It pleased her that she and Nancy got along so well.

"My life goes from one extreme to the other," Magdalena started in on one of her famous dissertations, speaking in a combination of English and Spanish. "For nearly twenty years I am married to a man who beats me, you know? He said I complained too much. But what am I to do? He would never work. He would only sit around and drink his tequila or go to the cantina and drink his tequila. He would come home and expect me to be his woman, and he would beat me if I told him no. Then he would take what he wanted from me anyway. And the children were hungry because he would not work. He was worthless, and I wanted to kill him. Instead, I left him. I took the children and ran away.

"Sometimes I would think that maybe he would sober up and come looking for us. Ready to change and be a man, you know? Instead, he went to the cantina and got himself drunk and stabbed to death in a fight. And now I am working for a woman who never knows when to *stop* working. It is too much, you know?"

She shook her head and headed for the house. "Your dinner will be ready in one half hour, señora. I will ring the bell so you will know when to quit."

Nancy watched as her short legs propelled her to the house. She had heard Magdalena's life story before, several times, but Magdalena had a habit of repeating herself just in case you might have forgotten or not fully understood. Nancy found it amusing that the woman could criticize her for working so hard, and yet she was up at dawn, cooking and cleaning or washing, and she never stopped until it was time for bed.

Hart had found her through Rachel Larkin, who happened to be the net for all the gossip floating up and down the coast. Magdalena had worked for a rich ranchero near San Juan Bautista before seeking new employment. It was said that the young, new *patróna* who had married the rich ranchero had an ugly temper and a very abusive vocabulary, and had treated Magdalena and her children like chicken dung.

Nancy's eyes roamed the small valley reaching out before them, dropping away very gradually from the higher ground where they had put the house and ranch buildings. Only children were missing—*her* children—and she would have them. Some day. For now, she had been using that "female preventative" which Rachel Larkin had ordered from Boston and kept in the back room of their store, all tucked away in a box with a dozen others.

"Not all Californio women want two dozen children," Rachel had said. "Their religion forbids them to do anything to prevent pregnancy, but there are still those who come to me in private and ask if I know of something."

Nancy lifted her hat from her head and wiped the perspiration from her forehead with her shirtsleeve. She missed Hart. He'd been gone nearly two weeks this time and she expected two more. He and the vaqueros had brought in several herds so far. After branding them and making a tally, they'd turned them back out on the new range. They anticipated their ranch could handle at least four thousand head of cattle, but until a market for meat was a viable option, it would do little good to raise more than what they could sell for hides and tallow, and what they needed to feed all the ranch employees.

Tugging her hat back down on her head, she rammed the shovel into the hole again with all the strength she could muster. It barely dented the soil. The ground was too dry this time of year to be digging post holes. It should have been done in the spring, but there had been too many other things to do at that time. Still, she wanted to finish this hole before going up to the house for dinner.

Suddenly she stopped short, listening. She cocked her head toward the sound—a distant rumble, like thunder from a far-off storm. But there was not a cloud to mar the perfect blue dome of the sky. She looked up and down the valley, searching for a clue to the disturbance. She saw nothing, only the calmness of the verdant summer day. The tall grass stood perfectly still without a breeze to stir it. Birds chirruped in the trees. The Indians' primitive hoes made a distant clink as they hacked away at weeds in the garden. A clatter of silverware from the kitchen reminded her of dinner.

Then, to the north, she saw the dust and recognized the sound now as one she had heard that night on the Platte. It was the thunder of hundreds of hooves. Leaning her shovel up against the last fence post she had planted, she reached for the rifle propped next to it.

25

A herd of approximately fifty head of wild horses, being driven by six vaqueros, were circled and brought into the wide valley below the house. They ran immediately toward the Cosumnes River to drink. Three of the men stayed with the herd while the other three kicked their tired mounts into a lope toward the house. The horses in the corral paced nervously around their compound, eager to be off with the wild bunch. Lady Rae released a shrill bugle to a stallion that returned the call from down on the river.

Nancy stood in the center of the yard, flanked by Thane and Torey, rifles in hand. The riders thundered into the yard, halting only a few yards away and filling the air with a cloud of dust. Instinct told Nancy that it wouldn't be wise to show intimidation or fear, although the encounter had the air of a challenge—or a threat. For a few seconds, she had honestly wondered if the strangers had had intentions of stopping, or running over them.

One man, stockily built with a swarthy, broad face and heavy sidewhiskers, smiled and pushed back his sombrero from a head of thick, curly, jet-black hair. "Señora Daniels. What a fine day this is."

"It is indeed," she replied smoothly, concealing her apprehensions about these visitors. "Although perhaps a bit too hot for my taste."

His dark brown eyes skimmed over the simple adobe house and the new two-story frame house being built by Thane and Torey. There was nothing that his surveillance missed, from the Indians working the vegetable gardens and orchards, to the saddle horses in the corral.

"*Sí*, it is hot, and very dry, señora. We could use some rain, no?"

"It might help to settle the dust."

His eyes continued to roam over the budding ranch in a way that went beyond simple regard for their accomplishments.

"There are many beautiful places in California," he said in his heavy Spanish accent. "You and your husband have picked one of the finest. Is your husband here?"

"Not at the moment. Is there something I can do for you?"

The man's eyes suggested that he had already known of Hart's absence, but he said, "Ah, such a disappointment to be in the vicinity and miss him. Especially since I have heard so much about him and Rancho Vallecito from many people in Monterey."

"I'm afraid you have me at a disadvantage, Señor—?"

He flashed an apologetic smile. "Forgive my bad manners, señora. I am José Castro, at your service."

The name struck fear in Nancy's heart. Few Americans in California had not heard of the infamous José Castro, a fighting man, who enjoyed being the spearhead for rebellion. He had been the prefect of the northern district under Governor Alvarado, and was presently Micheltorena's military commander. Three years ago, while California had been under the leadership of Governor Juan Bautista Alvarado, forty-six Americans had been accused of plotting a conspiracy to overthrow Alvarado and claim independence for California. The Americans, led by Isaac Graham, had been captured and sent to San Blás and then Tepic, Mexico.

Thanks to an American traveler, Thomas J. Farnham, who had worked on their behalf, the charges against the Americans had been dropped. Twenty-six had been expelled from Mexican territory, but the remainder had been acquitted of the charges and allowed to return to California.

Castro, the guard en route, had been tried and acquitted of extreme cruelty to the prisoners. He had returned to Monterey, but the incident had left the Americans hardened towards him. There were those who would kill him yet, given half a chance—Graham particularly, claiming Castro had tried to kill him in cold blood the night of the capture. Only the interference of an Indian had saved his life. Castro had also been heard to boast that he was going to destroy Sutter's Fort, which he considered a rising threat to the Californios.

Nancy did her best to hide her wariness and fear of him. "It is my pleasure to meet you, Señor Castro." She forced a smile, feigning ignorance of his notoriety. "There is fresh water in the well, and I'm sure my cook could find something for your men to eat."

"As much as we would like to accept your hospitality, señora, we cannot stay. We must keep the horses moving. But there is one thing you could do for us."

"I'll do whatever I can, Señor Castro," she responded cautiously, not liking the look that had entered his eyes.

"Our saddle horses are very tired. As you know, it is the Californio custom for rancheros to exchange horses to travelers. I see you have some fine horses in your corral, and we would like to know if we may leave our tired horses here to rest and use yours. You could claim your own at a later date—perhaps the next time you come to Monterey—but I can assure you the horses we are riding are among the best and would serve you as well, perhaps better, than the ones you now have."

This was one California custom Nancy did not favor. Horses meant nothing to the Californios. They rode them into the ground and cast them aside for another. The plentitude of the wild herds brought on this attitude, but Nancy didn't believe, as few Americans did, that a horse should be so misused.

She sensed in Castro's request an escalation of trouble. She saw the challenge deepen in his eyes, bordering on intimidation. She took in the pistols he and his men wore. All of them looked like men who took what they wanted and gave no quarter to their adversaries.

"There are several horses I could let you take, Señor Castro," she compromised. "But I could not let you take my personal mount."

Castro glanced at the corral, taking in the stock in one practiced sweep of his eye. "And which one would that be?"

"The dark bay mare. I rode her all the way from Independence, Missouri, two thousand miles on the overland trail. She has served me well, and I could not possibly part with her. However, we do have some good mustangs. They would be suitable for your purpose."

His visage darkened; his smile slipped. "If you will not consider a trade, señora, then would you sell the mare? I will offer you everything she is worth in American money."

Torey tensed next to Nancy. "Don't let the bastard have her," he mumbled so only she could hear.

"As I said," Nancy remained adamant, "I could not possibly part with her, not even for money."

Castro shifted in the saddle. Nancy sensed that this one exception she had made was going to turn the entire scenario into a battle of wills, or a play for power. He appeared the sort to bully women, frighten them, until they gave into his wishes. And why? More than likely so he could merely say he had won the battle.

He folded his forearms over the big horn of his California saddle. "I remember when I was very young. I had a horse I was so proud of. A ranchero offered me very much money for this horse, but I thought there was no other like him in all of California." He lifted an arm and passed it across in front of him in a sweeping gesture, as if taking in all the territory. "So I refused his offer. But do you know what happened, señora? I went out three days later, and I found that horse dead."

Nancy heard not an amusing anecdote but a disturbing parable. Surely he would not have the gall to come back and kill the mare in the night just to teach her that nobody denied José Castro? She shivered at the thought. She met his dark eyes and saw he waited with confident expectation for her ultimate capitulation.

"That is a very sad story, señor," she replied politely. "A very hard blow for a young boy, I'm sure. But, if that is so, why would you want to pay good money for a horse that might die in three days?"

His lips tightened into a line so thin they disappeared beneath his black, raven's-wing moustache. He pulled his black eyes, snapping fire, away from hers and made a show of looking around the ranch again. "I see you are quite undermanned here with your husband and vaqueros gone. I hope your husband does not leave you so unprotected very often. It could be very dangerous for a woman."

Another threat, thinly disguised. She was afraid of him and what he might do to her, but she would not allow the pompous bastard to intimidate her either. "My Indians are armed, señor," she lied with an ease that shocked even her. "So I do not worry overly much about bandits and renegades."

His gaze traveled the length of her, returning slowly to her steady gaze. "I did not know you Americano women were so impervious, Señora Daniels. It is a most admirable quality."

"*Gracias,*" she replied, not fooled by the words rolling off his silver tongue. "Now, are you certain you and your men wouldn't care for something to eat?"

José Castro gazed down at the fiery Americano woman with golden hair wisping down around her face from beneath her man's hat. The brim shaded her eyes just enough that he could see only a spark, a glint, but something about it suggested she would not hesitate to shoot him through the heart given the least provocation.

He had to admit he did not care overly much about her mare. Mares might be as high-spirited as stallions, even possess mean tempers, but when their bluff was called under the strong hand of a determined man, their spirits tended to break too easily. Like any woman's. No, he had only been persistent with the offer because he wanted to see how strong this woman's spirit was. How far she could be pushed before relenting. Breaking. It was always good to know where possible opposition might present itself, but what he had found in her troubled him. Most women would have given him anything simply out of fear of being raped or killed. This one was different, and he wondered if she wasn't a little loco. He would let it go this time, for a crazy woman might do exactly what she said she would do, and she clearly had him at a disadvantage. These Americanos invading his California—ah, he wished to see them all dead.

He smiled apologetically. "Your hospitality is greatly appreciated and will not be forgotten, but we want to get across the valley before nightfall. We saw another herd of wild horses on the San Joaquin not far from here, and we want to see if we can capture them. It has been my greatest pleasure to meet you, Señora Daniels. You will not soon be forgotten. *Buenos días.*"

Nancy stayed where she was until Castro's men had rounded up the horses in the meadow and driven them on down the valley. She was inwardly thankful he had refused her offer for food. She was glad to see him gone. Unless she was being paranoid, she had even heard a subtle threat in his farewell.

She retired to the adobe house in the shade of the big oaks, wondering if Castro would come back and kill her and her mare in the night. Wondering, too, if Lottie, Brenham, and the girls would be safe. They were right in the path Castro and his men were taking back to Monterey.

Nancy would bet the entire Rancho Vallecito that Castro hadn't stopped by to meet Hart. Nor had he stopped to pay his respects. As for trading horses—that, too, appeared to be a convenient excuse to get close to Rancho Vallecito's headquarters. What could be his real reasons for being so far from Monterey? *Was* he only looking for wild horses? Or for Americans and their gun power?

She might never know the real reason, but intuition told her there was more to his horse hunt than catching wild horses.

26

Hart leaned back on his chair and patted his full stomach. "That's the best fried chicken I think I've ever tasted, Miriam. It's no wonder your business is booming. You've found a veritable gold mine in this restaurant of yours."

Miriam finished pouring coffee for both Hart and Thomas Larkin. "I got me a California cook to help out and satisfy the tastebuds of the natives," she replied. "She can't speak a word of English but she can cook up a storm. Makes tortillas so fast you get dizzy just watching her hands. As a matter of fact," she added proudly, "you probably noticed I've had to hire several women to help, not only to cook but to wait tables, do dishes, grind meal, and procure food. Yes, sir. It's turning into quite a business."

Hart noticed that the women Miriam employed were those without men, or whose husbands were lazy or abusive. He supposed she had a special compassion for them since she'd been through an unfortunate relationship herself. But the sadness that had been in her eyes during those early days of the overland journey had been replaced by a glow of satisfaction and accomplishment. She walked lightly, even hummed on occasion. She hardly resembled the oppressed woman who had joined the wagon train last spring. Except for the three sons Waite had left her with, she maintained nothing of her former self or her former life. She had even dropped the Waite name and was using her maiden name of Rutledge. Her two older boys, just toddlers, had never known the difference and gave no objection to the change.

"Being a businesswoman agrees with you, Miriam," he said.

She rested the coffeepot on a pad atop the white muslin tablecloth and sat down on one of the four chairs that graced each square table. But she only perched on the edge of the chair, as if she knew her duties would call for her to be off in a minute or two. "I think you're one hundred percent right," she replied with pride in her voice again. "I've made enough money to pay Mr. Larkin the first payment on the loan, and ahead of time too."

Larkin had been listening to the conversation with a smile. "I never had any doubt that you would succeed."

Miriam stood up. "I certainly do thank you for having faith in me, 'cause I didn't have much in myself. Well, I'd better go get back to work before I start losing customers. Listen, Hart, you tell Nancy hello for me. I'm sure glad to hear she likes it out there. 'Course, I never doubted she would. That girl has a wild streak in her that would suit perfectly to being the *patróna* of a big ranch. Still, you tell her I'll be looking forward to the next time she comes to Monterey. Don't you wait too long to bring her to town."

Hart grinned sheepishly in accordance to her teasing tone of reprimand. "I've been so busy chasing cows and horses, and she's been so busy keeping the ranch in running order, that it hasn't worked out this summer."

Miriam patted his shoulder in a motherly way, even though she was probably only a dozen years older. "I understand, but you tell her I think of her. I worry about her out there with you gone so much. I know you've got trustworthy vaqueros and all but"—she stepped closer and lowered her voice to a whisper—"with the rumors of Mexico thinking of expelling Americans from California, I'm a little worried that they might resort to violence. Even those of us with bona fide citizenship papers and passports. I sometimes think those Mexicans believe we're all spies. I wouldn't put it past 'em to jail us all like Alvarado did Isaac Graham and his bunch—or worse yet, line us all up in front of a firing squad. I tell you, it's got me, and every other American woman in these parts, pretty darned worried. You be careful headin' back with those horses."

The men watched Miriam as she breezed around the tables filling coffee cups until her pot was empty. Then Larkin spoke in a low voice,

"Her intuitions aren't far from wrong, Hart. There's trouble brewing. Rumor has it that José Castro and Juan Bautista Alvarado are staging a revolution to overthrow Governor Micheltorena. Word is, they've been out rounding up wild horses to break for their volunteer troops."

Hart's eyes narrowed. "Have you got any idea when they plan to move?"

"Soon. Micheltorena is definitely in trouble. Last year he dispatched a letter to the Minister of War asking for clothing and money for his *cholos*. Because he had nothing to pay them with they resorted to rampant thievery all up and down the coastal towns and ranches. They steal out of hunger, but when their hunger is abated, they steal out of sheer pleasure. They take everything from food, to clothes, to money. It's not uncommon for them to stop people in the streets and demand their valuables at gunpoint. They've become more bold since Micheltorena has let their transgressions go unpunished.

"Alvarado is a native Californian," Larkin continued, "and he has never believed a Mexican should be governor of the province, only a Californio."

Hart stared contemplatively into his coffee cup. "What are Castro's and Alvarado's sentiments towards the Americans?"

Larkin observed the people in the small restaurant that contained ten small square tables, most of which were occupied. A few of the Californios occasionally glanced their way, but Larkin was satisfied that none were close enough to hear their conversation. "They think we're fine insofar as we will fight on their side. Personally, I believe they would rather we weren't here. But I would caution the Americans against taking sides. Repercussions could come of it, depending on who comes out victorious. As you well know, governors here are toppled under the continual power struggles like so many rows of dominoes.

"As Consul to the United States, I can only abide by the President's orders, which are to try and spread goodwill to the Californios about the Americans, and encourage an annex of California to the United States. Negotiations to purchase the province seem to have fallen through completely, in lieu of Commodore Jones's blunder two years ago, and because of the situation between Mexico and the United States over that disputed land in Texas."

"War is likely to erupt from that," Hart said. "And our situation here could be affected."

"Yes, and my explicit orders state that the United States cannot become involved in the struggle between Mexico and California, unless Mexico starts a war with us. If California herself were to assert her independence, then the United States could step in and offer annexation or protection to the new republic. If that plan were to succeed, the Californios must have a feeling of goodwill toward the Americans and want to join the United States."

"A lot of the incoming emigrants don't seem to want to be part of an independent California under the rule of the Californios, let alone a part of Mexico," Hart put in.

"Americans simply aren't tolerant of the relaxed Californio ways," Larkin responded passionately. "They want to take matters into their own hands. Their attitudes could make my job of fostering pro-American sentiment among the natives a difficult task at best."

"So you think some of the Americans might try to seize the country?" Hart questioned.

Larkin sighed, clearly discouraged by the impossibilities of his mission as peacekeeper. "War is not what we want when diplomacy will achieve the same end. Still, we need to be ready to step in if it looks as though another country might run up their flag. As for who would be best in power—Castro or Micheltorena—is anybody's guess. Micheltorena is not dedicated to California, but Castro ruined his reputation with the Americans when he mistreated Graham and the others during their imprisonment."

"Neither seems to like the American segment of the population. A man like Mariano Vallejo is better liked, but he tends to mind his own business up in Yerba Buena."

Larkin twisted his coffee cup around in its saucer. "There are Americans itching to settle the matter, but we don't want war. Nor do we want to seize this country. We want the Californians to make their own decision to join the United States."

"You can't blame the settlers for getting nervous," Hart countered. "They're isolated in the northern territory and when they hear rumors about being expelled, there's a natural tendency to react. Maybe even to overreact."

Larkin nodded. "I understand that, but I need to try to head off any revolutions from the American segment, so would you mind keeping me informed as to what those hotheads up around Sutter's Fort might be planning at any given time?"

"Sure, I'll let you know if I hear anything."

Both men pushed their chairs away from the table and stood up.

"Will you spend the night and dine with Rachel and me?" Larkin asked, glancing at his pocketwatch. "She would love to have you."

"Of course, but first I need to ride out and make sure my vaqueros aren't having any trouble with that herd of horses. Particularly that stallion I bought from Gilroy. Nancy wants her mare bred, but I wanted a stallion with some bloodlines."

"I'm sure she'll be delighted. She's truly excited about raising horses, isn't she?"

"It's what she came out here to do."

Larkin led the way from the restaurant. "I'll tell Rachel to expect you in a few hours."

Beneath the hand-painted sign and the word MIRIAM'S, Hart watched the consul head back up the hill to his own house. From his shirt pocket, Hart pulled some tobacco and papers and commenced to roll and light a cigarette.

He leaned against the hitching rail outside the restaurant to muse over California's situation as well as his own. Earlier, he had met with Micheltorena and had received the papers giving final approval by the Departmental Assembly for his land grant. Nancy would be relieved. With the anti-American sentiment on the rise among Mexican officials, she had been worried that the assembly might find a reason to deny the grant.

He'd been gone so much since they'd established Rancho Vallecito, and he was looking forward to being with his wife through the winter. His plan was to finish the big house for her.

"Ah, it is Señor Daniels."

At the voice, Hart turned, surprised to see the object of his and Larkin's conversation. "Señor Castro. It's a fine day, isn't it?" he said casually, hoping his surprise and distrust of the man wouldn't show in his eyes.

"It is indeed. But there are few days in California which are bad, no?"

Hart feigned a congenial attitude. "That's true. The sun nearly always shines."

"I was out at your rancho a few days ago," Castro said. "I visited with your lovely wife."

The comment had been made in an off-handed, conversational way, but wariness tightened Hart's gut into a knot. He didn't like the needling glow in Castro's dark eyes that suggested he had calculated his words to induce concern.

"I trust she was well," Hart said just as casually, as if Castro's visit to the ranch was nothing to illicit alarm. But just what *had* taken him to Rancho Vallecito? It was not on the beaten path to anything.

"Oh, *sí*. She was quite well. You should be very proud of such a spirited and independent woman. She is, I think, a true survivor, like the horses that run wild."

Even the compliment did not settle well with Hart, or perhaps it was only the gleam in Castro's eyes that hinted, despite his praise, that he did not like Nancy. Had something happened between the two of them?

"She's a strong woman," Hart conceded.

"Very admirable, señor, as long as she does not become *too* strong, no? Too much authority in a woman's hands can be a dangerous thing."

Hart took a drag on his cigarette. "Only to a weak man."

Castro gracefully sidestepped Hart's casual remark that bordered on insinuation. "Please give her my regards."

With nothing left to say, Castro strolled on down the street where he disappeared inside one of the cantinas.

As soon as Castro was out of sight, Hart headed up the hill on a brisk walk to Larkin's. He would have to decline dinner. He and his vaqueros could easily get the horses to San Juan Bautista by tomorrow tonight, then strike east and north up the San Joaquín River. Suddenly he felt an inexplicable urgency to get home.

Nancy rode her mare into the Indian village with Torey following in the supply wagon. Even though the Miwoks worked for Hart and Nancy, they preferred maintaining their own village a mile from the ranch. Always glad to see the supplies that Nancy brought to them once a week, they ran out to meet her with smiles and greetings. Children pushed their way past the adults to assume positions in the front of the circle that formed around the wagon.

Magdalena had come with Nancy once but had been so frightened that she had never returned. "What is to keep these savages from taking their hoes and knives to you and killing you?"

Nancy didn't share her cook's fear. She felt no hostility from the Miwoks. "They're here from choice," she had explained to Magdalena. "They're free to go any time it suits them. Most of these Indians have been born and raised on mission farms or have worked at Sutter's Fort for years. They have no desire to go back to the wild."

Magdalena could only shake her head. "You are a brave woman, Señora Daniels. I think you are brave just to ride that horse of yours."

The Indians ground their own corn into meal, did their own weaving, spinning, sewing, and cooking. They had been given permission to build their own adobes and most had done so.

This evening, with the work in the fields complete, they were lounging in the shade of their dwellings, relaxing with their families.

The group gathered around as Nancy pulled her mare to a stop. Behind her, Torey hollered "whoa" to the mules pulling the supply wagon. Nancy dismounted and removed from her saddlebags a cloth bag filled with gingersnaps for the children. The children had come to expect these little treats from her. Dropping to their knees, they kept their hands at their sides and waited politely with anticipation in their large, black eyes.

Most of the children were ten or under. Only a few were in their early teens, but Nancy excluded none of them. Starting with the oldest, she distributed the goodies. Each child showed his or her gratitude with a grin, sparkling eyes, and a thank you in one language or another.

Occasionally, one of the children had something to give to Nancy in return. Today, a little girl carrying the Spanish name of Rosita, shyly took the cookies in one pudgy hand and, with the other, handed Nancy a cornhusk doll she had made by herself.

Nancy, delighted by the girl's generosity and thoughtfulness, gave her a big hug. "Thank you, Rosita. I will cherish your gift always."

The children ran off to play and eat the cookies. Nancy helped Torey distribute the supplies.

On the way back to the ranch, they stopped to inspect the crops. Until harvest came in, they had had to buy everything from Sutter. A good yield was crucial so they could feed everyone on the ranch from their own produce. In a few years they would have their own fruit as well as vegetables.

The women did most of the weeding of the vegetable gardens and orchards while the men built irrigation ditches to carry water to the tender vegetables and fruits trees. The other crops had to depend on rainfall.

Until the ditches were completed, water had to be hauled to the plants in buckets. It was time-consuming, labor-intensive, and never quite provided adequate moisture. The area had received very little rain so far this summer. This dry climate was not unusual, according to Sutter and others who had been here in California for years. They assured her that the rains would come in full force in the winter. Nancy compared it to closing the barn door after the cows had gotten out.

Dusk was slipping down into the valley by the time Nancy and Torey arrived back at ranch headquarters. Her heart lifted at the sight of Brenham Royal's wagon parked outside the house. A visit from Brenham and Lottie was just what she needed to help pass the time until Hart returned.

But when Nancy rode past the wagon to tie her mare at the hitching rail, she was taken aback by the sight of blood-soaked blankets in the back of the wagon.

"Oh, no! I knew this was going to happen. Lottie's hemorrhaging."

She leaped from her horse and rushed into the house, halting so suddenly on the threshold that she nearly lost her balance. Prone and looking dead on a grass mat in the middle of the kitchen floor, and surrounded by no less than seven people, lay Brenham Royal. His clothes were nearly ripped from his body. His torso was a bloody mass of torn flesh.

A wave of nausea crested inside her. She gripped the door frame to steady herself. "Oh, my God, Lottie. What's happened to Brenham?"

27

"A goddamned grizzly, Nancy," Lottie said, rising to her feet. Her hands and clothes were covered with Brenham's blood. "He came right into the yard this morning while Brenham was out chopping wood. Harry tried to tackle him, but he was no match. The griz . . . killed him." Lottie took a sustaining breath and glanced at Josh. The boy, kneeling next to Elise and Beth, looked dazed.

"I've already sent a couple of vaqueros across the valley to get Dr. Marsh," Lottie continued. "Can you spare a man or two to ride to Sutter's Fort and see if there's a doctor there? I was going to try to get him to Sutter's, but I don't think he'll stand anymore jostling in the back of a wagon."

Nancy tried not to panic, but Brenham had lost an incredible amount of blood, and the bear had mauled his head badly. Blood had matted in his hair around ugly teeth punctures. Gashes on his arms and chest still oozed blood even though Lottie and the girls had wrapped them with makeshift bandages.

Elise, as blood-covered as Lottie, suddenly leaped to her feet and flung herself into Nancy's arms. "What are we going to do, Nancy? I'm afraid he's going to die!"

Nancy suspected the same thing, but kept her fears silent. "We're going to take care of him. But we must move quickly. Thane, you take one of the vaqueros and ride to the fort. Elise and Beth, I want you to make a pallet here in the kitchen where we can easily take care of him.

"Carmelita, you and Torey ride to the Indian encampment and get the medicine woman. Magdalena, Lottie, and I will see what we can do to clean up the wounds and stop the bleeding."

The vaqueros helped Beth and Elise prepare the pallet, but Nancy barely noticed their comings and goings as she and the other two women worked on dressing wounds. Magdalena had some experience with suturing—her husband had been knifed a few times in the course of his rowdy existence—so she took over with the needle and catgut. Running Cloud the Miwok medicine woman brought her bag of herbs and set about making a poultice which she carefully spread over Brenham's battered body.

Brenham's breathing was so shallow that Nancy expected each breath to be his last. Still, he lived. After what seemed hours of getting him cleaned, poulticed, sutured, and bandaged, the vaqueros moved him to the pallet.

Everyone was exhausted. Nancy encouraged them all to go to bed, especially the girls. Josh had long since fallen asleep on the floor. "I'll pull up my rocker and sit with Brenham for awhile," she offered.

Elise and Beth didn't want to leave their father, but finally, with worry and fear in their eyes, they accepted the offer of Nancy's bed. Magdalena and Carmelita retired to their own adobe. Lottie found a blanket and, after rolling Josh into it, curled up on the rug.

In the quiet of the house, with only one coal oil lamp left burning, Nancy wearily settled into her rocker. Leaning her head back, she closed her eyes and thought of the day she had rescued Brenham from the river. And about the day Lucille had left him for that worthless Arthur Waite. Brenham was a good man and had deserved a more supportive woman than Lucille. He deserved to live.

Unexpectedly, Lottie spoke, startling Nancy from her private thoughts. "I keep seeing that bear comin' at us, Nancy. Just coming and coming. He wouldn't be stopped. I've never seen anything like it."

"What happened?" Nancy whispered.

The brunette sat up. "I was in my adobe making cinnamon rolls for the girls, gettin' an early start so's I could get them baked for breakfast. Brenham was outside his own adobe, chopping wood. All of a sudden he let out a scream that nearly curled my hair. I figured he'd laid his leg open with that ax and I went running. But I saw that bear and stopped dead in my tracks. It had Brenham down—" She choked back a quiver in her voice. "I swear, Nancy. I've handled some bad things in my life, but that bear was the biggest goddamn thing I've ever seen. I screamed for the vaqueros and headed back to the house for my gun.

"The girls came out and that bear saw them. It left old Brenham cold and headed for them. I was screaming for them to get back inside the house. Anyway, before it was all over, every one of us who had a gun was pumping lead into that beast." Lottie's gaze drifted off, caught on the tiny flame in the lamp as she relived the horrible incident in her mind. "He finally fell, but it sure seemed to take forever."

Nancy shuddered, thinking of their bravery and how gallantly they'd risked their own lives to save Brenham. Then she put the imagined images from her head and bent over to touch Brenham's forehead.

"God, he's on fire, Lottie." Alarm lifted her voice. "We've got to do something to get this fever down."

They forgot their weariness. In minutes, they had collected water and clean cloths and had begun the ritual of wiping him down, a difficult task in itself in lieu of his heavily bandaged body.

Nancy didn't know how many minutes, or hours, had passed when suddenly Brenham opened his eyes.

"Lottie? That . . . you?"

"Sh-h-h, Brenham. You're in no condition to talk. I got you as far as Nancy's. We're waiting here for Dr. Marsh, and we've sent a messenger to Sutter's Fort to see if there's a doctor there."

He rolled his head on the pillow. His eyes were glazed with fever and pain. "Too late . . . Lottie . . ."

"Don't say that, Brenham," Nancy gently scolded. "I saved your life once, remember? There's no reason why I can't do it again."

"Need to . . . tell . . . Lottie . . . some . . . thing."

"It can wait, Brenham. Just rest."

"No, can't . . . wait. The . . . ranch, Lottie. Keep it. Somehow. For my . . . girls. They'll . . . need it. Take care . . . of them. Nobody . . . else . . . to . . ."

His eyelids started to close. Fear catapulted to Nancy's throat, nearly choking her. "Your girls need you, Brenham. Hold on for your girls."

His eyelids fluttered open again. "Take care . . . of them."

"Brenham, everything's going to be all right."

His eyes rolled back in his head and a rush of air escaped his lungs. Nancy and Lottie stared down at him in disbelief.

"God Almighty," Lottie whispered.

The clock ticked in the background, much louder than before. Marking the continual march of time. Never stopping for anything. Not even the death of a damned good man.

28

August

The white-yellow smoke from the longhorn's burning hair poured up into Lottie's face. She automatically held her breath until the worst of it had cleared. Her focus was on the red-hot branding iron, pressed against the cow's tough hide. It had to be applied with just the right pressure and for just the right length of time, which was a few long seconds. If held too long, it would burn through the hide and split it, creating a wound that would draw flies and infection. If it wasn't held long enough, the brand would be a "hair brand" and in a few months the hair would grow over it, obliterating it completely.

With the last names of Royal and England, she and Brenham had designed their brand and called it the "Crown." It had three interconnected peaks intended to resemble the front of a royal crown. Even though Brenham was gone, she kept the brand.

She had never considered her feelings for Brenham when he'd been alive, but in his death, she realized she missed his smiling face and his kind, gentlemanly ways. She and Nancy and the others had brought his body here to Rancho Corona and buried him up on the hill. Elise and Beth had been utterly devastated, but gradually they were learning that life goes on. They had found that work helped them to cope with their grief, and so they stayed busy taking on the responsibilities of the household like full-grown women. She couldn't have been prouder of them if they'd been her own girls. Josh was grieving, too, in his quiet way. He had started looking to Brenham in a fatherly capacity. The loss of Harry had also been a blow. When he spoke of the dog, though, it was with pride in his voice.

"He tried to take that grizzly, Ma. Harry was a good dog."

Lottie wouldn't have had to do the branding. She could have stayed at the house with the girls and simply given orders. Her vaqueros had even tried to talk her out of it. "Just because Señor Brenham did this while he was alive does not mean we would expect it of you," said Julio Fernandez.

To which she had responded, "I might eventually turn it over to someone, but I want to learn to do these things. What good is a *hacendada* who knows nothing of what is going on beyond her hacienda?"

Lottie knew vaqueros were adverse to any job that took them out of the saddle anyway. They were experts with lariats, laying their loops neatly over the horns of the mean, wild cattle, and then using their saddle horns to dally the ropes. Their horses did the rest of the work by dragging each cow, at the end of a rope, to the branding fire where two more vaqueros snared the front and hind feet with quick, accurate loops. The vaqueros pulled in opposite directions at this point. The cow's feet were literally taken out from under her and she invariably fell to her side. The two vaqueros continued pulling the ropes in opposite directions until the animal was stretched taut. In this position, the cattle could do nothing but bawl at their restraint, which, from their reactions, appeared to hurt their pride worse than the branding iron hurt their thick hides.

"Ma! Watch out for the horns!" Josh suddenly yelled from behind her.

Lottie jerked back just as a flailing head and its six-foot span of wicked horns slashed past her thigh, missing flesh but catching the folds of her skirt and tearing the cloth.

The smoke boiling up into her face made it difficult to see and she had to put her full concentration on the brand. She had messed up her share as it was. The vaqueros had laughed good-naturedly and told her she would learn eventually. She had burned a few too deeply, overcompensating the next time by applying only hair brands. She had put a few too far up on the back, and numerous brands had come out upside-down. But when the cow was stretched out on its side, it was sometimes difficult to tell exactly where the brand was supposed to go so that when the cow stood back up the brand would be in the right place.

"Are you all right, Ma?" Josh took the used branding iron from her and raced it back to the fire. There were a half-dozen irons in the fire so that one would be hot at all times. It was his job to keep the fire going and the irons down deep in the growing pile of coals. His face was flushed from the heat of the summer day and the heat of tending the fire.

Lottie moved out of the way, as the vaqueros expertly released the ropes on the cow's head and legs simultaneously. The cow leaped up with lightning speed, flinging her horns and a long string of snot from her nose, looking to attack someone—anyone—in compensation for the outrage she had suffered. The natural target was someone on the ground, so the vaqueros were very diligent about hazing her back out onto the range. Lottie, fearing more for Josh than herself, had had a heavy farm wagon pulled up not far from the fire so that either Josh or herself could leap into it in case one of the animals got past the vaqueros.

The vaqueros themselves were not entirely safe from the path of the wild cattle. One of the vaqueros was back at the ranch on his bunk with a nasty gash that ran from his thigh to his knee where a longhorn had, just two days ago, separated his flesh with one mighty swipe of its horn. Lottie and the girls had been forced to once again get out the catgut and indulge in some fancy skin stitchery.

Lottie removed her hat and wiped the sweat from her brow with her blouse sleeve. She looked out over the corraled herd of wild yearlings and two-year-olds that the vaqueros had gathered prior to Brenham's death. Normally, according to the vaqueros, the calves were branded in the spring. But until Lottie got all the cattle she would need to stock the ranch, they would have to continue to brand those brought in regardless of the season.

Bullocks had to be castrated. For breeding purposes as well as management, ranchers wanted only about one bull for every twenty-five head of cattle. The castrating was being done by an Indian who called himself Juan. Just Juan. He said he had no other name except his Indian name which, in English, meant Bird Singing. He was older than most of the vaqueros, probably in his fifties. Lottie had learned that all the original vaqueros had been Indians, having learned their craft while at the missions before secularization, and before they had been turned loose to make their own way. Juan was so quick at his job, it seemed his knife made a couple of flashes in the sun and he was done. There was usually very little bleeding, either. She had entertained the notion more than once that if mild-mannered Juan should ever decide to kill someone, at least it would be neat, quick, and probably painless.

Josh handed her the canteen of tepid water. "Time for a drink, Ma?"

"How did you know I was dying of thirst?"

He grinned. " 'Cause I was."

Lottie drank thirstily then handed the canteen to her son. He pushed his hat to the back of his head to drink, and Lottie didn't miss the chance to ruffle the sweaty curls matted to his forehead. Already he was looking out toward the herd, ready to continue. She thought the boy must never tire and she wished she had his energy, or even the energy she'd had ten years ago.

Suddenly his thick, brown brows shot together. "Hey, Ma. Who's that vaquero out there? He ain't one of ours."

Lottie looked across the herd of milling longhorns being held in the basin in a tight bunch by several vaqueros. The cattle had settled down and were just standing now, but she knew that at any given moment one might take the notion to bolt for freedom and a stampede would be on. She knew because it had happened the first day they'd tried to brand.

She spotted the man Josh was talking about. From a distance, he didn't look much different from the other vaqueros. All vaqueros rode as if they were part of their horses, and each one had his own form, figure, and style that could be recognized. But there was something about the way this man sat his spirited black horse that stirred a place inside Lottie that hadn't been stirred for years.

Juan came up beside her, quietly, as he usually did. "That is Carlito Palocios. He is one of the best *amansadores* in all of California."

Lottie's interest was piqued. She could use a good horsebreaker on the ranch. "I wonder what he's doing all the way out here."

"He roams about, going from ranch to ranch. Breaking horses and then moving on. But I am surprised to see him so far from the settlements. Maybe he has come only out of curiosity to see the rest of California and what the Americans are doing with it."

"Is he a decent sort?"

"*Sí*. We all know him. You could not go wrong to hire him."

Palocios's riata snaked out and easily settled over the horns of an un-suspecting cow, showing that he was also a very accomplished vaquero.

In the next instant his horse had leaned into the opposing force and was dragging the captured beast to the fire. The other men lifted their arms in greeting, apparently thinking nothing of his unexpected appearance.

Lottie wondered how long the man had been there, watching them, watching her. She was a mess. Her clothes were dirty, her hair straggling down out of her hat and down around her face. Her face was probably dirty, too, if Josh's could be used as a mirror.

She stepped closer to the fire as the vaqueros roped another cow and stretched it out. Gathering up the hottest iron, Lottie placed it on the critter's hide. The smoke billowed up into her nostrils again for lack of a breeze to blow it away. After a few seconds, she pulled the iron away in one quick, decisive movement to keep the brand from smearing.

Handing the iron back to Josh, she moved away from the longhorn and over to the new arrival. He had removed his rope from the longhorn's neck and was coiling it back up. He had done it all from the saddle, but now he stepped to the ground, his spurs with their five-inch rowels, dragging in the dirt.

"Can I offer you a job, señor?" she asked lightly as she pulled her leather gloves off. "Or do you just enjoy working for free?"

It was crazy, but her heart was pounding like a hammer against her chest. Never had she seen such a handsome man. Not even Major could compare. She had to force herself to breathe. The din of the bawling cattle faded away into the roar that began inside her own head, crashing there like the winter waves on the ocean's rocky coast.

The Californio, who was probably a few years younger than she was, flashed her a white-toothed smile, took her proffered hand and bowed from the waist, as if she were royalty. "It is my pleasure to make your acquaintance, Señora England. I am Carlito Palocios, born and raised near Monterey. I am indeed looking for work, and it was rumored that there was an incredibly beautiful woman who owned a rancho called Corona in the Great Valley. So I thought I would ride here and see if the rumors were true. I am pleased to say they were. It would be my honor to serve you in any way I can. I know most of your vaqueros. They will vouch for my skills."

The heat from his fingers was almost as hot as the handle of the branding iron. Her heart stopped, at least for the space of a few seconds. He released her hand, but clearly without haste.

"Juan says you're an *amansador*, Señor Palocios," she groped for words, feeling peculiarly rattled by his presence. "But I could use another man to do the branding. Since my partner was killed, I find myself one short."

She fully expected him to refuse the offer. An *amansador* may be too proud, and might consider himself too important, to stoop to the dirty job of branding cattle.

"I have learned that most vaqueros prefer to be horseback." She flashed a teasing smile from Palocios to her men. "At least the ones I've hired so far are of that mind."

His smile widened and his black eyes sparkled. His flat-brimmed hat rested on his broad back, held there by a string that pressed against a strong, tanned throat. A strand of black, short-cropped hair fell down onto his forehead. She guessed his age at about thirty-two or thirty-three, and while she suspected a man so handsome would surely have a wife, or at least a girlfriend, she found herself hoping he didn't.

There appeared no deception in his eyes. He seemed very forthright, and she liked that in a person. "I probably do my best work on my horse, señora, but I am very good on my feet, too."

And probably very good in a woman's bed, as well, she thought.

But the mention of his feet drew her eyes to the ground, to the heavy spurs with their five-inch rowels, and to the low-heeled boots made of soft buckskin. He wore the standard garb of the vaquero, with only personal touches for variation. His pants, with buttons down the outside of both legs, fit snugly across his hips and thighs. As was the style, the buttons were left undone from the knee down, flaring out to reveal the voluminous leggings beneath. Partially concealed in the flare on the right leg, he carried the ever-present long knife in its scabbard. In this position, it could be easily reached while on horseback.

Carlito Palocios was not a tall man, perhaps only five-foot-nine, and he was lean and evenly proportioned, his legs the strong, sturdy legs of a horseman. Because of the heat of the day, he wore only a loose-flowing white blouse, open at the throat, tucked into his trousers and circled at the waist with a red sash. His intelligent eyes were kind and friendly and offered no threat of any kind, and yet her sixth sense told her he could be a very dangerous man to a woman's heart.

"You can have the job if you want it," she said. "I wouldn't mind turning it over to a man."

"It would be the wise thing for you to do, señora. You are too beautiful to be out in this heat, doing work meant for a man." His chivalry seemed sincere, not practiced. "I would be happy to do this work for you."

"The job is yours then," she said, hoping her instincts were on target.

She felt Josh tugging at her hand, and finally looked down at his plaintive face. "What is it, son?"

Josh glanced askance at the new arrival, then blurted out his concern. "If you ain't branding, then I'm probably gonna have to quit too."

Carlito Palocios grinned and bent down to remove his spurs. "You are doing a good job, no? There is no reason for you to leave. I would much appreciate you to continue in your position just as you have been. That is, if your mother does not mind."

Josh's gaze shot back to Lottie's, this time with hope. "Can I, Ma?"

Lottie looked up at Carlito Palocios. His eyes sparkled back at her in such a manner that she felt he concealed nothing of himself. "Are you sure? He might get underfoot."

"So it is with all of us, from time to time. I have no sons, señora, for I have no wife, but I have nieces and nephews. I do not mind children. Were we not all children at one time?"

Lottie pulled in a deep breath and let it out. She'd been released from her job and wasn't sure she appreciated the freedom. The work was hard, but she liked to be in the middle of it. In charge. In control. Something told her that even though Carlito Palocios was the newest employee, he would be in charge now when she was gone, and the others wouldn't mind. They would gravitate to him, to his expertise, and they would look up to him and expect him to tell them what to do. She didn't know how she knew all these things. She simply did.

She ruffled Josh's hair one last time, then sauntered away from the branding fire. Mounting her mule, she watched for ten or fifteen minutes to make sure Carlito knew as much as he said he did. Admittedly, he branded with more ease and finesse than she did, and seemingly with less effort and sweat.

She turned her mule back to the house, wondering about Carlito. One would almost expect a man of his bearing to be a rich *hacendado*, not a drifting *amansador*, earning a little here and a little there.

She paused atop a knoll and looked back down at the branding scene again. A feeling stirred inside her. A feeling of restlessness, of need, of want. Carlito Palocios reminded her that she had been alone for many years without a man to hold her at night, to make sweet love to her, to whisper romantic words, to cherish her, to love her. To touch her. She missed being touched by a man. He reminded her that, in truth, she had *never* had those things she craved. Major had not filled that emptiness inside her. Major had never truly satisfied her lonely heart.

Releasing a sigh, she nudged her mule on down the hill.

29

"Come quick, señora. He is home! Señor Daniels is home."

Nancy set aside the pattern piece she and Carmelita had just made, and hurried outside. Shading her eyes with her hand against the bright glare of the afternoon sun, she searched the distant hills, golden now at summer's end.

She spotted the band of wild horses running down into the valley, being directed by four riders. Even at the distance, she easily recognized her husband. It was something in the breadth of his shoulders. Something in the way he sat his saddle.

Herded by the vaqueros, the wild horses veered to the river. Hart separated and loped his horse toward the ranch. He was out of the saddle practically before his horse had come to a complete halt. He pulled her into his arms, holding her so tightly she could barely breath.

"God, I missed you," he proclaimed in a husky whisper. "When Castro told me he'd been here . . . well, I was worried." He set her an arm's length away and looked her over as if to assure himself that she was unharmed.

Exalted by his unconcealed love, Nancy gave him a bright smile. "His visit *was* a bit unnerving, but everything is all right, except—"

His brows shot together. "Except what, Nancy?"

Her smile faded. "Brenham's dead, Hart. Killed by a grizzly." Briefly she explained how it had happened.

Hart released a deep sigh, shaking his head in disbelief and remorse. "How's Lottie doing over there by herself?"

"Faring. She's taken over a considerable amount of what Brenham had been doing. I hear she did hire a man who might eventually work into the capacity of foreman. A vaquero by the name of Carlito Palocios."

"And the girls?"

"Before Brenham died he asked Lottie to keep his girls."

"Boy, that's a tall order."

"We asked them if they wanted us to try and find their mother, but they said they'd rather stay here with Lottie. And Lottie doesn't mind. Unlike their mother, Beth and Elise are well-mannered, and they respect and like Lottie. They treat Josh like their brother. They're certainly not lazy, and I know they'll do more than their share of the work. Brenham's share of the ranch is theirs now. They miss Brenham terribly, but Lottie will treat them like her own. Now, tell me, do you have to leave again soon?"

"No. We've got all the cattle we'll need for a starter herd, and enough horses for a decent-sized remuda. The vaqueros will be sticking close to the ranch to break the horses, and I want to help Torey and Thane finish the house. We're going to be in it by Christmas, just like I promised."

He led her over to his buckskin. "Let's ride out so you can see the stallion. We can ride double on my horse."

Hart assisted her into his saddle then swung up behind her. She had a barrage of questions about the stallion until Hart started to nuzzle her neck with affectionate kisses. "I brought you a gift from Monterey," he whispered. "Something other than the horse. I have it with me."

There was such a mysterious quality to his voice that Nancy wondered what he had up his sleeve. Teasing was his favorite thing, next to lovemaking. She turned and saw the sly smile playing at his lips. "Is this going to be a joke, Hart? Something you learned in Monterey?" She looked him over good but saw no sign of a package bulging from his pockets or stuffed in his shirt. She even lifted his hat to find only his hair.

"Now, turn around, close your eyes," he said. "And no peeking."

She obliged but suddenly felt as excited as a child on her birthday. "What could you have possibly brought me that you have to be so secretive about? Come on, hurry. You know how I hate suspense."

"Patience, my lady. Patience."

He lifted her hand in both of his. Shortly she felt the circle of a ring slide down the length of her finger, and then she knew. She opened her eyes to a gorgeous cluster of tiny pearls and diamonds set in a thick gold band. Her wedding ring, at long last.

"Oh, Hart," she murmured in awe. "It's the most beautiful thing I've ever seen." She held her hand out, turning it this way and that, admiring the way the gems sparkled in the sunlight.

"I'm sorry it took me a year to get it," Hart apologized. "I hadn't forgotten. I was just waiting for the right one, and finally a shipment of jewelry came in on one of the trading vessels this time when I was in Monterey. Apparently jewelry is a popular item among the California women, but I got there first and got my pick."

She twisted in the saddle and gave him a hug and a kiss. "It was worth the wait, sweetheart. Truly."

"I hope you like my choice of horses as well as you do rings. There's the stallion, over by the river."

They had reached the herd, grazing in the wide valley below the ranch headquarters. The vaqueros were staying with the animals until they settled into their new surroundings. Ultimately, they would stray, but soon they would be branded, and some of them would be brought into the corrals to be broke for riding.

Osvaldo easily placed a rope over the head of the bay stallion and brought him closer for Nancy's inspection. Even though spirited, the stallion was broke to ride and well-mannered. He took a liking to Nancy and won her over immediately.

"He's everything I'd hoped for, Hart," she said, rubbing his velvety nose. "With him and Lady Rae as our base stock, we'll have the finest horses in Northern California. Maybe in *all* of California."

"It's my wish to see your dream come true, Nancy. It always has been, and I'll do whatever I can to help you."

On the way back to the ranch, Osvaldo led the stallion and rode on ahead. Nancy and Hart stayed behind to exchange all the information and news each had heard in the other's absence. Discussion of the stallion soon led to Castro and his men gathering wild horses in the Great Valley.

"Rumor has it that those mustangs are to be used by Castro's army when he and Alvarado stage their revolution against Micheltorena," Hart said.

"I had a feeling he had ulterior motives for being out here," Nancy replied. "I also think he was looking to see our manpower. I didn't like him, Hart. We could be in trouble if he succeeds in wresting power from Micheltorena."

"If he does and proves to be a dictator out to chase the Americans out of the country, then I feel confident that the United States will intervene."

"I think the Americans here would probably initiate their own uprising if José Castro got too heavy-handed. They're outnumbered, and aren't as good on horseback as the Californios, but they have better weapons and more fire power. And they won't put up with a dictator."

"No, they won't," Hart replied. "And I certainly don't like the idea of Castro coming out here trying to intimidate you into selling your mare. Be careful of his sort, Nancy. You never know what men like him might do. They don't like their authority challenged, and they don't like to be made to look foolish, especially by a woman."

"I wasn't going to let him scare me into giving him my horse, Hart," she responded defensively. "Once those kind of people know you're easily intimidated, they just take that much more advantage of it. They just keep pushing and pushing. I won't back down just because I'm a woman. But I'll use common sense, too, in how far I can take a bluff."

"Some people have good memories and a taste for revenge. Castro is a revolutionist, a natural-born military commander who likes a good fight. He's out to have the power over California because he feels it should rightfully be his. He might be all bluster, but one can't take the chance."

While Hart unsaddled his tired horse, Nancy watched in silence. At first he thought she might be considering Castro's true motives, but he soon sensed that something else was on her mind. A subject she was reluctant to broach. A subject that might not hold the same immediacy as the threat of war, but one that was troubling her just the same.

He pulled the heavy California saddle from his horse's sweaty back and tossed it over the hitching rail. "Has something else happened I should know about, Nancy?"

A startled expression crossed her face that he would be able to read her so completely. She hastened to resume a normal demeanor. "No, not at all. Nothing. Everything's fine. Almost fine. Actually, Hart, there is something. It's not all that important, I suppose. I mean we could discuss it later, but it's something that's been on my mind. I've been giving it a lot of thought."

Grinning, he rested his arm over his horse's back. "Tell me about it."

"Oh, we can discuss it later."

"No, let's discuss it now."

She hesitated, as if she might argue further, then finally she relented. "Very well. I'm twenty-seven now, as you know, and I was thinking that it's time I tried to have a baby again. If I'm ever going to get it done, I really should go ahead and do it. I mean, it's been a year and—"

He tossed his head back and laughed, pulling her into his arms again. "I can't think of a more pleasant duty," he whispered against her parted mouth. "I'll get started on it right away."

But that night as Hart held his sleeping wife in his arms, content from their lovemaking, he worried. What if they did end up in the middle of a war? What would happen to Nancy? To a baby?

There were times when he honestly believed in fate. Believed that he had been living each day, each year, just waiting for the moment when God deemed it time to set the two of them on a course toward each other. He loved Nancy more than any dream he could have ever dreamed. And he realized now that his dreams, however camouflaged, had always been of her, of love, of building a life together and sharing the intimacies of man and wife.

He worried, not about their relationship, but about her decision that he was obligated to honor. He wanted children, too, but he had come so close to losing her the first time. He could only hope that being at home, with proper care and good food, that this time she might fare better than last. There was already one grave at Rancho Corona. He wanted none at Rancho Vallecito.

30

November

"It's what you call a chocolate torte," Lottie explained to Elise and Beth. "And I've got a mighty big hankering for a piece. Hell, maybe I'll just eat the whole damn thing single-handedly when we get it baked."

Elise nodded and smiled, amused by Lottie's forthrightness. "Maybe I should make two, Lottie. If it's as good as you say it is, then I'm sure Beth and I will think it's wonderful, too. You show me how so I can do it by myself next time. We could take one to Nancy and Hart for Christmas."

"That's an excellent idea."

"Is Nancy feeling better now?"

"When I was over there last week, she was still sick in bed," Lottie said, her brow furrowing. "I just hope she can carry this baby to term and not lose it like she did the first one. She'll be going on four months by Christmas. Anyway, I think I'll go out and gather the eggs."

"I can do that," Beth volunteered.

"No, stay and help your sister. The mornings are the best time. My favorite time."

Lottie left the little adobe with basket in hand. The chicken coop was a fair distance from the main house, but, as she had told the girls, she enjoyed the mornings the best. Like now, just as the sun was coming up, spreading its golden glow down over the hills and valleys, making the ripened grass gleam as if it were swaying strands of gold, growing from the rich earth.

The chickens were setting up a commotion as she neared the henhouse. Thinking a weasel must be raiding the nests, she stepped up her pace, all the while thinking she was going to have to set a trap.

She flung open the henhouse door and stepped inside. The interior was still dim in the morning light. The chickens flapped about, hitting the roof and the wooden stanchions that held the nesting cubicles.

But in the next instant, she was seized from behind and a hand closed over her mouth and nose, silencing her startled cry. "So we meet the Americano woman who would dare refuse her horse to our *comandante?*" came a deep male voice, speaking mostly Spanish and some broken English. "Maybe we should teach her a lesson in respect, *amigos*. And then, when we are done, take her to our camp and let the others reinforce the lesson."

Lottie struggled to get away. "Leave me alone, you stinking bastard!"

"We only came for eggs," a younger-sounding voice objected. "You said so yourself, Reynaldo."

"*¡Silencio!* If you are not man enough to take your pleasures, then I have a big knife that will fix you so you will never take them again."

A third voice came from the other corner. "Gag her, Reynaldo, and we'll hold her down. I am not afraid to take my turn. We will teach the *puta* that she does not say no to Comandante Castro."

Fear nearly choked Lottie. These men thought she was Nancy! She knew all about the incident with Castro and the horse. These men must be from Castro's army. But dear God, she wouldn't betray her friend and send these animals her way. It would matter little anyway. They had her now and they would not release her until they got what they wanted.

She cursed her carelessness. Where was her goddamned gun when she needed it?

"You bastards! I'll see you in your graves."

They only laughed at her impotent threats. Reynaldo grabbed her legs and in the next instant she was on her back in the straw. While the other two held her arms, Reynaldo shoved her skirt and petticoat up to her waist and ripped away her drawers. She managed to scream out for help with all her gusto before Reynaldo slapped her face and shoved a dirty bandana in her mouth.

She didn't want to look at them, but she forced herself to so she could remember their faces and kill them. They were filthy in appearance as well as character. Grimy clothes, greasy hair, unshaven faces; greedy, evil eyes. Reynaldo tried to spread her legs but she kicked him in the face with her boot heel, bloodying his nose—maybe breaking it—and raising his ire. She continued kicking any part of him she could reach until she saw the gleam of his knife inches from her face.

"You will be still or I will slice your throat from ear to ear."

Lottie never doubted it for a minute. Her last hope plummeted. By the time anyone missed her, they would have completed their violation. Maybe even her murder.

Grinning now, like a man who knows he will be victorious, Reynaldo dropped his pants while keeping the knife pressed to her throat. His extended male organ sprang up from its ugly nest of matted, black hair. Chuckling, he positioned himself between her legs.

He put his hand on her private parts and started rubbing her with his dirty fingers. He spoke something in Spanish she couldn't understand, and didn't think she wanted to understand anyway. His friends' chuckles were low, restrained gurgles in their throats. Then Reynaldo circled his own manhood and pumped it a few times, grinning at her. To her horror, he got up from his position between her legs and straddled her chest, laughing and jabbing her face with his penis. She turned her head to avoid it, but felt the sting of the knife followed by the warmth of her own blood.

"Ah, see what happens when you resist?" Reynaldo said. "Now, I am going to remove your gag, but if you scream I will finish slicing your throat. ¿*Comprende?*"

Lottie struggled again, although there was no way she could win this battle. The gag was removed and immediately Reynaldo tried shoving his rigid male organ into her mouth. She clamped her lips tightly together, but he grabbed her chin and pinched on either side of her mouth.

"You will obey me, *puta,* and if you bite me, you will die."

Lottie prayed to God for someone to come and find her. Her fear and humiliation, her rage and her tears blurred the scene as she tried to separate herself from it. Revulsion rose in her throat as his organ slid into her mouth. Her stomach turned and heaved, spewing vomit up out of her throat. It spilled onto her face, choking her. Reynaldo cursed and pulled back as if he'd been snake-bit.

At nearly the same time, the henhouse door flew open and banged on its hinges. Through a blur, Lottie saw Carlito, his face a mask of rage. His shotgun boomed. Once. Twice. Two of her assailants were blasted from their positions, their heads and chests ripped apart, their blood splattering on the walls, on her face, her clothes, the squawking chickens. Reynaldo fell backward, gripping a long stiletto that had flashed across the distance from Carlito's hand to land with a heavy thud deep in his heart.

Reflexively, she rolled to her side and curled up, still vomiting and crying and wiping the vileness from her mouth with her hand and her blouse sleeve. All the while wanting to hide from herself, from Carlito.

Then he was there next to her, kneeling on one knee with his hand on her shoulder. "It is over now, Lolita," he said tenderly. "I am sorry I was not here sooner, but I came as quickly as I could when I heard your cry for help." He stroked her hair so gently. "It will be all right now."

"Don't tell Josh, and the girls. I don't want nobody to . . . know."

"Then they shall not."

She couldn't look at him. She would never be able to look at him again. But she was grateful. So very grateful he had come when he had. She could not even choke out words of gratitude; she could only stare numbly at the straw pressed against her face.

Carlito pulled her into his arms. She turned her face away from his, pressing her cheek against his strong, broad shoulder and the soft cloth of his cotton shirt. He continued to hold her and soothe her with comforting words and strokes of his lean, brown hand. She had no idea how long they remained in each other's arms. It couldn't have been too long, for soon she heard running feet and shouts from the other vaqueros as they came to see what had warranted firing the shotgun so early in the morning. One appeared at the door, but Lottie turned her head away, still pressing her face against Carlito's chest. He stroked her hair, running a gentle hand over her head.

"These men attacked our *patróna,*" he said. "But she will be all right. Remove them from here and throw their bodies in a wagon. I think they ride with Juan Bautista Alvarado and José Castro. I will return their bodies myself, for there are a few things I want to say to those two."

Carlito stood up and lifted Lottie into his arms. She was so shaken she allowed him to carry her all the way to the house and to her room, where he gently laid her on her bed and then sat down on the edge, next to her. Elise and Beth both wanted to know what had happened, but Carlito would only say, "She was attacked by thieves. Get some warm water. I think a bath will be what she wants."

"Is she going to die, too?" Beth asked fearfully. The young girl had turned to Lottie in the full capacity of a parent when her father had died.

"No, *chiquita*," Carlito said gently. "She will not die. She has many vaqueros to protect her. *I* will protect her."

The girls, deciding they would have to be content with that bit of assurance, hurried away, cursing the thieves and conjecturing on what exactly it was they had done to Lottie. Elise had heard of what men did to women, and she'd seen Lottie's torn drawers. But she didn't say anything to her little sister.

"If Carlito hadn't killed them first, I would go out there and kill them myself," Beth announced. "Just the way we killed that grizzly."

"You shouldn't talk that way, Beth."

"I don't care. Out here in California you can talk any way you please. You can do anything you please. You can even kill people if it suits you."

"You can't kill people in cold blood."

"Who's to stop me?"

The child's words troubled Carlito, but he understood that she was only afraid of losing another person she loved. He looked down at Lottie. Her eyes were vacant, distant, and she refused to look at him. He didn't think the men had raped her because he had been standing in the doorway of the vaquero quarters when she had come across the yard, headed for the henhouse. From the morning shadows, he had watched her while the fire in him burned for her. She was very beautiful, and his thoughts had been that he wanted her, but he saw no way that it would ever happen.

He was only her servant; he could not expect to attain a higher position in her life. He had been musing about her, there in the doorway of his quarters, when he had heard a cry and the commotion inside the henhouse. He had grabbed his shotgun and run, not knowing what he would find, but expecting something. His senses had been honed for danger his entire life. He had run toward the henhouse, seeing three horses tied a distance from the house, and he had smelled the evil doings inside.

He ran a finger along her cheek, being bolder than he should be. But she needed comforting and he wanted nothing more than to give it to her. He would take her in his arms again and lay with her this very minute, but he knew that would be one step too far.

"Please look at me, Lolita. You are a strong woman, but no match for Castro's men. Do not be ashamed. What those men did to you was by no means your fault. I am angry that they were there. That they were able to sneak in, past us all, and do this thing. From now on, I will post guards."

Lottie nearly cried again at his tenderness, but she couldn't look at him. Gently he took her chin in his hand and turned her head. Finally she lifted her eyes to his, and there she saw so much kindness and understanding, that emotion overflowed the weak wall of restraint she had surrounded herself with. She began to cry again, and he was there, comforting her in his arms.

"They thought I was Nancy. They thought they were paying her back for that incident with Castro and the horse."

That troubled Carlito more than he could say, and he wondered if Castro had sent them. "You are a loyal friend to lay your life on the line for Señora Daniels."

"She's good, Carlito. Better than I ever was or ever could be. And she's been a friend to me, the only real friend I've ever had in my life. I'm glad you killed the bastards. I had every intention of doing it myself."

Carlito didn't tell her that he didn't think they would have spared her life when they had finished with her. But she would be all right now. He knew this because she was already cursing again, something he found rather amusing. She tried to be so tough—and she was in her way—but underneath, she was a woman with a woman's heart.

Elise came back into the room. "I'll take care of her now, Carlito," she said with a frown, clearly not liking the intimate scene she had walked in on. Carlito reluctantly set Lottie away, pushing a strand of hair away from her face one last time before he rose from the bed and put the unwanted distance between them. He would never wish for Lolita to suffer in any way, but this incident of mistaken identity had allowed him to get close to her in a way he long dreamed of doing. Maybe it would be easier a second time.

"Our *patróna* will be fine," he said. "She is a woman stronger than any I have ever known. Now, I will take care of the matter of the thieves."

"Carlito," Lottie's voice halted him as he turned to leave.

Hesitating at the door, he lifted his eyes to hers, thinking, hoping, that the look she gave him was indicative of some sort of feeling for him. "Sí, señora?"

"Don't mention this to anyone, please."

"You have my word."

Gratitude washed over her face. "Thank you, Carlito. And be careful where Castro is concerned."

"I am always careful, Lolita. And I am not afraid of José Castro."

He left the room, returning to his quarters where he finished dressing and arming himself. Not bothering to eat breakfast, he put some jerky in his saddlebags and solicited the aid of an Indian fieldworker named Long Legs to drive the wagon carrying the dead men. His only regret was that he had killed the men so quickly. Looking back, he was thinking it might have better served his rage if he had made them beg first, just a little.

About two miles from the ranch, Carlito signaled for Long Legs to halt the wagon beneath a grove of sycamore trees at the crest of a hill. He backed his own horse into the shadow of the trees to get a better look at what he saw in the huge valley below them and removed an old spyglass from his saddlebags. "What is it you see, Carlito?" Long Legs urged. "My eyes are not so good any more and I cannot see clearly past the mules' ears."

After several minutes, Carlito lowered the spyglass. "As I suspected, it is Castro and Alvarado. There's probably about two dozen men, and they have a remuda of wild horses bunched down along the river. Come on, we're going to take the bodies of the thieves down there and let them handle it."

Long Legs' black eyes enlarged with fear. "Two dozen? Do you think it's wise for us to go down there? I am not even armed."

"Castro won't shoot me. We used to play together when we were children."

"But what about me, Carlito? Will he kill me?"

Carlito gave the old man a grin. "If he does, I'll kill him. He'll be smart enough to know that."

Long Legs wasn't completely pacified with the answer, but he tapped the reins over the mules' backs anyway and the wagon rumbled along down the hill behind Carlito.

They had not gotten very far when they were spotted by Castro's men. One rode out and escorted them back to camp where Castro and Alvarado were waiting.

Alvarado recognized Carlito first, or at least made the first acknowledgment by smiling and walking out to greet him. "Look here, José, it is our old *compadre*, Carlito Palocios, who went to school with us. So you have come to help us fight that dog, Micheltorena. I knew you would eventually see that it was your duty as a Californio."

Carlito crossed his arms over his saddle horn and gave Juan Bautista Alvarado his best smile. "I have been fighting, *sí*, but for no one's cause except my own. While you have been sitting here in the shade smoking your cigars and plotting your attack on Micheltorena's army, I have killed three of your men." He watched as their expressions changed from pleasantness to dismay. "Their bodies are in the wagon. You can do with them as you please. I will leave now, and with the suggestion that you stay off the Rancho Corona if you do not want the same thing to happen to you."

The men rushed to the wagon and looked at the bodies, two with their faces nearly blown away. "They are hardly recognizable, Carlito," Alvarado objected. "Did you have to blow their faces off?"

"There's one that still has his face. He only has a hole in his heart. I'm sure you recognize him as one of your men."

"What caused you to do this?"

Carlito gave a little shrug. "They were stealing chickens."

"What! You did this to them for stealing chickens? Oh, you are a bloodthirsty sonofabitch, Palocios."

Carlito's smile faded and he knifed José with a dark gaze. "Isn't this what the rebellion is all about, *amigo?*" He said the last word with a decisive bite. "You did not like the way Micheltorena's *cholos* were behaving? They were robbing and committing all sorts of immoralities."

"*Sí*, but—"

"It would seem your men are guilty of the same crimes. I'm going to leave their bodies here. You can bury them, if you want to. I only know that if anyone comes back to the Rancho Corona and tries to steal, or harm anyone—whether it's *your* army or Micheltorena's—they will get the same treatment."

He straightened in his saddle, preparing to rein his horse around when Alvarado caught his bridle. "So you are working for the Americano woman who owns the ranch? Are you bedding her as well? Could it be you are only using her to get that which you lost years ago?"

When Carlito did not answer, José added with a wicked grin. "From what I have seen of her, it would not be a distasteful liaison. It is no wonder you do not want to ride with us when you have such great plans for yourself. But what good will your plans do you, Carlito, if we stay under the thumb of Mexico? Or if we are taken over by these Americanos?"

"You fight for a worthy cause *mis amigos,* but a lost one. Besides, if I was to join your rebels, I would have to be their leader, and I do not think you would be happy with that. I take orders from no one."

"Except that woman."

"Ah, but she is an exception; a very beautiful exception. And her position is steadfast where your own is like the shadow of running horses across rolling hills."

"You are a coward, Palocios. You always have been. You like to ride around on your stallion, and shoot chicken thieves in the face with shotguns, but you do not want to risk your life on the battlefield."

Carlito was amused. "I don't see you doing much fighting, José. You are like a dog that barks because the moon has risen and has frightened him to death. But the dog, in all his stupidity, still knows, somehow, that he is relatively safe to bark and bluster because the moon will not come down out of the sky to silence him."

Carlito wanted their reaction. He saw only sheepishness. "You will learn this eventually," he continued, "but I will tell you now so you cannot say you weren't warned. There are not enough Californios to fight either the Mexicans, the Americans, or the British. Whichever one should decide to take over. We would have been better off if we could have kept California a secret for another hundred years. But it was not to be. So go mount your rebellion and get your power back for a little while. I can tell you it will not last. The Americanos will keep coming. And others from other countries. Even the Mexicans you are trying to drive out will return when they see that California has more to offer than their own country.

"We Californios have seen our time, *mis amigos.* The tide of people from overland and over the sea will not stop now."

Carlito trotted his horse to the rear of the wagon and expertly looped his lariat around the six feet of the dead thieves. Urging his stallion into a lope, he jerked the bodies out of the wagon. They hit the ground, hard and heavy. A few more flicks of his wrist and the rope came clear again. Coiling it, he gave one last look to José Castro and Juan Bautista Alvarado, then headed back to the Rancho Corona.

31

December

Nancy ate. She ate everything placed in front of her and then asked for more. The nausea had finally lifted, returning only occasionally in the early morning or late at night. With each new day, she had feared she would wake to pain and blood and the loss of another baby. But each day came and went, and she was encouraged by the continuing improvement of her condition.

A few weeks ago, Hart had carried her over the threshold of their new home. Although there was still some finishing work to be done and furnishings to order from back East, they were officially moved in.

To add to the heightening of Nancy's spirits, she was surprised two days before Christmas by a party of visitors from Monterey and another party from Napa Valley. They brought with them letters from Amherst. From Grandpa.

The other members of her family still refused to acknowledge her existence, apparently as some sort of punishment for her moving away. But Nancy recalled her grandfather saying "the past is the past, and the only way to go is forward." So she refused to dwell on anything that would cause her heartache. She preferred to celebrate the holidays, joyfully, with her many new friends.

Practically everyone they'd ridden the California trail with had come: Miriam, Garnet, Lottie, J.B., Billy. Only Frances and Elizabeth were absent, having sent their regrets that they were spending Christmas with their father, George Yount, at Frances's new home.

Vaqueros from Rancho Corona came with Lottie and the children. Nancy noticed the handsome Californio, Carlito Palocios, acting as if he were Lottie's personal bodyguard. He helped her from her horse, carried her bags, tended to her every need, and stayed right by her side until there was nothing left for him to do but join the other vaqueros out in the bunkhouse. There, they commenced to make music on their guitars which lasted all day and into the night. During the ten-day visit, they were frequently joined by Hart on his harmonica and J.B. on his fiddle.

Miriam, escorted by some Californios who worked for her at the restaurant, brought her three boys. The youngest, over a year old now, still clung to Garnet as if she were his mother, but Miriam still didn't seem to mind. The other two boys were better behaved than her older children had been who had gone with Arthur to Oregon. These boys treated her with respect and were well mannered. Miriam's life with Arthur had been nothing short of a nightmare. Now she was in control of her own destiny, and the burdens of her previous existence were lifting.

Through tears of delight, Nancy hugged each and every one of her friends. "You all planned this behind my back."

Lottie strode into the new house, glancing about with obvious approval. "Well, girl. You were too sick to come to us, so we all figured we'd just come to you."

"I'm better now, much better," Nancy assured them.

Miriam patted her on the shoulder. "That may be, young lady, but we won't have you waiting on us while we're here. We don't mean to have you down sick in bed again. You're as thin as a reed, and our intentions are to place enough food in front of you that you'll gain back all you've lost."

And so it was. The women were always eager to help Magdalena and Carmelita with the cooking and whatever else needed to be done. They spent long hours, when not engaged in kitchen duties, making quilts and clothes for Nancy's baby and getting caught up on everything that had taken place while they'd been away from each other.

Nancy found it most rewarding to hear that each and every one of them was well toward bringing their dream to its fullest capacity.

Miriam had been dragged out here against her will, but her circumstances had summoned her inborn strength and allowed her to reach for things she would never have considered had Arthur not abandoned her. Her restaurant was a booming success, and she had started work on her hotel.

"It'll be finished in the spring," she said proudly. "And I insist you come and stay with me, Nancy. I wouldn't want you out here by yourself when you have that baby. There are no reputable doctors around, and I sure wouldn't put my trust in that Dr. Marsh for anything more than smearing salve on a cut. No, I've delivered plenty of babies, and I'd like to be there with you. My hotel isn't big, mind you," she quickly amended. "But I'll have a room set aside especially for you."

Garnet seemed content enough now. She hadn't accomplished what the others had, nor expressed an interest in trying any business enterprise on her own. She seemed content to work for Miriam and to take care of the children. She showed no interest in marrying again either, or having her own children. The baby, Laramie, seemed all she needed in her life.

Torey and Thane had joined them for meals, but Garnet showed Torey no more interest than she ever had. Torey was showing less attention to Garnet, too, though. The young man was twenty now and was clearly more intrigued by the budding beauty of sixteen-year-old Elise Royal. As for Thane, he found excuses to wander out in the kitchen, or onto the veranda, or anywhere else that Carmelita happened to be.

J.B. and Billy were working together on the ranch in Napa Valley with plans for a flour mill. Since arriving in California they had seen that people here preferred adobe over milled lumber, and they had decided that a flour mill would be a more lucrative business than a lumber mill. They had also been busy clearing land for fields and vineyards, and collecting cattle and horses to round out their herds. J.B.'s main interest was still his mules. Already he was acquiring a reputation for having some of the finest in Northern California.

Lottie was never one to boast or brag, but Nancy thought she was being unusually quiet. All she really said about Rancho Corona was, "I keep busy just telling other people what to do. But, then, I sort of like it that way. A few years ago I never would have dreamed of being a big landowner, of having dozens of people in my employ and being responsible for them all. But they know their jobs and they do them well. I trust their judgment and learn from them. Maybe someday I'll truly warrant being called *patróna.*"

While at the ranch, the young boys found plenty of mischief outdoors. Elise and Beth stayed with the women. The men, of course, found
politics to be the most enduring topic. When the house became too con-
fining, and if it wasn't raining—as it was wont to do this time of year—
they often rode out with Hart over the ranch and conjectured on what
was taking place in the province.

Occasionally they brought their discussions to the table. The most disturbing topic was the buildup of John Sutter's army. Everyone had heard
by now that some two hundred twenty rebels, led by José Castro and Juan
Bautista Alvarado, had faced Micheltorena's army of one hundred fifty a
month ago in the San José Valley. The rebels had demanded that his *cholos* be expelled from the province and sent to San Blás. The governor,
overpowered, had capitulated to their demands and signed the Santa
Terésa treaty.

Rumor was now that Micheltorena intended to violate the treaty because of the firepower at Sutter's Fort. Sutter had always been faithful to
the Mexican government and had been appointed militia captain by
Micheltorena back in July. He had vowed at that time that he would
come to Micheltorena's aid if ever he needed him. Not only had Micheltorena held Sutter to his promise, but he had *ordered* him to support the
Mexican government. Sutter, keen on the idea of being in command of
an army, and garnering all the glory of such a position, had willingly answered the call of duty.

He recruited two hundred men, uniformed them, armed them, and
drilled them. One hundred were Indians; the rest were a combination of
sharpshooting American backwoodsmen, trappers, and a few deserters
from the Navy.

But not all Americans were eager to jump into the fracas. J.B. Chiles
leaned back in the easy chair in Hart's new den, took a puff of his cigar,
and blew the smoke to the ceiling. "We stopped at the fort on our way
here," he said, "and damned if Sutter didn't try to recruit us. Because
we're not married, he saw no reason why we couldn't just leave our
ranches and do his bidding. I've never been one much for intrigue, you
all know that, and I had my fill of fighting in the Florida Wars and the
Battle of Lake Okochobee.

"Frankly, I think it would be wise to stay out of the middle of this
petty power struggle between Alvarado and Micheltorena. Today it'll be

the two of them; tomorrow it'll be somebody else. If there's a coup going on, you can just about figure José Castro will be headin' it. I think the bastard just likes to fight and be in the middle of a turmoil, even if he has to create it himself."

"We may have to choose sides one day whether we want to or not," Billy put in passionately. "The man who straddles the fence usually ends up with slivers in his ass."

"Very true, Billy. But did you all know that Micheltorena wrote to the War Ministry in Mexico, concerned about the number of Americans coming into the country?" Hart countered. "According to Larkin, he's asking for assistance in keeping them out. You can't tell me he's loyal to us, so why should I fight on his side of the battlefield? There are no true loyalties here. I'll fight when the line becomes more defined."

J.B. rallied his agreement. "Those in Sutter's army who don't have passports, let alone citizenship papers, could find themselves on the losing side and end up in a Mexican prison with no angel of mercy to negotiate their rescue."

"You're a Mexican citizen," Billy countered. "We all three are. We came here to give the country our allegiance. Shouldn't we be aligning ourselves with Micheltorena?"

"It's not wise to show hostility to the Californios," Hart warned. "They're the people we're wont to live side by side with, not the people of Mexico. We all know that if the United States succeeds in annexing California, without war, it would be better accomplished if the Californios considered us their friends and didn't mind having us as neighbors. I employ a few Californios, and have a lot more who are my friends. Micheltorena and his army of ex-convicts are *not* my friends, and certainly don't have my respect."

"I wouldn't want Castro or Alvarado in charge either," J.B. responded. "They certainly make no bones about their contempt for Americans."

The whole mess annoyed Hart immensely. "I'd rather fight the goddamned Pawnee single-handedly than to get in the middle of the storm that's brewing over California. At least I'd know who my enemy was."

On New Year's Eve, knowing the guests would be leaving soon, Hart collected all the musicians on the ranch, and soon a fandango was underway.

Because the ground was a little wet from occasional rains, the dancing was mostly on the huge veranda that went all the way around the new house. It was a little cold, but hardly anyone noticed once the dancing started.

Nancy didn't do much dancing, just some slow waltzes with Hart, for she hadn't gotten her strength back.

Around midnight, happy but tired, she collapsed in the porch swing to watch the doings. By someone's suggestion, Carlito had agreed to do the lively *pasodoble,* and he was trying to convince Lottie to be his partner.

"Good God Almighty," Lottie proclaimed, balking at the prospect. "I can't do nothing but the waltz and the Virginia reel. Well, maybe a square dance. But I can't do all that arm-raising and foot-stomping stuff that you Californios do."

But Carlito had a most persuasive smile, and he pulled her next to him, striking a pose. He looked terribly alluring in his tight pants that flared out at the knee, and in his fitted, waist-length jacket that hugged his wide shoulders.

"I will show you how to do it, *mi* Lolita. It is very easy. Just relax and do what I do. Allow yourself to feel the music and move your body accordingly."

Lottie was clearly self-conscious at first. But soon, as Carlito had predicted, she was dancing as if she had always known how even if she couldn't take it quite as seriously as he did, preferring the part of a "good sport" who was only humoring the master. The veranda was soon vibrating beneath the vivacious pounding of their heels against the plank lumber. Lottie let out a few squeals of delight and soon everybody else was hooting and clapping their hands in time to the passionate movements of the dancers.

But the way Carlito's arm curved around Lottie's slender waist, and the way his dark eyes probed hers with a serious sensuality, made Nancy, and possibly a few other onlookers, wonder if his movements went beyond the mood of the music. If, per chance, they came directly from the heart.

The dance ended and the applause was deafening. Carlito and Lottie bowed, holding hands, then Carlito returned to his guitar. Lottie leaned back against the veranda railing, next to the porch swing where

Nancy was sitting. A silence fell between the two friends as they watched the others dance to another waltz. Then Nancy said, "Tell me about you and Carlito."

Lottie feigned surprise at the request, and her attempt to look completely confused and innocent was more telling than words. "What do you mean? I only danced the *pasodoble* with the man."

Nancy chuckled. "Did you think I wouldn't notice when my best friend fell in love?"

"Good God." Lottie rolled her eyes and released a deep sigh. "Don't be ridiculous."

"I've never been ridiculous. It's not part of my nature." Nancy continued, driving home her point with a knowing smile. "I noticed how he looks at you. How he holds you—as if you were the most fragile piece of china. And a person would have to be deaf if they didn't hear the softening in his voice and in his eyes when he calls you '*mi* Lolita.' I didn't know that was your full name."

"It isn't." Lottie tried denial again. "My name's Charlotte. But he doesn't know that and never will because I hate the name. He just took to calling me Lolita. I've never bothered to correct him. It sounds good, rolling off his tongue. But then, a damned cuss word would sound good coming out of his mouth." She shrugged her shoulders and sought out the subject with huge, adoring eyes.

Nancy's trilling laughter sounded over the music, drawing a few eyes. Oh, how she enjoyed her friend's lovesickness.

"Nothing's happened between us, if that's what you're thinking," Lottie was quick to clarify.

"Do I hear a tone of regret?"

Lottie's gaze strayed to Carlito, still singing and strumming his guitar. Carlito made her acutely aware that she was a woman without a man. He made her acutely aware, too, that in a few more years she would be too old to have another baby. She wouldn't mind having another child by a man who would want to share the joys and responsibilities. A man who would love and cherish a child of his own seed. She sensed Carlito would be that kind of man, but she also surmised that he would probably want a younger woman to have his child. One who could give him not one baby, but many. But because of the way she bled every month, if she didn't drink the bayberry bark tea, she wondered if she would even be able to carry a baby full term.

"Maybe I wish something would happen," she finally said in response to Nancy's remark. "But it's better if nothing does. A relationship with him wouldn't work out. He needs a woman who's softer, more feminine. Younger."

"If I recall, you said something similar about J.B. But that poor man came all the way here just to see you."

"You don't know that. And I'm *certainly* not the right woman for him, even though I do like him a great deal. I respect him, you know?"

"I think you should quit deciding what's best for the men, Lottie, and start letting them make up their own minds. If Carlito loves you, it's because of who you are. I trust he knows you fairly well by now."

"Maybe."

"I guess this explains why you've been so quiet. Completely out of character," Nancy teased.

"Thanks," Lottie quipped in kind, but looked away, afraid her friend would see the flashes of remembrance reflected in her eyes. Remembrances of the day those men tried to rape her because they thought she was Nancy. She would never tell Nancy about that. There was no point in putting that kind of guilt on a friend. Nor would she ever hold it against her. If she'd been the one who Castro had tried to bully, she'd have done just what Nancy did and suffer the consequences later.

Besides, she didn't want anybody to know about that horrifying and humiliating incident that had left her feeling tainted. She didn't want people to look at her and think less of her, knowing she'd been pawed and violated. She didn't want to always be thought of, or remembered as, "the woman who got assaulted by those men of Castro's." It would somehow make her look weak. And she was not weak.

But there was one person who knew. One who had seen.

She was afraid that every time Carlito looked at her, he saw her in that ugly scene. Maybe if she told Nancy about it, it would help her put it behind her. But she looked over at Nancy's pure, smiling face and she could not bring herself to dampen the spirit of the visit with such a dark subject. Talk of the war was dark, but not as dark as that violation of pride and body she had experienced. Not as dark as the utter helplessness she had suffered at the hands of those men. Lottie England had never been helpless, or at anyone's mercy. She'd never been humiliated beyond words. It was a feeling that, even now, could put her into a blind rage.

She didn't care much about the political struggles, except that they might somehow separate her and Carlito and force them to take opposite sides of the issues—this man she hungered for, but did not dare open her heart to. She suspected she would only have to give him a bit of encouragement and he would come to her bed. But would he stay? Would love keep him there? Or would he, like Major, use her, tire of her, leave her with a child, and then never look back.

It was better not to talk about it at all, not even to her best friend. When you voiced your fears, they had an uncanny way of materializing.

"Maybe I'm just learning to keep my mouth shut for a change," she quipped, forcing a sassy grin. "That would be an improvement, don't you think?"

Nancy reached over and squeezed Lottie's hand. "Do you remember that advice you gave me when I fell in love with Hart?"

Lottie smiled wryly. "If I was spoutin' philosophy, you shouldn't have listened."

Nancy proceeded despite Lottie's cynicism. "You said that true love shouldn't complicate life. It should make it easier."

"Yes, but does he love me? If he doesn't, that's going to complicate the hell out of things."

"Could it be he's just waiting for a sign from you?"

"If I knew anything about men, I wouldn't have lost Major to that whore."

Nancy left the swing and linked arms with Lottie. "Major sounds as if he wasn't worth fighting for. Now, go ask Carlito to dance again, or at least go over there and gaze fondly at him. Look enraptured by his singing and his guitar playing."

Lottie scowled, but it was all in good humor. "You know, girl, I think I liked you better *before* you got experience."

Nancy just chuckled and gave her a nudge, then leaned back and watched the magic of love take its course.

32

April, 1845

The Californios called it *matanza*. No, not the battles at Cahuenga and Verdugo Ranch where Sutter's army had met Castro's opposing forces in January and lost. Those confrontations had turned out to be nothing more than mere exchanges of gunfire and cannon shot at long range. There had been Americans fighting with both armies, and when they had learned of this, they had refused to fight each other, resulting in the loss of Micheltorena's principal strength.

The Mexican governor had surrendered, and both he and his troops had been deported to San Blás. Pío Pico stepped in as governor, and José Castro held his position as comandante-general. Sutter, after having gotten lost on the battlefield and been taken prisoner by Castro's men, was finally released to return to his fort, albeit in humiliation.

But this killing, this slaughter taking place on this spring day at Rancho Vallecito, was the annual cattle slaughter. Most ranches conducted the *matanza* once a year, following the spring *rodeo,* or roundup. For many ranches near the seaports, *matanza* was held any time they needed or wanted something from the Yankee traders. This selling of hides and tallow was the ranch's chief livelihood, and therefore a big event that required additional temporary help in the form of skinners, butchers, vaqueros, and extra cooks to prepare the meals.

By midsummer, there would be a lull in the ranch work and only the vaqueros who were needed for horse breaking and training would remain on the ranch—perhaps four or five. Those not needed would wander back to the settlements, usually with promises to return for the fall roundup when calves born during the summer would be branded and accounted for. At that time, another *matanza* might be held, depending on the need of the ranch, or if the range was getting overstocked.

Since there was virtually no meat market for the thousands of California cattle, their hides and tallow were collected, taken to the trading vessels and shipped back East. Most ranchers sold the hides green. The Yankee ships had their own hide-curing grounds in the sunny, dry clime of San Diego, and their own crew did the backbreaking work of curing the hides for shipment back to Boston.

Nancy turned away from the ground that had once been verdant with spring grass but now ran red with gallons of spilled blood. Since she'd been pregnant, her constitution had not been strong. Even though she was eight months along now, it was still easy to become ill. Gripping the side of the wagon, she pulled in several deep breaths to help stay the nausea, but found it was only made worse by the smell of the blood. The clouds of dust churning under hundreds of bovine hooves did not help either. Both Magdalena and Hart had told her not to come, but she had refused to listen.

She had thought that her journey across the continent, and her experiences with the struggle of life and death on that journey, had sufficiently prepared her for whatever the wilds of California could offer. After Brenham's mauling by the grizzly, she had thought she could see just about anything and handle it. Last year, she had even helped with the branding and castrating. But nothing had prepared her for *matanza.*

The cattle were bunched in a natural bowl of the hills, at the head of where a large, blind corral had been built back in the trees to trap wild horses, or to confine the saddle horses being used for *matanza.* The vaqueros also had taken to using the corrals for breaking horses because it was much larger than those at ranch headquarters, approximately three miles away. A few other smaller corrals were attached to the large corral, and were used for sick cattle or calves needing special attention.

Facing away, Nancy could still hear the sounds of the vaqueros, on horseback, as they moved among the cattle and, with their well-placed long knives, leaned down and severed the nerve at the nape of the cattle's necks. The latter seldom cried out; they simply fell dead. Ropes were tossed around legs or horns and the dead bovines were dragged to the place where *peladores,* skinners, stepped in and opened their throats to bleed them before stripping off the precious hides. The *tasajeros,* butchers, then took over, saving the best portions of meat to be salted, jerked, or cooked fresh.

The third team was usually the Indian women who collected the tallow and fat from the dead cattle, piled it on the fresh hides which were folded over and secured with thongs then dragged to the fires. Here, at the trying-out grounds, the fat and tallow was lowered into huge kettles dangling over large firepits. The fat and tallow were constantly tended until it had cooked down to a liquid that could be cooled to workable temperature and poured into hide containers. These *botas* were then sewn up with gut strings. Twenty-five pounds of tallow sold for two dollars, and the Yankee traders usually offered half in cash and the other half in goods from their ships.

This tedious rendering of the fat and tallow kept the Indian women busy, but none minded the hard work. Nor did they mind the blood and were covered with it from head to toe. They were given much of the fresh meat for their families, and found uses for practically every part of the animal that was not going to be hauled to Monterey. They were also allowed to keep many of the hides for tanning.

Nancy, with stomach protruding and creating an obstacle in itself, climbed back into the small spring wagon. She was desperately anxious to be away from the smell of the blood and the bellowing cows; the skinners peeling off the warm hides; the butchers opening the cattle from end to end to pull out the gut bag; the dogs, tearing at the fresh, bloody piles of offal.

She was also more than anxious to be over her pregnancy. It was getting tiresome, and it limited her too much to what she could do. She yearned to ride Lady Rae again, to gallop over the golden hills. To be free, unrestrained, unhindered both mentally and physically. It was that same inexplicable, elusive yearning that had left her restless in Amherst and had driven her to California, and was driving her still.

Lady Rae had not gotten with foal yet, which was another cause for concern. The men were saying she was barren. Nancy refused to accept that, nor to give up hope.

She was about to snap the reins when Hart rode up alongside the wagon. "Are you going to be all right? You look a bit pale."

She flashed him a sheepish grin. "I should have listened to you and stayed home. I think I'll go back and help Magdalena render the tallow."

"Nancy."

She lifted her eyes to his and saw apology there. "You know this is a necessary part of ranching here in California. This is what takes place in any slaughterhouse back in the states."

"You don't need to apologize, Hart. I understand."

Hart glanced back at the operation, but Nancy kept her eyes trained on the ears of her horse. "I wish there were some meat markets," Hart said in frustration. "I would much rather drive the cattle to market and leave this part up to somebody else. It's an awful waste besides. So much of the meat isn't even used. I keep thinking of those starving Digger Indians over on the Mary's and how much they could use it. But, hell, there's no way to get it to them."

Nancy fidgeted with the reins, trying to hold onto the contents of her stomach but not wanting to tell Hart just how close she was to losing it.

He leaned down from his saddle and kissed her cheek. "Take a rest when you get back home. I don't want that baby to come early."

With a smile that bordered on flirtation, he slid his hand down over her breasts and rested it on the growing mound of her stomach. She didn't know how he could still find her attractive, but he constantly told her how beautiful and desirable she was. To her amazement, making love during her pregnancy had oftentimes been even better than before.

She forgot the *matanza* as her thoughts drifted to the more important matter of the swiftly arriving birth of their baby. She was getting so large she really wondered how much more her skin could stretch before it burst. She didn't think it was her imagination either because both Lottie and Magdalena commented constantly about how huge her stomach was becoming.

She placed her hand over Hart's. "Personally, I'd like to get it over with. I'm beginning to feel like a bloated cow, ready to pop."

"Lovely correlation," Hart teased.

There were more complaints, of which she didn't mention too often to Hart, but which she did ask Magdalena about. There was the inability to sleep at night because the weight of the baby prevented her from sleeping on her back. Sleeping on her side was better, but then the baby didn't seem to like it and would kick her furiously and sometimes painfully. She didn't throw her food up as often, but everything gave her indigestion.

She often found it difficult to breath as the baby seemed to be pressing into her lungs. It was getting hard to walk, and when she sat, her legs would oftentimes go to sleep. Magdalena just chuckled at her complaints and told her that everything was normal. But the housekeeper's assurances did nothing to allay her secret fears that she might lose the baby as Garnet had hers. Or that she might die right along with it.

Hart straightened in the saddle and gathered his reins. "I'll ride back to the ranch with you. The wild animals will smell the blood and some of the bolder ones will make their way here, even in broad daylight. Those damned grizzlies aren't afraid of anything. Instead of messing with the tallow rendering, why not get our bags packed. As soon as we're done with this—hopefully by the end of the week—we'll be heading to Monterey."

Around midnight, the night before they were to leave, Nancy was pulled from her sleep by sharp pains in her abdomen. She laid next to Hart in the silence of their bedroom, listening to an owl in the sycamore tree outside their open window and thinking the pains would go away. She was three weeks early, from her calculations. But the pains began to come closer together and with more intensity. She remembered Garnet crying and screaming out there on the prairie; remembered Miriam coming out and saying the baby was dead. And Miriam, qualified as a midwife, wasn't here. No one here was qualified to deliver a baby.

Another pain tightened her stomach. Fear set in. Instinctively she knew it wasn't false labor.

Not wanting to alarm Hart, she laid her hand on his bare shoulder and gently shook him until he turned groggy eyes to her. "Is it morning already?"

"No, I think my skin has stretched about as far as it's going to stretch," she said, trying to keep calm.

His only response was a confused stare.

Realizing he was still half asleep, she added, "I think I'm going to have the baby now, Hart."

He shot out of bed like a bullet from a rifle. "You can't."

"But I am."

"Damn it." He groped for his pants and skipped across the room while yanking them on. "I'll get Magdalena. And Lottie. I'll send a rider for Lottie. She'll know what to do."

Nothing could have prepared Nancy for the pain. She had heard about it. She had been told about it. But she never would have been able to imagine it until she had actually experienced it. The hours went by—morning, noon, afternoon. The pain gripped her, one wave of it after another, coming increasingly closer and closer together. The women assured her that first babies were slow in coming and that everything appeared to be progressing normally.

Magdalena, who had delivered a few babies in her life, including Carmelita's little boy, tried to chase Hart out of the room, but Nancy wanted him there. And he wanted to be there. They'd made the baby together; he couldn't imagine standing outside the room, pacing with fear and worry while she needed him close. He held her hand and wiped the sweat off her face with a cold, damp cloth. He made sure she had cold water to ease her thirst.

In the evening, her water broke. She thought the baby would be born soon now. The pains, which she had thought were excruciating before, increased to an intensity that rolled over her in one horrific wave after wave. Worse in her lower back than in her stomach, they lifted her up off the bed and arched her spine with their force. Screams rose in her throat but she bit them off, fully believing that if she ever started she would never be able to stop.

She held onto Hart's hand, not realizing her crushing grip was nearly sending him to his knees. But he held onto her, knowing that from the extent of the pain she was inflicting on him, her own was tenfold.

When the bearing-down pains began, it was almost a relief. For awhile she rode through them with the force of her own pushing. But two hours went by with no progress. She became exhausted and fell asleep between contractions that were now barely a minute apart.

Hart left her side for a moment to whisper to Lottie, "My God, is something wrong? Why isn't the baby coming?"

Lottie tried to conceal her own concerns from Hart, but didn't know how successful she was. Her own labor hadn't been this hard or long, although she had heard of women who had gone on for days. "I don't see anything out of the ordinary, except that Nancy is small in the hips, and first babies are generally always slow in making their entrance into the world anyway." What she didn't tell Hart was that she hoped the birth canal was large enough for the baby to pass through, or Nancy might die.

Nancy suddenly awoke screaming as the next contraction seized her with its cruel force.

"Push, Nancy," Magdalena encouraged. "The baby's head is showing. It shouldn't be much longer now."

"Just make it end," Nancy mumbled weakly after the pain had subsided. "My God, make it end. I don't care if I die. Just make it end."

Hart looked worriedly at Lottie, but she focused her attention on the child trying to emerge into the world. Lottie answered her friend's fears with assurance she didn't feel. "I know how hard it is, Nancy," she said. "And I know you feel like you want to die, but you're not going to. Everything will be all right. You'll see."

"Just end it. End it." She looked at Hart this time, pleading. "Hart, I don't know how much more—"

"Hold on, Nancy. For me." Tears stung the backs of his eyes. "God, I'm sorry I did this to you."

She squeezed his hand, not in pain this time, but in understanding. "It's not your fault, Hart. I . . . wanted this baby." Then she managed to quip, "Although for the love of God, I don't know how I could have been so naive."

Hart didn't smile at her attempt to lighten the moment. He had put her in this position. What if she really *did* die? She was so weak from the hours of labor. It wasn't right that a woman should have to suffer so much just to bring a baby into the world.

Diligently, he wiped her face again with the cool cloth on her forehead and lifted the glass of water to her dry lips, wishing he could just reach down and somehow pull the baby out like one did a stubborn calf that refused to be born.

Another pain ripped through her body. The grip she held on his hands literally brought him to his knees this time. He had to bite his lip to keep from crying out. But Nancy screamed for him. A long, hideous scream that chilled his blood and brought the roots of his hair up on end.

The silence that followed was almost more unnerving than the heart-wrenching cry of agony. Nancy fell back to the pillow, eyes closed. Hart thought she was dead. But Magdalena, beaming, stood up from the foot of the bed. In her arms she held a tiny, wet creature with black hair and flailing arms that was covered with blood and something white over most of its body. Carefully holding its ankles, she tipped it slightly upside-down and slapped its bottom. The baby gasped and released a lusty squall of indignation. Hart felt Nancy's limp hand stir in his, and he looked down to see her eyes open.

"You've got yourself a baby girl," Magdalena said proudly. "A very beautiful baby girl."

Gently the housekeeper placed the infant on Nancy's stomach, and Nancy automatically spread her protective hands over its small body.

Fifteen minutes later, another baby arrived. A boy. Stillborn.

33

December

The beautiful orange poppies would grow on the little mound of dirt eventually, the same way they did across the hills in the spring. But in the eight months since Nancy and Hart had buried the dark-haired baby boy up on the hill overlooking the house, nothing had grown over the grave except weeds.

They had planned to name their first boy Flynn, after Nancy's grandfather, but since he had been stillborn, Hart had simply carved the words BABY DANIELS on the grave marker. The death had been particularly hard on Hart. He would have sold his soul to the devil to prevent the grave of one of his children on the hill above the house.

So many times, as Nancy watched her little girl grow over the past months, she, too, had felt the pang of loss, and wondered what her other baby would have been like. She was only thankful that God had not chosen to take Angelica as well. She could fully appreciate now what poor Garnet had gone through.

But there would be a new life in the spring. Lady Rae was finally with foal. Now that it had finally happened, her progress was being carefully monitored by everyone on the ranch. Even Magdalena went frequently to the corral to hand-feed her carrots, believing that they would be good for the colt growing inside her.

Eight-month-old Angelica, sitting doll-like in the brown grass of early winter, bundled in her tiny coat and leggings, suddenly reached out and picked up a handful of dirt in her chubby fist. Laughing, she flung it into the air, only to be amazed and confused when it came back into her round, cherubic face. Although her eyes watered, she didn't cry at this unpleasant discovery. She just bounced up and down on her diapered bottom a couple of times, waving her pudgy arms before dropping to hands and knees. Crawling rapidly, she covered the distance to Nancy's lap, climbed up and laid her head against her mother's breasts for consolation.

"Mum-mum. Go bye-bye."

Nancy finished blinking the dirt from her own eyes and laughed at her energetic daughter who had been jabbering, it seemed, nearly from birth. Everyone had commented on how unusual it was that Angelica had spoken so early and so clearly, but Nancy attributed it to the fact that because Hart was gone on ranch duties or to Sutter's or Monterey so frequently, Nancy spent much time with Angelica, reading to her at naps and bedtime and talking to her as if she could understand it all. Naturally, Angelica's vocabulary was simple as she learned her first sounds—da-da, mum-mum, bye-bye—but nearly every day she tried a new sound. Yesterday it had been ba-ba after Magdalena's baby goats.

Suddenly tired of being immobile, Angelica plunged off Nancy's lap and crawled around behind her. Using Nancy's shoulders as an anchor and would-be ladder, the baby pulled herself up and kept trying to climb higher up Nancy's back as if her goal was the top of her mother's shoulders. Finding it useless, she pointed toward the valley and made bending motions with her knees, trying to jump up and down.

"Mum-mum! Da-da!"

Nancy heard the excitement in her daughter's voice and followed the direction her pudgy little hand was pointing. She saw the dust first, from the direction of Sutter's Fort, then the long military-style column of men, probably fifty in number, whose identities were indiscernible from the distance.

Nancy's heart thudded with immediate alarm. Hart was out on the range with all the vaqueros today. He wouldn't be back until dark. The only men here were Torey and Thane, working on building a barn.

She hated to be suspicious of every person that came onto the ranch and most people traveling to Sutter's Fort stopped for the night. But out here, alone, it was necessary to be suspicious of strangers. Still, if this army of men chose to kill her and her hired help, she and the Indian field-workers would be no match for them anyway.

She grabbed up Angelica and ran as fast as she could go, something that Angelica liked immensely. By the time she reached the house, the Indians and house servants had all been alerted to the advancing party of men. Carmelita was out on the porch with a rifle in hand. Thane and Torey were in the barn, taking defensive positions behind the finished walls of the structure, out of sight of the approaching battalion of men.

Nancy deposited Angelica in her crib. The baby did not appreciate it and immediately threw herself down on her back and started screaming. Before Nancy could even get out of the room, Angelica had rolled over and pulled herself up to the crib's bars, reaching out her hands to Nancy.

"I'm sorry, sweetheart, I have to leave you for just a little while," Nancy tried to assure her, but the baby would have none of it. Her screams continued as Nancy, wielding the shotgun, hurried from the room to join Carmelita and Magdalena on the porch.

The column of men were considerably closer now and Nancy's eyes were drawn to the buckskin moving alongside the head of the column. With a sigh of relief, she lowered her weapon. Hart was leading the men to the house.

Curious to find out who the group was that moved in the precision lines of an army battalion, she leaned her shotgun against the porch railing and waited on the top step. The column was strung out for a considerable distance, the riders moving two by two and kicking up an immense cloud of dust that hung over them for lack of a breeze to push it on.

The man riding next to Hart was spare of build but rode the saddle like an army general—or like a man who perceived himself to be of that eminent status. None of the men wore uniforms, and as they grew closer they materialized into a motley group, bedraggled and weary. A few Indians rode next to the leader in the capacity of personal servants or body-guards. Because of the season, they all wore coats which were mostly belted at the waist with cotton rope or leather belts.

Hart nudged his gelding into an easy lope and rode the rest of the way to the house, dismounting in front of the steps. "Thought I'd better let you know who we were so you wouldn't open fire." He grinned and glanced over at the shotgun.

"I recognized you," she said simply. "But who are they?"

"Captain Frémont and his men."

She remembered Frémont all too well from the overland trail, and the incident with the deer had strengthened some growing prejudices against him. "What's he doing in California again?"

"Says he's surveying a road to the coast, orders of the President. Anyway, I've invited him and a couple of his men to supper, so maybe he'll tell us more. But one way or the other, I don't think Larkin is going to be too happy to hear about him being here with what looks like an invasion of U.S. troops."

Frémont, now just twenty yards away, lifted his arm in the fashion of a cavalry officer and brought his highly disciplined brigade to a halt. He trotted his horse up to the house and dismounted, then strode to the steps and jerked his hat off with a flourish. "Mrs. Daniels. What a pleasure to see you again."

Frémont was as trail-worn as his men. All had hair and beards that needed scissors and razors. Their clothes weren't fit for much more than a bonfire. Nancy understood the rigors of the overland journey all too well, but she was still quite startled to see the fastidious Frémont in such personal disarray. On closer inspection, she sensed an agitated air to his demeanor, as if he were not in the best of spirits. Of course, the trials of the journey itself could be responsible for the latter.

Nancy offered her hand. "Captain Frémont. This is indeed a surprise to see you again. You are more than welcome to camp here for a day or two and rest up. We can provide you with plenty of beef and some vegetables from our gardens. They came in quite well this fall—only our second year, too."

"I see you've started some orchards," he said, glancing over the land with steady, deep-blue eyes that shone brightly with approval. "It's good to see this land under cultivation. I always suspected it would be excellent for farming. As for your offer, I will most certainly take you up on it. The men have been living on nothing but meat for months now. We had hoped to get supplies and fresh horses at Sutter's Fort." Testiness sharpened his tone. "But Sutter said his wheat crop has been a dismal failure for two years running. He could offer us next to nothing, save a passport, which I shall present to Consul Larkin in Monterey. We are hoping he will be able to re-outfit us."

"Sutter is getting a tremendous number of people around him over there," Hart defended mildly. "The last time we were there, he was making plans to start a town because he can't take care of them at his fort anymore."

"Sutter always has had big plans," Frémont said derisively. "If he had his way, he would be provincial ruler of all California." He slapped his gloves against his thigh, revealing a private annoyance at the man. "Well, enough about Sutter. Where shall I tell my men to camp so they won't be a bother to you, Mrs. Daniels?"

"Down by the river should be fine," Nancy replied. "But you will join us for supper at the house, won't you? And I have room at the table for a couple of your men as well."

"I would be greatly honored, Mrs. Daniels, but are you sure you don't mind having such ruffians sitting at your table?" He asked the last with a winning smile.

"Of course not. You've come a long way. No one would expect you to look otherwise. At least no one at Rancho Vallecito."

Frémont candidly explained over a plate of roast beef and mashed potatoes that he had indeed been sent West again by the President to survey a route to the Pacific. "We are headed south to rendezvous with Joe Walker who is leading another division of my party. They're coming into California by way of Owens River and Owens Lake. Since Sutter could not be of much help to us, and many of our animals need a rest on good pasture, I was hoping you would have a few horses you could trade."

"That can be arranged," Hart replied. "Some might be a bit green, though, since the vaqueros can't keep them all ridden down the way they should be."

"Anything will be greatly appreciated," Frémont replied. "My men can finish them." He wiped his mouth on the napkin and slid his chair back, standing up. His two men followed his lead. "It was a lovely meal, Mrs. Daniels. I've had so few good meals since I began my explorations of the West, and now the surveying. When I do get one, it is long remembered and greatly appreciated."

Nancy and Hart showed Frémont and his men to the door, then watched as they rode back to camp. Leaning against a porch brace, Hart draped his thumbs at the corners of his front pockets and looked clearly disturbed. "If Frémont's heading south, I think I had better prepare to ride to Monterey and warn Larkin about his arrival in the country—if he hasn't already heard."

Aside from Frémont's explanation of his presence here, he had only spoken of things back East and the journey itself. Nancy saw no reason why any of it should have Hart looking so worried.

"He's only here on official government business. Why is that cause for alarm?"

"He's not telling us everything, Nancy. He got a passport from Sutter to be in the country, but I wonder if he has papers from President Polk giving him authorization to be in California. Frémont's men too closely resemble an army. If his arrival gets Castro and Governor Pico worried, it could very well undermine Larkin's efforts for a peaceful annexation of California to the United States."

Nancy followed him up the stairs to their room, her heart filling with trepidation. "What could Frémont possibly be here for if *not* to survey a route to the Pacific? You're not suggesting he might have plans to instigate trouble? There's enough unrest as it is."

"Right now the Americans are like a powder keg that only needs a match to send it sky high. Maybe Frémont *is* only going to Monterey to get the supplies he couldn't get at Sutter's, but his presence in the settlements is going to have every government official on edge, and maybe even in arms."

Hart went to the armoire and pulled out his saddlebags.

"Can't you send someone else?" Nancy watched him roll two shirts and tuck them in the bags. "You're gone so much as it is. I miss you, and Angelica misses you. Won't a letter to Tom suffice as well as a personal visit? You could send Thane and Torey to Monterey to deliver it. They could use a holiday from the ranch."

Hart abandoned his packing. With a bit of a seductive swagger, he crossed the distance separating them and pulled her into his arms. "Miss Nancy Maguire wanting a man around?" he teased. "Isn't that a different tune from the one you sang two years ago?"

She lifted an eyebrow, trying not to be amused. "That might have been my tune, sir, but since you talked me into marrying you, things have changed. Now that I *do* have a husband, *and* that husband's daughter, I expect that husband to stick around once in a while."

He grinned. "*I* talked you into marrying me? And all this time I thought you said yes because you just couldn't stand to live without me."

She gave him a playful shove. "Don't be so proud of yourself."

His laughter filled the room. He caught her arm and pulled her back into his embrace. "If you want me to stay home and warm your bed, I'd be more than happy to oblige."

"There you go, being cock-proud again. I want more than a man in my bed, Hart. I want you to be *here,* to talk and laugh and share things, like Angelica's growing up. She's eight months old and you've been gone at least half of it. I know the ranch keeps you busy, but just this once, send somebody else. I never did like the idea of Larkin asking you to be a spy."

"A spy?" His eyes twinkled with amusement.

"Call it a courier if you will," she conceded, "but technically you're his informer."

He chuckled. "Don't make it sound so unethical."

"It could be dangerous, Hart."

He slid his arm around her waist and pulled her down beside him on the bed. "It's no different than your grandfather sending you letters telling you everything that's going on back in Amherst. I'm only keeping Tom informed of the sentiments here in the north. Much of it is only gossip from a bunch of men sitting around complaining about the way the Mexicans are not running things. Don't worry about it, Nancy. Nothing is going to become of it."

34

April, 1846

The supply wagons from ranchos Corona and Vallecito creaked and rumbled their way along the road to Sutter's Fort. About a quarter of a mile from the big gates of the fort, Hart brought his team of mules to a halt. Behind him, Carlito did the same, but not before drawing the wagon up alongside the other.

From her position next to Carlito on the wagon seat, Lottie was the first to speak. "What in the hell's going on up there? Is that what I think it is?"

Outside the eighteen-foot-high walls of the fort, an American "officer" was putting one of Sutter's battalions of Miwok Indians through a highly disciplined, military maneuver. Across the training field, a brigade of American riflemen was engaged in a similar drill, only mounted rather than on foot.

Hart fidgeted with the reins threaded through his fingers and felt an unpleasant premonition roll over inside him. "I'm surprised Sutter hasn't had enough of doing battle after Castro outsmarted him a year ago."

"I would bet that what you see is a direct result of Frémont being here," Nancy said, sitting next to Hart. "He's got everybody war-crazy."

"Only the hotheads who don't have anything better to do with their lives," Lottie said, "and who think the rest of us don't either."

"We might as well head on in and see what in the hell's going on,"

Hart mumbled, snapping the reins over the mules' backs. "See if the bunch of damned fools has gotten us into war yet."

The arrival of the two wagons with numerous outriders was a curiosity to the soldiers, but they managed to keep their formations. One would hardly recognize the soldiers as the same ones Sutter had outfitted over a year ago in smart, colorful uniforms manufactured by the Russians.

The Indian troops were now pathetically garbed and poorly armed. Most still had their white trousers, albeit covered with several months' worth of dirt. Their jackets hung open, missing nearly all the gold buttons. It was common knowledge that Indians would gamble just about anything, and the buttons had been dispensable baubles literally at their fingertips. One quarter of them had no muskets, only bows and arrows. The Americans had managed to hold onto their rifles, or at least to replace any taken from them during the battles of Cahuenga and Verdugo Ranch. Being a rather undisciplined group anyway, many had abandoned their uniforms and gone back to wearing their buckskins.

The guards swung open the big gates, hinged on the thick adobe walls of the fort, and the wagons rumbled through into the fort's plaza area. Sutter, having been notified of their arrival, was there to greet them with his usual charm and generosity.

"My friends, it is so good to see you all again!" His blue eyes danced with genuine delight. "You have arrived just in time to join me for supper. I have already told my cooks to put a few more plates on the table. And would you look at little Angelica," he cooed, reaching up to take the baby from Nancy's arms. "I do declare, you are growing much too fast, little one!"

Angelica beamed, finding no person to be a stranger. She tumbled, laughing, from Nancy's arms into Sutter's. Clapping her hands on either side of his face, over his bushy sideburns, she gave him a wet kiss right on the lips. Then she turned in his arms and grinned at everybody while Sutter hooted with delight.

"Ah, she likes me very much, don't you think?" he queried no one in particular. "I believe I can find a little treat for you, sweet one." With Angelica bouncing on his arm, he led the way into the main house.

"Well, I hope he finds a treat for the rest of us, too," Josh said, scowling after Sutter and Angelica. "Why, the way everybody goes goo-ing and gaa-ing over that baby, you'd think she was the Queen of England."

"Do I detect a note of jealousy?" Lottie teased.

Josh replied with a glare and stayed on Sutter's heels all the way up the stairs to his living quarters.

Nancy, Hart, Lottie, and the Royal girls followed Sutter, leaving the wagons and mules for the vaqueros to take care of. As they crossed the plaza not far behind Sutter, each took note of the hustle and bustle of the fort and the signs of military preparations. All that appeared lacking was the artillery Castro had captured in the previous confrontation.

A bell from below clanged loudly, sending notification to the troops that it was supper time. The drilling halted and everyone hurried inside the fort's walls to take their meal. The Indians rushed to their communal "trough" and to food prepared by their women. The Americans lined up with tin plates in front of the fort's cook. The military leaders and guests joined Sutter in the main dining hall, and included John Bidwell as well as several of the men from the Chiles–Walker party of three years ago: John Gantt, Pierson Reading, and Samuel Hensley.

Hensley slapped Hart on the back. "It's good to see you again, Daniels. Did you come to sign up with our army?"

Hart, having always considered Hensley swift on action and slow on thought, gave the man a tolerant smile. "No. I came to get supplies."

"If you change your mind," Captain Gantt put in, "we won't turn down another rifleman."

"So what makes you think you'll be fighting again?"

Pierson Reading, always eager to insert his opinions, was the first to answer. "Things are heating up, Hart. We want to be ready. Even Frémont says it's a good idea."

Hart noticed Sutter was particularly quiet and sensed that he was not getting involved with the army this time. He had apparently had his fill of military glory.

The cooks arrived and filled the table with bowls of steaming food. Sutter began, serving himself, then passing the bowls to his right.

"We're thinking of stepping things up a little," Reading said, plopping a huge portion of mashed potatoes onto his plate. "Get this matter settled once and for all."

Hart had been hearing similar warnings on every trip he'd made to the fort since last fall, but a tension in the air this time, coupled with the intensive drilling of the men, gave him the cold feeling that it might not be just talk anymore.

"How do you plan to go about it?"

"We're just waiting for the right moment. When we see it, we'll know it, and then we'll take action."

"And if it doesn't come?"

"Oh, we think it will. Castro is itching for battle with the Americans, and he'll keep pushing until he gets it."

"I guess you have heard," John Sutter said casually, "that Prefect Manuel Castro is still seriously considering expelling all foreigners, especially Americans, from the province. In accordance with the colonization law, he has recently reiterated that any purchase of land by foreigners will be considered 'null and void.' "

"Americans are getting nervous, Daniels," Gantt put in.

"They're feeding the flames with their own fears," Hart replied. "They hear rumors and act on them instead of finding out the truth of the matter."

"Governor Pico is afraid of the province changing hands," John Bidwell inserted. "He's the one causing the unrest. Did you know he has issued over one hundred land grants in the northern province to all his friends and relatives and other Californios as a tactic to keep the land from getting into the hands of Americans?"

Hart took the bowl of hot rolls from Nancy. Removing one, he said, "Yes, I've heard about it. A confrontation may become inevitable, men, but I don't think the Americans should be the ones to start it."

"Oh, we won't," Reading said confidently, if not slyly. "They'll start it, and we'll finish it."

"Don't you believe that Governor Pico is nervous because of Frémont entering the province with what looks to be an army battalion?" Nancy asked, knowing these men they had traveled overland with didn't mind female inclusion in their political discussions. "From what I've heard," she continued, "he was ordered by José Castro to leave the boundaries of the department since he had entered illegally."

"Yes, and instead of obeying the order, he threw the equivalent of a temper tantrum," Lottie added. "Not only did he erect a military fortification at Hawk Peak, but he ran the American flag up as well. It's not surprising that Castro met him with an army of two hundred men."

"It didn't help the situation when Frémont proclaimed that he would fight to the end," Nancy said. "What is the man trying to do anyway, if not start a war?"

No answers were forthcoming because no one really knew what Frémont's function in the province was, although he did clearly seem to be keeping the Americans rallying for battle.

"It was fortunate for him that the wind knocked his flag down," Hart said sarcastically. "Otherwise, he might have been encouraged enough to proceed with his idiocy."

"It might have helped that Larkin informed him it wouldn't be wise to raise the ire, or the enmity, of the Californios," Lottie said. "Where has the strutting little bandy rooster flown to anyway?"

Sutter supplied the answer. "After his flag fell, he gathered it up, along with his men, and set off on a slow march to Oregon. He stopped here briefly for supplies."

"Mexico wants war," Reading insisted, refusing to let the subject fade away. "And the Californios want war. Hell, the United States even wants war. There just isn't a one of them who wants to throw the first punch and get all the blame. President Polk has tried to buy the confounded place for years. His last offer was for fifteen million dollars."

"The Mexican government didn't care a hoot about this place until the Americans started pouring in," Hensley complained with a sour face. "Now they don't dare give it up for fear there's a damned gold mine under every hill."

"The Mexicans are the ones who broke off the diplomatic relations back in December when Congress accepted Texas into the union," Captain Gantt said with considerably less emotion than the others. "Between the land dispute in Texas, and the American settlement of California, they're running scared. The smoke of war is slowly being fanned into flames, ladies and gentlemen, and we had all better be prepared to fight or we'll find ourselves heading back over those mountains."

"Or being hustled off to a Mexican prison," Bidwell put in snidely.

The conversation continued, but nothing more than various repetitions of what had already been said. After supper, Nancy retired to the room Sutter had given her and Hart. It took patience, but she finally convinced Angelica that it was her bedtime. The baby hated to miss out on any of the action even though she was rubbing her eyes, sucking her thumb, and nearly having to prop her eyelids open.

Lottie and the girls were in the next room. Josh refused to share quarters with "a bunch of women," so he threw his bedroll down in the plaza with Carlito and the other vaqueros.

Nancy listened to Lottie and the girls talking and giggling on the other side of the wall. She would have joined them if she hadn't had to rock Angelica to sleep in the old rocker Sutter had provided. She was just laying Angelica down in the crib when Hart came into the room. There was no fear of waking the baby; she was so tired that not even cannon shot could disturb her now.

"I've got all the supplies loaded," he said, peeling off his shirt. "We'll be able to leave right after breakfast. As soon as we get back to the ranch, I'll be heading to Monterey with the hides. Are you sure you won't change your mind about coming with us this time?"

Nancy turned away from the crib. "I'd like to, Hart, but I'd also like to be on hand when Lady Rae has her foal. I've been waiting a long time for this."

"I hate leaving you at the ranch, virtually alone, Nancy, but I need all the vaqueros with me to drive the hide wagons. You know I'd wait for the mare to foal, but I want to trade with Captain Kane, and he's leaving for Boston the first of May.

"Lottie and her vaqueros and the kids will be coming along, too," he continued, trying to change her mind. "Not to mention, I'll be in big trouble with Miriam and Garnet and Rachel if I show up without you and Angelica. You really shouldn't worry about Lady Rae. She'll have the colt easily enough on her own. She hasn't even begun to make a bag. She could be two weeks yet."

A trip to town *would* be a nice break from caring for the garden and the new fruit seedlings. But regardless of what Lady Rae looked like, she was closing in on her due date. They would be hard-pressed to get to Monterey and back in two weeks with the hide wagons.

"I've waited three years for Lady Rae to have a colt and start my herd," Nancy finally said. "I would just feel better being with her. And I won't be alone at the ranch. Magdalena and Carmelita will be there, and the Indian fieldworkers. If we have any trouble we'll fire the signal—three rifle shots—and they can be at the ranch in a matter of minutes."

Both Hart and Nancy knew that wasn't true, but Hart didn't argue the point. He had come to know that when her mind was set there would be no changing it. He also knew how important the parturition was to her.

"Do you really need to go with the vaqueros?" Nancy chanced the question. "I mean, couldn't they handle the sale of the hides without you being there this time?"

Hart sat down on the edge of the bed to remove his boots and socks. "I could probably trust Thane and Torey to handle the sale, but I need to talk to Larkin anyway."

Nancy settled next to him. "I wish this political trouble could be settled so we could live without the threat of revolution hanging over our lives like a gathering thunderstorm. I know you men seem to thrive on the intrigue, but none of us women do."

Hart put a comforting arm around her shoulders and drew her close. "Larkin believes California will be under American rule in a couple of years. He's even heard José Castro insinuate that he wouldn't object to that as long as he and certain other leaders could be guaranteed their positions and salaries under the United States government."

Nancy sighed and pushed a loose strand of hair away from her cheek. "I wish I had Tom's confidence in the matter. I'd really like to see our lives take on a semblance of normalcy."

"We all would."

She searched his eyes, not wanting to think of him going to war, but the image of Miwok and American soldiers training outside the fort wouldn't leave her mind. "Be careful going to Monterey this time," she cautioned. "If Castro steps up his actions against the Americans, there is no telling what he might do to isolated travelers."

35

May

On the seventh night after Hart's departure to Monterey, Nancy paced the floors of the quiet adobe. During the day, Lady Rae's small udder had swollen and filled with milk, and she had begun to restlessly pace the corral as if searching for a way out and pawing the ground irritably. Because of the mare's nervous behavior, Nancy checked on her every thirty minutes or so, suspecting that these were indications of early labor.

Around midnight, Nancy went to the corral with her lantern and found the mare lying on her side. The mare leaped to her feet, glaring at Nancy as if her presence was not at all welcome. Nancy noticed, too, a bluish-white membrane protruding from the vulva and knew it was the sack that envelops the colt while in the uterus.

Certain Lady Rae was in labor, Nancy forked fresh straw into the corner of the corral where the mare had chosen to deliver. She then retired to the house to allow the mare the privacy she needed. Nancy didn't know a lot about parturition, but she did know horses preferred their privacy, and if a human was present they would oftentimes be too nervous to get down to serious labor. But every thirty minutes Nancy snuck out to check on the mare's progress, being careful to stay in the shadows so her presence would not be detected.

An hour went by, then two. The fluid sack surrounding the colt broke and the front hooves and colt's nose became visible. There progress stalled.

Nancy grew increasingly nervous as another hour passed. Finally she woke Magdalena for a second opinion and any advice the woman might be able to offer. "Give her time, señora," the cook said calmly. "Have you forgotten so soon how it was when you gave birth to Angelica? It is probably not much different for animals, you know?"

"She's straining, she's tired, and there's no progress, Maggie. The foal's nose is finally showing, but it's been like that for an hour. What should I do?"

"I don't know that there is anything you can do, señora."

"I can't let her die having this colt."

"I will go take a look, although I am no expert on the birthing of foals. I only know of babies."

"They can't be that much different, can they?"

"I know that when babies are born feet first, there is big trouble."

"Well, that's the natural way for animals. I know that much from eavesdropping on my father."

"You should have eavesdropped more, I think."

"I wanted to." Nancy flashed an impish grin. "I wanted to watch the colts being born, but my father refused to allow any of us girls to be present for either the birthing or the breeding process."

"Ah," Magdalena clicked her tongue disgustedly. "Men. They are so silly, you know? They think they protect us women by keeping us away from such things, when we are the ones who *should* know since we are the ones who have to have the babies." As an afterthought, she said, "Maybe we should go get the medicine woman. Do you think she would know anything about delivering colts?"

"I don't know, but I don't think there's time to ride out to their camp. Unless my intuitions are wrong, the mare needs help right now. I should have gone for Running Cloud sooner, but I didn't anticipate the mare having trouble. Hart assured me everything would be fine."

"Even men are wrong sometimes."

Exhaustion and pain dulled Lady Rae's big brown eyes. She no longer tried to rise when Nancy came out to check on her. She even allowed Nancy to kneel by her side. The contractions came hard now, but the colt's nose came no farther out from the restricting vulva. Gauging by the size of its hooves, the mare's birth canal might be too small to allow passage.

It was when the foal's nose began to turn blue that Nancy started to panic. She knew it would die, maybe taking the mare with it. She remembered one time when she had snuck out to the stables while a mare was having a colt, and she had hidden where she could hear but couldn't see or be seen. She had overheard her father say something to one of the men about "pulling" the foal or it was going to die. She suddenly faced the fact that she was going to have to do that, although she knew nothing of how to go about it.

"I'll have to try and pull it out, Maggie," she announced.

Magdalena's eyes filled with terror. "Do you think that is wise?"

"At this point, I think it's necessary."

Nervously, Nancy positioned herself at the rear of her suffering mare. She circled the foal's protruding hooves with her bare hands, but quickly realized the legs were too wet for her to get a good grip on them. "I need something to tie around its hooves that won't slip off, Maggie," she said, getting back to her feet. "I'm going to run to the tack room and get a rope."

"Don't be long," Magdalena said, kneeling next to the mare's head. "This situation upsets me more than I can say, you know?"

Nancy hurried to the tack room, her lantern casting a dancing, yellow circle of light in front of her. Glancing over all the bridles, halters, hackamores, harnesses, and ropes, she spotted a relatively new and clean cotton lead rope that wasn't too thick or bulky. She snatched it from its nail and hurried back to the corral. The mare was bearing down again, still with no progress.

"Here, Maggie. Hold the lantern up so the light will shine on the colt's feet."

Magdalena did as she was told, all the while looking very frightened. Nancy fashioned some small loops in each end of the lead rope and slipped one over each hoof. She hoped that the rope tightening just above the hoof wouldn't damage the foal's legs in some way, but if the loops remained too loose, they would slip off too easily.

When the next contraction came, Nancy sat back on her fanny in the straw for leverage and pulled on the hooves. She saw a little progress and kept pulling until the contraction ended. After a few contractions, she saw that if she pulled first one hoof, and then the other, and if she pulled more in a downward direction toward the mare's rump, that a larger portion of the foal's nose would appear beyond the lip of the vulva. But as soon as the contraction stopped, the head would recede again.

"Maggie, come and hold the ropes. When she pushes again, I'm going to see if I can lift up the skin of the vulva to enlarge the passage. If the colt's forehead would just slip past it, I think—I hope—the shoulders will follow more easily."

Magdalena looked scared out of her wits but did as she was told. Nancy wiped any dirt or straw from her hands onto her skirt, and when another contraction gripped the mare, she carefully slid her fingers, up to her thumb joint, between the foal's head and the heavy membrane of the birth passage. Gently she lifted it up and over the colt's eyes and forehead. She saw good progress almost immediately and continued this procedure for the next few contractions until the head was nearly all the way out.

Rejoining Magdalena on the ropes, she said, "We'll alternate. You pull one hoof, I'll pull the other. Back and forth. Back and forth. Yes, that's it. Come on, girl," Nancy encouraged the mare, but the words were as much for herself and Magdalena as the horse. "That's it, keep pushing. That's it."

Once the shoulders were through, the colt slid out as far as its hips. The contraction stopped, and the mare rested. Nancy stared at the colt's limp head, resting in the straw and partially covered with the bluish-white membrane that had surrounded it while in the uterus. The colt looked dead. Its nose was blue; its eyes closed. With one hand, Nancy finished pulling the membrane off the foal's nose, refusing to believe the colt was dead, and vaguely remembering how her own baby had looked until it had taken that first gasp for air. The colt's umbilical cord hadn't broken, so it was probably still getting oxygen from its mother.

"I think she'll be able to get it on the next contraction, Maggie. Okay, here she goes. Pull, Maggie. Pull."

The mare gave one tremendous push, Nancy and Magdalena pulled for all they were worth, and the remainder of the colt slid out in a long, wet gush of birthing fluids and blood. Nancy quickly removed the ropes from the colt's hooves and waited for a sign of life, for movement of any kind. The flick of an ear; the twitch of a muscle.

"The poor little thing is dead," Magdalena almost wailed. "It is not breathing, señora. After all we have done."

"It can't be dead," Nancy insisted. "It just needs to breathe."

She couldn't pick the foal up by its feet and swat its butt the way Magdalena had done with Angelica, so she started rubbing the colt, lifting its head and moving its legs, wiping the mucous from its nose with the clean straw. "Live!" she cried in mounting frustration. "Me and Maggie have worked too hard, and your mother has worked too hard, for you to just lay there and not even try to take a breath."

One of the pieces of straw stabbed the colt in the nose and he twitched. Hope filled Nancy. She took another piece of straw and poked it at the foal's tender nostrils until it opened its mouth and pulled in a breath of air. Then another, and another. Finally it opened its eyes and twitched its ears and tried to move its head away from the annoying stab of the straw.

Lady Rae lifted her tired head, too, and after a moment's consideration, mounted the strength to struggle to her feet. Almost simultaneously, the colt came to life and began moving its head and legs as if to rise. The mare saw her baby and turned toward it, sniffing to see what her labors had produced.

"She'll take care of it now, Maggie," Nancy said, rising to her feet and moving out of the way. "Let's let her handle it."

They moved back to the poles in the corral with their lanterns and watched the mare as she nosed her baby and licked it. Her rough tongue encouraged it to lift its head, to rise, to face the new world it had so unceremoniously been brought into.

Joy rose inside Nancy at the miracle of birth, and she wiped away tears of relief that had crept down her cheeks. She and Magdalena watched the young colt get its wits about it, sit up, and finally try propping itself up on long, wobbly legs. They worried when it fell time and time again. The mare was worried, too. She would hurry over to nudge it back up, to nicker at it, and to give its wet, curly hair a few more licks.

As the first gray of morning spread out above the Sierras, the foal finally got its legs under it and began nosing around its mother's stomach, instinctively looking for nourishment. Another few false attempts passed, frustratingly so for Nancy who had to hold herself back from taking the foal's head in hands and showing it where the two taut teats were. But finally it found its mother's milk and began sucking vigorously. The nourishment gave it strength, and when it had had its fill, it made a couple of hops in the straw before tumbling down again. Tired from the exertion, it decided to stay there and sleep. The mare laid back down, too, and shortly expelled the afterbirth.

Morning's glow fell into the corral as Nancy and Magdalena, tired from their ordeal, headed back to the house. They hadn't noticed if the foal was a filly or a colt. It didn't matter. It was alive.

Hart smelled the unrest as soon as the hide wagons rolled into town. Like fish cast up on the beach and left to die and rot by the outgoing tide, the distinctive scent of nervous suspicion wafted down the unusually hushed streets of Monterey.

They halted the hide wagons a short distance from the customhouse. The Yankee traders were there, as always, along with a few fishing vessels, but it was the warship out in the bay that drew Hart's keen eye.

"So you see it, too, *amigo*," Carlito said, drawing one of Lottie's wagons up alongside Hart's. "What do you suppose it means?"

Hart saw the Mexican flag still flying over the customhouse. "I don't know, Carlito, but we'll see what we can find out. Let's go ahead and talk to Captain Kane of the *Phantom* and see if he has anything left in his stores to trade."

Several Yankee vessels were in port, reporting to customs and taking on trade goods. Monterey was only one stop for the Boston brigs. They customarily sailed up and down the California coast for as long as two years, trading goods as opportunity arose. They might lay anchor as many as fifteen times in each port before they sailed back to Boston.

Captain Jack Kane, along with nearly everyone in the village of Monterey, had seen the arrival of the hide wagons from ranchos Corona and Vallecito. With a smile, he clamored down the gangway to greet them and escort them on board his sleek new clipper. "Where's Mrs. Daniels? I hope she isn't ill again."

What he meant was that he hoped she wasn't suffering from morning sickness again, but he had been too polite to say it. It was common knowledge around Monterey now that she did not carry babies very well.

"No, she's fine," Hart replied. "But her mare is about to foal and she didn't want to leave the ranch. It seems the birth of babies—of any kind—never comes at opportune times."

"So true," Kane said jovially. "I have never been fortunate enough to be at home any of the three times my wife has given birth. She holds it against me mightily, I fear, but she loves the finery I keep her in, so she doesn't complain overly much."

He turned his attention to the children. None of the three had been on board a ship before and their eyes resembled Spanish *reales* as they craned their necks to take in the height of the masts and the bewildering array of ropes and sails. "You're here to shop, I presume, so let me take you below deck to the store. I have some more of those silk shawls from China you were looking at last time, Mrs. England. Perhaps this trip, you will decide to indulge yourself."

Lottie made a little snort through her nose and flashed him a half-grin. "And I'm sure my mules will be impressed when I wear it on the way home."

Kane smiled, enjoying her dry sense of humor. "You never know, Mrs. England. They might like it so well that they will be like all foolish males and rush to please you in any way they can."

Giving her one last teasing grin, he led the way below deck to a won-derland, gleaming with polished wood paneling, drawers, lockers, shelves, and glass-enclosed showcases. The children's eyes bulged in awe at items they had not even known existed and were all brought together in this one small space. To them, Captain Jack had forgotten no necessity nor luxury. There was everything from expensive furniture to candlesticks. A shiny harmonica caught Josh's eyes, while the Royal girls gravitated toward the bundles of laces and velvets, and jade jewelry from the Orient. Lottie kept herself more focused, gathering into a basket the practical things on her list; needles, candles, threads, a new pair of scissors. Carlito fingered an embroidered Chinese shawl of the finest silk, known to the Spanish as *el mantón de Manila*. Carefully he lifted it from the shelf while glancing often and surreptitiously at Lottie.

"I agree with Captain Kane," he said when Lottie looked up to see the item in his hand. "You would look very beautiful in this. You could wear it to the next fandango."

"I don't believe in squandering money on such frivolous stuff, but thanks for the compliment, Carlito."

"Perhaps you are above frivolity, Lolita, but I am not such a saint. Therefore, it will be my gift to you."

Lottie was initially at a loss for words. She coveted nothing more in this storeroom than the gorgeous embroidered shawl, but how could Carlito have known? She had never said a word on any of the previous vis-its to the ship. She had only looked at the darned thing, maybe fingered it one time too many. Never in her life had she had the luxury of splurg-ing on nonessential items.

Finally she rallied an objection. "That's thoughtful, Carlito, but if your money is burning a hole in your pocket, just buy yourself a new shirt or something."

"My pocket is not even warm, Lolita." He smiled in that rakish way of his. "I simply believe that beautiful women should have beautiful things. Besides, a man can only wear one shirt at a time."

He draped the shawl over her shoulders. Lottie ran a hand over the fine silk again, but it was Carlito's hands lingering on her shoulders that drew the deepest sensation. His eyes, like black, liquid magnets, summoned hers. Slowly, she lifted her gaze to his, and her breath caught at the tenderness she saw there.

Oh, Carlito, don't do this. Don't make me fall in love with you.

"Well, Lolita?" he urged. "Your wish is my command, but *my* wish is for you to say yes."

Yes, to the shawl, Carlito? Or yes to love?

"Say yes, Ma," Josh encouraged. "You look real pretty in it."

"Yes, Lottie," Elise said. "Go ahead and let Carlito buy it for you."

Carlito's hands moved along her shoulders, just slightly, but enough that she thought the movement strongly imitated a caress. At last, Lottie caved in under everyone's good-natured urging. Or maybe she gave in to her own desire. Looking away from the Californio's hot, waiting eyes, she said, "Thank you Carlito. It is the most beautiful thing I have ever had."

"It pales in the light of your own beauty, señora."

He removed the shawl from her shoulders to drape it over his arm until he paid for it. Lottie, embarrassed by his attentions, yet warmed by them, was relieved when Hart changed the subject.

"People in town seem to be a little nervous," he said to Kane. "Has something happened that we don't know about?"

The captain of the *Phantom* pushed his cap to the back of his head. "Aye, apparently so. Or it could just be rumors. But there's talk that José Castro is increasing his threats towards the Americans, and that he's mounting an army. Word is that his first target will be Sutter's Fort and the settlers up on the Sacramento River. Apparently he figures to take the fort over and prevent anymore foreigners from coming in over the mountains."

"Well, hell," Lottie said, voicing Hart's thoughts, "the Sacramento ain't but a day's ride from Rancho Vallecito and another day's ride from Rancho Corona. I figure that puts us right in his path of destruction."

"No place will be safe from Castro's army if he decides to carry his threats through," Kane replied. "Every American here in Monterey is getting nervous. Most are starting to sleep with their doors bolted. They're afraid Castro and his men will break in on them in the middle of the night and either kill them on the spot or take them prisoner. The Californios are afraid, too. Afraid of war and how it will affect their lives. Some who have American friends are afraid for them and don't want to see this rift that will invariably force loyalties to one side or the other."

Hart lost interest in the supply list Nancy had sent with him. He thought again of her being out there without any protection except for the Miwok fieldworkers. What if Castro went back to the ranch for some reason? "Do you think Castro will have any problem raising an army among the Californios?"

"Maybe you should ask a Californio." Kane turned to Carlito. "What do you think, Palocios?"

Carlito shrugged. "Who is to know? Many people do not like José Castro, but even those who don't might very well rally around him for the sake of honor and country. There is jealousy among the Californios towards the Americans and the changes they bring. I believe many are ready to fight to hold onto what has been theirs for many generations. A few years ago they accepted the Americans, made friends, and even allowed your men to marry their women. But with so many Americans coming in now, and with Captain Frémont showing up with what appears to be fighting power . . . well, they are beginning to feel they will be driven out. Their numbers are small, and they know they can expect no help from Mexico. Many feel that if they don't stop the emigration now, they will lose their country.

"As for me personally," he continued, "I would not ride with Castro because I do not respect him. He stages revolutions only for the sake of power. If he succeeded in winning such a revolution with the Americans, I would not want to be under his rule because he knows nothing of running a country. But I am sure there are those who would follow him into war. Although, I think a battle might be won, but never a war."

"What do you mean, Carlito?" Lottie wanted to know.

"Because California has been discovered by the world, mi Lolita. And because it is an untouched paradise, people will come to reap her golden fruit and will not be deterred even by threats to their lives. It is human nature to want paradise. There is no way to stop the tide."

"What about that warship out in the bay?" Hart asked Kane.

"Larkin sent for it," the captain replied. "Right after your last trip here, José Castro sent Andrés Castillero to Mexico to get munitions. He then called a military conference here in Monterey. Let me tell you, that upset Pico tremendously. It upset Larkin, too. He wrote to Consul John Parrott at Mazatlán to send the Portsmouth. It laid anchor just yesterday.

"Lieutenant Archibald Gillespie, naval officer for the United States, came in here with dispatches. One was for Larkin, appointing him as confidential agent for the United States. He had another dispatch for Frémont. Couriers were sent out to try and catch up with Frémont in Oregon and bring him back to meet Gillespie, who's headed that way to deliver them in person."

"I don't suppose you'd know what was in the dispatches?"

"No. Gillespie wouldn't even tell Larkin, and he was fit to be tied. But with Governor Pico and Comandante-General Castro at odds with each other, we have internal strife in California, as well as external."

Hart's brow tightened into worried furrows. "I think we'd better complete our business quickly and get back to our ranches. I should never have let Nancy talk me into letting her stay there without adequate protection."

"Be careful on your trip back," Kane said. "With Castro firing everyone up for a revolution, there are those who might decide to start killing Americans for target practice."

"Don't forget Frémont," Lottie replied dryly. "He's doing his fair share of firing up people's imaginations."

"Every American in Monterey is damned curious to know what Gillespie had to tell him that he couldn't tell the confidential agent."

"That might be something we'll never know, Jack," Hart said grimly. "You know how Frémont likes to work on his own."

"Yes, and that's what worries us all."

36

June

Hart held Angelica in his arms. With Nancy, they leaned against the corral poles and watched Lady Rae's colt bound around the enclosure, trying to entice his mother to play with him.

Hart had been home several weeks now, and Angelica would hardly let him out of her sight. When he needed to work he practically had to sneak out of the house, or wait until she was asleep because she raised such a fuss. Her fear was that he would leave and be gone for weeks, as he often was.

"Ride pony," she said. "Me." She held out her arms toward the colt, and Hart had to pull her back to his chest to keep her from tumbling right out of his arms.

"The colt is just a baby, like you," he explained patiently, his eyes twinkling with joy and love for his dark-haired daughter. "He's too little to ride."

"Me . . . lit-el. Me ride."

"I'll take you for a ride later, on one of the other horses," Nancy promised.

Angelica's lips puffed out in a pout but she gave the explanation considerable thought. Finally accepting it, she slid her thumb into her mouth and sucked vigorously as a means of consolation.

At the unexpected sound of a galloping horse, they turned from the corral and toward the road leading north to Sutter's Fort.

Hart handed the baby to Nancy and automatically lowered his hand to the revolver he'd started wearing in a holster on his hip. "Maybe you should go inside with the baby."

"It's only one rider, Hart. Probably a messenger from the fort."

Nancy was right. A young man of about eighteen, his chest puffing from exertion, pulled his horse to a stop in the middle of the yard. He saw the two of them and anxiously nudged his tired horse across the distance. It stopped a few feet away, its head drooping to the ground.

Hart's brows shot together. No one but a Californio rode his horse that hard for nothing. "What's wrong, young man? Can you come inside and get a drink, maybe something to eat?"

The boy gladly dismounted and followed them to the house on weak legs. By the time he got there, he had caught his breath. "I was sent from Sutter's Fort, Mr. Daniels. William Ide received a message from an Indian just yesterday that there are two hundred fifty armed Mexicans coming right up the valley. They're supposedly destroying everything in their path—crops, houses, cattle. And Frémont has sent out a request for every man who doesn't have a family to come to his aid at Sutter's Buttes. Immediately. To stop the enemy."

"Who's leading this army?"

"I don't know, sir. But I was told to warn every ranch in the area to be on alert."

"Has war been declared?"

"Not that we've heard."

Hart would go in aid of the Americans, if necessary, but he didn't want to leave the ranch in the hands of his vaqueros, who, except for one, were all in their early twenties. "Thanks for letting us know. We'll prepare ourselves for possible attack."

After feeding the young man, Hart took him to the corral and mounted him on a fresh horse so he could ride on to Rancho Corona and warn Lottie. When the dust of the departing horse's hooves had settled, he returned to the house. Nancy was standing on the veranda holding Angelica.

"I'd better arm the Indians and the vaqueros," he said.

"I'm wondering if that army is Mexican or Castro's rebel Californios. If it's the latter, the vaqueros might not wish to align themselves with Rancho Vallecito."

He nodded grimly. "Yes, I know. We will simply have to wait and see."

Late that afternoon, the thunder of hooves once again brought Hart and Nancy and everyone on the ranch, reaching for their weapons. Hart instructed Nancy to take cover with the baby, but the thundering hooves turned out to be a herd of approximately one hundred seventy-five horses being driven by ten men. While the men circled the animals into the valley, down by the river, one of the men left the herd and rode up to the house. Hart was waiting for him in the middle of the yard.

The man, a Californio, held up an arm in greeting as he pulled his horse to a halt in a swirl of dust. "Señor Daniels, *buenos días.* I hope our arrival has not alarmed you." He glanced nervously at the rifles aimed at him from every barn and house window.

Hart made no pretense at friendliness. "We have word that there is an army coming this way, destroying everything in its path. You wouldn't know something about that, would you?"

The man's smile placated. "An army? No, señor. I do not think so. As for us, we are just an army of riderless horses. I am Lieutenant Francisco Arce, under the command of General José Castro. I have with me Lieutenant José María Alviso and a few vaqueros. We have requisitioned these horses from Comandante Vallejo in Sonoma for military purposes."

"And what military purposes would that be, Señor Arce?"

"Comandante Castro is mounting a force to ride against Governor Pico. They do not see eye to eye, you know? And Comandante Castro thinks it is time for a new leader. We would welcome any citizens such as yourself to ride with us in this worthy cause."

Hart wondered who he should believe. The boy last night, or Arce. Something in Arce's eyes left Hart suspicious that he would not be above a lie. But it didn't matter. He would ride with Frémont and the Americans before he would ride with Castro.

"I can't leave my family and my ranch, Señor Arce. I hope you will understand my position."

Arce smiled slyly. "From what I hear, Señor Daniels, you leave your family quite frequently. You make many trips to Monterey these past six months."

Hart didn't like the needling suggestion. "All the more reason to stay at the ranch when business does not call me away."

Arce lifted an eyebrow in skepticism, as if he didn't believe Hart. Did he and others in Castro's regime know he was delivering information to Larkin? Would they consider him a spy for the American government?

"You have some large corrals about three miles from here." Arce said, changing the subject. "We would like to know if we can corral our horses there tonight. It would allow us to rest and not worry about the horses wandering away."

Outside of being suspicious of Arce's true intent, Hart had no good reason to refuse him his request. It would be better not to show hostility at this point. "You are welcome to use the corrals."

Hart loitered around the yard with the vaqueros until Arce and his men had driven the horses on down the river. "You can go back to your quarters now, men," Hart told them, finally relaxing the grip on his own rifle. "But don't trust Arce. Be on guard, just in case he and his men return."

Neither Nancy nor Hart slept well that night with Arce and his men so close. They talked deep into early hours, then spent the remainder of it tossing and turning.

The next morning, pounding on the door brought them from the breakfast table. Osvaldo was there, his eyes large, his voice excited. "There is dust on the road, señor. Many riders from the north are heading toward the holding corrals. They ride hard, like men with intent."

"Stay here with Angelica." Hart shot the order to Nancy as he went for his weapons. But Nancy was right on his heels.

"I'm going with you. Magdalena and Carmelita can stay with the baby. You might need my help."

"I don't want you getting hurt. *Stay* here."

There was no room for argument in his tone, but when he took a rifle from the rack, Nancy removed the shotgun.

"I'm going with you," she said stubbornly. "We have only six men on the ranch right now. You'll need every gun you can get."

He glared at her. "All right. Come on. I don't have time to argue with you."

Together, they raced from the house. The four vaqueros, along with Thane and Torey came running from their quarters to join them. Hart and the men ran to the corral to catch the horses; Nancy hurried to Magdalena's *cabaña* to tell her and Carmelita to go to the big house, bar the doors, and tend to Angelica. Then she met the others as they brought the bridled horses from the corral. They had not taken the time to saddle them. Hart gave Nancy a leg up on one of the geldings, then swung onto the back of his own. In a cloud of dust, the eight of them galloped from the yard.

Hart slowed his mount some distance from the holding corral. They noticed a group of rough-looking men had surrounded Arce and his men. The latter had their arms reaching for the morning sky at the encouragement of twelve long rifles.

Hart nudged his horse into a fast, but cautious walk as he approached the situation, rifle ready. Nancy rode next to him, the heavy shotgun wedged under her arm but aimed and ready to fire. They soon recognized the captors as Americans from Sutter's Fort, commanded by the hard-drinking Ezekiel Merritt. His bloodshot eyes suggested he'd tipped a bottle or two prior to this excursion.

"What in the hell's going on here?" Hart demanded.

Ezekiel rested a hand on the handle of the tomahawk protruding from his belt and spat a stream of tobacco juice into the dirt. He always spoke with a stutter, but managed to say, "We're confiscating these horses, Daniels. I guess you didn't know Comandante Castro is planning on using them to mount a military force against the Americans. They plan to kick us all out of the country—those that they don't kill—and then start up their own fort on Bear River to keep any more of us Americans from coming in over the mountains. Arce himself insinuated as much to William Knight when they used Knight's landing to cross the Sacramento."

Hart's gaze locked with Arce. "That's not the story the Lieutenant told me. Perhaps he would care to clear things up."

Lieutenant Arce slid a nervous tongue over dry, cracked lips. "I was only making, with Señor Knight, what you Americans call a joke. It is all one big misunderstanding. These horses are to mount a force against Governor Pico, not the Americanos. José Castro wants to put him out of power."

Merritt spit another trail of tobacco juice onto the ground, emptying his mouth so he could talk. "We're taking these horses, Arce. You go tell Castro that if he wants them back, he'll just have to come and get them."

A pained expression streaked across Arce's face. "But it is a long way to Monterey, señor. Surely you do not expect us to walk?"

Merritt spat again, while considering. His dirty fingers traced the notches in his tomahawk. It was rumored there were in the vicinity of a hundred—one for every Indian scalp he'd taken. "All right, Arce," he finally said. "We'll let you have two horses each and your rifles. But only because I have a message I want delivered to Comandante Castro."

"We are very grateful, señor, for any kindness," Arce feigned humbleness. "What is this other message, *por favor?*"

Merritt's lips curled into a smug smile. "Tell him that we're going to take Sonoma and declare this republic an independent nation."

Hart, like most people who had ever come into contact with Ezekiel Merritt, knew of his hatred for Mexicans. Salvador Vallejo, Mariano's brother, had taken Merritt prisoner not long ago on some fabricated charge and had beaten him severely, going so far as to use his sword for the lashings. But this bold and dangerous declaration to take Sonoma, the headquarters for Colonel Mariano Vallejo in the northern district, surprised Hart as much as it did Arce.

Hart waited until Arce and his men had saddled their horses and fled down the valley before turning to Merritt. "Have you lost your mind, Merritt? You'd damned well better be prepared to carry this through all the way to the end because you've just issued a declaration of war. Are you sure you're not just wanting to get even with Salvador Vallejo?"

"I take it you don't approve?" Merritt spat tobacco juice at Hart's feet.

"No, I don't. And I certainly don't approve of capturing Sonoma. But now that you've stolen these horses, there may very well be no turning back."

"Stolen? Let's just say they've been 'requisitioned' to head off a coup against the Americans. Whose side are you on anyway, Daniels? Maybe we ought to string you up right along with those other Mexicans, the natural-born ones."

Hart ignored the threat. "Did Frémont put you up to this? We all know he's itching to take California and claim a higher degree of glory for himself."

"Frémont didn't tell us what to do, but he's let us know he'll stand behind us. At least he's a *true* American, which is more than I can say for you." With no further word, Merritt mounted, reined his horse around, and hollered to his men to head the horses back to Sutter's Fort.

Hart and Nancy and their vaqueros watched them go, knowing there was no way to stop them. And knowing, too, that Larkin's hopes and plans for a peaceful annexation of California into the United States had just been destroyed.

37

July

The Miwok messenger from Sutter's Fort doused his hot, sweaty head in the horse trough while Hart read the missive he had brought. Hart's lips thinned to a grim line as he handed it back to the Indian. "You may take it to Señora England. Get yourself a fresh horse from the remuda."

Hart waited on the veranda, thinking about the message while he watched the Indian cross to the corral. It wasn't until the Indian had kicked his fresh mount into a gallop, heading for Lottie's place, that Hart went inside, wondering all the while what he was going to do and how he was going to break this latest news to Nancy.

Since Merritt had ridden out of here a month ago, news of numerous events all over the province had been flying in from every direction. Most of the American settlers, like Hart, had not approved of Merritt taking Sonoma. But he had managed to collect about thirty volunteers to assist him in capturing Mariano Vallejo and his family right out of their home at daybreak on the morning of June fourteenth. The group had thrown up a crude flag, sporting a star and a bear, and had declared California as the new "Bear Flag Republic." They had drawn up a proclamation stating such and had escorted their prisoners to Sutter's Fort for incarceration.

Captain Frémont had denied having taken any part in the capture, but he had given the orders to arrest Jacob Leese, an American and brother-in-law to Mariano Vallejo. Leese, acting as interpreter for the proceedings, had also been put in jail with the others.

This harsh action taken by Merritt's "band of robbers," as Sutter called them, had not only illicited the anger and contempt of the Californios, but of the Americans who were married to Californios, and the Californios working on American-owned ranches.

Two days before Merritt and his men had stolen the horses from Arce, José Castro had declared martial law in the province. Eight days later, Governor Pico, with a military force of his own, had headed north from Los Angeles to engage Castro and regain control. With news of the Sonoma capture by the Bear Flaggers, Pico, after considerable discussion with Manuel Castro at Santa Barbara, had decided to set aside his personal differences with the comandante-general and join forces with him against the Americans.

A retaliation against Merritt had come swiftly. José Castro had gathered an army of one hundred sixty men and sent Joaquín de la Torre with about one-third of them to engage Merritt in a counterattack. They had captured two Americans on the Russian River who had gone there to get gunpowder for William Ide, one of the American leaders. The two Americans had been tied to trees and brutally butchered by Torre's men.

A few days later some more Americans were captured. Lieutenant Henry L. Ford of the Bear party took eighteen men to attempt a rescue. They, too, had been attacked by the Californios, but the Americans managed to kill one of the enemy and wound several more.

Frémont, now in charge of the new republic's army, had retaliated by having three Californios shot as they left their boat at Point San Pedro. It turned out, however, that they were innocent men who had no connection with Castro.

Wearily, Hart removed his hat and draped it on the hat rack in the foyer. Knowing what he had to do, he mounted the stairs. Nancy was usually with Angelica this time of day, reading to her before she put her down for a nap.

He heard her animated voice, softly husky, drifting down the carpeted hallway. He sat down on the top landing to wait for her to finish the story, wanting to delay the inevitable as long as possible.

Nancy came out of the baby's room quietly, and Hart knew Angelica must have fallen asleep before the story was over. She spotted him as he rose from the landing, but wariness leapt to her eyes, for it wasn't customary for him to be inside in the middle of the afternoon.

"I heard the rider coming in from Sutter's Fort," she said, moving down the hall toward him. "Is something wrong, Hart?"

He took her by the arm and led her to their room, closing the door behind them. He sat her on the edge of the bed and joined her. "Yes," he said softly. "The United States and Mexico are at war."

"What?" Her voice rose in alarm. "Is this for certain or only another rumor?"

"It's official." He sighed, releasing all the air from his chest. "Mexican troops went over the border into Texas and killed a bunch of Americans, so the United States declared war. That was clear back in May, and we just now got the word. Commodore Sloat sailed into Monterey a few days ago and raised the American flag. It went up over Sutter's Fort yesterday, and Frémont and his California Battalion have been ordered to Monterey."

Nancy was confused. "But what about the Bear Flag Republic?"

"It's over. Maybe it never really was. Even as Merritt and his men were capturing Sonoma, the United States had already declared war on Mexico."

Hart stood up, pacing back and forth on agitated strides. "I keep thinking of Torre's men tying Cowe and Fowler to trees, torturing them, and then butchering them. I can't sit by and watch my fellow Americans being killed and not do something to help. I wouldn't be surprised if José Castro tries to mount an army and overthrow the Americans, despite the declaration of war.

"It's crucial now that the Americans move in and occupy every major town in California," he continued. "In a sense, things haven't changed between the forces of Frémont and Castro except that the Americans now have the support of the United States for what they're doing."

Something else was coming. Something that would affect Nancy directly. And she knew what it was. "Will you join Frémont's army?" she asked softly.

He sat back down next to her, taking her hand in his. "There are men who haven't and probably never will, Nancy. They're staying with their families, tending their ranches. I know J.B. and Billy won't get involved. He stayed out of that Sonoma incident, even though they tried to recruit him. But the Americans are going to need every gun they can get if Castro and his men put them to the test. Yes, I have to join up."

"There's more, isn't there, Hart? What is it?"

He looked at her beseechingly, wanting her understanding, her consolation. "I have Californios working for me. Californios who are my
friends. God Almighty, but I feel like my heart's being ripped out, Nancy.
I want California to be under American rule, but I didn't want it to come
to this. I didn't want to fight my friends and neighbors. And I don't want
to leave you and Angelica. Your safety is my prime concern."

Nancy placed an arm around his shoulder and he turned into her
soothing embrace. "I know, Hart. I understand. And if it wasn't for Angelica, I would go with you."

A soft chuckle, breaking the tenseness of the moment, slipped
through his lips along with his warm breath against her neck. "Yes, you
probably would. But I would refuse to let you go. War is no place for a
woman."

"You're wrong," she countered, searching the depths of his eyes,
thinking in that moment how fiercely she loved him. "No one can fight
more passionately than a woman protecting her family."

"And that is the only time a woman should fight," he said. "Only when
it's a matter of life or death."

"Sometimes we are all called to fight, Hart. If we sit back and wait
until death threatens us personally, we could find that the battle is won
but the war is lost."

"Then you understand why I have to go?"

"I would rather keep you here safe with me, but, yes, I understand.
And don't worry about us." All the while she spoke, her heart ached with
fear about him leaving, and about her own position in being left behind
for an indefinite period of time. But she would not cry nor curse. She had
known when she left Amherst three years ago that war might decide the
future of California, and that by coming here, she would have to suffer
the consequences. It was a risk she had taken, and it was a reality she
would now have to face.

She spoke again to reassure them both. "The fighting seems to be isolated to the coastal settlements. The main objectives of both armies will
be the occupation of the towns. Isolated ranches would serve no purpose.
We'll be fine here at Rancho Vallecito."

But neither of them believed that, not one hundred percent.

"It's hard to say what Castro will do," Hart said irritably. "He doesn't
seem to be happy unless he's fighting. The fool would probably fight if all

odds were against him. It's the damage he can do before he surrenders that worries me the most."

Hart set her away from him, hoping she was right about the Californio armies not being interested in ranches this far from the main settlements. With the men gone, there were plenty of women and children being left alone. Many along the coast would be sent to missions for protection. Out here, in the Great Valley, they would probably go to Sutter's Fort. But Nancy and Lottie wouldn't go. He knew that much without even asking. It would leave them as prime targets for unscrupulous men. The Indian fieldworkers would be here, tending the crops. At least they would be loyal to Nancy. He was positive of that.

"There's one more thing I have to do," he said. "In the morning, I have to tell the vaqueros of my decision. And I have to give them the chance to make their own."

At the break of dawn, Hart had his horse saddled and had two extra mounts tied on lead ropes. His saddlebags were tight with food packed by Magdalena. His bedroll was tied on top of the saddlebags behind the cantle. He'd called the six hired men together, Thane and Torey included. They stood now, having heard his words and the choice he was placing on their shoulders. They said nothing at first, just shifted their weight from one foot to the other, looking at the ground and keeping their gazes hidden beneath the shadows of their hats and big sombreros.

It was Osvaldo who stepped forward first, his hands resting on his narrow hips. "Torre is a bad *hombre*, Señor Daniels. You are right to want to stop him before he kills any more of your people. I cannot speak for the others, but I will say that I have nothing against the Americanos governing the province of California. Mexico does not care about us. They send stupid people to be our rulers. They set ridiculous rules that are impossible to enforce, that have no meaning for the rancheros of California. I do not want to join forces with José Castro and his other men, Torre, Carrillo, and Manuel Castro. I could not do the things that they would ask of me. I could not tie men to trees, even men who might be enemies, and cut their limbs off, one by one. Castro and his officers only want power and glory for themselves and what riches they can steal from the common people. While you are gone, I will stay here and protect Rancho Vallecito, which I consider my home."

"We trust you, señor," another said. "But we do not trust Frémont and some of the others we do not know. I fear they might try to make us leave California, the way Castro has threatened to make the Americanos leave. Only we would have nowhere to go. If the Americanos win this war, we hope they will speak in our behalf and let us remain in this place of our birth."

His statement moved both Hart and Nancy, and made Hart feel guilty again for leaving, guilty that he might somehow be betraying them. Guilty because *he* should be the one to stay behind and protect his family. And yet, there were fellow Americans fighting for him, for his cause, and he could not sit back and let them die while he reaped the benefits of the blood they shed.

"The Americans don't want to remove the Californios from the province," he said.

Two other vaqueros stepped forward and said they agreed with Osvaldo. They would stay. Torey and Thane felt they should go with Hart and fight with the Americans. Only one vaquero, an older man and the last one to be hired, remained in the background. When all eyes turned to him, silently asking for his position on the matter, he finally spoke.

"I am your friend, too, Señor Daniels, but I am a Californio first, and I must go to fight on the side of my countrymen. It is not that I have a personal dislike for the Americanos. It is a matter of honor and loyalty. Can you understand what I am saying?"

"Yes, it is for the same reason I must go."

"I can assure you of one thing," the older man continued. "I will not ride against the families of the Americanos, only against the armies."

Hart nodded. "*Gracias.* Nor will I ride against the families of the Californios."

The man shook Hart's hand and parted by saying, "I hope we do not meet on the battlefield, señor. I do not believe I could kill you."

The vaquero swung into his saddle and rode away down the valley to the south, probably heading for Los Angeles where Castro now had his headquarters. Thane and Torey saddled their horses, too, and brought them up to the house.

Hart gathered his reins and was preparing to mount when a sleepy-eyed Angelica toddled from the house. She saw him and hurried precariously across the porch and down the steps. Nancy scooped her up to keep her from running under the horses' legs. The baby reached her arms out for her father. "Daddy go," she insisted. "Me go Daddy."

Hart took her in his arms, hugging her one last time, and smoothing her dark locks that had fallen down around her face, framing her huge blue eyes. "Not this time, Angel," he said tenderly. "But I'll be back soon, and I'll take you for a ride. How will that be?"

Angelica clapped her hands together and grinned. "Ride hoese."

Hart pulled Nancy against him with his free arm. Their passionate kiss delighted Angelica who giggled and covered her mouth with her tiny hands.

"My two sweethearts," he murmured. "I love you both so much."

"It seems we are always saying good-bye, Hart."

"It won't always be this way. I promise."

He handed Angelica into Nancy's arms. His feet had barely slid into the stirrups when he pushed his horse into a lope. It was as if he had to leave quickly or not at all. Thane and Torey scrambled to catch up.

The three remaining vaqueros, all just boys under twenty, wandered away, returning to their duties. Angelica got bored and squirmed from Nancy's arms, toddling off on her chubby little legs to the veranda. Finally, Nancy turned back to the house, feeling the loneliness of her husband's absence as she never had before. The ranch seemed oddly quiet with him gone this time. Empty. And she had the horrible thought that it would be this way forever if he did not return.

38

Angelica could sit for hours with her mother atop the pole corral, watching nineteen-year-old Osvaldo educate the young horses which were being brought into the remuda. Osvaldo preferred breaking the horses in the big, blind corral three miles downriver from ranch headquarters.

The baby girl had straddled the corral's big top pole and was pretending it was her horse. She had even wrapped an old horsechair rope around the pole's rough bark and was using it as her reins. She could bounce for hours, it seemed, and keep Nancy, who was sitting next to her, clutching the back of her dress so she wouldn't fall to the ground—a drop of eight feet.

The corrals had been built high and strong for the express purpose of keeping the wild horses and cattle from jumping over them, or crashing through them, in their occasional frenzied attempts at freedom. But Angelica wasn't afraid of the height. Angelica wasn't afraid of anything.

Today Osvaldo was patiently teaching his young mount the art of reining and backing up. He had a knack for making a horse eager to learn. Nancy determined it was because he made the horse his friend before he ever attempted to make himself its master. The two-year-old colt which he was working with today was one of his favorites and showed a great deal of promise in becoming a top-notch cow pony.

Nancy could have stayed all day and watched the young *amansador*, but it would soon be time for Angelica's nap. From the way the baby was rubbing her eyes, she would be asleep in Nancy's arms before they got back to the house.

Anchoring Angelica under one arm, Nancy got down from the corrals. The baby didn't want to go and raised an immediate fuss, but Nancy quieted her by telling her that it was time to ride Lady Rae again.

The mare was tied to a corral post. Her vivacious colt, which the vaqueros had named Lightning, or Relámpago, was nosing around the corrals, sniffing at some chipmunks that were running back and forth along the poles. The vaqueros claimed the young colt was going to be faster than his mother. To date, there wasn't a horse on the ranch that had been able to beat Lady Rae in a race. But she was getting older, Nancy reasoned, and someday another would take her place. If it happened to be her own colt, then all the better.

Osvaldo rode his horse up to the gate, opened it without leaving the saddle, and closed it behind him in the same fashion. He had left his pistols atop one of the gateposts and paused to gather them up and tuck them into the bright red sash at his waist. "I will go with you, señora," he said. "Enough has been taught today."

"Are you sure, Osvaldo?" she questioned. "I don't want to keep you from your work."

The young man, in truth, had taken on the role as her personal bodyguard since Hart had been gone. He seldom let her get away from the ranch but what he didn't ride along.

"I am certain. A young horse is like a young child. He gets bored easily and his attention span is short." Osvaldo reached over and chucked Angelica playfully under the chin, making her smile shyly. "Isn't that right, *chiquita?* We will ride together, *sí?*"

"*Sí*, ride Osva," Angelica reached her arms out for the handsome young man.

"Ah, pretty señorita," he crooned, holding her only long enough for Nancy to mount her mare. "My horse is much too wild for a *chiquita* like you. You will be much safer with your mother."

"No safe." Angelica shook her head and frowned. "Go Osva."

He chuckled, handing her over to Nancy, who settled her in front of her in the big California saddle. "*Sí*, I know you do not like to play it safe, Angelica, but you must. My pony might buck us both off and we would go sailing into the sky. Maybe all the way to the moon."

"Go moo," Angelica pointed to the sky. "Me go moo."

Osvaldo laughed again. "That would be fine, *chiquita,* but if we got there, there would be no way to come back and you would not have your mama with you. Only me, Osvaldo, and I do not know how to cook. I definitely cannot make cookies. And do you know something even worse than all that? I have been told that there are no horses on the moon."

Angelica shoved her thumb in her mouth and sucked purposefully while considering these new obstacles. She pulled the thumb out long enough to shake her head and say, "No hoeses. No go moo."

The ride back was kept lively by watching Lady Rae's blood bay colt run around the saddle horses and race ahead for short distances, then race back and gallop wide loops around them.

On an easy lope they traversed the green, rolling hills, slowing occasionally to a walk to give their horses a breather. Nancy's mare fretted more than usual when her colt bounded out of sight over the edge of an oak-rimmed hill, and Nancy had to maintain a tight rein to keep her from racing after him.

"Don't worry," Nancy patted the mare's neck consolingly. "He won't get too far away before he returns."

As predicted, the colt suddenly burst onto the horizon again, running hell-bent for his mother. But almost immediately, Nancy detected a difference in the way the colt was running. It was as if he were fleeing from the devil himself.

The thought had no sooner crossed her mind when four riders, with their lariats twirling in big loops over their heads, galloped over the hill, spreading out to surround the colt.

"*¡Dios mío!*" Osvaldo shouted. "Renegade Indian vaqueros after the colt! And he is bringing them straight toward us!"

The Indians, surprised at seeing her and Osvaldo, reined up slightly, but then a signal of agreement must have passed between them for, once again, they set out on the chase. Their quest for the colt took on new proportions and new meaning as they saw they easily outnumbered Nancy and Osvaldo. With ropes whirling, they came onward, spurring their horses at full speed.

"They've seen us!" Nancy shouted in fear, not knowing what to do. The ranch was too far away, and the renegades were right in the path.

"We must run, señora!" Osvaldo reined his young mount around. "Run. Get to the safety of the Indian village with the baby! If they catch us, we are dead!"

Nancy whirled the mare, who didn't want to leave her colt, and forced her after Osvaldo's mount and toward the river, all the while trying to turn Angelica around to face her so she could ride faster. "Put your arms around my neck, Angel," she instructed in a frantic voice. "Wrap your legs around my waist. Don't let go no matter what. Do you hear me? Mommy can't hold onto you. You must hold onto me."

Angelica, sensing her mother's fear and the urgency of the situation, whimpered slightly in objection but ultimately turned into her mother, and, burying her face in Nancy's neck, clung to her as she had been ordered to do.

Nancy pushed the mare into a full gallop after Osvaldo. They fled across the valley, over and up a long hill that was a short-cut to the Indian village. The incline wasn't steep, but it was long, and their horses quickly became winded. The mare could have easily outrun the Indian ponies but her instinct was to hold back and protect her colt which was still somewhere behind her, and she refused to go full speed. With Angelica hanging off the front of her, Nancy was unable to lean out over the mare's neck as much as she needed to for maximum speed and balance.

The rumble of hooves grew louder, closer. Nancy switched the reins to her left hand. With her right, she fumbled to pull her Allen pepperbox from the hip holster.

The mare hit a low spot. Nancy lost a stirrup and lurched forward, grabbing Angelica as she came dangerously close to losing her seat. A quick glance over her shoulder showed the colt gaining on them, but the renegades were too, and the Indian village was still a good mile away. If those lariats settled over them . . .

"We're not going to make the village, Osvaldo!" she yelled to his back. "We've got to take cover!"

She veered her mare toward a pile of deadfall on the river where an ancient oak had fallen into a tangle of bushes and underbrush. Osvaldo followed. They reached it just minutes before the renegades, but long enough for Osvaldo to pull both single shot rifles from their saddle scabbards and for Nancy to push Angelica down under the brushy limbs of a fallen oak.

"You must not move, Angel!" she commanded. Yanking her hat from her head, she handed it to the baby. "Hold mommy's hat very tightly and don't cry. Lie very still and don't cry! If the Indians hear you cry they'll take you away from me. Do you understand?"

Angelica's big blue eyes were as large as saucers and welled with tears, but she didn't cry. She clutched the hat tightly, as if it were Nancy herself, and did not move from the concealing branches of the big tree. Nancy wanted to hold her, to protect her with her love and her body, but the only thing that would protect her now was a gun.

Osvaldo crossed his chest and mumbled a prayer to God, readying his rifle. "We cannot fend them off for long, señora," he said hopelessly.

"They'll split up and try to surround us," Nancy said, exchanging the pepperbox for her rifle. "Be ready."

The renegades came, yipping and screaming. The sounds froze Nancy's blood. She knew they would give no quarter. Both she and Osvaldo fired their rifles. One Indian tumbled backwards over the rump of his horse and hit the ground. There was no way of telling if he'd been hit. The other yelped in pain as blood burst from a wound in his thigh.

Nancy reached for her pepperbox. Osvaldo pulled both pistols from his sash.

Still the Indians came, undeterred, not giving their victims time to reload, only to counterattack with whatever skill and weapons they could as quickly as they could. Within seconds, two of the Indians had separated to either end of the barricade while the third expertly lobbed arrows over the fallen tree and brush, keeping Nancy and Osvaldo pinned down. The wounded one vanished from sight.

Nancy sent three shots from the pepperbox at the man closing in on her end of the barricade, but he hit the ground rolling, avoiding injury. Osvaldo fired off one pistol, but missed his target, too. An Indian burst from behind the fallen tree and came at Osvaldo with an upraised tomahawk. Osvaldo lifted the pistol in his left hand and fired. The lead caught the Indian in the chest, flinging him backward into the tree branches, dead.

The arrows stopped falling, and in the unnerving silence that followed, Nancy could hear nothing but the pounding of her own heart and the sucking sound of Angelica furiously working on her thumb. Nancy could not spare a glance at her baby. A split second of inattentiveness could spell death. Only one Indian was dead for sure, and the others were closing in.

Rapidly she calculated three shots left in the pepperbox. The rifles were empty. The pistols were empty. The ammunition pouches were back on the saddles, and the horses had run for cover.

She gripped and regripped the handle of the pepperbox, then broke off some branches of the dry, old tree. The noise filled the deathly silence with a loud crack. She hunkered down closer against the trunk of the fallen tree and sank again into that silence.

Osvaldo pulled the long knife from his leg scabbard.

"Why do they want to die trying to kill us?" she whispered to Osvaldo. "We've done nothing to them."

"It was a game in the beginning," he replied. "But we have killed one of them, so now it is a battle. And they will not back down to a battle."

Osvaldo let out an abrupt cry and Nancy's head snapped around to see an arrow running straight through his forearm, a few inches above his wrist. The knife he held fell to the ground. She reached for it, her hand closing over the handle just as one of the Indians let out a war cry from just above her. She jerked her head around in time to see him leaping from another tree whose branches extended out over the barricade. She shot to her feet, whirled, and flung the knife. Like lightning it flew threw the air and met his freefall, ending his hideous shriek with a heavy thud in the center of his torso. He crashed heavily onto the branches of the dead oak, directly over the top of Angelica, spurting blood. The baby started to scream hysterically just as Osvaldo yelled, "Look out! To your left!"

Nancy whirled again, firing the last three shots from her pepperbox into the face of the third Indian, simultaneously feeling the sting from his knife as it sliced past her, cutting open her upper arm.

"¡Dios mío!" Osvaldo cried out. "We are dead."

The fourth Indian, with blood streaming from the thigh wound Osvaldo had inflicted, stepped out from behind the base of the fallen tree with his bow and arrow raised and pointed at Osvaldo's heart. "Sí," he spoke in Spanish. "You are dead."

Seeing they were defenseless, a cold malevolence entered his black eyes. Smiling evilly, he lowered the weapon. "I think it more fitting that you should both suffer for killing my compadres," he said. "I will drag you, vaquero, to death behind my horse. I will bash the baby's brains out against a tree. And the woman—she will be my prisoner and I will have my pleasure with her until I tire of her. Then I will slit her throat from ear to ear."

Slowly and menacingly, he started toward them. As he bypassed Osvaldo and came closer to Nancy, she backed against the tree limbs trying to protect Angelica. The baby had given up on her orders not to cry and was screaming convulsively while trying to crawl out from her hiding place and away from the dead Indian staring down at her through the branches. But the tree limbs stabbed and jabbed her every attempt at escape.

Nancy backed deeper into the tangle of limbs and one of the smaller ones, about an inch in diameter, snapped from the pressure of her weight. Her fingers curled around the branch. With a slight twist, she pulled it free and felt the stabbing, spearlike tip where it had broken off.

The ensuing silence was filled with Angelica's terrorized screams, and with the pounding of her own blood in her veins. Her grip tightened on the severed branch.

The Indian was so close now she could smell his sweat and the blood oozing from his leg. Osvaldo kicked him in the shin, trying to draw him away from Nancy, but he ignored the boy, knowing he was completely helpless. His thick lips twisted into a gloating, sinister smile. He reached for Nancy.

With a burst of ice-cold fear and utter desperation, she thrust her arm forward with every ounce of strength she possessed and rammed the broken branch deep into the tender, boneless flesh of his abdomen. His eyes bulged in shock as he lurched slightly forward, staring down at the branch protruding from his stomach. He stumbled backward, lifting his eyes to hers in abject shock. He tried reaching for the knife in the scabbard at his waist but couldn't seem to work his fingers. He staggered forward and back, losing his balance and finally made a pirouette into the river, landing facedown.

Knowing he could not harm her now, Nancy dropped to her hands and knees. Breaking and shoving branches out of her way, she reached Angelica and dragged her into her arms, clutching her as tightly to her chest as she possibly could. The baby was shaking violently and gasping for air between shuddering sobs.

"It's all right, Angel. All right," Nancy soothed. "The Indians are dead. Everything's all right."

Nancy began to shake uncontrollably now herself, and tears took a course down her face in a quiet, ceaseless stream. Osvaldo moved next to her and pulled both her and Angelica against him with his good arm. He was shaking badly too, and no doubt needed their comforting arms as much as they needed his.

After a time, when Angelica's sobs had softened to hiccups and

Nancy's own tears had slowed, Osvaldo moved away and stood up, weaving on his feet and looking pale.

"We need to get that arrow out of your arm." Nancy forced herself to her feet and balanced on trembling legs. She sat Angelica down again, against her cries of objection. Osvaldo clenched his teeth and grabbed a tree branch with his good hand, bracing himself for what was to come. Carefully Nancy snapped off the feathered end of the arrow as close to his arm as she could. Before Osvaldo knew what had happened, she had yanked the remaining shaft all the way through his arm with one swift, downward pull. He cried out briefly in pain, then it was over.

Nancy removed the bandana at his throat and bound his wrist. She took her own bandana and, with Osvaldo's help, tied it around the wound on her arm. "We'll go to the Indian village and have Running Cloud treat the wounds."

"You are a valiant woman, señora," Osvaldo said in a voice which he strained to hold steady. "I will go into battle with you anytime."

Nancy swallowed convulsively. "*Gracias,* Osvaldo. You didn't do too badly yourself. I just hope we don't have to do that again anytime soon."

His lips split into a quivery, white-toothed grin and he put an arm around her waist. "We will help each other to the horses. I think my mother will be very happy to see us."

39

The American flag billowed and waved on the flagpole over the custom-house at Monterey, its colors bright and confident against the hot, azure sky. The breeze, thick with the scent of salt and sand, of seaweed and fish, ran along the half-moon bay and brushed at the faces of Frémont's California Battalion, lounging in the sun while awaiting their next orders.

Hart had overtaken Frémont's California Battalion at the San Joaquin River and had been with them when they'd ridden into San Juan Bautista and raised the stars-and-stripes. They had occupied the village briefly along with some dragoons sent by Commodore Sloat. Comandante-General José Castro had been invited by Sloat to come to Monterey and sign articles of capitulation.

Instead, he sent a message stating that he was not the proper authority to sign the capitulation. In a message sent to Sloat, he had informed him that, as comandante-general, his duty was to defend the country "at all sacrifice," and that if Sloat wanted capitulation he would have to take the matter up with Governor Pico in Los Angeles. Sloat had put Commodore Robert F. Stockton in charge of all land forces and operations, washed his hands of the matter entirely, and prepared to sail for home.

Castro's refusal to appear in Monterey had been the cause of a meeting at Thomas Larkin's house shortly after Frémont's arrival in Monterey. Commodore Stockton, who had arrived not long ago from Norfolk, lifted his militant voice to a level that easily carried across the room to everyone present. "We will not confine operations to the possession of Monterey and San Francisco," he said. "If not challenged, Castro will continue to keep California in a state of revolution. He has apparently joined Pico in Los Angeles, making it time for us to demand their surrender.

"I will take some three hundred sixty men to Los Angeles. Captain Frémont, I want you and your battalion to set sail for San Diego. Raise the American flag there and then march up to Los Angeles from the south to meet us." He turned to Thomas Larkin. "I would greatly appreciate it if you would go with my battalion as conciliator, Consul."

Larkin was not happy with the turn of events, bemoaning the demise of his plan for California's quiet annexation into the United States, which would have helped his own political standing and place in history. But, having no choice but to reconcile himself to the situation, he graciously accepted the request. "I would be happy to help in any capacity I can."

"Very well, men." Stockton rose. "I will issue the proclamation tomorrow, then we will proceed with the plan."

August

The cloud of dust on the road north drew Lottie's attention. It wasn't a big cloud of dust, just a stirring caused by three or four riders.

"You can't be stubborn and stay there all day, sitting on your contrary fanny, you stupid jackass," she said to the mule who had, for thirty minutes now, belligerently sat on its rear end, refusing to budge. "Company's coming, and if you don't get up I'll be forced to put a bullet between your sorry eyes. I've about run out of patience with you, just in case you were wondering."

As if to prove her point, Lottie reached for the pistol in her hip holster, drew it, and pointed it at a spot between the mule's large eyes. She pulled back the hammer. "Well, are you gonna sit around and see if I'm bluffing? You ought to know by now that I seldom bluff. But I've got to hand it to you. In all my years of working with mules, I've never dealt with a critter as damned contemptible as you."

The mule flicked his ears, either at the sound of the hammer clicking in place, or at the sound of the riders coming down the road. Lottie would never know exactly which motivated the creature, but with a bray of defeat, he pulled himself back up onto all fours and stood there, spay-legged, with his head hanging remorsefully between his knees.

"That's more like it," Lottie said, lowering the hammer and sliding the pistol back to its holster. Inwardly, she was relieved he hadn't called her bluff. She never would have been able to pull the trigger anyway. "Now, I'm going to let you think about the lessons you've learned today while I go see who's coming down the road."

She tied the mule to one of the corral posts, left the corral and was in the middle of the yard by the time the riders were close enough to rec-ognize. She had a big smile in place when Nancy, with baby Angelica rid-ing in front of her on the California saddle, pulled to a stop a few feet away. Two vaqueros had ridden along as bodyguards.

"Well, hell, girl! It's good to see you. It's almost gettin' to where I hate to see somebody comin' down that road for fear its a bearer of bad news. You didn't come with any, did you? Here, let me take Angel and you can light for awhile."

Nancy handed the baby down to Lottie then swung to the ground herself. "Actually, I just got word from Hart that the war—as far as Cal-ifornia is concerned—is over. Stockton's and Frémont's battalions scared the daylights out of Pico and Castro. They forked their horses and took the road to Sonora. Everyone will be coming home as soon as all the loose ends are tied up. I can't believe it, Lottie. We're part of the United States again."

Lottie's smile spread from ear to ear. "That's cause for celebration, girl. I say we plan one hell of a party when the men get back. We'll have it here at Rancho Corona."

September

"What are the crazy fools going to do?" Hart asked, watching Frémont and a number of the men leaving the dancing platform and heading for the horse corrals.

Carlito grinned, showing a set of pearly white teeth made even whiter by his deeply bronzed face. "Frémont is taking them out to catch a griz-zly. But I tell them they are wasting their time. It is dark and the grizzlies will hear the music and not come within a mile of this place. But they must show the señoritas their *machismo*, no?"

Hart's arm tightened around Nancy's waist. A melancholy Spanish tune, strummed on the strings of several guitars, filled the air. "There are better ways. Don't you agree, Carlito?"

The Californio, who had been dancing nearly every dance with Lottie, flashed her a seductive smile. "*Sí, amigo.* I think the señoritas are more impressed by a man who can do the *pasodoble* than a man who can kill a grizzly. Is that not true, Lolita?"

Carlito's passion burned as hot as a prairie fire pushed by the wind. For months, the two of them had tried to squelch the growing flames rising between them, threatening to consume their common sense. But the way he held her tonight, the way he looked at her, the way he moved his body for her during the sexually suggestive *pasodoble,* was a bright, clear banner displaying his feelings for her. And she needed a man. She was tired of lying alone in her big bed, night after lonely night.

Yet, Carlito frightened her in many ways. He was always protectively by her side, a self-appointed bodyguard since that day with Castro's men. They could laugh together, work together, play together. They had confided in each other about things from their pasts that had left their scars. She had told him about Major. In turn, she had learned something of him. She had always suspected aristocracy running through his veins, and her intuitions had been correct. He was indeed from a wealthy Spanish family. His father had sailed to Mexico as a young man, married an Indian woman, and the two of them had come to California to make a life for themselves. When he had been a boy of only eight, a jealous uncle had killed his father and taken over the Rancho Palocios which his father and mother had built just down the coast from Monterey. His mother had taken him and his siblings and made a living for them the best she could. At nineteen, more tragedy had befallen him. His young wife of seventeen had died in childbirth, taking their unborn baby with her. His life after that had contained no ties to anything or anyone. No ties, that is, until he had come to work on Rancho Corona.

Despite everything he had told her about himself, Lottie still found him to be something of an enigma. Often she wondered if the face he showed her was his true self or only that which he wanted her to see. And sometimes she believed he was possibly *too* handsome, *too* aristocratic, for a plain woman such as herself. Could she compete with his first love, his lost love? That lovely girl he had spoken of with such pain in his eyes. It was hard to fill the shoes of a beautiful memory.

She feared that if she took him to her bed, she would wake up one morning and find him gone. But when those doubts pummeled her, as they frequently did, she would always chuckle and bring herself back down to earth with the simple truth. She was *not* a beautiful woman whom a man would sacrifice months of hard labor for just so he could find a few moments of pleasure with her. There were other women more beautiful, younger, and desirable to which a man would turn. Surely then, she reasoned, his feelings for her had to be genuine.

"You know women well, Carlito," she finally said. "There is much to be said about a man who can dance."

His dark eyes sparkled in the lantern-light. "Then I will stay here and dance the night away with you. I do not care to track down and kill a grizzly who is minding his own business anyway.

"What will your decision be, *amigo?*" He turned to Hart. "Will you stay with me and entertain the ladies, or go with Frémont and torment a poor, unsuspecting beast who is just searching for nuts and berries in the forest?"

The Spanish guitars flowed on, enticing movement of the feet, the body. Hart took Nancy's hand and started toward the dance floor in the middle of the yard. It was a large platform which the men had constructed of milled lumber, and strung around with lanterns. "I'm not going anywhere. They can catch their own grizzly."

And indeed they did. The men, drunk with spirits and the adventure of the hunt, returned around midnight with a poor, dead grizzly, tangled in a dozen lariats, dragging along behind their tired horses and covered with dirt that had turned to mud from his lather. Proud of their prowess, however, the dancing and drinking picked up for a couple of hours until fatigue overcame most of the women. Too much liquor was the culprit that finally forced the men to call it a night. A few didn't even make it to their bedrolls, but passed out in the dirt.

When the messenger from Sutter's Fort came riding onto the ranch at daybreak, he was met by a few clucking chickens, one barking dog, and a group of giggling, drunken young people who were carrying on the party to the best of their ability while the musicians dozed.

"I'm looking for Captain Frémont," the courier said anxiously to the young people who stared at him with glazed eyes and silly smiles. "Where is Captain Frémont?"

One of the young men, an American boy named John Jenkins, staggered off the dance platform, tripped down the stairs, and swayed to a semi-stop in front of the messenger's horse. "He killed a grizz last night. The biggest sonofabitchin' thing I've ever seen in my life. Do you want to see it? It's right over there." He pointed lamely at a pile of matted fur in the shadows of the toolshed.

"No, I don't want to see it," the messenger said. "I need to talk to Captain Frémont." Suddenly losing patience with the scene, the messenger pulled a pistol from his holster, aimed it at the sky and fired it off, three times. By the third blast, Frémont and every other person was groping for consciousness and their weapons, which none of them seemed to be able to find.

The messenger spotted Frémont and rode up to him. "I have a message from Commodore Stockton, sir."

Frémont tried to stand straight but weaved unsteadily as he continued to grope for his weapon, which wasn't on his hip or anywhere else nearby. "Well, what in the hell is it, man?"

The young man straightened in the saddle, lifting his shoulders long enough to deliver his message. "There's been an insurrection, sir. California is at war . . . again."

40

"It seems, sir," the young courier continued, "that demonstrations in Los Angeles, led by Sérbulo Varela, have turned into an insurrection. Varela may have started it, but José María Flores, and two of Castro's other officers, José Antonio Carrillo, and Andrés Pico, have taken over. They have seized Los Angeles and left Gillespie and his men completely without power. He has sent for assistance from Commodore Stockton in Yerba Buena.

"We have also learned that at least seventy rebels have ridden east to engage Benjamin Wilson and his command of twenty Americans stationed on the Colorado to keep José Castro from sneaking back into the country. They might be able to take a position at Chino Ranch, owned by Isaac Williams, but his entire family could be in jeopardy, and we have no idea how long they might be able to hold off the rebel attack."

While Frémont and the others tried to absorb the information in their liquor-soaked minds, the messenger added, "Commodore Stockton wants you and your men to make haste to the port of San Francisco where boats will carry you to Monterey."

Balefully, Frémont eyed him, as if questioning whether he had heard correctly, and clearly annoyed if he had. "You picked a hell of a time to deliver a message of war, young man. Few of us are in any condition to ride."

"I'm sorry, sir, but you picked a hell of a time to get drunk—if you'll pardon me for saying so."

Frémont, surprised by the youth's counterattack, finally conceded the truth of his statement with an indifferent shrug. Elevating his voice, he spoke to the crowd that had gathered. "You heard the man. Let's get our drunken asses in the saddle. Once again, duty calls."

While the men scurried about, trying to collect their gear and their wits, the sun bowled over the horizon full bore and shot into the eyes of the quickly sobering bunch. Coffee miraculously appeared and was downed by the gallons. The woman cried, a few cussed. Lottie complained that her party was supposed to have gone on for three more days at the very least.

Nancy followed Hart to the corral and tried to get a few words exchanged in the melee surrounding them. "Is this ever going to end?" she asked, angry that because the rebels had refused to accept a superior power, Hart was going to have to go to war again.

He was none too happy either as he cinched the saddle down on his buckskin. "When I think of what nearly happened to you and Angelica the last time I was gone, I've a notion to tell Frémont he'll have to fight this round without me. Ideals fade in the face of reality."

But Nancy knew he had his honor, and she wouldn't ask him to forsake it. "We'll be all right. You'll never feel good about yourself if you don't go and fight with the Americans. There would be those like Reading and Hensley, Merritt and Ide, who would call you a coward if you didn't. They gave you a bad enough time about your reluctance to get involved with that Bear Flag incident.

"The attack by those renegade Indians was an isolated instance, Hart," she continued. "And one unlikely to ever happen again. Besides, I never go anywhere now without at least three vaqueros. Osvaldo and I learned our lesson."

Hart drew her into his arms. "I don't know, Nancy. But I'd never forgive myself if something happened to you and Angelica."

At that moment, Frémont strode up, looking quite sober now despite the dark circles under his bloodshot eyes. "Daniels, I need some special help from you."

Nancy and Hart exchanged a look. Hers said, "Go ahead. The Americans need you worse right now than I do."

Hart acquiesced. "What is it, Captain?"

"Quite simply, we're going to need horses. As many as we can get our hands on. I'm going to have to requisition anything you and the other ranchers have that can be spared. I would be interested in some of Mrs. England's mules, too. And any horses she might have, as well. The United States government will reimburse you, of course. Just prepare a statement and I'll sign it."

"I can supply about seventy-five."

"I imagine I can give you fifty head of mules," Lottie answered, having come up behind Frémont. "I got a jim-dandy in the corral. I'll make sure you get him."

"Excellent. Just excellent," Frémont replied. "Take a couple of men to drive the animals to Monterey, Daniels, and the rest of us will meet you there."

Frémont strode away, walking only slightly off center. Lottie and Carlito went to select the mules and horses she could spare. Nancy moved back into Hart's arms, with the fleeting and disturbing thought that it might be the last time he ever held her.

They spoke words that had been said before, but needed to be said again. Words of love. Words extending well wishes and good health. In the end, Nancy stood in the yard of Rancho Corona with the other women, watching the men ride out, and silently wondering which ones would be coming back.

Silence. Days and weeks of silence. September slipped into October. October into November.

Nancy supervised the harvest, the canning and pickling, fussed occasionally over her rapidly growing orchards, and kept a close eye on the meat curing out in the smokehouse. She helped Osvaldo teach Lady Rae's colt to lead. And on these long autumn days, she took Angelica for daily rides across the golden hills, stopped for picnics beneath the fall colors of the sycamores and oaks, but never did she go out of sight of the ranch.

Often she and Lottie sent word to meet halfway between the two ranches, always accompanied by vaqueros. Nancy didn't know what it was, but something—maybe the grizzly attack—had Lottie spooked too. On these occasions, Angelica rode in front of Nancy on the big California saddle. Nancy had practically given up her sidesaddle except when she went to town or to Sutter's Fort. Occasionally, eighteen-month-old Angelica would ask if the Indians were going to come again. Apparently they were the one thing that had elicited fear from her. Mostly, though, she just urged Nancy to gallop Lady Rae and keep up with the horses ridden by Elise and Beth and Josh. Those three had turned so wild since being in California that they could have put on war paint and fit right in with the Indians.

"Run," Angelica would chirp. "Run, Mum-mum. Like boy. Like girls." Except that she couldn't say girls. It came out sounding like "gulls."

When Nancy and Angelica rode alone, they usually went to Nancy's favorite old oak just a quarter of a mile from the ranch. There, Nancy would read aloud the letter she'd received from Hart right after he'd arrived in Monterey. She had memorized it, but being able to touch the paper and see the words he'd written made her feel closer to him.

The letter hadn't told her very much. Just that he had arrived in Monterey with the horses. There still weren't enough, and Frémont was trying to requisition more. He said nothing of any battles, only that the men who had been captured at Chino Ranch and imprisoned in Los Angeles had been set free. Most of them were married to native women who had raised a ruckus over their imprisonment and forced the new governor, José María Flores, to release them. Flores had been briefly arrested himself, but the people had been pacified in the end to acquit him and have his subordinate imprisoned instead.

Hart had also written,

> Frémont has recruited over four hundred men, some of them Indians, along with those we already had, including several hundred seamen and marines. We can't get enough horses around here for the ground troops. Most were driven south by the enemy. It looks like a few of us will be making a run back to the ranch to get what we can there. Have the vaqueros round up and break as many wild ones as they can. I'm looking forward to seeing you again. It's lonely without you.

But it was the middle of November now, and he had not returned. Nor had she received another letter from him.

Nancy would have relished the sight of a rider on the road, for riders meant news. But no one came, save Lottie, Carlito, and the children on their way to Sutter's Fort for supplies in early December.

"Why don't you come along with us," Lottie insisted. "You'll need some spices and sugar and things like that to fix up your Christmas dinner."

Nancy wanted nothing more than to go somewhere, to ease the worry about Hart. But she was afraid if she left, she'd miss him.

"Maybe he's just changed his plans," Lottie said after hearing Nancy's concerns.

"She is right, señora," Carlito seconded. "It is a good possibility they found horses elsewhere. If he was going to come, he probably would have done so by now."

What they said was true, but something clawed at Nancy's insides. A feeling she couldn't express. *Wouldn't* express for fear it might somehow come true. Something was wrong. Hart had sounded so confident in the letter that he would be coming back for the horses.

Finally she forced herself to accept their explanation. She bundled Angelica up in her winter attire and rode along to the fort. One of the Indians was elected to drive the supply wagon. Osvaldo and Antonio came along as outriders.

The road to Sutter's Fort was quiet. One could almost fall into the comfortable notion that there was nothing beyond this isolated existence, and certainly not the discord of war. But at Sutter's, the world intruded again, in a most frightening manner.

John Sutter greeted them warmly, as always, but the usual sparkle was absent from his eyes, and he could barely force a smile. When asked what troubled him, he sucked in a deep breath that stretched his vest to the limit of its seams. Releasing a long, worried sigh, he said, "I have received word just today that an American force led by Charles Burroughs and Bluford Thompson was set back by Torre. Castro's men came in for support and five Americans, including Burroughs, were killed. That many more were wounded.

"Along with that message came notice that Thomas Larkin was taken prisoner about a month ago. I hope the same dilemma has not befallen your husband, Mrs. Daniels."

A deathly silence fell over the group that still stood in the fort's spacious plaza. Indians and emigrants hustled and bustled around the fort, tending to duties, but Nancy felt merely a spectator in an audience, watching a scene on stage as it was played out before her. Then even that complacent scene vanished to be replaced by the imagined picture of Californio rebels torturing and butchering their prisoners.

With a shake of her head, she forced the horrendous thought from her mind. "Who?" She spoke the strangled question. "Who captured Thomas Larkin?"

"José Antonio Chavez and some of his men captured him at Joaquín Gomez's ranch," Sutter replied dismally. "He had stopped there for the night on his way to Yerba Buena. Apparently he has been taken to a prison in Los Angeles."

Nancy could not speak, silently fearing that Hart might be in the same predicament. Why else would he not have come back after the horses?

Lottie finally broke the silence that had emotionally crippled the group. "You shouldn't worry needlessly, Nancy. If anything had happened to Hart we would have heard something. Frémont would have been wondering where he was. Where the horses were."

Nancy's head began to spin. She had to force herself to breath. "Yes, if Frémont had time to inquire of the matter. If they are engaged in battle, he might have had to leave the matter unresolved."

The group broke up to attend to errands before they joined Sutter for supper in the main house. There, they discussed what had been learned about the happenings in the south, which wasn't much. Kit Carson had met a United States army battalion, led by General Stephen W. Kearny, coming in from his previous assignment in New Mexico. Along with Captain Mervine's men, they had been confronted by sixty horsemen led by José Antonio Carrillo. Mervine casualties had been four dead and six wounded. At San Diego, Ezekiel Merritt, in charge of a small garrison, had fled to a whaler and stayed out at sea when the guerrillas came riding in.

"To top it off," Sutter said, sighing again as if very weary of it all, "word has reached us of a party of emigrants—the Donner party—that is supposed to be coming in over Truckee Pass. They should have been here by now, and we are all beginning to fear they are trapped on the other side of the Sierras—or worse, *in* the Sierras. The snows and blizzards up there in the early part of the season are the worst. I don't know if a rescue party could even survive. But, as soon as the storms over the mountains break, we will have to outfit a group to go looking for them. It is the only humane thing to do."

That night in the little room Nancy and Angelica always used while at the fort, Nancy tossed and turned. Thinking. Thinking of the Donner party up in the mountains, hungry and stranded in the deep snow and not knowing what was ahead of them in California. Thinking of the months she had spent on that overland trail with Hart, the nights in his arms, sharing dreams. Wondering now if he was lying somewhere wounded. Or in a prison along with Thomas Larkin, being tortured. Or maybe already dead.

If something had happened to him, surely word would have reached them? But maybe not. If he had set out with only a couple of men across the San Joaquin Valley, he could have been killed and left for the buzzards and no one would be the wiser.

As soon as the first gray light of dawn touched the eastern horizon, she and Lottie set their wagons for home. They were never more surprised to meet J.B. Chiles and Billy Baldridge just a few miles north of Rancho Vallecito.

"You're a little far from home, aren't you, J.B.?" Nancy inquired, giving him the best smile she could muster as she pulled her mare to a stop alongside his big, black mule.

"Yes, ma'am, I reckon I am. I've been over in Monterey delivering some mules to Frémont. Him and his battalion are headed to Los Angeles over the Santa Inez Mountains. That's going to be tough going this time of year. Stockton, Kearny, Mervine, and Gillespie are converging on Los Angeles from all directions to see if they can force a surrender out of Flores and his men. Anyhow, Hart was supposed to have come back and gotten some more horses but he never did show up. Me and Billy came back to see if he needed help."

The cold feeling that had been in the pit of Nancy's stomach for weeks suddenly turned to a solid chunk of ice. "He wrote and said he might be coming back for horses, but that was two months ago. He never did show up, J.B. We just figured his plans had been changed. Was he alone?"

"No, he had Thane and Torey." J.B. pushed his hat to the back of his head and folded his forearms over his saddle horn. Furrows developed in his forehead as he considered the meaning of Hart's tardiness. He could only come to the same conclusion that Nancy herself had come to late last night.

He tugged his hat back down. "I'm going to ride back to Rancho Vallecito with you. Me and Billy, and maybe a few of your men, had better head back to Monterey and see if we can find him."

Nancy didn't say what was on her mind, but there were those who knew about Hart's close association with Larkin, and who might consider him a prime source of war strategies and information.

"I'm going with you," she announced without reservation. "I'll leave Angelica with Magdalena."

J.B., Lottie, and the others saw the stubborn set to her jaw and knew that once her mind was set there would be no changing it. As a matter of fact, they knew she would go looking for Hart now even if she had to go alone. No one blamed her, considering what had happened to other Americans at the hands of the rebel Californios.

"Well, I can damn well tell you that I'm not going to sit home pacing the floor while you all are out carousing the countryside," Lottie said.

"You will have the assistance of all of us, Señora Daniels," Carlito added. "This is one thing that cannot be left to chance."

41

December

Angelica's cries echoed in Nancy's ears long after the thunder of the horses' hooves had muffled the plaintive sound. She had never left Angelica for any length of time. As a matter of fact, she had taken the baby practically everywhere with her. The baby had come to expect her father to leave, but never her mother.

"I'm going to help your daddy," Nancy had explained to her the best one could explain such a thing to a child not yet two years old. "He needs my help, sweetheart. Daddy needs Mommy's help."

Angelica's eyes had lit up. "I go. Me hep Daddy."

"No. This is one time I can't take you, Angel. You must stay here with Magdalena and Carmelita and be a good baby."

Thoughts fluttered across Angelica's eyes as she had lifted her thumb to her mouth, clutching her blanket tightly so that one corner of it touched the end of her small, straight nose. She had sucked the thumb vigorously, popping it out only long enough to say, "Good baby. Me."

Now, Nancy laid in her blankets on the edge of the western side of the San Joaquin River, listening to the haunting cry of a nightbird, and the snores of the men outside the tent she shared with Lottie. Had she made the right decision in leaving Angelica to search for Hart? What if by some perverse twist of fate, she lost them both? Or what if something happened to both her and Hart, and Angelica was left alone with no parent at all? Magdalena knew about Nancy's family in Amherst, but would she contact them? Would Nancy even want those puritanical relatives of hers in Amherst clipping her daughter's wings as they had done hers? Would the child be better here, raised by Magdalena, or Lottie?

She smiled. Lottie the mother of orphans. Orphan herself.

Nancy sat up, drawing her knees to her chest and resting her chin atop them. Despite the shelter of the tent, it was cold. She didn't like being in the tent tonight. She wanted to see the sky, the clouds, and anything that might be out there in the dark, closing in on her and the others.

"We'll find him, Nancy," Lottie said softly from her blankets. "And don't worry about Angelica either."

"You always know what's on my mind, don't you?"

Lottie chuckled. "I was thinking about Josh and the girls, too."

Guilty heat flashed up Nancy's neck and scorched her face. How selfish of her not to think of what she was putting Lottie through. "I appreciate you standing by me, Lottie. I've never had a friend as loyal as you."

"Now, don't go getting sentimental. Everything will turn out okay."

Nancy clung to that small ray of hope. "Do you remember what you said about raveled ends of sky, Lottie?"

"Vaguely."

"Well, right now I feel like my sky is fraying, slowly unraveling, like a chain stitch on a crocheted neck scarf. I have to find him alive, Lottie. I have to, or my coming to California was all for naught. I didn't know it, but he was my destiny, my reason for jumping off into the unknown. I thought I could make a life out here alone, but there was so much I didn't know."

"You still could make it alone, girl," Lottie said. "You would do what I'm doing. Have the men do the hard work."

"Don't you ever get lonely, Lottie? Without a man, I mean?"

Lottie released a wistful sigh. "Guess I wouldn't be human if I didn't. But a person has to go on, to think of the others needing and depending on him. You have Angelica. No matter what happens, you have to think of her."

Nancy laid back on her blankets and said no more. Eventually she slept, but not until well after midnight.

The next day they rode hard, maybe too hard. If it hadn't been for the buzzards, they would have ridden right past the bodies. Carlito saw them first. The buzzards, that is. They rode closer, cautiously, and it was then that they saw the remains of two bodies tied to trees.

"*¡Dios mío!*" Carlito shied away from the sight. "Do not look, señoras."

But it was too late. Both Nancy and Lottie had already seen the faces of the two men, their heads drooping down. Each with a bullet hole between his eyes.

A tortured moan escaped Nancy's lips. Pain crashed over her. This couldn't be. Couldn't.

She left the saddle, but J.B. stopped her from going near the men. "Don't, Nancy. It's not a sight fitting for a lady."

She turned away and tried to breathe as the pain kept coming in wave after smothering wave. She went to her knees, unable to stand up. Lottie and Carlito rushed to either side of her to offer support and sympathy, but nothing helped. She had come to care a great deal for Torey and Thane, treating them like brothers and friends. The crux of it rammed into her heart like the blade of a bayonet.

"My God, why would anyone do this to them!" she screamed. "They didn't deserve to die, let alone to be executed! They were only helping Hart with the horses." She threw herself into Lottie's arms, unable to control the fear swelling inside her, choking her. "Oh, God, Lottie. If they've killed Hart, too—" the sobs overtook her and, trembling violently, she could say no more.

She didn't know how long she clung to Lottie, accepting the soothing stroke of her hand and her comforting words. She wanted to be strong, but this was one time she simply could not be. She closed her eyes to the world, hearing distant sounds of the vaqueros cutting the bodies down, digging graves. And all the while fear clawed at her. Where was Hart?

She didn't know where strength came from, but slowly it returned, and with it, a burning rage. She swore that whoever had killed Thane and Torey would pay for it. But deep inside she doubted she would ever find the one who had given the execution order. Still, it was the fire for revenge, surging hotly through her veins, that gave her the strength she needed to go on into Monterey.

It was not the same town they'd ridden into three years ago, exhausted and hungry from their ordeal crossing the continent. Gone were the friendly, carefree smiles of the Californios. Gone were the happy, singing voices and strumming guitars.

The town seemed to be holding its breath, waiting in hushed antici-pation for something, anything, to happen. The Californios who did not know them eyed them suspiciously, some with open contempt. Those who did know them, greeted them, but with cautious reserve as if maybe they should no longer be their friends. For the first time ever, Nancy did not feel overly safe on the streets of the little village.

The party of six stepped down from their horses in front of Miriam's restaurant and looped their reins around the hitching rail. They'd ridden hard and were tired and dusty. They needed food and rest, and infor-mation.

Miriam was delighted to see them and verified their suspicions that the town slumbered in quiet confusion over the war. Her business had fallen off; few Californios came in for meals since the uprising. She was more than a little frightened herself, but she gave them a free meal and all the news she knew, none which was about Hart.

"There's a new *alcalde* named Walter Colton," she said. "I'd advise you to talk to him. He might be able to tell you something, or at least find something out for you."

But Colton knew nothing either, although he said he would do some investigating and "get to the bottom of things." They asked questions of everyone they trusted. They searched every building or adobe shack that might possibly serve as a prison. They rode up the hill to talk to Rachel Larkin. She was sympathetic to Nancy's fear, experiencing her own over the imprisonment of her own husband.

"I didn't know Hart was missing," she said. "There are others, too. A Mr. Bartlett was captured outside San Francisco just a few days ago. A rescue party has been sent, but I fear for the man."

"What about Tom?"

"I received a handwritten letter from him, allowed by Governor Flo-res. Tom assures me he is being treated almost royally, and for me not to worry. I suspect that because he is Consul, they will be careful not to abuse him, as he could be invaluable in a prisoner exchange. He says not to attempt a rescue, fearing it could endanger not only his own life but those of the liberators. He is confident he will be released in due time. I hope he's right. I do not trust the rebels heading this revolution. Some can be quite bloodthirsty."

"Did he mention seeing Hart? Or knowing anything of his where-abouts?" Nancy asked anxiously, feeling all hope dwindling away.

Rachel shook her head regretfully. "I'm truly sorry, Nancy. He didn't mention Hart in the letter. What will you do next?"

Nancy had already considered her next option. "We'll head to Los Angeles. Since they're holding Tom there, they might be holding Hart there, too. Assuming—" she took a deep breath "—assuming they haven't already killed him."

"Try not to think that," Rachel said. "You must have hope."

"I am trying, Rachel. I really am. The rebels know that Tom and Hart were friends. They probably know, or suspect, that Hart was one of your husband's informants from the northern district. They might think he has secret information pertinent to American maneuvers and are holding him until they can get it from him."

Rachel took Nancy's hands in hers and clasped them tightly. "Maybe you should leave it up to the men, Nancy. Right now, Los Angeles is no place to be. A few weeks ago sixteen Americans under the command of Kearny and Gillespie were killed in a battle near San Pascual. Fourteen more were injured, including Kearny and Gillespie and some of the other officers. Captain Johnson was shot through the head.

"The Californios, led by Andrés Pico, pretended to be outnumbered and fled, scattering. Then they closed ranks on the Americans and trapped them. Kit Carson, Lieutenant Beale, and an Indian set out for re-inforcements from Commodore Stockton. Two hundred marines went to their rescue. The last I heard, the Kearny–Gillespie force was in San Diego. Frémont and his land force of a hundred sixty men are heading that way, too, through the Santa Inez Mountains. They left here the end of November."

The news of more dead Americans, and the escalation of war, made Nancy that much more determined to find Hart, if it wasn't already too late. "I have to try to find him," she said. "He doesn't carry the political clout that your husband does. If he's been taken prisoner, they might find him dispensable if he can't tell them what they want to know."

Rachel looked at her sadly. "I wish I could offer something more helpful, Nancy. I'll do what I can, using the tailings of Tom's influence to open doors and pull strings. But you'd better not go by land, it would take too long, and you're liable to end up in the middle of warfare. Troops are converging on Los Angeles from all directions, and from both enemy and American forces. I have connections with most of the Yankee traders through Tom's business. If you'll be patient for a few days, I'll see if I can find one who will take you to Los Angeles, no questions asked."

New Year's Eve

On a rough sea, slashed by cold rain and wind, they sailed under cover of darkness. The Yankee trading vessel had taken them as far as Santa Barbara, where they had been able to charter a fishing boat owned and navigated by an old, leather-faced fisherman originally from New England. He called himself J.J., short for Jerry Jeff James, and he'd been traversing these coastal waters for twenty-five years. He caught enough fish to feed himself, and a few to sell and trade for the things he needed. He had never married, and lived in a little shack on the beach. He had no qualms about taking them the rest of the way to Los Angeles; he relished the intrigue of the mission.

Every boat in the area knew J.J.'s rig by sight and ignored his comings and goings. Hiding his passengers under a fishy-smelling canvas, he sailed past every boat in the coastal waters, warships and all, in broad daylight with no detainment or questions asked.

The weather warmed the closer they got to Los Angeles, but the winter winds were still cold. A pale quarter moon hid behind the winter cloud cover and did little to light their way. But J.J. knew every inch of the coastal water, as well as the shoreline, and expertly maneuvered his boat through the darkness.

Around midnight, as they neared Los Angeles, he ordered all lanterns doused. The town of some twelve hundred lay several miles away, invisible in the darkness, but they could not be sure that the rebel forces did not have guards patrolling the beaches.

J.J. dropped anchor in a secluded cove north of the pueblo, and lowered a little rowboat. In three trips to shore, he had delivered all his passengers onto the sandy beach.

"I will be here at three in the morning," he said. "If you're not here just before daybreak, I'll have to sail without you. If that should happen, I'll come back for two consecutive nights. If I still don't see you, I'll assume you've all been killed." He flashed a teasing smile. "If I'm caught in these waters, this close to shore, those damned men of Flores's might think I'm a spy or something and run me through. So I hope you'll understand that I can't linger around too long."

"We understand," Nancy said. "We'll be back here by three in the morning, if all goes well."

He touched the bill of his grimy cap in farewell and leaned into his oars, pushing the rowboat quietly back out to sea until it was swallowed by darkness. They waited on the beach until all they could hear over the brush of the wind was the fading murmur of J.J.'s oars kissing the water.

Nancy turned toward the dark bulk of the land thrusting up and away from the ocean's edge, toward the velvet blackness that presently hid their destination. "Does anyone know where Flores's headquarters are? Or where they keep prisoners around here?" she whispered.

"Sí, señora," Carlito replied. "I have been to Los Angeles many times. We will go to the prisons first."

42

January 1, 1847

Dressed in sombreros and serapes to hide their identities, and carrying their concealed pistols and knives, Nancy and the others moved toward the lights of Los Angeles that had appeared in the darkness like stars popping out from behind a heavy cloud cover. Rude huts and rambling adobes, with their whitewashed walls and tiled roofs, crouched near the central plaza as if it were a fire that would keep them warm and protected. Those adobes on the outskirts looked woefully vulnerable in the darkness of this chilly, starless night. Normally lively with fiestas, fandangos, and rodeos, the pueblo was hunkered down beneath the threat of war.

Although most people slept at this hour, there were a few cantinas still open and music spilled out into the quiet night. Their lights were beacons that the searchers avoided. They stayed to the back streets, moving as quietly as possible through the alleys, disturbing only a few dogs and sending numerous cats scrambling for cover. Once an ugly mongrel dog, surprised by their approach, let out a yowl. A sharp, low-throated command by Carlito frightened the creature back into the alley from whence he had sprung. On this first day of the new year, the only resident of the village that they actually came into contact with was an old man who was passed out in the alley from drinking too much tequila.

Stepping over him and his empty bottle, they moved on.

As they approached the jail, Carlito slipped into another dark alley and drew the others around him. "There are two guards out front," he whispered. "We need to make sure there are none in the back, behind the jail. J.B., you and Osvaldo circle around and check it out. Osvaldo can speak for you if you should be stopped by anyone. But stay low, *por favor.* Your height alone will draw attention and suspicion."

Carlito briefed everyone on what his part in the plan would be. Agreeing, Lottie, Nancy, and Billy stayed in the alley as the men moved off. Carlito cut back behind a few adobes and came out on the narrow, dirty street that ran in front of the jail. He began to stagger, as if he had been tipping the bottle at one of the cantinas, and he hummed a drunken tune under his breath.

As expected, the two guards stood up from their chairs positioned on either side of the jailhouse door. One of them stepped out in front of Carlito and placed a hand on his chest, halting him. Carlito feigned surprise and swayed at the end of the man's hand.

"You are a long way from the cantina, *amigo,*" the guard drawled the words in Spanish slow enough for the observers in the shadows to understand.

"*Sí,*" Carlito replied with a convincing slur that was also in Spanish. "I am on my way home."

"Where is your home?"

"It is around here, somewhere. Close, I think."

"Maybe the best place for you is in the jail over night." The guard's tone sounded vaguely sinister.

Carlito tried to take another step and stumbled to the side. "No, no. It will not be . . . nec . . . necessary. I have some *amigos* around here who will take me home. Yes, some . . . *amigos.*"

Realizing Carlito had given them the signal to move, Nancy and her companions stepped out from the shadows. J.B. and Osvaldo appeared from around the corners of the jail. Carlito simultaneously sobered and lifted his pistol from beneath his serape, jamming it against one of the unsuspecting guard's midriffs.

"It's only the two of them," J.B. said.

"*Bueno.*" Carlito smiled at the guards. "Then I am sure they will not mind opening up the jail and allowing us to see who is inside."

The two men were more than compliant, even going inside with lanterns and shining them on the faces of each man. There were six prisoners but none were American.

"Where is the governor keeping the American prisoners, Larkin and Daniels?" Nancy asked, speaking for the first time. The guards' heads jerked up in surprise as they realized she was a woman.

"Americanos?" one said innocently. "I know of no Americano prisoners."

It was either the insolent gleam in his black eyes, or merely Nancy's intuition, but she sensed he was lying through his tobacco-stained teeth. Time was running out. Morning would be here soon. J.J. would be waiting for them at the rendezvous and he would leave without them. Even though he had said he would come back, it was too dangerous to prolong their search in the city. By morning, the guards would have told the authorities of their presence and they would become the hunted instead of the hunters.

"Something tells me you're not taking this too seriously, señor," Nancy said, in the best Spanish she could manage.

"No, we are very serious," he replied. But his eyes lied, and Nancy had seen the change in his attitude when he had discovered she was not a man. So he didn't think she would kill him? How little he knew. Her husband's life was at stake, which put his at stake too.

"I saw an old well not far from here," she said. "It didn't have any water in it, but it was filled with rats. I think that if a man was tied and gagged and lowered down into that well by his ankles, he might just remember all manner of things he thought were long forgotten. Don't you agree, Carlito?"

Nancy's Spanish was not so good, but the guard understood enough of it, mixed with the English, to know what she had said, and his face paled in the dim lantern light.

"Well, señor?" Nancy prodded.

To her surprise, he sneered. "I heard an Americano was shot yesterday. Maybe he is the one you search for."

Nancy's restraint crumbled like a sandstone cliff beneath the hungry, nibbling mouth of the ocean. She moved forward, step by slow step, until she was within a rifle's reach of the insolent guard. She drew her pepperbox from its holster and pointed it at his ugly face.

The six barrels, regardless of how small, were daunting when one was on their receiving end. A bead of sweat broke out on his forehead and squirmed its way down along the side of his rough face. Still, he would not back down. "You will not kill me, señorita. You are only making threats."

"If you will notice, my weapon has no hammer. If I should decide to kill you, all I have to do is pull the trigger and you would have no warning whatsoever. And, regrettably, no face either."

"Do not be a fool, Rodrigo," the other guard spoke up, his eyes darting nervously over their captors. "The Americano is nothing to us. He is probably dead anyway. Take them to where he was being held."

Pursing his lips beneath his drooping moustache, Rodrigo considered his friend's suggestion for the space of another long moment before finally capitulating. "All right, but the governor will not be happy, Francisco. If I lose my job over this . . ."

"Which would you rather lose?" Nancy inquired. "Your job, or your life?"

Sighing, Rodrigo made his decision. Turning down a series of back streets, he led them to an old adobe sitting alone outside of town. From all appearances it looked uninhabited, and had clearly been used as a prison. The mud overcoat was crumbling off its bricks, but the latter were good and strong and had been put together like a fortress. It had only one heavy, wooden door and no windows. The door had been reinforced with one-inch rough lumber and was secured with a huge iron lock.

"There was an Americano in here," Rodrigo said, "but I do not know if he is the one you are looking for. And I do not know if he is still here. We heard they were going to execute a spy yesterday."

Nancy's heart began to pound, anticipating what she would find—or what she would not find—on the other side of the door. "Open it. ¡Dése prisa!"

Rodrigo fumbled with the keys on the ring, and finally found the right one. The big lock opened with a decisive click. The heavy door swung wide to reveal an interior as black as pitch. They were hit with the stench of human excrement, rats, of earth and dampness.

Nancy took the lantern J.B. had been carrying and stepped inside with her heart pounding in her temples. She lifted the light higher. A man leaped up from the corner nearest the door, almost putting himself in her face. Gasping, she stumbled backward into J.B.

"What the hell—"

But the man wasn't Hart. He was a pathetic-looking Mexican, half-starved and half-clothed in rags, and shielding his eyes from the lantern light. It was doubtful that he could even see who any of them were. He was only hoping they were his saviors from this hell hole he'd been tossed into.

"Are you going to let me go back to my family?" he jabbered in rapid Spanish.

If he was the man the guards had brought her here to see, then they had sent her on a cruel, wild goose chase.

"What are you in here for?" Nancy asked, trying to see around him, but his body blocked her view to the rest of the dark room.

He moved his arm away from his eyes to peer at her in surprise. "You are a woman."

"*Sí.* Are you the only one in here?" she asked impatiently, trying to see past him.

He answered her first question. "I am in here for murder, but I killed nothing but a stray pig. Are you someone in authority who can release me?"

"You stole the pig," Rodrigo interjected.

"*Sí,* to feed my family," the prisoner replied defensively. "It was no reason to beat me and lock me up for weeks and starve me nearly to death."

Nancy's patience snapped. Precious time was being lost. She tried to step around the prisoner but he moved in front of her again, as if afraid she would forget about him. "Is there an American in here with you?"

"Oh, *sí.* He is there in the corner, but he is either dead or unconscious," he replied, launching into a rapidly spoken, lengthy spiel. "He has not moved for hours, not that I could hear anyway. It is so dark in here I could not see anything, only listen to movement, to his breathing. They beat him badly, you see, to get information from him about the Americanos and the war. They claimed he was a spy, but he told them nothing. They said the next time they came, it would be to execute him. I do not want to watch that for he is not a bad sort for an Americano. Now, may I go? My family will think I am dead."

Nancy nearly shoved him out of her way. It was in the third corner her light touched that she finally saw another man curled up on his side with his back to her. He had nothing to protect him from the cold, bare earth. No blanket, no shirt, no shoes. Only a pair of dirty trousers covered his lower half. His bare back was unusually dark, as if coated with mud, but after a few faltering steps forward, Nancy saw that the "mud" was actually blood caked over open wounds. If he was breathing, it was too shallow to detect from the distance. She might not have recognized him had she not known him so well.

The lantern dimmed; the darkness tightened. The image of Thane's and Torey's bodies, tied to the trees, flashed before Nancy's eyes. Fighting back a wave of emotion that rose up in her throat to choke her, she rushed to Hart's side and gently turned him over into her arms. A cry of anguish tumbled from her lips at the sight of his battered face, bruised and bloody from a horrific beating. His eyes were swollen shut and the eyelids gleamed purple in the dim light.

"Oh, my God, Hart." With his head cradled in her lap, she reached for her serape to remove it from over her head and cover him with it.

"No, señora." Carlito caught her hand. "You will need the serape for yourself to protect you from the cold when we leave here. Let our guards offer up their clothing. Rodrigo would like nothing better than to donate his shoes and his blanket."

"I did not do this to him," Rodrigo objected. "Why should I be made to suffer?"

"Because it is your lucky day, *amigo.*"

Feeling Billy's pistol near his right ear, and Osvaldo's near his left, Rodrigo released another gargantuan sigh and relinquished the articles of clothing they wanted.

"You were going to leave Daniels here to die, weren't you?" J.B. accused.

Rodrigo's face fell. "No, no, señor, but Governor Flores sort of . . . forgot about him, you know?"

"You should have helped the governor remember," Carlito said. "But because you didn't, you and your friend here are going to find out what it feels like to be forgotten. Billy and Osvaldo, could you spare me your bandanas?"

"What are you planning to do?" Rodrigo tried to back away, only to come up against the wall of J.B.'s six-foot-four frame. "Surely, you do not mean to tie us up and leave us in this place?"

"You are a lot smarter than you look, Rodrigo." Carlito said. "But you will only be prisoners until they come with your breakfast."

"But they may not—"

Carlito shook his head. "Ah, that is what I thought." Seeing just how mistreated Hart and the pig thief had been, he turned to the latter. "Go home to your family. And, *amigo,* you would be wise not to steal any more pigs."

"Oh, you can be assured I will not. *Gracias. Gracias."* The man fled the jail with no delay, nearly knocking J.B. down on his way out.

While the men tied the guards up, Lottie joined Nancy and tried to get some water between Hart's swollen lips from Nancy's canteen. Finally it hit the back of his throat and he started to cough. The reflex brought him to consciousness. He looked up at Nancy through eyes that were barely slits, but he did not appear to recognize her immediately.

"It's me, Hart," she whispered, her heart breaking for him. "I'm here."

He made a feeble attempt to lift his arm to her face but it fell back weakly to his side. "Tried to . . . escape . . . they . . . caught me."

Nancy pulled him against her to protect him from the cold and the pain. "Don't try to talk now, Hart. You can tell me all about it later. Later, when we're safe at Rancho Vallecito."

EPILOGUE

May, 1847

Nancy leaned out over Lady Rae's neck, laughing with the exhilaration of the race as the mare took the hill in giant, eager lunges. Neither of them was ready to stop when they reached the top of the poppy-covered hill, but Nancy pulled the mare up and reached down to pat her neck.

Hart came to a thundering stop next to her on a new gelding he'd been riding lately, a horse broken from the wild bunch. He tried to look irritated, but his smile shone through his words. "I swear, I don't think I'll ever find a horse that can outrun that mare of yours."

"Oh, you will someday. When she gets too old to beat the young ones."

Hart reached across the distance and his fingers slid into the mane of Nancy's loose, flowing hair. He leaned from his saddle and kissed her in the few seconds before their horses both pranced sideways, eager to be off again.

"We'd better get over to the old oak," Nancy said. "Carmelita will be there by now with Angelica and our picnic lunch."

"Then we'd better not keep her waiting. I heard from Osvaldo that Antonio is planning on taking her for a ride this afternoon."

"They're getting pretty serious, aren't they?"

"It would seem."

They gave the animals' their heads and directed them down the hill and through the valley for about a half mile to a big oak whose roots reached out into the creekbed. The latter wound through the mountains, bringing melted snows from the Sierras. As expected, Carmelita was waiting with Angelica. The two-year-old was squatting on her chubby legs next to the creek, playing in the cold water. Carmelita hovered over her, fussing that she didn't fall in. Antonio leaned his lanky frame against the oak, watching. And they were both surprised to see Osvaldo a short distance away with a scowl on his face, apparently assuming the role of chaperon.

"Thanks for bringing her out here for us, Carmelita," Nancy said. "Hart and I enjoyed our morning ride."

"We didn't mind at all." Carmelita cast enamored eyes at her handsome young suitor. "We are going to ride out toward Lottie's place."

"Enjoy yourselves. It's your day off."

Hart and Nancy watched the young couple, and their disgruntled chaperon, mount their horses and ride away, suspecting that in the very near future there would be a wedding at Rancho Vallecito.

Hart spread a blanket over the carpet of orange poppies, and Nancy laid out the food for the picnic. Magdalena had sent cold chicken, yeast rolls, cheese, fruit, and apple-filled *empanadas*, her personal specialty.

After they had eaten their fill, they laid back on the blanket to bask in the warmth of the sun. Angelica toddled back to the shallow creek to splash the water with the flat of her hand. Nancy didn't really worry about the child falling in. The worst she would do was get her drawers wet. The water was no more than a few inches deep.

Since the war had ended, Nancy and Hart had made a point of getting off to themselves at least once a week. These were days of peace. This was the California Nancy had dreamed of. The California she had left home to see, to experience, to take into her heart and soul and to become a part of. This was the life she had been destined to live.

Hart patted his full stomach and stretched onto the blanket, tossing his hat aside. He closed his eyes against the sun that was not yet too hot. Nancy's gaze fell on the thin, red scar that ran nearly the length of his cheek. It was fading gradually, but she knew it would never go away entirely. Hart had said it had been put there by the blade of a knife; the scars on his back, from a whip. But she had never known the details of his capture or his imprisonment because he had preferred not to expound on the pain, the humiliation, and the fear he had suffered. All she really knew was that she had come close to losing him. Dangerously close.

It had been a struggle to keep him alive. That night in Los Angeles, after the rescue, J.B. had carefully placed him over his broad shoulders and carried him all the way to J.J.'s waiting boat. At Monterey, Rachel Larkin had taken him into her home. There, they had spent weeks trying to keep the infection from his wounds. Larkin had fared better. He had not suffered any brutality. He had actually been treated like a guest rather than a prisoner of war and had been released when the Americans had taken the city.

He'd been taken aboard the *Cyane* and returned to Monterey. He told them later that he could have escaped several times but feared such action might have forced them to kill him. He had seen no point in taking such a chance since they had not mistreated him. Some of the women in the village had even gone so far as to bring him gifts.

Like the hardships of the overland trail, Hart's brutal imprisonment had reminded them again that life and love could not, and should not, be taken for granted. He hadn't been fed by his captors for days, nor had he been given water. There was no doubt in anyone's mind that if they had been a day or two later in finding him, they would have found him dead. Or not at all.

The Mexican-American war in California ended shortly thereafter. The Americans marched into Los Angeles ten days after Nancy and the others had rescued Hart from his death. On January 13, a treaty had been signed at Cahuenga. The insurrectionists surrendered their arms and artillery, and were given the choice of leaving the country or staying and enjoying the same rights and privileges as all citizens of the United States of America. Governor Flores relinquished his command to Andrés Pico, and, with his companion, Manuel Castro, left the country like those leaders before him.

Hart had not yet been able to put behind him the executions of Thane Lewis and Torey Porter. Occasionally, he still had nightmares about being forced to witness it. And the ranch was not quite the same place without them.

Nancy sighed, pushing the thoughts and memories out of her mind again. She leaned back against the oak tree and watched Angelica. The two-year-old squatted next to the grassy edge of the little creek and splashed in the water. The toddler had been instructed not to get in the water, but she was wet to her elbows, and her leggings were soaked at the knees. There seemed to be something in the water that had caught her attention, something she was trying to reach with concentrated effort.

She must have accomplished the task because she suddenly sat back on her bottom, looking earnestly at something in her tiny palm. Letting out a squeal of delight, she leaped to her feet and ran toward her parents. "Mumma! Daddy! Look! Pitty wock!"

Hart wasn't asleep, and Angelica's excited cries roused him from the warm blanket. He sat up, pushing the hat that he'd had over his face to the back of his head. "What's she got?"

"I don't know." Nancy laughed. "Something about a pretty rock."

Hart held out his arms to his daughter and she rushed into their protective circle. "Let's see what you have there, Angel."

"Pitty wock, Daddy." The toddler held out her hand and uncurled her chubby fingers from around the object: a gold nugget.

Hart and Nancy stared at it, awed to speechlessness for several moments. Finally, Hart lifted it up and held it to the sunlight, turning it this way and that, exchanging a glance with Nancy that almost registered concern.

"What is it, Hart?"

"It's a pitty wock," Angelica supplied, as if her mother were foolish for asking a question that had such a definitive answer.

Unexpectedly, Hart dug in his vest pocket and pulled out a shiny gold coin. Smiling at Angelica, he said, "Let's trade. You have my gold coin, and I'll have the rock. The next time we go to Sutter's Fort, you can buy anything you want with that coin."

Angelica beamed and carefully tucked the gold coin in her dress pocket. Then she hugged Hart and ran back to the stream. "I find 'nother pitty wock," she announced to her parents.

Nancy slid her hand up Hart's back, leaning closer to look at the nugget he was again scrutinizing with keen eyes. "It looks like pure gold," she whispered.

His lips thinned to a compressed line; his eyes narrowed as he watched his daughter go in search of another. "It is."

Nancy's hand on his back halted. She stared at him as if she thought he'd lost his mind. "Are you sure?"

"Positive. I've found it out in these parts before."

"And you never said anything?" She leaped to her feet. "I'm going to go see if I can find some myself."

He caught her hand. His eyes beseeched her. "Don't, Nancy. Just let it lie. Pretend you never saw it."

She returned to the blanket. "But why, Hart? If it's gold . . ."

He seemed to have trouble putting his reasons into words. "Because if people know—"

He stared off across the beautiful hills dotted with oaks and sycamores, poppies and larkspur, cattle and horses. Nancy saw the love in his eyes for the land. *Their* land. They'd left their families, their homes, their pasts behind to get this land. They'd nearly died for this land.

"The war's over," he continued, his voice low and earnest. "California is ours right now. It's the dream we both had, and the dream we came here to live, to share. As far as you can see, the land is ours. The fields of poppies are as close as I care to get to gold. Gold ruins men. It ruins dreams like yours and mine. Do you understand what I'm saying?"

The spring day suddenly lost its warmth. Yes, she understood, or she thought she did. People would come here looking for gold, and they wouldn't care that this land wasn't theirs. They would destroy it in their quest for riches.

She moved to a position behind her husband. Remaining on her knees, she put her arms around him and kissed the back of his ear. She watched Angelica, understanding why Hart had exchanged the gold coin for the gold nugget. He hadn't wanted the child to know what she'd found so she couldn't tell everyone. But wouldn't she anyway? Or would they just have to explain it away by saying that she had found fool's gold? Yes, that's what they would say, for Angelica was sure to show everyone the gold coin Hart had traded her.

"Let's go back to the house," Nancy whispered, thinking, *let's go back before Angelica finds another nugget.* "We'll forget about what we found here today."

They gathered their picnic basket, blanket, and child. Hart put Angelica in front of him on his saddle. Squealing with delight, she temporarily forgot about the stream and the pretty, golden rock.

At the top of the hill, Nancy paused to look back at the spot where Angelica had found the gold. It was so peaceful down there. So far from civilization and prying, searching eyes. She looked across the hills. *Her* hills.

Hills that represented the freedom she had come to California to find. To never give up. Never. For nothing. Not even gold. It was Daniels land, and there would be no reason for anyone to come out here . . . as long as nobody ever knew.

Unexpectedly, a cloud slid over the sun, and a chill rippled down Nancy's spine. The clouds had crept in and congregated on the edges of the sky, raveling away, bit by bit, at the clear blue dome. And Nancy knew with a falling heart that there would be no way to hold onto that precious piece of sky.

But she wouldn't think of that now. She would think of it when the time came.

Turning her face into the wind, she set Lady Rae into a gallop after Hart and Angelica.

SELECTED BIBLIOGRAPHY

Bidwell, John. *Echoes of the Past.* Chicago: The Lakeside Press, 1928.

Colton, Walter. *Three Years in California.* New York: Arno Press, 1976.

Eide, Ingvard Henry. *Oregon Trail.* New York: Rand McNally, 1972.

Geiger, Vincent, and Wakeman Bryarly. *Trail to California: The Overland Journal of Vincent Geiger and Wakeman Bryarly.* Ed. David Morris Potter. New Haven: Yale University Press, 1945.

Giffen, Helen S. *Trail-Blazing Pioneer: Colonel Joseph Ballinger Chiles.* San Francisco, CA: John Howell Books, 1969.

Hook, Eileen. "Suttersville, A Pipe Dream at Best." *Dogtown Territorial Quarterly* no. 19 (Fall 1994).

Hughes, Benjamin M. "Ezekiel Merritt, The Leader of the Bear Flag Revolt." *Dogtown Territorial Quarterly* no. 13 (Spring 1993).

———. "William Brown Ide: Pioneer, Bear Flagger and Builder." *Dogtown Territorial Quarterly* no. 19 (Fall 1994).

Johnson, Paul C. *Pictorial History of California.* New York: Doubleday, 1970.

Kelly, John, and George Stammerjohan. "John Sutter and His Fort." *Dogtown Territorial Quarterly* no. 19 (Fall 1994).

Lavender, David. *California: A Bicentennial History.* New York: W. W. Norton & Co., 1976.

McDonald, Lois H. "John Bidwell and the Bear Flag Revolt." *Dogtown Territorial Quarterly* no. 13 (Spring 1993).

———. "Larkin and Frémont: Protagonists on the California Stage." *Dogtown Territorial Quarterly* no. 13 (Spring 1993).

Mora, Jo. *Californios.* New York: Doubleday, 1949.

Nelson, Maidee Thomas. *California, Land of Promise.* Caldwell, ID: Caxton Printers, Ltd., 1962.

Paden, Irene D. *Wake of the Prairie Schooner.* New York: Macmillan, 1943.

Richman, Irving Berdine. *California Under Spain and Mexico 1535–1847.* New York: Houghton Mifflin, 1911.

Schlissel, Lillian. *Women's Diaries of the Westward Journey.* New York: Schocken Books, 1982.

Stammerjohan, George R. "The Popular Movement, and Sutter's Fort: An Interpretive View." *Dogtown Territorial Quarterly* no. 13 (Spring 1993).

———. "Sutter's Indian Guard, To Defend the Establishment." *Dogtown Territorial Quarterly* no. 19 (Fall 1994).

Stone, Irving. *Men to Match My Mountains.* New York: Doubleday, 1956.

Unruk, John D. Jr. *The Plains Across.* Chicago: University of Illinois Press, 1979.

Van Every, Dale. *The Final Challenge 1804–1845.* New York: William Morrow, 1964.

Watkins, T. H. *California: An Illustrated History.* Palo Alto, CA: American West, 1973.

AUTHOR'S NOTE

In the writing of this book, I have tried to follow as closely as possible the journey undertaken by the Joseph Ballinger Chiles company of 1843. Chiles did not keep a journal. Information about the journey, and about Chiles, came from the journals and writings of others.

There were some historical instances which, for the purposes of this story, I took the liberty to alter. It was Martin Murphy's corral on the Cosumnes River where General Arce and his men held their horses just prior to the Bear Flag Revolt.

I also placed John C. Frémont at the fictitious Daniels ranch when the news of the Californio insurrection was delivered. In truth, he had returned to his camp in the Sacramento Valley, believing the conquest for California was over.

And last, Nancy's confrontation over the horses with military commander José Castro was not based on any historical account involving the commander, other than the fact that the opposing faction was known to round up horses for the predicted revolution. It does attempt to reveal something of Castro's cruel personality, his political position, and his intent in the struggle for possession of California.